INTO THE NIGHT

C.K. Bennett

First published by Claire Bennett 2021

Third edition

Editing by Nicola Lovick

Artwork by Caracolla

https://ckbennettauthor.com

Instagram: @ck.bennett

Into the Night

By C.K. Bennett

The Night series

Skin of the Night
Into the Night

To A., for being more than I would have thought possible.

Acknowledgements

Again, I need to give a special thanks to my partner, A. You are an exceptional and exemplary man. I am so grateful to have caught your eye, and to have the privilege of being able to tease and spend time with you anytime I like.
I love you.

I also need to thank author Darla Cassic again, who is always there to offer sound advice and insight anytime I need it. You're amazing. Thanks, also, for your Frenchness, which has added further substance to this book.

I'd also like to thank my siblings, M., H., and B., for being prime comedians, the best chefs (honestly, wow),
for being exceedingly annoying on purpose, for spotting the most humorous ironies in situations, for offering impeccable banter,
for humbling me, and for always being interested in entertaining philosophical and intellectual debates with me for hours on end.
You have taught – and continue to teach – me so much.
I am honoured to be your sister.

Thank you, Nicola (Nicky) Lovick, for being such a wonderful editor to work with. I've learnt so much from you.

Chapters

One must still have chaos in oneself to be able to give birth to a dancing star.

– Friedrich Wilhelm Nietzsche

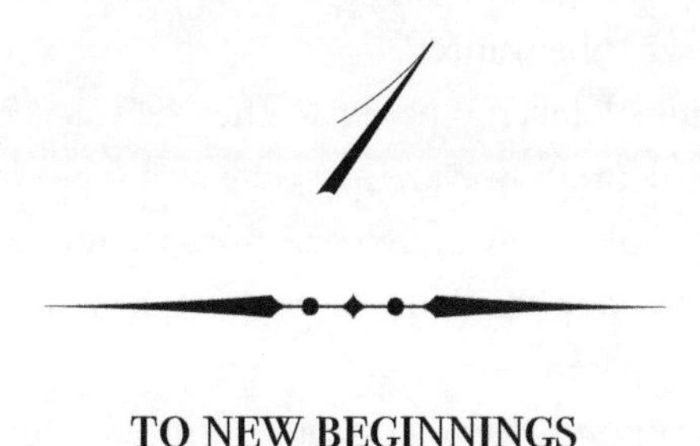

TO NEW BEGINNINGS

THE SHATTERED LOOK IN HIS EYES HAUNTED ME. Through their warm brown colour, I'd seen his heart break into pieces. My best friend; heartbroken, because of *me.*

A shudder ran through me, my hand gripping the pole on the train. Biting into my lower lip, I fought back the urge to cry. What a sight that would have been for these poor strangers. A grown woman, noisy tears erupting from her as though someone close to her had just passed away into the unknown.

Perhaps I was being dramatic, but I did draw a parallel to death when it came to my ruined friendship with Aaron. Who knew if he'd ever want to see me again? Then again, he hadn't told me to stay away from him for ever. He had only said he would require time, so perhaps death was too final a concept to signify what I felt. Either way, I would respect his need for space.

I missed him already. We had shared so many fond memories,

and I had thought a lifetime of them remained to be crafted. To think it might not happen was brutal. For three years he'd been one of my closest friends, a companion I had never wanted to lose. I wasn't one to get attached to people easily, but Aaron I was certainly attached to. He had slipped under my skin and straight into my heart, though the space he had carved out for himself couldn't offer what he wanted.

What would I tell my parents? They had never been aware of our arrangement. However, they were aware he was one of the few precious people in my life, so questions would certainly ensue. And if there was one thing that I couldn't bring myself to do, it was to lie to my parents.

Trying to suppress the rising rage of my emotions, I blew my cheeks out and released a loud breath. I'd have to tell Olivia as well, but, since I hated crying in front of others, I would delay it till my feelings had settled somewhat and I was confident that I would be able to speak without being interrupted by sobs.

Then there was dear Mary-Anne, Aaron's mother. What would he tell her? Would he tell her anything at all? Like my parents, I knew she would be asking questions if she heard nothing about me for a while. In the end, it had been somewhat of a tradition that Aaron brought his closest friends to dinner with her once a month. Now that I was no longer invited, she would surely grow suspicious.

I hoped he wouldn't paint me in an awful light. I adored Mary-Anne, so the idea that she might think badly of me after this was adding further pain to my misery.

I sighed. At least I still had Olivia and Jason. I supposed I had William, too, although he was hardly the person that I would seek comfort in about this. Knowing him, he would probably be over the moon to hear that Aaron and I had cooled our friendship, and I wouldn't be able to stand the concealed satisfaction in his eyes.

I was convinced he wouldn't be able to sympathise with my

distress sincerely. To him, Aaron was a threat. So his withdrawal from my life was probably a dream come true. However, to me, it was anything but. He was my best friend and knew me better than most. A friendship like ours was irreplaceable, and the recent absence of it brought sorrow that I would require plenty of time to recover from.

But, like I always did, I suffered in silence. I hadn't told Jason anything yet, and I dreaded having to. When I'd arrived home after visiting Aaron yesterday, I had shut myself into my bedroom and locked the door. Jason had been out for dinner with Jon and Stephen, and I'd pretended to be asleep when he got home and knocked on my door. He'd tried to open it; he even called my name, but I hadn't answered.

I was sure he had found it strange that it had been locked. After all, I usually kept it open in case he wanted company while asleep. Questions about my deviation from the norm were likely to come my way the instant I arrived home from work today, but perhaps I would have recovered a small portion of myself by then so that I'd be ready to answer them.

My low mood persisted as I entered through the Day & Night building's revolving door on Cannon Street. It was half seven, so I had arrived earlier than usual, but I'd had poor, restless sleep and was already awake when my alarm rang at half six. While part of me wasn't looking forward to seeing William again so soon after my conversation with Aaron, I hoped his company would treat me to a few moments of forgetfulness.

After settling into my chair by his desk, I wrote down my to-do list for the day. I had to stop by Clifford Paints to collect more files before our meeting with Craft Interior's lawyers on Friday, so I thought I'd make the trip shortly after lunch. I wished they'd stored their data virtually rather than physically. It would have saved us all a lot of time, and paper. Then again, if the congeneric merger went according to plan, the new company would certainly opt for a virtual solution to store their data – hopefully.

I knew William had a meeting with Bo Zhang – Clifford Paints' financial advisor – and the representatives from the bank this afternoon, but I supposed he would fill me in later. Right now, I had too much grunt work to look over regarding the due diligence process for the transaction between Elixerion Pharmaceuticals and Porter BioScience.

My first weeks here had consisted of getting familiar with everything. Even though I was still a novice, William had seen me capable of managing both my work and time somewhat independently, which I appreciated. He wasn't the type of supervisor to micromanage. Instead, he encouraged independence, and that was an effective method to employ on personalities like mine.

After writing my to-do list, I got straight to working on the material William had emailed me yesterday, and I was grateful for the mental escape. I did not want to face up to my feelings right now. They were scattered into a seemingly unsolvable mess while I wondered if I'd ever know Aaron again.

Moments later, I heard the door open behind me. My fingers paused on my keyboard for a beat, but I didn't turn to acknowledge him, as I was afraid that the sight of him would trigger my tears to return.

"Here already?" he questioned, amazed.

Looking at the time in the corner of my screen, I saw it was a quarter to eight.

"Mm," I said with a slight nod.

His familiar footsteps drew nearer, but instead of rounding his desk like I had expected him to, he grabbed the available chair beside mine. Leaving his bag on the desk, he pulled out the seat and sank into it.

Curiosity drove me to glance over. With a vague smile on his mouth, he studied me. The sight of him made my heart tingle, but it was a bittersweet sensation. Though I did smile, it wasn't from the heart.

A worried look crossed his face then. Leaning forward, he put a Starbucks coffee on his desk absentmindedly. At that moment in time, I didn't have the strength to look at it, or him. Instead, I relocated my focus to my laptop.

"What's wrong?" he asked, gently, and continued to analyse my profile.

I shook my head and willed for my tears not to surface.

"Cara. I can tell something's wrong. What's the matter?"

Again, I shook my head, but my feelings ran amok within me, so I could no longer concentrate on the words on my screen. Instead, my entire focus was on keeping a lid on my emotions.

I sensed him watch me for another minute until he reached forward to place his large, warm hand on my thigh. "I won't ask again, but if you find yourself wanting to talk about it, I'm all yours." He squeezed.

I'd never seen this side of him before, and it nearly devastated my efforts to maintain my equilibrium on the surface. He was being unbearably tender, and it made my heart throb.

"If you want to cancel our date, I'll understand," he continued, and I was shocked by his statement. For the first time, he was placing me before himself. I knew how much our date meant to him, how hard he had strived for it, and now he was willing to cancel it? Without even knowing the reason behind my misery?

His searing gaze burnt my profile as he tried to gauge my thoughts. Hoping to be relieved from it, I shook my head again. I didn't want to cancel our date. Right now, nothing was more tempting than letting William distract me. In all honesty, what I would have loved more than anything was to discover genuine sympathy in him while I wept in his embrace.

"I don't like seeing you like this," he said softly and took my hand.

"I'll be fine," I mumbled. It was all I could manage.

"That tone is not very convincing." He sandwiched my hand between his. "Let me know, yeah?"

I still hadn't looked at him when I nodded my head, but I heard him sigh. Lifting my hand to his mouth, he gave the back of it a few pecks before he released it to face his day at work. As he was walking away, a tear leaked from my eye, but I rushed to wipe it away before he could notice. Just as he rounded his desk, my eyes flickered to the Starbucks cup to avoid his gaze.

To new beginnings, it read. I smiled. Genuinely, this time. Unwittingly, he'd told me exactly what I needed to hear. To new beginnings, indeed. Aaron hurt, but I'd chosen to give William a chance, and now I had to embrace my decision. I couldn't let my hurt over Aaron ruin what I could build with William. That would be letting the past ruin the future, and I was not inclined to allow it.

We worked with a razor-sharp focus that I, ironically, found relaxing. Neither of us said much, but, just before lunch, William broke the quiet by saying he had to consult Lawrence about some tax issue he had discovered, which might pose a liability in terms of the deal between Elixerion Pharmaceuticals and Porter BioScience.

After his departure, I worked until my stomach reminded me that it was time for lunch. Hearing it complain, I turned my head and noticed that Elisabeth hadn't gone to the canteen yet. I considered whether to approach her, but at the same time, I wanted to wait for William. However, I knew Lawrence specialised in matters relating to corporate tax and had an office in the floor below ours, in the tax department, so perhaps William meant to go straight to the canteen after consulting him.

Standing up, I decided not to wait. As I made my way over to Ellie's desk, she caught my eye and raised a finger in the air. "Hang on. I've only got one page to go."

With a nod, I sat down next to her desk and zoned out of the present. Seeming to understand that something was on my mind today, she sent me a curious glance, but didn't pry, which I was grateful for.

It didn't take long before Andy exited his office to approach Elisabeth's desk. I ignored most of their conversation because I couldn't be bothered with socialising today, but, eventually, Andy's jovial presence barged into my brooding, melancholy zone.

"Seriously, you need to try these." He shoved a box of chocolates into my face, which a client had brought with them from Belgium. "The best I've ever tasted. Come on. Where's your bravado, Cara? Did Will finally manage to kill it off?"

I glared at him. "Christ, Andy. Give me a break, yeah?"

Taken aback by my hostile tone, he blinked. "Damn, what's with the fire-breathing dragon? You on your period?"

My glare persisted. "Is that what you think every time a girl doesn't smile? We're allowed to be unsmiling, you know."

He hollowed his cheeks as he sucked on the chocolate, and, after swallowing it, glanced at Ellie. "She alright?"

"Andy," she replied with a sigh.

He shrugged his shoulders and threw another chocolate into his gaping mouth. "Only saying. Every time Chloe's like that, there's either something serious on her mind, or she's on her period – or both."

"And after ten years of it, you still haven't learnt how to treat it?" I fired back, annoyed. "Poor Chloe, having to deal with you."

"Whoa." His lips curled up into a humoured grin. "Shots fired, indeed."

"Andy, leave her alone," William grumbled from my right, and his presence startled me. Whipping my head around, I saw him arrive from the lifts whilst scowling at his best friend. Meanwhile, his graceful deportment filled my stomach with ticklish sensations.

Dropping the box of chocolates onto Ellie's desk, Andy threw his hands up. "I was only offering her chocolate, mate, and she chewed my head straight off. She's all yours. I'd like to keep at least my cock while I still can."

William's lips twisted with amusement. "We both know you're a dickless twat already, so I wouldn't worry if I were you. They any good?" Halting in front of Ellie's desk, he reached for a piece. While he unwrapped it, Andy chuckled at his banter and smacked his arm, playfully.

Hyperfocused on William, I watched as he placed the sweet in his tempting mouth. Saliva gathered in mine when I saw his strong jaw flex as he chewed.

"They're better if you suck them," I murmured. "Lasts longer."

Andy pressed his lips together before he spun around to face away. A heartbeat later, laughter burst out of his mouth.

"Oh, for fuck's sake, Andy. When was the last time you got laid?" William muttered.

"Not recently, clearly," Ellie said with a giggle.

Andy's laughter ceased instantaneously. "Well, Will's always cock-blocking me, so what's a man supposed to do?"

"Fix his relationship," William replied and reached for another. An irrepressible smile made its way onto my lips. Again, I was reminded of his admirable virtue – unquestionable loyalty.

Before placing the chocolate in his mouth, he studied the texture of it. "These really are quite good. Where did you get them? Are they Belgian?"

"Yeah. Client," Andy said and tucked his hands into his pockets. "Anyway, lunch?"

William nodded his head as he resorted to sucking on the chocolate this time around, and the sight made my mouth bend into another small smile. He was heeding my advice. Headstrong as he was, I hadn't expected that. Then, suddenly, his gaze shifted to me. Surprised by his attention, I stared back, wide-eyed, feeling caught. When he winked, it said more than a thousand words ever could. Completely smitten, I nearly sighed – what a man.

Smiling at me, he faced Andy and Ellie again. "Cara and I

aren't having lunch with you lot. I need to hear how things are going for her," he informed us.

Puzzled, I frowned up at him. Was he doing this solely because he wanted to know what was bothering me, or was he doing it because he wanted to spare me from having to endure small talk over lunch? Both? Either way, I appreciated the gesture.

"Right." Andy smirked and looked directly at Ellie. "Let's go then, shall we?"

"Yeah." She shut her MacBook, pushed her seat out and smiled at us.

Andy headed towards the lift and we all followed. As we rode down to the lobby, I stood next to William, whose alluring scent drifted in the air around me like a custom-made drug. Inhaling it, I lost focus on everything but him. When his arm suddenly brushed against mine, my breath caught in my throat. At first, I thought his touch had been accidental, but when he did it again, I realised he was seeking my attention. Looking up, I saw him smirking at me. Then, while withdrawing his hand from his pocket, he lowered his gaze, silently signifying mine to follow. I studied his fisted hand. Opening it, he revealed a single piece of wrapped chocolate.

To hide my smile, I pulled my lower lip between my teeth when he nudged it against me. Meeting his eyes again, I took it, unwrapped it quickly, and tossed it into my mouth.

Grinning, he winked at me as I shoved the sweet confectionary into my cheek and smiled back.

Andy had been right. The chocolate was indeed delicious, and William had saved me one. It was a surprising, sweet gesture. Today, William was chasing the clouds away.

"See you later then," Andy said once we reached the lobby.

"Yeah," William replied, but didn't bother to look at him. With his hand on my back, he ushered me through the security gates, beyond the revolving door, and out on the streets.

"Thank you," I said and smiled up at his profile as he guided the way along the pavement. He reached for my hand, entwining our fingers, and the action made my heart melt. *Oh, Will.* This was exactly what I needed.

I was still enjoying the electric feel of his hand around my own when he lowered his head to press a firm kiss to the top of mine.

But he said nothing – only squeezed my hand in his. The whole way there, my heart was beating so hard that I worried it'd break my ribs. Each second that ticked by was intense. He was being agonisingly sweet today. I could hardly fathom this side of him. I hadn't endured such delightful emotions in a very, very long time, and I frowned to myself when I wondered if I ever truly had.

By the time we got to the place where he meant for us to eat, we hadn't shared a word. However, just as he reached the door and was about to open it, he broke our silence with a certain look on his face.

"Just to be clear," he said, "this does not count as our first date. This is lunch. Work lunch."

A giggle escaped me before I stretched up on my toes to plant a kiss on his mouth. "Here's your good morning kiss," I said. "And if that's the case, I'll be allowed to pay for my share, correct?" I said, teasing, watching him tense. It tickled me that he wasn't one to accept his generosity being turned down.

"Cara, till you've completed the LPC, you're essentially a student," he reminded me. "Don't be ridiculous. Besides, this was my idea – *and* I'm your boss. It's etiquette that I should pay."

I rolled my eyes. "Have you always got ten arguments to back up any—"

"Yes." His smile was shrewd. "You'd better get used to it. This," he motioned between us with his free hand, "whatever this is, will prove most beneficial for you. You should be taking notes. Watch and learn, and I'll make a great solicitor out of you." Finally, he opened the door for me.

"You've got an inflated ego, Will," I countered, amused.

He scoffed. "It's not inflated."

"Confidence is indeed your forte." I bowed to him, imitating a Japanese greeting. "Sensei."

"That's more like it," he said with a laugh.

We were shown to a table at the far end of the restaurant by the windows. Suddenly the gallant version of himself, William helped me into my seat. The restaurant was light, airy with floor-to-ceiling plate-glass windows. Sheepskins covered the contemporary chairs of various colours.

"What's this place called?" I asked, realising I hadn't spotted a sign outside.

"The Listing," he murmured and peered at the street outside. "Good food, quick service."

I smirked at his comment. "Efficiency is your bible, isn't it?"

He looked at me then, and a sly smile rested on his mouth. "Sounds about right. Why, are you religious?"

"Very." Since I'd always considered myself an agnostic atheist, I barely managed to keep my smile at bay.

Judging by his astonished expression, I had surprised him. "Really? Which religion?"

"Christianity," I lied.

After scrutinising my features, he looked far from convinced. Dubiousness crowded his brows while he asked, "And what does Jamie make of that, given he's a philosophy teacher and all? I mean, yes, there are plenty of Christian philosophers. I'm just not entirely convinced that dear Mr Darby is one, and I'm even less convinced that he would raise his daughter a Christian. After all, critical thought is at the core of philosophy. Surely, he must have raised you to consider religion with a critical eye, rather than shove it down your throat?"

I laughed at the mention of my father. It was charming that William remembered all these details about him when I hadn't mentioned him since our lunch at Farm Girl in May – over a month ago. Dad was also precisely the character William seemed to have deduced. It impressed me that William could consider my personality traits combined with such few details about my father, and thereafter craft a reasonable impression of him.

"You're right. I'm not religious at all," I admitted. "None of my family members are. Are you, though?"

The grin he presented was winsome. "Yes, of course. I'd kiss your feet right now if you asked me to."

The unexpected twist led heat to gather in my cheeks. By insinuating that I was his god, he made it clear that he wasn't taking me seriously at all.

"Foot fetish?" I replied, nose wrinkling somewhat. "We're going to have to work on that," I said and rested my cheek in my palm. "Not judging those who are, but I am not into that."

He chuckled and leaned back in his seat. "Not into it myself, but I gather there must be a reason for its existence. The fetish, I mean. Perhaps there are some erogenous zones there."

I shook my head. "Listen, I'm all for exploring limits, but not that one."

"Done anal?" he asked with a face that was devoid of emotion. I wished I had something to smack him over the head with. Vulgar William had returned.

"Christ, Will," I growled under my breath and glared at him while my cheeks burnt hotter.

He laughed; I adored the sound. In many ways, he truly had become a version of sunlight in my world in such little time. Odd as it were, he always seemed to know what to say.

Though we had only known each other for a few months, I often felt like I'd known him for a lifetime. So yes, his company never failed to leave me tense, but it was only because he stirred such intense feelings in me. But, if I were to overlook that, his existence had always been strangely familiar, as if we'd known each other in a past life and were just learning to know each other all over again. Truthfully, I had never connected with anyone as instantly and as profoundly as I'd connected with him.

"You've definitely done it," he said when he stopped laughing.

Pursing my lips, I looked away from him. Indeed, I had done it, and it was in fact something I quite enjoyed when done right. Aaron and I had done it several times, and while it had been an uncomfortable sensation in the beginning, we'd eventually cracked the code. These days, using butt plugs during sex was one of my favourite things because the fulfilment was unlike anything else.

The thought of Aaron and all the things we'd done together made my mood plummet in the span of a mere breath.

"I have," I confessed, pouting.

He seemed to notice the drop in my mood, but it was evident that his curiosity got the better of him. "Do you like it?" he probed. Lust flared up in his eyes as he leaned forward to arrest mine.

My blush was constant at this point. "I can't believe we're discussing this over lunch, in public," I replied quietly and glanced around to see if anyone were eavesdropping. There was only one other couple here, however, and they sat several tables away from us.

"You do," he said, grinning widely.

This topic, as well as the excitement in his eyes, made it impossible to hold his gaze. "I prefer regular sex with butt plugs over anal sex," I mumbled, embarrassed, while I studied the street outside.

"Duly noted," he replied, satisfied.

"Do you like it?" I stole a glance at him.

He shrugged. "I don't really have an opinion on the matter. I'm into it if my partner is, but it's not something I desperately need to do. Regular sex is equally pleasurable in my experience."

"Good to know. I don't think I could take you up the arse anyway," I replied boldly.

His eyebrows twitched. "Are you saying I'm bigger than—" He turned mute upon my glare.

"Don't compare," I insisted, defensive of Aaron. I hadn't meant to expose the truth like that, and I regretted it profusely. While he wasn't William, Aaron was surely adequately endowed, and I hated the idea that William might gloat about this. "Besides," I continued vehemently, "size only matters up to a point. After that, how you use it is much more important."

Before he could say anything else, the waiter approached to take our orders, and I was relieved by his arrival. I settled for a duck salad as my appetite had essentially vanished upon the thought of Aaron.

After the waiter left with our orders, William was wise enough to avoid returning to the subject. Instead, we discussed work for some time until he turned quiet altogether. Since I appreciated the silence, I didn't say anything either, but I didn't fail to notice that he spent it studying me.

Just before the waiter reached the table with our orders, he asked, "Are you going to tell me what's eating you?"

I waited till the waiter had left again. Wearing a pout, I averted my eyes and said, "Doesn't matter. There's little to be done with it."

"Please don't tell me someone has died."

Frowning, I turned my gaze to his. "If someone had died, I would have cancelled our date."

"All grandparents alive, then?"

I chuckled against my will. "Alive and well."

"Good. Parents, too?"

"Unless something's happened since last week, yes."

"Is it Aaron, then?"

My breath hitched.

Upon my delayed response, he nodded. "Hit the nail on the head, didn't I?" Folding his arms, he looked away.

"How?" It was all I could manage.

He grimaced and shrugged his shoulders. "Don't know. Call it intuition. He did seem rather infuriated last Saturday. Can't imagine he was thrilled if you've told him about our date."

Trying to calm the uprising of my emotions, I faced the window beside us and focused on breathing slowly for a few seconds. "I didn't tell him," I eventually murmured. "I meant to, but he broke things off before I could."

"Did he?" he questioned sympathetically and tilted his head. "Did he say why?"

I directed my wet eyes to him. He didn't look smug, and I appreciated it immensely. I couldn't tolerate a smug William right now. I'd tear his guts out. "Yeah," I replied, upset.

With a sigh, he leaned forward again, and his eyes roamed across my face for a brief while. "Was it because he's got feelings for you?"

"Ye-es." My voice broke. Hurriedly, I shielded my face with my palms and continued to focus on my breathing. I did not want to cry, especially not in public.

"I'm sorry, Cara. Honestly, I am. Obviously, this was what I wanted, but I still hate to see you like this. I'm aware he was, and probably still is, one of your best friends."

Sniffing, I spread my fingers apart to look at him through the gaps. "Who are you, and what have you done with my entitled arsehole of a boss?"

He smiled crookedly. "He'll be back later – when he isn't going to do any serious damage."

Despite how sorrowful I was, his reply made me giggle. "Can't wait."

Hearing me, he sent me such a gorgeous smile that I had to catch my breath. He truly was an outstandingly handsome man.

Rubbing the back of his head, he said, "I'm happy to hear that you still want to go on a date with me despite everything with Aaron." He reached across the table for my wrists. Dragging them up to his mouth, he granted them each a tender kiss precisely on my pulse. My heart jerked within me when the same feeling I'd sensed earlier streamed through it.

Was I starting to fall in love with this man?

"Yeah, well, you'd be a bloody thorn in the side if I didn't, wouldn't you?" I replied dryly and retrieved my hands from his grip.

A cunning gleam entered his eyes. "In Ancient Rome, they called it 'divide and conquer'."

Incredulous, I reclined deep into my seat and folded my arms over my breasts. That had been his tactic in all this? "Will, are you implying that you tried to separate us? On purpose?"

He shook his head. "No. Happy accident, though."

It was in moments like these – when he shamelessly confessed to his selfish feelings – that I questioned both him and whether we had a future worth pursuing. "Do you read strategy during your spare time?" I asked, astonished.

He chuckled and scratched his stubble. "I'm an avid reader. Always have been, and I played lots of chess growing up. Everything's strategy, Cara, and I've always had a flair for it. Anyway, I was drunk on Saturday. I spoke without thinking. So, I meant what I said. It wasn't my intention to divide you and Aaron quite like that. I had hoped you would simply dump him." He shrugged. "Now, I'm not sure exactly how things played out, but I wouldn't be surprised if he gave you an ultimatum. If he did, I'm sorry. That really wasn't my intention."

Sometimes, his perceptiveness truly got on my nerves. "You're outrageous," I grumbled, annoyed.

He sighed, and his shoulders sank with it. "Cara, I told you I'm not going to waste your time, and I meant it. You won't regret this. On a completely different note, try not to chew off Andy's balls when we get back to the office. I know you're having a rough day, but so is he. He and Chloe had another big fight about whether to have a baby yesterday, but he's always goofing around, so I can understand that you find it difficult to tell if something's bothering him."

My blood stilled. "Christ," I breathed, upset, "that didn't even cross my mind. God, I'm so sorry."

"Don't worry about it. Just thought you should know. Besides, it won't be long till they're reconciled. He's lonely without her. It's only a question of time before he'll realise that a baby is the right thing for them both."

"Poor Andy," I mumbled, pushing my long, wavy brown hair back behind my ear. I genuinely felt for him. I couldn't imagine how painful it must be to be in such different places within a relationship, and they had been together for a whole decade, too.

"Poor Chloe, if you ask me," William muttered.

I tilted my head. "How come you're siding with her?"

He shrugged again. "I have my reasons."

"And?"

He shook his head. "I'm afraid I can't tell you that without first receiving both Andy and Chloe's explicit consent."

I was astonished by that, and it revealed itself in my smile. "Wow. You really do keep secrets, don't you? Why wasn't I treated to the same luxury?"

His expression was sober. "To the grave – unless permission to spill is granted. And I spilled your secret to Jason because it wasn't only yours. It was mine as well."

I nodded. "True."

"I'd never spill a secret that wasn't any of my business."

"I love that."

"Good. Anyway, did you say you're unsure about whether you want children?" he asked then, and I wondered for a moment if he'd brought Andy up simply to create an opening so that he could ask. Knowing how slick he could be, it wouldn't be surprising, and I did recall telling him that I was uncertain about whether I did or not.

"I did say that, didn't I?"

He nodded. "Did you mean it?"

"Yes."

"Why are you unsure?"

"I'm just not sure it's for me."

"So, you don't dismiss the idea completely?"

"No." I narrowed my eyes at him. "But I've got ambitions I'd like to see through first."

He snorted. "Ambitions are subject to constant change, Cara."

A valid point. I cocked my head from side to side, not disagreeing.

"I want five," he stated. Upon my gape, he asserted, "Yes, five, so you ought to prepare." The grin he flashed me made me realise that he was joking.

"You're crazy, and you're getting far, far ahead of yourself," I fired back. "Let's start with dating, and, if you're lucky, maybe I'll grant you the title of my boyfriend."

Again, his laughter sounded through my ears, making my heart contract. "Allow me to make this clear, once and for all," he said and pointed his finger at me while his grin persisted. "If you upgrade me to the status of being your boyfriend, *you'll* be the lucky one." Suddenly, he frowned. "Actually, I take that back. We'll both be most lucky."

I shook my head in comic despair. "Where does this confidence stem from? How can you be so sure when you've only known me for a few months?"

"It just…feels right. Is that entirely one-sided?"

I blushed and looked away from him. "No."

"Thought so."

Always so self-assured.

A comfortable silence sat between us for a moment, and, when I realised it, an affectionate, shy smile claimed my mouth. I loved that we could spend silence in comfort. It was a feat, and it was also evidence of our compatibility, so I savoured the moment.

"Will?"

"Yeah?" he replied nonchalantly, swallowing a mouthful of the Chicken BLT sandwich he'd ordered.

"Thank you," I said and held his gaze. He frowned and took another bite.

Another swallow and he responded affectionately, "Anything for you." Amidst the affection was a casualness that I adored.

Combined with his tone, his words struck me as one of the sweeter things I'd ever heard. They echoed round my mind, and I wondered if I would ever forget them.

He chuckled at my smitten expression. "There's plenty more where that came from, darling," he assured me with a smile.

I sighed, content.

YOURS ENTIRELY

Jason had made dinner when I got home from work. It smelled wonderful, but I couldn't deduce what was on the menu. Little did it matter. I had blind faith in Jason's cooking. He could as well have served a bull's testicles without me knowing, and I would have devoured it all.

Like his elder brother, he was an excellent chef, and I knew their mother, Daphné, was to thank for their skills. While she had been born and raised in England, Daphné's parents were French. Her father, Thibault Bellamy, was a renowned chef who had moved to London with Daphné's mother, Sophie, in 1956, where Daphné had been born in 1963. Together, her parents had started a restaurant that had been awarded two Michelin stars, but they had sold the business upon their retirement in 1997, and it had lost its fame since then. I'd learnt this over dinner with the Night family back in April, which was the first time I'd met Daphné.

Either way, Daphné had honoured Thibault and Sophie's legacy by nurturing a passion for cooking ever since she was a little girl.

Due to her and John's demanding jobs, I was aware they had employed a chef to cook most of their daily meals, but when I'd been over for dinner in April, Daphné had been the chef, and it had been an unforgettable experience. Though I would never dare to tell Dad for fear of breaking his heart, I'd never had a better meal in my life. In light of it, it was no wonder that both Jason and William were excellent cooks. Daphné had obviously taught them well.

"What's for dinner? It smells wonderful," I asked as I sauntered into the kitchen.

Standing in front of the stove, Jason glanced at me across his shoulder before he dipped a spoon into the casserole to have a taste.

"Boeuf bourguignon," he replied in perfect French, but it made no sense to me. After all, I'd opted to learn Spanish during my days in school. It had seemed more practical at the time since Spanish was the national language across several countries around the world. However, these days, I regretted my choice, as French was, in my opinion, the most beautiful language in the world. Moreover, I'd hardly used my skills in Spanish since my days in school.

"That is?"

"Essentially a beef stew, but with a loud presence of red wine," he explained to my amusement, "which means it needs to cook for several hours. I've been working on it all afternoon."

I raised a brow. "Sounds luxurious. What's the occasion?"

He put the spoon aside and turned to face me properly. "I was in the mood to spoil you."

I smiled. These Night brothers were surely going the extra mile to brighten my day, weren't they? I wondered if William had spoken to Jason and warned him that I was feeling low. If he had, I appreciated the sentiment, because it could only mean he was trying to look after me.

"How come?"

"Will called this afternoon," he said, confirming my suspicions. "Said you aren't having the best day."

Holding his gaze, I nodded.

Wrinkles formed across his nose. "Honestly, I already suspected since your door was locked when I came home last night. Did things end badly when you spoke to Aaron?"

Without saying anything, I nodded again.

The bright blue in his eyes mellowed, and the view inspired me to think of William. Like Jason, his eyes had conveyed the same compassion over lunch today. Sometimes it was odd how similar they looked when expressing their emotions. Then again, their eyes were nearly identical, and since so much emotion was borne through them, I supposed it made perfect sense.

"I'm not going to ask if you're alright, because you're obviously not, but if you want to talk about it, I'm all ears," he said.

Tears threatened to run down my cheeks. Truly, nobody could console me as well as Jason. He always knew what to say, and, in the wake of losing Aaron, I was more grateful for him than ever.

I released a pent-up breath. "There's not much to say. What did Will tell you?"

"Nothing, really – only that you aren't having a great day and that I ought to tread gently." As if Jason ever did anything else.

"Right, well, Aaron confessed to having feelings for me last night. Gave me an ultimatum. Said we had to upgrade things to an exclusive relationship or cut contact. Until he's moved on, he doesn't want anything to do with me."

Seeing the misery that revealed itself in my subsequent grimace, Jason said, "Oh, Cara. I'm so sorry." He pulled me into his embrace. Trying and failing to suppress my sobs, I shook in his arms. *God*, the relief of unleashing the full extent of my sorrow into his embrace.

"He'll come round." He tried to soothe me.

"I don't know, Jason," I replied, my voice high-pitched. "He looked so heartbroken. Honestly, the whole thing has made me question whether we were ever friends or whether it was all based on an ulterior motive."

"Shh, Cara," he mollified me. "Don't speculate like that. Just give him some time. He might have feelings for you, but I'm sure friendship is at the root of it all. Time will tell."

I tilted my head to look up at him. "I hope you're right. I really don't want to lose him."

Tucking my head under his chin, he continued to hold me.

"I just feel so guilty," I mumbled. "Like I've betrayed him."

"That's just your feelings, Cara," he reassured me patiently. "You've done absolutely nothing wrong. Aaron knew what your deal was. He should have told you the instant he realised his feelings for you, but I suppose he was scared about the potential consequences."

I nodded. "Still, I can't help feeling culpable. Part of me thinks I ought to have suspected." Another grimace crossed my face while I paused to catch my breath. "I never meant to hurt him," I insisted, like it would somehow repent my sin.

"He knows that, Cara. It's his own fault it turned out like this. Really, he should have warned you."

Disbelieving of my obliviousness, I said, "I can't believe I never suspected it."

He made a noise of hesitation. "I don't mean to be annoying, but I had my doubts all along. Perhaps it's because I'm also a man, but, from the way he treated you, I've always suspected that he was sweeter on you than he cared to admit."

"I was completely blindsided," I replied with a shake of my head as I wiped my cheeks.

"Please, stop being so hard on yourself. You can't always see things when you're in the middle of it. Sometimes it's easier for an outsider to spot the warning signs."

I puffed out a blast of air. "I recall asking him sometime in the spring whether he'd ever considered dating someone during our arrangement, but he made it crystal clear that he wasn't interested in anything romantic. I don't know – I just perceived it as a confirmation that we were on the same page."

Cupping my cheeks, Jason leaned in to place a tender kiss on my forehead. As he pulled back, he stared compassionately into my eyes. "Like I said, he was probably scared that admitting his feelings would mean losing you. In the end, you've always been unequivocal on your lack of interest in relationships, and, unlike Will, Aaron's probably been intimidated by that."

I sighed. It was possible he was on to something. "Yeah. Maybe. Would make sense."

Jason pouted. "Your fling with Will must have inspired him to act. Now or never, sort of thing."

"Maybe," I said again. "Either way, I guess I'll just have to wait and see what comes of this."

"I'm afraid so," he agreed. "If it's any consolation, you'll always have me. I don't love you that way at all."

I laughed. I could always count on Jason to make me laugh even when I was at rock bottom. "Thanks for reassuring me, Jase, but I've never thought anything else."

He gave a lopsided smile. "Good."

The doorbell rang then. Puzzled, I pulled out of his arms and said, "Are you expecting anyone?"

He frowned. "No."

I wondered aloud, "Could it be Will?"

He shook his head. "I invited him for dinner actually, but he turned me down. Said he thought you'd appreciate some time alone with me."

How considerate of him. It was true that I preferred to be alone with Jason tonight. "Hm," I uttered and turned on my heel to open the door.

Speaking into the intercom, I said, "Hello?"

"Hello, this is Yusuf from Appleyard. I've got a delivery for a

Cara Jane Darby?"

What on earth? "Um, yes, that's me. Hang on." I pressed the button to let him in downstairs.

Opening the door, I waited for him to exit the lift, and, once he did, my eyes went wide open. I could hardly see his upper body behind the huge bouquet. The flower arrangement consisted of pink and white flowers, blended with a bit of green, and its beauty took my breath away.

"Oh, my gosh!" Astounded, I took a hold of it. It had even come with a vase. "Jason!" I called.

"Christ," he replied, right behind me. Turning, I glanced up at him.

"To Ms Cara Jane Darby," Yusuf said, "from Mr William Night."

I looked at Jason again when the deliveryman uttered William's name, and we both stared at one another, astonished.

"Did you know?" I asked him.

"No. This is all him."

"There's more," Yusuf said.

"Of course there is," Jason murmured, amused. "Here." He took the flowers out of my hands to proceed into the flat with them.

What on earth had brought this on? Was this how William romanced his women? Lavishing them with gifts out of the blue? I'd never been a target of such courteous and romantic treatment in all my life, and it made me feel a bit awkward, as I had no idea how to handle it.

Presenting a stylish paper bag, Yusuf said, "The card's inside."

I reached for it. "Thank you." It was heavy.

"Of course, Miss. May I have your signature, please?" he asked politely and withdrew an electronic device from his back pocket.

After wishing him a pleasant evening, I locked the door and headed towards the kitchen. On my way there, I saw that Jason had left the bouquet on the dining table in our dining room.

"What's got into him?" I wondered as I walked into the kitchen with the paper bag.

"What do you think?" Jason replied, amused. "You're dating now. He obviously wants to show you he's serious."

"We haven't actually been on a proper date yet," I corrected him as I opened the bag to peek inside, wherein I discovered a bottle of Pinot Noir as well as a box of handmade chocolates. "Christ, he's pulled out all the stops, hasn't he?"

Jason laughed at my obvious amazement. "I'm amused to see this romantic side of him," he admitted. "Honestly, I'm taking notes. I've much to learn."

"It must be the French in your blood," I replied, and I couldn't hide my smitten smile. Within me, my heart was going on a rampage. Being doted upon like this was a novel experience, and it filled me with giddiness.

"Perhaps," Jason replied with a shrug.

Once I found the card at the bottom of the bag, I pulled it out of the white envelope to read the content. It wasn't written in William's sharp and elegant handwriting, but electronically, so I suspected he must have ordered it online, but when? Today? If so, before or after he'd learnt about me and Aaron?

To Wonder Woman (aka Cara Jane Darby)

This wine should go well with your meal tonight. The chocolates are there to offer the sweetness that I won't be able to since I thought you might appreciate being alone with your very best friend tonight.
Despite everything, you've still got us.

Yours entirely,
Will

And you are more than enough, I thought to myself.

Since he was clearly aware of what was on the menu, he must have ordered the flowers shortly after speaking to Jason today. That notion made me smile. He was truly going out of his way to boost my mood.

"Wow," I breathed out, entirely wooed. While my on-hold friendship with Aaron would continue to hurt for quite some time, William's tenderness was surely numbing some of my pain.

"What's it say?" Jason asked.

"The wine should be paired with the meal. Other than that, it's private," I replied sassily and pressed the card to my bosom.

"Oh come on! Tell me what it says!"

I laughed. "No. I'm not going to expose your brother like that. This is between him and me."

He rolled his eyes. "Urgh. How am I supposed to learn how to woo a woman if you won't show me his tricks? He's obviously a master of the art."

I giggled. "Ask him for lessons. And I wasn't aware you were even interested in 'wooing' any women at the moment."

He scoffed and changed the subject. "Dinner should be ready in half an hour."

"I love you, Jason."

"I know," he smiled coyly. "I love you, too."

"I'll set the table for us. But, first, I'm going to send a photo to Will and thank him."

I went to get my phone from my purse in the hall. Eyeing my screen, I saw that I had an unread message from Olivia.

> Are you free anytime soon? I know you're busy with work these days, but I miss your face x

I smiled. Her message was yet another reminder that I still had precious people in my life even though Aaron had taken a –

hopefully temporary – leave from it. I decided I'd call her straight after sending William a message.

> Thanks for the flowers, the chocolates, and the wine, Will. But, most importantly, I'm thankful for you. I've never been treated to something similar before. You spoil me. Thanks for being the wonderful man that you are. I'm glad we're giving things a chance x

I sent it on Instagram. However, he hadn't been active for several hours, so I didn't expect him to see it straight away. I rang Olivia without further ado, but, to my disappointment, she didn't pick up. Oh well. She'd probably ring me back soon, so, in the meantime, I went to help Jason set the table.

§ § §

Halfway through dinner, I heard my phone ring from the hall. Looking up from my plate, I met Jason's gaze and said, "It's probably Livy. I'll call her back later."

Nodding, he swallowed a mouthful. "How's she doing?"

I frowned. "Um, fine, I think?" Since I got the feeling he was aiming at something in particular, I followed up with, "Why? Anything in particular on your mind?"

Suddenly he seemed engrossed by his dish. "Well, she and I don't really talk about our love lives to each other, which makes sense considering she's more your friend than mine."

"Oh," I said as I understood. "You're wondering about Colin?"

He nodded. "Has she managed to move on yet?"

It was charming that he took such a genuine interest in Olivia's wellbeing. Then again, Jason has always been remarkably empathic, and I knew he had a soft spot for her. Thinking back to January, I recalled how infuriated he had been when I'd explained that she and Colin had broken up after she had uncovered his frequent infidelity.

"I think so. She's not mentioned him much lately."

He glanced sideways, but I wasn't blind to his elusive behaviour. He was acting strange, I thought.

"Is she seeing anyone, then?" he eventually asked.

His question stirred suspicion in me. It wasn't like him to dig so deeply into Olivia's love life, or anyone's for that matter.

"Er, not that I'm aware of. Why? Do you mean to ask her out?" The last bit was intended as a joke, but when he faced me again, the expression he wore made my eyes widen. I had clearly hit the nail on the head.

"Oh my God," I uttered disbelievingly. "You fancy Livy?"

"Maybe a bit," he confessed with a casual shrug of his shoulders.

"Jason. Why haven't you told me?"

He grimaced. "Well, she wasn't single, was she? Didn't seem like something worth telling."

Stunned, I continued to stare at him. "I honestly can't believe this. I didn't suspect a thing! How long have you felt this way?"

He chuckled. "About a year. Please don't tell her."

Offended by his momentary display of doubt regarding my loyalty, I paid him another frown. "Of course I won't."

After a sip of wine, he said, "It's not that I doubt you. I'd just prefer if nobody meddled, that's all."

I went quiet for a minute as I processed his confession. I couldn't believe he'd kept this to himself for an entire year; I'd never suspected his interest in the slightest. Like Aaron, he was clearly adept at keeping secrets.

Still trying to recover from my shock, I said, "Is Will aware of this?" I looked back to see him shake his head.

"Haven't told a soul till now. Besides, I already know what Will would've said. He would have told me to pursue her, but since she's been in a relationship I didn't want to. It's against my values."

I couldn't help reflecting that his approach could hardly be more different to William's. They were polar opposites. In fact,

I remembered vividly what Will had told me the very first time we met: he would've tried to lure me away from my boyfriend if I'd had one. And, in some ways, I supposed he had lived up to his word by tempting me away from Aaron.

"You're quite right," I said. "That would be typical of him."

He nodded. "Yeah, so, I just haven't bothered. I try to limit the amount of nagging he can do."

Laughter burst out of my mouth. "Teach me your ways, J."

"I'll do my best." He smiled. "Anyway, I'm not sure whether it's smart to ask her out yet. She's still relatively fresh out of a long-term relationship after all, and she's the one who got dumped. I don't expect my chances are at their peak right now."

I pondered the situation. "I could do some digging for you, if you like."

The light-blue in his eyes softened. "Would you?"

I grinned and reached across the table for his hand. "Yes, of course. I'd do anything for you. Would you prefer daily or weekly reports?"

He laughed as I released his hand. "Weekly."

"As you please."

We gave each other demure smiles then, and it made me laugh again.

"I'm sure she'll accept," I told him. "She'd be an idiot to reject you. You're the whole package. Clever, tender, handsome as hell, fit, a wonderful cook, the list goes on."

"I hope so." He sighed. "I really like her. She's so sweet, you know?"

"She is," I agreed. "And she's also a hopeless romantic. You'd make for a lovely couple, and I'd be very happy third-wheeling you."

He chuckled. "Idiot."

I gave him another smile, but I couldn't ignore the concern that crept into my mind upon the news. Regardless of how much I wanted to support him in this, the realist in me warned that things might become awkward if she didn't return his interest. However, I knew I wasn't one to talk, so I didn't voice it. After all, I was currently seeing his brother. Things would surely become awkward if that didn't work out, either. So, like him, all I could do was cross my fingers and hope for the best.

"One thing's been bothering me a bit, though," he suddenly said.

"Oh?"

"Yeah. Remember when you first met Will?"

I raised a brow. "Hard to forget."

He chuckled, but it wasn't genuine. "Well, do you remember what you texted me that night?"

I frowned. "Um, not precisely."

He nodded, avoiding my eyes. "Well, you told me you'd insulted a man that Livy wanted to get off with. That man was Will, Cara. Livy wanted to get off with Will, didn't she?"

His statement sucked the air straight out of my lungs. *Shit.* I hadn't thought of that. Poor Jason. This must have bothered him ever since he found out that it was William I had slept with in April.

Sympathy formed in my features while I searched for his gaze. "Jason, if anything, that works in your favour considering the resemblance between you two. Really, as soon as he opened his dreadful mouth, Livy was appalled. And, where William failed to live up to her expectations, you won't, because you're not rude the way he can be."

"It still feels a bit weird to know that she was sexually attracted to him at one point."

I wasn't sure what to say, so I spent some time contemplating how to reply. "I get that. But, seriously, Livy's interest died the minute he opened his mouth, Jason. I promise you. She even went so far as to give me her blessing straight away – said I could have him instead. She wouldn't have done that if she were genuinely interested in him."

He shrugged. "Maybe."

"Jason, she wasn't aware he was your brother. Neither of us were. It's not fair of you to hold that against her."

Finally he faced me, but it was with a frown. "I'm not holding it against her. I'm just saying I'm a bit uncomfortable knowing she finds him physically attractive."

"I understand, but really, Jason, she's only human. What's more, she's a straight woman, and – just like you – your brother happens to be a remarkably gorgeous man. Either way, he's not a threat to you. Is that what you're worried about?" Since he didn't immediately refute it, I continued, "*I'm* dating him now, Jason. He's into *me*, and Livy is definitely not interested in him. To be fair, Livy will probably be really happy to hear that I'm seeing him now. Will's not a threat to you at all."

"I shouldn't have said anything," he eventually murmured. "You've got the wrong end of the stick. I don't feel threatened by Will per se. It's just…weird. I can't really explain it. But now that I've said it out loud, it seems like a much bigger deal than it really is. It was only a thought that's crossed my mind – that's all."

Seeing his point, I nodded. "Right. I'll pretend you never said anything."

He sent me a grateful smile. "Thanks. It was silly."

"It was."

After a brief moment of silence, he asked, "Is Will aware that she was initially interested in him that night?"

My grimace exposed the truth. "He deduced it."

Jason sighed. "Brilliant. So, if I were to tell him about Livy, he's going to feel awkward as well."

I shook my head. "I seriously doubt that. Perhaps for a second, but he's a rational man. He'll consign it to oblivion."

"Imagine what a story it would be to tell our kids," Jason murmured and leaned back while folding his arms. "Oh, yes, you see, your mother tried to chat up your uncle first. Fortunately for you guys, he put her off by being his usual self – an absolute dickhead."

I laughed. "Jason, come on. What's done is done. And it really doesn't matter. Just let it go."

He chuckled. "I'm only joking. I do dread telling Will, though. He'll definitely tease me about it."

"I'll tell him not to."

He scoffed. "As if he'd listen."

"I think you underestimate him. Obviously you know him far better than I do, but I'm not sure he's as big a dick as you would have me believe. When it really counts, he's a brilliant person. If you make it clear that you don't want to be reminded of that piece of *history*," I emphasised, "I'm sure he'll respect it."

Releasing a loud, long breath, he rubbed the back of his head. "Yeah, perhaps you're right. I ought to give him the benefit of the doubt."

"You do."

He smiled then. "I'm amused you're defending him. You sound like his girlfriend."

I snorted. "Don't be ridiculous. I'm only being reasonable."

"Whatever you say."

§ § §

After dinner, I insisted on doing the dishes since Jason had cooked me such a lavish dinner. That said, he was determined to help, so, whilst listening to Foals playing in the background, I washed while he dried whatever couldn't go into the dishwasher, such as the expensive crystal wine glasses which he had been gifted by his parents some years ago.

"Right," I said once we'd finished. "I'll be rolling into my room now, if you don't mind."

My joke earned me chuckle before he slapped my stomach.

"Jason," I scolded as I recoiled. "Careful. I'm seriously full. I'd hate to vomit up your amazing cooking."

His chuckle transitioned into laughter. "Sorry. Couldn't resist."

"Idiot," I said with a smile and shook my head to myself as

I approached the hall to find my phone. Entering my bedroom, I closed the door after myself and got comfortable in bed, then FaceTimed Olivia. This time, she picked up immediately.

"Hi," she greeted fondly, and the sight of her cute face made me smile. There was a childish beauty about Olivia. She had small features, and her cheeks were still quite round, like she'd never grown off the baby fat. However, it worked in her favour as it made her look younger than she truly was. She looked forever twenty years old.

"Hi, darling. How are you? Sorry I've been so absent lately. A lot's been going on."

"Well, that makes one of us. Summer holidays are boring as hell. I never thought I'd say this, but I actually miss coursework. At least I always had something to do."

I chuckled. "Aren't Jess and Nora keeping you entertained?" I asked, referring to her flatmates.

Before moving in with Jason, I used to live with the three of them, but since Nora and Jess had always been Olivia's friends, more so than mine, I had never really felt at home living with them. That was why I had been eager to accept Jason's offer. Olivia had been slightly upset about it, but since she had understood my reasoning she hadn't given me a hard time for it.

In the end, Nora and Jess were too dramatic for my liking and tended to gossip more often than not. We simply hadn't clicked, but I hadn't really expected anything else; we weren't friends at college either. It was Olivia who had begged me to move in with them shortly after graduation, and since I'd wanted to fledge the nest, I had grabbed the opportunity.

"They're in Spain with Elinor," she explained with a sigh. Right. I'd forgotten about that. Elinor was the girl who had moved into the room I had vacated. I was aware that Olivia had been invited to join their trip to Spain, but she had declined in favour of our plans to visit Jason's holiday house again, on the

Isle of Wight. However, following the prolonging of my vacation scheme, I'd cancelled, so Olivia was now unsure about whether she still wanted to go. If she did, it would only be her and the lads.

"Right," I murmured. "I'm sorry. Suppose you've seen Dawn a lot, then? And Christian?" I asked, referring to her mother and her elder brother.

"Yeah."

"Well, tell them I said hello."

"I will."

Recalling Jason's confession earlier, I pursed my lips for a second. "Have you made up your mind about whether to go to the Isle of Wight with Jason, Stephen and Jon yet?"

She looked away. "Not really. Since you can't, I feel like it would be a bit weird. I don't know them as well as you do. I'm not really part of their group."

I snorted. "Livy. You know what they're like. They'd welcome you like you've belonged all along."

"Still. At this point, I think they're hoping for an all-lads' trip."

I begged to differ. "Have you talked to Jason about it?"

"Yeah. We discussed it when we were in the park with Stephen and Giselle two weeks ago. He sounded like he really wanted me to join, but I'm not sure."

"You should absolutely go," I said. "It will be great fun, Livy. I'm sure of it."

"I'll see. I've still got a few weeks to decide."

"True."

"Anyway, how have you been? Work stressing you out?"

Knowing I had quite the bomb to drop, I blew my cheeks out and looked away for a beat. "You could say that."

She frowned. "You alright?"

"Sort of."

"Cara, spill it already."

"Right," I murmured and turned my gaze back to my phone.

"Well, there's really no way to say this, so I'll just put it plainly."

My heart started hammering in my chest. For some odd reason, telling Olivia about this made the whole thing seem even more real. William was becoming a larger part of my life by the second. Yet, somehow, bringing it to the awareness of the people I cherished seemed to grant him even more space, while simultaneously increasing the pace of things. Telling people about us was a manifestation of my choice, and with it came graver consequences. If things didn't work out, interrogations would ensue. People would inevitably care about the outcome. While I enjoyed the thrill of it, I also found the risk involved rather intimidating.

"I'm growing old here," Olivia complained.

"I'm going on a date with Will on Friday," I blurted out.

"What?" she exclaimed, and I could tell from her wide eyes that she couldn't believe what she had heard. "You're going on a date with *Will*?"

"Yes. On Friday."

She gaped for a good while before she gathered her wits. "To be clear, you mean William Night, right? Jason's brother? Your *boss?*"

"That's the one."

Her jaw fell to the floor. "What the actual hell, Cara? I thought you didn't like him!"

Redness crowded my cheeks. "Yeah, well, I might have been in denial."

"Oh my God. I bloody knew it. I knew it!" she insisted. "You'd have to be a robot to resist that sort of chemistry. Cara, fucking yes!" she cheered. "I am *so* happy for you! And for William. He must be over the moon. I'm sure he's been pining for you ever since you met!"

"Thanks."

"Tell me everything! What happened? What changed your mind?"

"It's a long story."

"I've got time!"

Her excitement made me laugh. Before long, I was sharing the whole story, and her engaged responses charmed me to my toes. For the first time in my life, I felt like a proper teenager.

"I honestly can't believe this," she said before I'd reached the part about Aaron. "You're really going on an actual date with someone? Despite your reservations?"

I chuckled. "Yes."

"But you've always avoided romance as though it were a plague. William must be wielding some serious magic. Especially considering he's your boss *and* Jason's brother. You've been crystal clear about how much those circumstances have bothered you."

I giggled. "I know. He really does."

Looking sideways, she pondered for some time, and I spent it observing her with some curiosity. What was on her mind? After a while, she faced me again, and from her sober expression, I could tell something serious was headed my way.

"Cara, does this mean you're in love with him?"

Her question took me aback. Speechless, I stared straight at her as blood warmed my cheeks. My pulse drummed behind my ears.

"Gosh, look at you. You're a tomato," she remarked, amused.

"I'm not sure," I finally answered. "I've never experienced this before. But I think I'm getting there."

She smiled sympathetically. "Do you think he's in love with you?"

I hadn't thought my blush could intensify, but it did. At the same time, alarms went off in my head. I didn't want to entertain that thought. Frankly, the mere idea that William's feelings might be that profound unsettled me, because if our chemistry failed to transition into love on my end, I'd have to break his heart, and – for an abundance of reasons – I dreaded that potential scenario with all my heart. Work would become a place worse than hell and Jason would be stuck in the middle. And, worst of all, I would be rejecting a man who absolutely deserved to have his feelings reciprocated.

"I don't think so," I said. "Like me, I think he's just curious to see where things lead. He's certainly optimistic, but I don't quite think he's in love."

"I think he is."

I hated her certainty. "Livy, please don't. I'm uncomfortable." I shook my head vehemently.

Realising that she'd crossed the line, she pouted. "Sorry. I shouldn't have said anything. I got a bit excited."

To change the subject, I said, "Anyway, there's more, but it's not happy news." The thought of Aaron made my giddiness plummet into misery.

Her intuition served her well when she asked, "Let me guess. It's about Aaron, isn't it?"

With a loud sigh, I started explaining everything that had happened last night, and recounting it out loud made guilt bloom in my chest again. Soon enough, the awful memory triggered my tears to return. Olivia did her best to console me, but I could tell from her responses that she was too excited about my date with William to really sympathise.

By the time I finally hung up, my tears had stopped flowing. We'd agreed that she would come over on Friday before my date to help me mentally prepare, although, in truth, I had mainly invited her because I thought Jason might appreciate her company. I hadn't managed to ask her whether she'd met anyone else yet, but, knowing her, I wouldn't have had to ask if it were the case.

After our call ended, I opened Instagram to see if I had received any new messages, and, sure enough, William had replied.

> Hi, love. Glad you liked them (and me).
> Sorry about the late reply. Went training.
> Anyway, how was dinner? Jason's cooking
> raise your spirits? x

I grinned as I started typing my response.

His cooking, like yours (and Daphné's), is out of this world. I'm a beached whale rn. Can't move, and I'm huge as hell x

My heart did a flip when he immediately saw it. An instant later he was typing a reply.

I actually just laughed out loud. Can't imagine that, fit as you are. Either way, I'm glad you ate to your heart's content x

I'm about to fall asleep btw. Been a long day, and I plan to train again before work tomorrow x

Glad I could put a smile on your face. I've been wearing the one you put on mine all day x

Right. You're a machine… Anyway, sleep well. See you tomorrow x

Yes. Looking forward to my good morning kiss. May I have two?

I sniggered. His greed was oddly charming.

How about a full-on snog? You deserve it x

Fuck yes. Thank you x

Despite the odds, I went to bed with a smile on my face, and I knew I mainly had William to thank for it.

3

WHEN ONE DOOR CLOSES

Even though I had last seen William just hours ago, I could not seem to calm the frantic march of my heart. "I'm growing really nervous," I mumbled as I paced around my bedroom after work.

Walking in circles, I shook my hands in the air to expedite the drying of my nail polish. I had only just painted them – something I seldom did – a light shade of blue, and I'd realised too late that the colour matched William's eyes. At that point, I'd decided that in the incident of another Freudian slip like that, I would head straight for the mental hospital.

Olivia smirked from my bed as she studied her own nails, leisurely. "Cara, you'll be fine." She took her glass of iced tea from my nightstand. "Are you spending the night at his?"

My head spun to face her, and I stopped pacing. Eyes wide, I studied her, stumped. "Shit. I forgot to ask. What do I do? If

I'm spending the night at his, I'll need clothes to wear in the morning, and bringing a change of clothes now that I haven't asked will come across as presumptuous. Desperate, at best!"

She rolled her eyes as she sipped on her cold brew, and I envied her state of relaxation. "Stop making problems for yourself. Just bring a bag. He doesn't need to know what's inside. If you don't want to do that, you can either head home early in the morning or head here after your date – or he could lend you some clothes of his own. Wouldn't be the first time."

I took a deep breath and nodded. "Right. You're right. It's not a problem."

"I am so amused that this is your first date ever." She laughed. "You're something else. All the men you've slept with, and you haven't been on a single date – ever. Finally someone's challenging your commitment issues."

"I haven't got commitment issues."

"Er, yes, you do. 'I don't have the talent of growing easily attached to people'," she quoted me.

I scoffed. "That's different. I'm not afraid to commit, per se."

"Cara."

"You're right. I'm not being honest with myself. But it's not been commitment issues in the stereotypical sense. I've never shied away from romance because I've been scared of getting hurt. I just haven't been so ensnared by a man before, and I've been committed to my education. So, that's why I haven't wanted to date before."

"And those reasons are perfectly valid, but the result is the same. You've had issues with commitment."

"I don't see the point of continuing this debate."

"Me neither. It's bagatelles."

I looked into the mirror. Who was I becoming? "Attachment isn't really my forte," I said and glanced back at Olivia. "But there's just something about him, Livy. He just gets me, you know? I find it really hard to explain. It's like I've known him for ages. He doesn't freak me out, and that speaks volumes, because he's a fast-paced man."

She studied me for a short while, brown eyes analytical. Then she sighed and sipped on her drink again. "Cara, I cannot possibly say how happy I am for you, but I'm also a bit worried. From what you've told me, he does strike me as an intense man, so just be sure to take this at your own pace, yeah? Don't let him rush you into anything you're not ready for. That's bound to end in tragedy."

I nodded. "Yeah. I've already told him this."

"And how did he respond?"

"Said he'd try to be patient."

"Try," she echoed under her breath. "He ought to do more than that. You're a complete novice. He's far more experienced – and older. You're at quite different stages of your lives."

"I know. I've reminded him of this, too. But let's worry about that bridge when we cross it, alright? So far, he's been an absolute daydream."

There was a knock on the door then.

"Yes?"

Jason stepped in, and his eyes sparkled with evident joy and brotherly affection when they met mine. "Well shit, Cara. My brother's a lucky man," he said, taking in my simple white off-the-shoulder summer dress.

I inhaled sharply upon his compliment while my heart skipped a beat. I hoped William would think so, too. "You think?"

Directing his attention to Olivia, he frowned and cocked his head in my direction. "Where's her confidence gone? Thought you were here to offer moral support?"

Amused by his banter, Olivia smirked back and returned her glass to my nightstand. "Well, I'm doing my best. Besides, I'd say it's a sign she's serious about this. First time a man's actually got to her. I can barely recognise her, and I've known her all my life."

"Guys, that's not helping," I whined. "I don't understand why I'm suddenly so nervous. I mean, I saw him just a couple of hours ago and I was totally fine then. This whole dating thing is changing me, and what if he doesn't fancy this new version I'm turning into? In case you've forgotten, the woman he first grew interested in accused him of sharing a bed with his mother! This shitty, nervous girl isn't going to do the trick."

"Oh my God!" Jason laughed. "I'd completely forgotten you did that! That just took on a whole new dimension, seeing as it's *my* mum you were talking about."

I blushed profusely. "Sorry. Daphné didn't deserve that."

"Cara, calm your tits." Olivia groaned. "You'll be fine. Just enjoy it. Being infatuated is exhilarating. Alas, it doesn't last forever, so enjoy it while you can, yeah? Stop fighting it, and quit getting these silly ideas. Will strikes me as pretty confident about what he wants. Besides, I'm sure you're changing him as well. You're not alone in this. He's right there with you."

The idea of William being as affected as I was in all this was a flattering thought, but I found it hard to imagine. Except for when he was drunk, he always practised such impeccable control of himself. Though he could be vulgar and blunt, I knew that everything he said was a decision consciously made, not an impulsive response. So, was it truly plausible that he was sitting at home right now, mustering up courage the same way I was, to face the other on a proper date?

I couldn't see it. On the contrary, my overall impression of him suggested that he was probably feeling completely calm and relaxed about the evening and what it held. It was likely that he was excited, but I couldn't imagine he was nervous. After all, I'd never seen him nervous – ever. It simply wasn't in his character. Rather, he was the embodiment of confidence. Even when he showed me his vulnerable side, his confidence shone through. Had he been insecure, he would have been far more reluctant to confess his weaknesses.

"Maybe," I said. "Either way, I don't understand myself at all right now," I confessed. "I feel like I'm thirteen."

Jason laughed. "I don't understand this, either. You've been interacting – frequently – for months. Just because it's an official date it doesn't mean everything needs to be different. Just treat him like you always have."

That was precisely what I needed to hear. Looking over at him, I breathed out in relief. Finally, I was liberated of some anxiety. As ever, I could always count on Jason to know what to say.

"Thanks, J. You're right. It's just a date. It's not like it warrants any panic. He's still the same man I saw mere hours ago."

"He is," he assured me with a nod. "And you're going to have an amazing time. I'm sure of it. I already know what he's got planned, and I'm positive it's right up your alley."

"You do?" Olivia and I questioned in perfect unison.

He looked cunning. "Yes. He called me a couple of days ago, asking for advice. When I heard his plan, I had nothing to add. I found it perfect. He's really understood who you are, Cara. I'm sure you'll love it."

A massive grin spread my cheeks apart. "Really?" Excitement saturated my tone, joy replacing my anxiety.

"Really. It's quite casual, just like you wanted."

"Ah, this has calmed me down a bit," I said. "Thanks, Jase."

"Here to help. Always."

"You're rendering my purpose of being here redundant, Jase. Anyway, what time is it?" Olivia asked.

Eyeing the same Rolex wristwatch that his brother had, Jason said, "Half six."

Nodding, I acknowledged that I ought to leave. Being late was out of the question; William wasn't the type of man to be late for anything. I'd learnt as much from working under his leadership for nearly a month. He always arrived early for every event in his calendar.

"I should probably think about leaving," I murmured.

"Yeah," Jason agreed. "Will doesn't make a habit of tardiness. Never has." He watched as I picked up my pastel blue purse matching the colour of my nails. While I collected my things, he asked, "Have you got any plans tonight, Livy?"

Avoiding a glance in her direction, I struggled to hide my amusement.

"No." A smile dwelled in her voice.

"Want to hang out for a bit?"

Say yes, I begged in my mind.

"Sure."

My amusement revealed itself as a grin, but I kept it hidden from her. After I'd packed the essentials, I turned towards them. "Right. I'm heading off."

"Did you remember chewing gum?" Olivia asked with a mischievous smirk.

"Yes. Lip balm, too."

Jason chuckled. "You're all set, then."

"Yes. Have fun, you two." I picked up my plain white trainers from the hall outside. As I opened the front door, I shouted, "Wish me luck!"

"You don't need it!" Jason yelled back.

"Don't come home without at least having kissed him!" Olivia commanded.

I skipped down the stairs.

§ § §

Just as I exited the Tube station at Leicester Square, I spotted him across the street, leaning against a streetlamp. My lips parted and I reached an abrupt halt. Was it truly him?

For a moment, I couldn't be sure. Black Ray-Bans with a golden frame shielded his eyes. He was wearing blue jeans and a white T-shirt that clung to his muscular body in a way that shouldn't be legal. However, his grin gave him away, and my heart threatened to combust upon the sight of it. He had the most amazing smile.

Despite the cluster of people between us and the heavy traffic in the street, I saw only him. This was truly happening. I was going on a date with William Night. Had someone told me three months ago that this would happen, I would never have believed them. Frankly, I could hardly believe it now.

He nodded in acknowledgement as he pushed himself away from the streetlamp. As he crossed the street, the view accelerated the beats of my heart. At that moment in time, I caught myself wanting to jump on him, ravish him with kisses, rip his shirt off and praise his beautiful body. Had we been alone, I would absolutely have done it all, but we weren't.

He'd nearly reached me when he withdrew something from his back pocket. Into my field of vision, he brought a single red rose. My blood simmered in my veins, and I was certain that my pupils were dilated to absorb the entire beauty of him. Every single one of my senses heightened the closer he drew. The purest form of electricity charged between us.

A foot in front of me, he stopped. Taking off his sunglasses, he let them hang from the collar of his white T-shirt. Then, he raised the rose to his mouth, bit off most of the stem, before tucking the beautiful flower behind my left ear and smiling crookedly.

"Hi," he greeted tenderly, and I couldn't stop myself from blushing at the affection that emitted from his eyes.

Utterly taken with him, I replied feebly, "Hi."

"Initially I meant to give you another bouquet, but I thought it would just be a hassle to have to carry it around," he said, as if I'd expected more than this.

I could hardly breathe. His romantic side was blowing my mind. Since I wasn't remotely accustomed to being treated like this, I had no idea how to react. The fact that I was a complete novice in this arena had never been more obvious.

When I failed to reply, he chuckled and placed his curled index finger beneath my chin to tilt my head back. Lowering his head, he left a tender kiss on the middle of my forehead. His lips burnt straight through my skin, and, even when he pulled away, the spot still tingled.

"Is it just me or does this feel a bit different?" he asked.

I shook my head. "It feels very different."

"In a good way, though."

"I think so. It feels good."

He grinned. "I saw you hours ago, and yet, somehow, I feel like I'm seeing you for the first time."

"I know what you mean."

"Like the confines are finally gone," he mused.

I nodded. That was exactly it. After everything we'd been through, this was the first time I was seeing him without worrying about potential repercussions. For the first time ever, external factors didn't spur me to resist him. There were no colleagues here to inhibit me from kissing him. Jason had already given us his blessing, and Aaron was out of the picture – at least for now. And, perhaps most importantly, I was finally allowing myself to consider what my feelings wanted.

William had told me I ought to start listening to my heart more, and I intended to heed that advice. However, that didn't mean I meant to ignore my head completely. On the contrary, I would bring it with me. I was eager to explore where the reign of my heart would take me, but I wouldn't be reckless. I had to be somewhat sensible.

For instance, I was still keeping a watchful eye on whether any new red flags would pop up, or whether old ones would resurface. Thus far, I'd detected none, but only time could ensure me that they would not make an appearance later.

At least from here on out, the only thing that could sabotage us was ourselves. That reality was rather liberating. If neither of us fucked up, and if both of us fell in love, I couldn't see any reason why a relationship wouldn't succeed.

He jolted me out of my thoughts, "Ready, then?"

"Yes." Nervous, I adjusted my purse on my naked shoulder.

"You look edible," he said, eyes devouring my body. "So much, in fact, that I'm seriously considering whether I should just have you for dinner instead."

I had no idea what my facial expression conveyed when his eyes returned to mine. My mind had resigned from the present. Instead, it was entertaining sensuous scenes in his penthouse – a place I hadn't seen for months, but recalled vividly. His naked body above mine, glistening with sweat in the dim light of his living room while he thrust me into total delirium upon his dining table.

Reality struck me all at once when he suddenly clasped my hand in his much larger one. Hyperaware of his touch, I swallowed. I was terribly nervous, so my hand was clammier than usual. I was certain he noticed, but he didn't seem to mind.

"I'm clammy," I apologised.

His eyebrows twitched with some amusement before one arched. "Are you nervous?"

"Of course," I admitted without shame. "I've never done this before."

"Well, you needn't be," he tried to soothe, hand squeezing mine. "I already like you rather a lot, and you'd have to fuck up spectacularly to change it."

My cheeks warmed upon his heartfelt statement.

"Right back at you," I murmured, embarrassed, and looked away. I couldn't help it – I was rigid. This entire experience was nothing short of overwhelming. I didn't know how to behave or what to expect.

"Fancy seeing me out of my suit, do you?" he teased, and I did not miss the reference.

I appreciated that he was trying to lighten the atmosphere by spiking it with humour. Smirking up at him, I said boldly, "I fancy you in all sorts of ways."

"Why, Cara, what could you possibly be getting at?" He chuckled and raised my hand to his mouth to offer the back of it a peck. As he was lowering it, he studied my freshly painted nails.

"Lovely colour," he remarked, and I could hear he meant it. I decided not to tell him that it matched his eyes. Knowing how conceited he could be, I was reluctant to feed his supermassive ego. He might misread it, thinking I'd done it on purpose, and, if he didn't, he would gloat over the subconscious implications of it.

"When did you leave the office today?" I enquired as he started leading the way towards Chinatown. Was that where we were going? I was weak for Chinese food, so I hoped so.

"About two hours ago."

My eyebrows jumped. "That's very early for you."

He shrugged, and his characteristic crooked smile dominated his lips. "Well, I was scared of being late. You made yourself abundantly clear on Sunday – if I stood you up, that'd be it. That's why I stayed at work till midnight yesterday, so that I could leave earlier today."

I pressed my lips together to hide my smile, but it was doomed to failure. Perhaps Olivia had been right. Maybe William was as affected as me. Either way, he hid it well. Did I, too?

"I hope you like Chinese," he murmured, bringing me out of my thoughts.

"I love Chinese, and I eat everything. I'm not particular."

"Good to know. Low-maintenance trait."

"And you?" I asked, curious.

I watched as wrinkles formed across the straight bridge of his nose. "No allergies, but I'm not very fond of ketchup. Tastes far too synthetic – too sweet." His eyes flickered towards me to gauge my reaction.

I giggled. That was rather specific. "You don't fancy sweet?" My tone was playful as I fluttered my lashes at him for comical emphasis.

In his hypnotic eyes, sincere amusement lurked. "Considering who I am on a date with, no, I definitely do not fancy sweet. Spicy is more like it. Hot, sarcastic, sassy – and you're the whole package," he answered and squeezed my hand.

I laughed, and it was a carefree, genuine sound deriving from the depths of my stomach. "Having you break a sweat, am I?"

"Later tonight, sure – if I'm lucky," he said, and my laughter immediately ceased. Instead, my face flushed, and I harboured no doubt that he could see it.

"We'll see."

"I've no expectations," he assured me. "Don't worry."

"If we end up at yours, I might require another T-shirt. I didn't bring any clothes."

The reference made him chuckle. "I'd be more than happy to provide one."

"Will you make me scrambled eggs for breakfast?"

He flashed me a grin. "I'd be delighted."

"Okay, I'll consider it," I replied sassily, although it was clear from my tone that I was joking.

"Would you be willing to close the deal if I told you I've already stored up butter just for you, to be on the safe side?"

"Sold!"

The sound of his laughter set my system alight. It was the most charming melody I'd ever hear.

He released my hand to wrap his arm over my shoulders instead. Welcoming his embrace, I circled his muscular waist with my arm. Walking with linked hands along the crowded streets of London was never an easy feat, and it was especially challenging amidst the tourist season.

Overlooking the financial benefits, I'd always dreaded the number of tourists that flooded London during summer. Very few of them seemed to adjust to Londoners' innate practice of quick speed when walking along the pavements. Tourists would flock around red telephone booths to snap photographs, sightseeing groups would block the pavement whilst they admired historical monuments, and squeezing into the Tube amidst extra humid and sweaty bodies was never pleasant. They never seemed to consider that the people who lived here were trying to get from A to B as swiftly as possible.

So, holding each other like this was undoubtedly the more practical solution – as if that was why we were doing it.

It struck me as a revelation that I just couldn't keep my hands off him. I wanted to touch him constantly, and, whenever I couldn't, I yearned to. It was a longing that resonated through my core, echoing through my bones. Truly, I had become addicted to his touch. It was ridiculous. I felt completely unlike myself.

Men had never intimidated me like this. I'd never felt a single thing under their caress. However, under William's, the sheer magnitude of a feather-light stroke triggered emotional and sensational mayhem within me.

§ § §

"Open yours first," he ordered, authoritative. Whenever he used that tone of his, you'd be a fool not to listen. Still, it both amused and agitated me. Mercurial William Night could switch between being the most tender of men to the most commanding in the span of a mere breath, and, without exception, it kept me on my toes.

He'd just bought us a fortune cookie each after we'd walked around Chinatown with our dinner in our hands. Fortune cookies didn't taste great in my opinion, but the real treasure wasn't in the flavour.

I scowled up at him as I broke mine apart. "So domineering," I grumbled.

He answered with a wolfish grin. "Well, forgive me. I'm only trying to speak in a language that a stubborn woman like you will understand."

I pulled the small scrap of paper out of the pastry. As I read the tiny slip of paper, I frowned.

"What's it say?"

"It says, 'When one door closes, another opens'," I murmured and felt chills down my spine. I'd never been one for superstition, but that was nothing short of eerie. What the hell? All I could think of was my ended relationship with Aaron and my new start with William.

"Uncanny," he commented, thoroughly amused.

I looked up at him again. "What about yours?" I asked before I took a bite out of the cookie.

Snapping his apart, he pulled out the paper and read it. Then, after leisurely devouring the entire biscuit – probably to taunt me – he met my impatient glare and gave me a smile. He really was exceptional at pushing my buttons; especially when he did it on purpose. Did he truly get that much joy from teasing me? He must, because he was expert in the art, and he never overlooked an opportunity to do it.

"Says, 'Look around. Happiness is trying to catch you'." His gaze turned astute and then burrowed into mine. "I'm looking, alright," he said and gave me a playful wink.

My face flushed again. Suddenly hyperaware of myself, I crossed my arms and rocked back and forth on my heels, nervous.

"Think Cupid's lurking around somewhere, messing with our fortune cookies?" I wondered out loud. His eyes were smouldering when they watched me after what I'd asked, so I inhaled a sharp breath.

"Hard to say," he murmured. "His arrow struck me some months ago. He might be following up on his work, though," he continued, and, before I could gather myself, threw his arm around my neck to bring me against his chest. The intoxicating scent of him flooded my nose, leaving me lightheaded. *Christ, this man.* I was defenceless against him, and what he had said had completely stunned me.

In that intense moment I was too shy to look at him, so I wrapped my arms around his strong frame and buried my face in his chest. It shook against me, so I knew he was laughing at me – again.

When he'd composed himself, he dropped a chaste kiss on my head and pushed me away from him. A playful look dwelled in his features as he studied me. "Our date's not finished yet. We've got a reservation in less than half an hour, so we best get going."

Puzzled, I watched him as he grabbed my hand to drag me down the street. He had more on the agenda?

He guided the way for some ten to fifteen minutes till he reached a place called Swingers on John Prince's Street. As I read the sign, I saw that it was miniature golf.

"Oh my God!" This was unexpectedly creative of him. Clearly, he didn't suffer from a shortage of ideas in the dating department. Just as William was an original man, he was an original suitor, and I adored him for it. If things worked out between us, I doubted I would face a boring day for the remainder of my life.

"I should warn you," he said smugly, "I'm a mean swing." The sexual insinuation dripped from his tone.

I knew full well what a mean swing he was. Over my shoulder, I peered at him with a libidinous glint in my eyes. "Good at putting it in the hole, are you? Try me."

Pulling his lower lip between his teeth, he grinned back. "Cheeky."

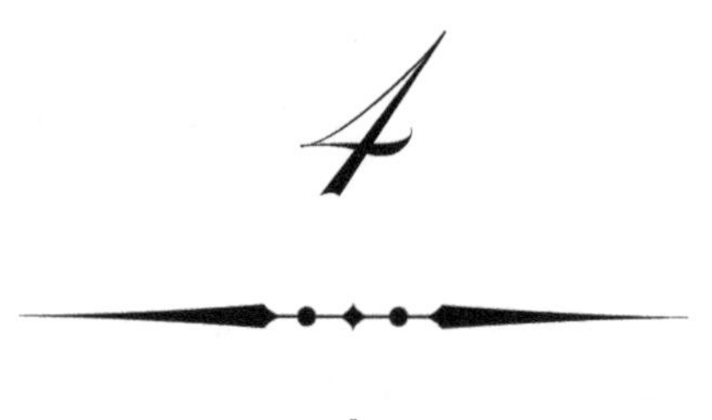

CHÉRIE

We were on the seventh hole of Helter Skelter when he returned with another two cocktails. Thus far, we'd had three each. In his hands were one mojito and one martini. I hoped the mojito was for me, as I didn't particularly enjoy martinis, but then I'd also said "surprise me" when he'd asked what I would like. So, if he'd opted for a martini, I wouldn't be so rude as not to drink it.

"How many tries?" he asked when he saw that I'd finally managed to send the ball into the hole.

"Like twenty," I muttered, annoyed. A humoured look crossed his face while he lifted the sheet of paper which kept our score.

"We'll say ten, then." He winked.

"These courses are impossible." I had wanted to sound annoyed again, but, instead, I started laughing because I felt so comically useless. I'd always been the best athlete out of the girls at school, but today's presentation did not serve as evidence.

Caught by my laughter, he chuckled after a sip of the martini. "You're a bit tipsy. Perhaps that's why. This course is all about physics. Maths and alcohol don't tend to blend well. In any case, let's move on to the next one." Upon that note, he guided the way to the eighth course.

Earlier, I'd insisted that he should start so that I could watch what he did wrong or right and apply it to my own swings, but it hadn't helped much. He was far, far better than me. When he nearly managed to send the ball into the hole on the first strike, he looked over with a smirk. "Tell me, darling. Where about in London did you grow up?"

I sighed and sucked on the black straw of my mojito. "West Hampstead."

"Cool area," he commented when he made another calculated swing and tricked the ball straight into the hole.

I narrowed my eyes at him. The insufferable bastard was too good at this, and part of me worried that he was even being merciful. This was becoming humiliating. Nevertheless, his skill aroused me. I'd never doubted that he was a capable man. However, seeing him prove it in all areas of life made him all the more appealing.

"You think?"

"Yeah." Leaving his putting stick to rest across his broad shoulder, he approached me. "Your turn."

As I approached the course, he reached for his martini. "Your mother's name is Lillian, right? And she's an economist?" he asked as I dropped my ball to the respective starting point.

"Yes," I replied whilst calculating my swing. He'd exerted some force, so I would try to emulate it.

"And which parent should I be most careful with?" he asked then, leaving me to freeze for a second. Gazing towards him, I blinked twice over. He was surely taking this in big strides, wasn't he? For the first time, it scared me a little.

When I failed to answer, he queried, "What?" After a chuckle, he spread his arms apart. "It's only fair I get to meet them sometime. You've already met both my parents, thanks to Jason. Besides, I'm interested to meet the people that made you into the bewitching woman that you are."

I shook my head. "If you make it to ten dates, I'll consider it," I replied, reserved. "And my dad would be the one to worry about, but not in the stereotypical sense. He's just a bit of a...challenge. Hard to understand, and he makes a hobby of annoying people with Socratic questioning. Mum's easier on the mind."

He laughed. "I'm intrigued."

I struck the ball then, but failed miserably. He was distracting me with all of these intimidating questions. "My turn to do the interview," I said.

"What would you like to know?" he asked as he watched my ongoing parody of attempted miniature golf. Meanwhile, blatant amusement lurked in his eyes.

"When did you realise you wanted to become a solicitor?"

"I realised that I wanted to study law when I was six. Dad's the inspiration. A solicitor? I made that decision while I was studying it."

I nodded to myself and looked between the ball and the hole. That bloody hillock in the middle was a complete nightmare. How was I supposed to send the ball over it?

"Have you always been this driven and ambitious?"

He cocked his head from side to side. "Yes."

"I know you've always played chess, but did you play any sports?"

"Yeah. Started playing tennis when I was seven."

"Like a true snob," I teased. "Badminton, too?"

"Football," he corrected. "Striker. Started when I was eight. But at Cambridge, it was all about the rowing."

I took note of the fact that he was obviously an athletic nerd. Well, we had that in common.

"You into any sports?" he asked.

"Not at the moment. In terms of watching sports, I'm a neutral observer. Let's just say I prefer playing sports rather than watching them."

"Which sports have you played?"

I laughed. "The list is endless."

He seemed intrigued. "So is my attention when it comes to you."

His slick response earned him a chuckle. "Well," I let go of my putting stick to count on one hand, "I've played football, basketball, volleyball, badminton, and tennis. I did gymnastics for a year, too, and contemporary jazz dance, with Livy. However, football is the sport I stuck with for the longest. I was the goalkeeper, though." I arrested his eyes with a taunting smile on my lips. "You see, I'm good with my hands."

A grin crowded his mouth before he whistled through his teeth. "Damn. That's impressive. And now you lift."

I laughed. "Yes. Sports are fun, but the gym offers more flexibility in terms of my schedule."

He nodded. "I can see that."

"How long have you been lifting for?"

"Twelve years or so. Started when I was sixteen."

My gaze swept over his robust physique. "And it hasn't been for naught."

Smiling, he took another sip of his martini. "So you've danced for a bit, too?"

"Yeah, for two years. I was okay, but I quit because I've always preferred playing with balls." I glanced at him with a smirk, only to see him cough on his drink as he caught on to my innuendo.

He cleared his throat before a grin took over his mouth. Meeting my eyes, I saw his radiate humour. "Fancy chasing balls, do you?"

"Chase them, dribble them, play with them...I could go on." I winked. "But, most of all, I love scoring them."

"Bet you were the MVP at that."

"I was, actually." I laughed. "Anyway, this is still my interview," I reminded him and eyed him sternly. Amused by my strict character, he tittered.

I turned my attention back to the course and refocused on my swing. Taking my time, I continued, "Jason's told me he lived in Chelsea growing up, so I suppose the same applies to you."

"Yes. Well, apart from one year."

This was news, so I glanced at him with a frown. "What do you mean?"

He shrugged. "I lived in Paris for a year as an exchange student, during secondary school."

Right. I recalled Jason had done that, but it hadn't occurred to me that William might have done the same. "Jason did that as well."

"Yes."

"How come you decided to, though?"

He shrugged. "Well, as you may recall, my maternal grandparents are French, and ever since they gave up their business back in 1997, they've lived in Paris. They've got a place in Cannes as well, and Bretagne. Love those places." His perfect pronunciation made me pause. I hadn't thought of this before, but if Jason was fluent in French, it was likely that William was, too.

The idea made my body behave in strange ways – it was rather arousing. The French language had always had a direct line to my carnal preferences. If William were a fluent speaker of it, I'd stand no chance against him.

I swallowed. "Oh. So, you speak French fluently, then?"

He raised a brow, and the view revealed that my question hadn't impressed him. Promptly, he responded exclusively in the alluring language, but all I could comprehend was the word '*chérie*'. Jason had said it to me before, so I was aware it meant 'darling'.

Instantly, heat flooded my face and neck. Trying to calm the rising demands of my libido, I cleared my throat and looked away.

"I've no idea what you just said."

Sweet laughter erupted from him. "I said Mum spoke French to us while we were growing up, and I studied French in school, too. That's why I wanted to do an exchange year in Paris, to solidify my bilingualism.

Have you been to France?"

I nodded. "Been to Paris. It's my favourite city, out of the few I've visited."

"Mine too."

"I took Spanish, though. Seemed more practical at the time. Alas, I've hardly used it since."

Just as I was about to perform my swing, he said something else in perfect French, and the sound of it led me to exert much more force than I'd intended, so I missed the target by several feet.

"Ugh!"

He laughed. "This is wildly amusing."

"Stop speaking French," I chided. "I can't concentrate."

"You shouldn't have exposed yourself like that. I'll take advantage."

I glared at him. "William. People are waiting for us to finish."

His mouth took a cunning shape. "Let them wait, *chérie*."

I groaned and looked away from him. Since I knew he wouldn't be able to resist teasing me again, I would need to divert his attention somehow. A smile formed on my lips when the perfect idea occurred to me. I had wondered about this for quite some time, and this was surely an appropriate time to ask.

"I want to know about your ex, Kate," I said as I walked over to my ball.

My plan proved effective. Glimpsing him, I saw his smile fading.

"I was wondering when you'd ask me about her." He sighed. "There's not much to say. It lasted for about two years until we mutually decided to break up. We weren't compatible, and I was never in love with her – merely very fond of her. It was more of a convenient relationship than anything else."

I was intrigued. Since I was still a stranger to the world of relationships, I considered two years to be quite a while, especially if he claimed he'd never been in love with her.

"I can't believe you've been in a relationship with a Kate."

I sensed him watch me with circumspection. "Her name was – is, seeing as she's not dead – Katelyn Wrightington, but I called her Kate."

"Still, it's hilarious. William and Kate?" I laughed. "This will never work out. How could I ever beat such royal appeal?"

He rolled his eyes. "Give it a rest, yeah? I've heard that joke too many times now. Anyway, we met in Cambridge. She studied chemical engineering. Brilliant mind. That was what piqued my interest the first time we met."

"How come you broke up?"

He shrugged. "Well, as I got to know her, I found that there was little else that I found intriguing about her. She was a bit dull, and sort of insipid. While her dedication to her course was admirable, and clearly a calling, it was essentially her entire identity. I'm weak for bright minds, but I prefer a brain that's got a broader range of interests. A single topic can only stimulate me for so long. That's why I love working with the law – it touches upon almost everything."

"I see." I nodded. "Well, she sounds like an admirable person. I'm sure I would've liked her."

He looked incredulous. "Strange thing to say."

"Why?"

"Well, she's my ex."

"So? Why should that prevent me from liking her?"

His eyes filled with wonder as he continued to study me. "Usually, an ex would inspire jealousy – or at least insecurity."

I snorted. "That's ridiculous. I mean, she's your ex for a reason, isn't she?"

He frowned. "Well, yes, but it's not always that simple."

Seeing as it would depend on the circumstances of a couple's failed relationship, I could agree with that. However my general opinion was that an ex was no reason for concern.

"Then have you still got feelings for her?" I enquired.

"Of course not. As I've told you before, I haven't spoken to her in ages."

"Then I don't see the problem. Clearly, she's old news and no reason for concern."

His head tilted while fascination poured from his expression. "You're remarkably rational about this."

I chuckled. "Thanks, I think?"

"Anyway, she was the perfect partner during my studies. Very low maintenance, rarely insecure, experimental in bed, and we worked well on those rare occasions when we decided to study together. I harboured great respect for her – I still do."

I was nodding my head as I processed their history. It was original, and I found myself intrigued by this Katelyn Wrightington. Like William, I was weak for bright minds, and Katelyn's intimidated me somewhat. If she'd bored him, how on earth wouldn't I?

"You said you were never in love with her. Why did you stay with her for two years if you weren't?"

A rueful expression surfaced on his face. "I…It's complicated. It was my first relationship, and I'd never been in love before. For quite some time, I thought I was, but part of me always doubted it. I realised too late that I had mistaken fondness for love."

Since I'd been in a similar situation with Aaron, his explanation earned my sympathy. In the end, I had frequently wondered whether what I had shared with Aaron was actually love. So I supposed William must have endured the same emotional confusion during his relationship with Kate.

"Besides, how we entered the relationship was a bit equivocal as well," he continued, and I noticed that shame was preventing him from meeting my gaze. It was evident that he hadn't forgiven himself for his time with Kate, and I pitied him for it. Although he had said that ending their relationship had been a mutual decision, seeing his reaction aroused my suspicion. If he had been the one to break her heart, I would not have been surprised.

"Oh?" I uttered, to encourage him to continue.

After a single nod, he drained the remainder of his cocktail. "Yeah. Like you and I, we met in a bar, actually. As it happens, Andy was there then, too."

I raised a brow. "Perhaps Andy's a bad omen."

"Don't say that."

"Sorry. Just a joke. Continue."

He took a deep breath to refocus. "Our chemistry was undeniable, and her intellect fascinated me. However, at that point in time, I was going through a promiscuous phase."

I laughed. I could not imagine William as a promiscuous man. After all, his unquestionable loyalty was one of his most prominent characteristics. Had he learnt a lesson the hard way?

"Really?" I asked disbelievingly. "You? Promiscuous?"

He groaned. "I was very young when I met her, Cara. Settling down wasn't a priority."

"But sex was?"

He groaned again. "I had needs, so I slept around, but I was always transparent about it. I went out of my way to avoid playing with anyone's feelings. To be honest, one of the main reasons I didn't stick to just one woman was that I considered it more likely that one of them would grow attached if I went about it that way. Having more than one partner and being open about it seemed the best course of action for everyone involved. It made it obvious where I was at, so they didn't have to speculate on my feelings. Personally, the variation was something I enjoyed as well."

This information surprised me. I found it difficult to reconcile the past version of him with the present one. Did they still share a few traits? I wanted to find out which. "Do you still enjoy it? The variation?"

He scoffed. "Not in the slightest. Back then, I was too immature to realise that the depth you can achieve when you only have one partner is invaluable. However, to reach it, it's necessary to sacrifice the others. Ironically enough, the variation thwarts you from recognising the significance of your partner. It distracts you instead. Your brain isn't – or at least mine wasn't – capable of processing all the impressions and information about them before I met the next girl, which ultimately enabled me to keep all of them at arm's length. My impressions of them didn't get sufficient time to settle since I never had time to reflect on each encounter much. That made it easy to avoid getting attached to any of them. So, it's my experience that once you become exclusive, you can focus on that partner alone, which in turn allows your bond to flourish, because the impressions get sufficient time to settle."

He gave me a sweet smile before continuing, "In other words, Cara: quality over quantity."

Hearing that, I doubted that he'd become so loyal because he had made mistakes in the past. He had simply evolved – that was all.

Impressed, I said, "Sounds like you've reflected on this quite a bit."

"I enjoy reflection in general."

"Which is one of the things I cherish and admire the most about you," I confessed, and his responding smile was unsullied. "Anyway," I continued, "you still haven't told me exactly what happened with Kate."

He sighed again. "Well, when we met, I got the impression she was interested in the same as me – a one-night stand – but when I invited her back to mine, she rejected me."

I pressed my lips together to prevent my laughter from

spilling out. "That seems to do the trick," I joked. "How to seduce William Night – reject him."

He actually laughed, and I appreciated that he had a sense of humour about himself. "It would seem that way, but, to be fair, it was you who seduced me, Cara – not your rejection. And, as opposed to you, Kate didn't reject me because she wasn't interested in a relationship."

"What was her reason, then?"

"She was just careful about whom she slept with. To Kate, sex wasn't something to have with random people. She required a bond to be present. Not necessarily a romantic one, but at least friendship, or some version of a connection that would last longer than a night."

My arrangement with Aaron notwithstanding, Kate and I sounded like polar opposites. The less my partners knew, the more comfortable I was, and therefore the more excited I was. There was something about the mystery of not knowing one another that aroused my sexual fantasy. The lack of knowledge about their character allowed my imagination to run free, and since we weren't ever going to see each other again, I'd never have to endure the disappointment of finding out that they were not, in fact, quite as ensnaring as I had initially wanted to believe.

However, since I respected Kate's approach to sex, I said, "Right. Cool."

"Yeah. Anyway, initial plan was to get her into my bed that night, but she refused, saying she never slept with men without knowing them. So, I asked to meet her again, and she agreed. After a while, we started sleeping together regularly. We'd been seeing each other like that for about three months when she asked if we could be exclusive. For egotistical reasons, and medical, I preferred having her to myself, so I agreed. Besides, since my studies demanded most of my time, I'd eventually stopped seeing other women. Kate already sufficed all my needs.

"We'd been sleeping together for six months or so when she confessed that she had developed feelings for me and asked why we couldn't just call a spade a spade. I remember I found that moment quite problematic, because while it was true that we were essentially already a couple in terms of exclusivity, how often we hung out, what we did together and things like that, I only agreed to it because she preferred it. It wasn't because I intended to pursue a relationship with her. In hindsight, I've realised that was her tactic, which was rather shrewd. I'll have to give her that."

If it was true, I found her actions rather appalling, but at the same time, I was incredibly impressed that she had managed to lure William – the cunning mastermind himself – into her web. "That's so cunning!"

"I don't think it was entirely deliberate," he said, eyes narrowing while he gazed absentmindedly upon the course we were at. "I'm sure she was merely hoping that I would change my mind about wanting to be single. She must've surmised that being exclusive for long enough might encourage me to consider a relationship. Eventually, she got impatient and forced me to decide, that was all – which is fair."

"Still, she wasn't acting *bona fide*."

The legal terminology made him chuckle. "Perhaps. I'll never know for sure. She's never admitted to it even though I've confronted her several times."

"Hm. Either way, I still don't understand why you would decide to enter a relationship with someone you didn't love."

He shrugged. "Well, by that time, I had grown so fond of her that I decided I might as well give things a go. Even though I didn't feel the same way, I didn't want to lose her. I sincerely cared for her, and it wasn't like I wanted anyone else, either. So, I decided that I ought to give us a chance. I'd never been infatuated before, so I suppose I mistook friendly affection for a potential of love. I hoped I could grow to love her – romantically

– so I agreed. Unfortunately, my feelings never escalated beyond friendly affection during the two years we spent together as a proper couple."

This story had made my mood turn sober. "So, she was in love with you the whole time?"

He looked so ashamed of himself then that I got the urge to reach out and console him, but our surroundings prevented me. It would have summoned unwanted attention from other guests.

"Yeah. She was. But ending our relationship was a mutual decision. She didn't want to be with me if I didn't love her. She had enough integrity to realise that."

"When did you break up?" I asked and looked to my hands around my putting stick.

"Five years ago – a bit more. I don't remember exactly to be honest. Things were a bit…vague at the end. Our relationship had been over for a while before we actually acknowledged it, if that makes sense."

"And you've hardly talked since?"

He folded his arms. "That's right."

"How come? Did you end things on a bad note?"

"No, but I personally believe that hanging out with exes is toxic behaviour, for a list of reasons. Firstly, the relation could stir insecurities in potential new partners. For instance, if I frequently kept in touch with Kate, it could trouble you. I'm not inclined to let that happen when I can prevent it.

"Secondly, it's my understanding that the person that was rejected in a relationship will always seek to be validated by the partner that rejected them – meaning Kate is likely to want to acquire my affections, even if she's moved on, just to prove to me that she was deserving of them. Generally, that's just the way the human ego works.

"Thirdly, it's confusing – role-wise. How do you go from being so intimate with someone to being strictly platonic? There's such a dreadful risk of someone misreading the signals. Don't get me wrong – I know there are people out there who manage it, but I don't think I'm one of them. She's history, and I prefer to keep it that way. I can be very cold about things like that."

I put my hand on my hip and watched him for a moment. He was clearly a reflective man, far more than I'd given him credit for, and I found it captivating. What other ideas did he store in that beautiful mind of his?

"I hear you, but you're a jealous person. I'm not. And I can't help but hear the insinuation towards Aaron," I pointed out and focused on my swing again.

He rolled his eyes, so I decided to change the subject before he got too worked up. "When's your birthday?"

Taken aback by my change of direction, he frowned. "April ninth. Yours?"

I gaped. "Really?"

My reaction confused him. "Yes?"

"So, we met mere days after your birthday?"

Realising my thoughts, he grinned. "Yes. Best late birthday present ever."

I giggled. "You're welcome."

"When's yours?"

"December twenty-first."

"That's very close to Christmas," he said, and I could tell from the absent look in his eyes that he was currently lost in the vast space of his mind.

A wry smile crept across my mouth. "Trigger your fantasy, did it?"

He bit down on his lower lip. The glance he gave me confirmed my suspicions. "I believe you'd suit red, but I will make no further comment."

I giggled and shook my head. "If you find out that I'm merely 'convenient' like Kate, you'd better hope you're not still around by then. I will personally emasculate you," I warned.

His lips twisted with amusement. "Cara, don't be silly. If anything, you're completely *inconvenient*. Firstly, you're currently my colleague. Secondly, you're my brother's best friend and flatmate, and thirdly, you're the tenant of my parents' flat. To make matters even worse, you're a bloody challenging woman, and I am completely mad about you. To be perfectly frank, if you knew how much I think about you, you'd be looking at me like I'd grown three heads right now."

Baffled, I asked, "Then why do you bother with me? If I'm such an inconvenience?"

He laughed. "Did you not just hear what I said? I can't stop thinking about you. Pursuing you doesn't feel like a choice. It feels like a need."

Astonished, I blinked. "Well, you've been warned," I murmured and took another swing.

"Duly noted. But, speaking of dating others..." he murmured as he watched the ball fall off the hillock prop. "While we're seeing each other, I expect your exclusivity. I'm a possessive man. I get intensely territorial, and it's impossible to switch off. Trust me – I've tried."

"You? Territorial?" I gasped, feigning surprise.

"Fuck you," he grumbled and tucked his hands into his pockets. I laughed at him, but when I looked over again, I saw that he did not share my amusement.

After gnashing his teeth for a beat, he continued, "So I'd appreciate it if you respected it. I'm aware you're not accustomed to monogamy, but you'll have to adjust if this is going to work out. Obviously, I'll return the favour."

I approached my ball with a shrewd look on my face. "Sounds fair to me. And it's not going to pose a problem, Will. When I slept around before, I wasn't seeing anyone. Yes, I had Aaron, but we had a specific arrangement, and it wasn't romantic. Hell, you're the first man I've ever dated. This is my first date! Ever!" I waved my arm in the air. "That should speak volumes. Seriously. You ought to feel special."

He shook his head to himself. "I don't understand that. It's ridiculous."

"What don't you understand about it?"

"Surely you must have been asked on a date before," he replied, bewildered.

I blushed again, though faintly, and averted my eyes. Modestly, I answered, "Well, yes, I have been asked. But I've always said no. I mean, do you remember when we first met? I didn't even give you my real name. I've always been ambitious, Will, and I've always avoided anything that could come in the way of that."

"Cupid's definitely been lurking behind the scenes of this," he then mumbled to himself. "I can't believe I didn't even know your real name that night, and yet here we are, three months later."

"Strange world."

"Indeed."

§ § §

Once we stepped outside after the travesty of my defeat, it became apparent from our hesitation that we were both uncertain about how to proceed from here.

"That was fun," I said, and my sigh betrayed how smitten I was. "I had a lovely time. Thank you."

A bashful smile reached his lips before he looked shyly away. "I'm happy to hear that."

"You weren't lying when you said you're a mean swing," I added with a grin.

His subsequent chuckle informed me that his shyness hadn't passed, and I found it awfully charming. While raising a hand to rub his neck, he said, "I'm not sure how you'd prefer to proceed from here, but, regardless, I've got something for you."

Frowning, I watched as he reached into his back pocket.

Humour etched through his gorgeous features while he held whatever it was behind his back.

"Do you recall last Saturday, when you accused me of being more exhausting than a marathon?" he enquired.

I couldn't help but giggle. I had said that, hadn't I? "Yeah."

"Well, do you remember what I replied?"

I grimaced. "Not really?"

He gave me a crooked smile. "I promised to give you a medal if you lasted an entire date with me, as well as a reward. So here goes the first part. The reward I'll grant you tonight – if you want."

Wide-eyed, I watched him lift a golden medal with a red ribbon into my field of vision. As he dangled it in front of my face, I read the number one on the front of it, while the initials W.N. were engraved on the back. He'd had it custom-made? How much thought had he put into this?

Overwhelmed, I stood frozen as he moved to hang it round my neck.

"Congratulations, Cara. You survived," he teased and lowered his head to place a kiss on my forehead. However, just before he reached his destination, my hands shot up to grab his sharp jaw so that I could instead lower his mouth onto mine.

My heart fluttered at the delicious taste of him, as well as the feel of his perfect lips against my own. They moved with such uncanny precision, expertly synchronised with mine, as if we'd always been meant to do this. This was how it was supposed to be. I just knew, because until I'd met this spellbinding man, I'd never experienced anything remotely similar.

Giving him a chance had been the right choice, which he proved right in that moment. In fact, I had a feeling he would continue to prove it, time and again.

Surprising me, he groaned against my mouth and suddenly moved away. Out of breath, I watched him with a worried expression on my face, scared I'd done something wrong. Using the back of his hand, he discreetly wiped his mouth and shook his head.

"Sorry," he panted. "I can't be doing that right now. You've no idea what it does to me."

I grinned and reached for the belt loop of his jeans. Hooking my fingers into them, I tugged him towards me again. "Then we've got a problem, because I am desperate for your mouth on me," I confessed, staring at his tempting mouth. I wanted it to devour the entirety of me. It was sent straight from heaven – I was sure.

Chuckling, he cupped my cheeks in his large, warm hands as he stared into my eyes. "How would you like to spend the night at mine, then? I'd hate to get arrested for public indecency."

"Dogging not your style?" I joked, and his astonishment was obvious from the sound of his laughter.

"Exhibitionist, Cara?"

I gripped his T-shirt to pull him closer. "Hard to remember my whereabouts whenever I'm with you."

He exhaled loudly before he suddenly moved to place a hard kiss on my mouth. "Fuck," he mumbled against my lips.

I pulled back, full of glee. "It's a ten-minute walk to your place."

"Let's go." Without further ado, he clasped my hand and strode down the street.

My shoulders sank as my body mellowed. I was completely smitten for the first time in my life.

PLAYING WITH FIRE

THE MOMENT HE OPENED THE FRONT DOOR DOWNSTAIRS, memories of our first encounter burst into my mind. Just like then, the marble covering the floor and walls summoned a feeling of stepping into a past era, when aristocracy had been at its prime. Apart from a few flower arrangements that decorated a vacant desk, the grand lobby looked precisely the way I remembered. An old scent was etched into the walls, and as I inhaled the fragrance, my memories grew even more vivid.

"What's the desk for?" I asked as he led the way to the lift. My eyes drank in the surroundings, and I found myself thirsting after the memories that the place elicited. My pulse drummed, but, unlike earlier, I didn't sense it mainly in my chest. Instead, the place between my thighs throbbed with anticipation. Already, I could feel my fluids trickle out of me, generously lubricating my underwear – just like last time.

"The porter," he murmured as he pressed the button. The doors slid apart to reveal the same cage I had been standing in three months ago. Mirrors made up the walls, and, in them, I caught a glimpse of my flushed face.

"Porter?" I echoed, and a mocking laugh escaped me. "Your building has got a porter?"

"Four," he specified as he entered the digits of a code to bring us up to his penthouse. "They work shifts. Garrick's my favourite. He works full time, mainly in the weekdays from seven till two."

"I didn't see a porter last time I was here."

"They work till nine. If my memory serves me right, we arrived after that."

"Oh."

The doors drew shut. Watching them, I folded my arms to hide my erratic heartbeats. Being here again was strangely intimidating. The first time I had been standing in this lift, I had been sure it would also be my last, but the arbitrariness of life had proved me wrong.

Looking over, I noticed that he was less composed than he had been the first time. His stance had been relaxed then, but now his shoulders were tense, and I noticed that he was consciously keeping his gaze from meeting mine. Was this William being nervous?

"Are you nervous?" I teased.

A crooked smile flirted with his lips as he glanced in my direction. "Nervous isn't the word I'd use."

"Which word would you use, then?"

"Stunned, maybe."

"Stunned?"

"Yes. I find our circumstance stunning. I've been standing in this lift god knows how many times, and yet, ever since you stepped foot in it, your absence has been sorely felt – every morning and every evening." He shook his head, evidently overawed. "And now you're here again."

I sucked in a sharp breath. "Wow. Really?"

I was surprised when I saw that he didn't look satisfied with such a reality.

"Yes."

Immensely flattered, I sensed blood tickle my cheeks. "You always know what to say, don't you?"

"Do I?" He didn't sound convinced.

"Yes. I had no idea you harboured such a romantic side."

He smirked. "Till I met you, neither did I. Safe to say, you're the muse at the root of it."

"There you go again."

A chime informed us that we had arrived on our floor. A moment later, the doors slid apart to reveal the same vestibule I had seen so often in my dreams. His front door was still the same dark shade of brown that I remembered. My heart skipped a beat. I wondered if what lay beyond it had changed at all, or if everything looked the same.

He ushered me forward without a word. As I approached the door, the beats of my heart increased in strength. I found the sensation rather peculiar because it wasn't like I hadn't had sex with him since then. We had shared intimacy on several occasions. Yet, somehow, being here again was kindling the very same intensity that I had experienced the first night. Anticipation took the shape of something thick and dense in my chest – merely breathing required conscious effort.

Tension filled the air between us when he reached over to my side to enter the code to unlock the door.

"Is your girlfriend home?" I joked, but he missed the reference.

"What?" He gripped the handle before his head turned to analyse me.

I chuckled. "Last time, you pulled my leg by saying you were expecting your girlfriend home soon."

He flashed me a devilish grin, and sin was spinning within it.

"Right. Sounds like something I would do."

"Yeah. Prick."

Laughing, he pushed the door open, and my eyes instantly scanned the interior of his flat. The view led my grin to widen. The same contemporary paintings decorated the cream-coloured walls. Indeed, everything was exactly how I remembered.

To appreciate my surroundings, I halted after a few feet to gaze around. As I admired his sense of style, I asked, "Did you furnish this place yourself?"

He shut and locked the door. "No. Mum helped. I've always found her taste most agreeable."

Considering their home in Chelsea, I could understand why. "Her taste is exquisite."

"I think so, too. I'm particularly fond of her respect for the old-fashioned. She's amazing at blending it with modern artefacts."

"I can tell. Did she select these paintings?"

His eyes followed the direction that my index finger pointed in. "No, we picked them together. The whole interior design was a collaboration between us."

"How long have you lived here for?"

"Three years."

My eyebrows arched. "It's not every day that you hear about a twenty-five-year-old living in a penthouse in central London."

"I'm privileged," he agreed with a nod.

"Will, I'm curious."

He chuckled. "Aren't you always?"

"It's a bit of an imposing question," I warned, "so you don't need to answer if you don't want to. It's really none of my business, and I would just like to clarify that I'm sincerely curious. I've no ulterior motive asking this. I'm not interested in you for your fortune."

He frowned. "You've already made that abundantly clear, but I appreciate you stressing it."

"Really," I emphasised. "I mean to build my own fortune, so

yours doesn't tempt me in the least."

Affection spilled from his eyes while a gentle smile climbed to his mouth. "Cara, I know. Don't worry. You're strong and independent – I get it."

"Yes. Neither my values nor my integrity would ever let me chase a man for his wallet."

"Had you been that type of woman, I would have noticed by now."

"Good."

"What's your question, then?"

I hesitated for another moment, gathering courage. Somehow, it felt rather rude to ask him this, but I was just so inquisitive. Besides, if we were going to be in a relationship, I ought to have at least a vague idea of his financial status. "Do you own your flat? Or is it your parents'? Or are you renting, perhaps?"

His left eyebrow curled upwards. "I own it. Why?"

"Because it must have been ridiculously expensive. Did John and Daphné help you out?"

"Of course."

"Has Jason been treated to the same generosity?" I wondered.

"Yes. Hasn't he told you?"

I shook my head. "I've never asked, though. Besides, he's always uncomfortable whenever the subject of money is brought up. He's always been inherently modest and reserved about it."

"It's how we were raised. Anyway, since you ask, he owns a place in Chelsea, close to our parents. He rents it out, though."

"How come?"

"Well, Mum and Dad allow him to live for free in the flat you're sharing with him in Notting Hill. However, he's only allowed to live there for free for as long as he's a student. Our parents are very strict about education. They never wanted us to get distracted by a job while completing it, hence why he's living there for free. The money he earns from renting out his own place he saves in a mutual fund."

His family's wealth had never been more apparent. Regardless, it didn't intimidate me. While I came from a humbler background, it didn't mean I wasn't deserving of William's attention. My origins were what they were, and, thankfully, William didn't seem to care in the slightest about it. Instead, it was evident that my personality was all that mattered to him, and I adored him for that. Then again, I would never have fallen for a man who was preoccupied with shallow criteria.

"I see," I murmured. "Wise, I suppose."

"It's the crux of capitalism," he stated. "Say what you want about it, but it makes rich people richer."

"That, it does."

"So I make it a point to give back. My whole family does. We're involved with several charities. Anyway," he said, "I'd like a glass of white. Would you?"

Wine? Weren't we going to have sex? I hesitated. Still, the remnants of alcohol in my blood were vanishing by the second, so perhaps a glass of wine wasn't a bad idea. It might even aid me overcome the tension that lingered in the air between us. However, when it came to wine, I could, in fact, be somewhat particular.

"I don't mean to sound rude, but it depends."

His head tilted. "Oh?"

I was embarrassed to say this, but I did it anyway. "What grape? I don't like Riesling much."

His smile revealed astonishment. "I'd no idea you were a snob about wine."

"Dad's an enthusiast about wine and whisky. He's rubbed off on me. That said, he enjoys Riesling."

"What's your favourite, then? I've got a whole collection."

My embarrassment intensified while I shook my head. "I'd hate to be impudent."

"Cara, come on. It's good that you're telling me this. Imagine if I served you Riesling."

I allowed a faint chuckle to slip out. "Then I would've drunk it."

"Of course you would." He shook his head, despairing. "What don't you like about it?"

My nose wrinkled. "It's a bit too...fruity for my taste. Reminds me of cider, in a way. I prefer drier and more bitter white wines. Those based on Sauvignon blanc are always a safe choice."

"How about Chardonnay?"

I was thrilled to learn that he was knowledgeable about wine. At the same time, I wasn't surprised when considering his heritage. If he ever met Dad, at least they'd have something in common aside from their fondness for reflection.

"Yes." I smiled. "Chablis is lovely."

"But Sauvignon blanc is your favourite grape for whites?"

"Yes."

"I'll open a Sancerre."

His French pronunciation triggered my impatience. To hell with the wine. I wanted him undressed.

"Or we could skip the wine?" I proposed and reached for his shirt to tug him closer, but he didn't move an inch.

Unmovable, he towered in front of me while a slow and wicked smile presented itself on his tempting mouth. "Impatient, Cara?"

Was he making me wait on purpose?

"Yes." I stepped closer and tightened my grip on his shirt. Stretching up on my toes, I grazed his lips with my own, but he bruised my ego when he seemed entirely unaffected.

"Good."

Puffing out a noise of complaint, I landed on my heels again and scowled up at him. "You're playing with fire, Will."

Smirking, he reached for my hands to unlock them from his T-shirt. "Can't wait to see you ablaze."

With a glare, I watched as he turned to approach his kitchen, and I was confident he could sense the heat of it burning into his back. Sulking, I kicked off my shoes and went into his living room to wait in one of two black-leathered sofas. As I sat there, a mischievous idea occurred to me. Two could play this game.

With a sly smile on my mouth, I lifted my dress' skirt to pull down my underwear. Sliding it down my legs, I dropped it on the floor and proceeded to lie down. My legs pointed in the direction of the kitchen, which he was bound to return from, but I kept my thighs together as I awaited his presence.

A minute later, he sauntered round the corner with two glasses of chilled white wine. The moment our gazes collided, I presented a lascivious smile and slowly spread my legs apart to bare my flesh to him.

Although it was barely noticeable, he paused on a step during his approach. My glistening folds didn't trigger even a twitch of his eyebrows, but at least his gaze fastened on them.

"Well, then. Ablaze indeed," he said, and I could hear I'd humoured him. Surprising me, he approached the lounge chair that stood at a right angle next to the sofa I was lying on.

The distance he demanded was somewhat offensive. Why was he resisting me? I had meant to drive him wild – senseless with lust. Instead, all he offered was a display of maddening self-discipline.

Ripping his eyes from the view of my beckoning wetness, he sat down and leaned forward to place a glass on the table between us. The other he brought with him as he reclined into his seat, leisurely. With a smile, he raised the glass to his mouth. "To the beauty of your flames," he said for a toast.

I frowned in bewilderment. Wasn't I arousing him? Was he trying to stall things because I'd been unable to get him erect yet? That led me to feel somewhat insecure, so I closed my legs.

"Please," he said after a sip. "Keep them spread."

His statement restored my confidence. I was arousing him after all. Smirking, I shook my head. "You don't deserve it."

He leaned forward to arrest my eyes, and the lust they

contained nearly overpowered me. "Spread your legs, Cara."

Feeling sassy, I raised a brow. "Or what?"

"Or you'll leave this place more sexually frustrated than you've ever been. I'd advise you not to test me."

Sensing that he had meant every word, I gulped. If there were one thing I would never do, it was to question his self-control. He had proved before that he was perfectly capable of turning down sex. I also knew that he was religiously committed to his practice of delayed gratification. So, seeing as listening to him was in my best interest, I slowly spread my legs and watched as his gaze slid to observe my saturated folds.

Satisfied, he leaned back again. "I'm curious to see just how hot you can get."

Pinkness flooded my cheeks upon his request. "Hot" was too poor a word to describe how searing my body felt. Nevertheless, I utilised every ounce of courage I had left to say, "Oh, Will." A confident smile tugged on my lips. "I'll incinerate you." I slowly traced my hand across my stomach. Seemingly hypnotised, his eyes followed its motion.

Just before I reached my throbbing wetness, I said, "Sometimes when I'm alone," my index finger circled my aching bud, "I imagine you touching me," I confessed, "just like this." Closing my eyes, I lubricated my finger in my juices and drew slow circles round my clit. Meanwhile, my hips started moving of their own accord to synchronise with the pressure I applied.

"Ah," I groaned as I brushed my finger with perfect precision across my most sensitive bundle of nerves. "I imagine your fingers inside of me," I told him before I inserted my middle finger into my body, "pushing through my wetness to bring me ecstasy. Your lips on my skin – pleasuring me the way only you can."

Excited by the sensation, I truly fantasised that it was actually him who was touching me, strong finger thrusting in to extract all my passion. Lowering my remaining hand, I used it to rub myself while the finger inside me continued to strike my front wall. "Fuck, Will. You feel so good."

Opening my eyes, I glanced over at him, and the view inspired me to grin. From the intensity of his eyes and rigid figure, I could tell he was holding on to his self-control as though his life depended on it. Still, he was on the cusp of losing his grip.

"Are you hard for me, Will?" I asked seductively.

His jaw flexed repeatedly. Spreading his legs wider apart, he revealed the bump of his erection. It strained against the firm material of his jeans, begging for liberation.

"Hard barely covers it." His voice was rough. "I'm in pain for you."

"Let me ease your suffering," I purred, but he shook his head.

"Make yourself come," he ordered instead. "Come the way you do whenever you imagine me fucking you."

His words fuelled my fantasy. Closing my eyes again, I withdrew my finger from within me to instead drag my dress down to free my breasts. Gathering my fingers around my erect nipple, I tugged it harshly. The sensation was acute, and it led me to arch my back.

"Ah," I moaned. Caressing my way to the apex of my thighs, I inserted my finger again and grimaced at the delicious feeling. *God,* how I wanted him inside of me – thick and hard while he penetrated me like he meant to ruin me. Curling my finger inside, I rubbed my front wall and imagined it was him who was doing it. To sharpen the sensation, I increased the speed of the fingers that rubbed my clit.

"Fuck," I groaned and ignored the strain that emerged in my hand. My hips continued their rhythm, intuitively knowing when to push forward and when to pull back. Tension coiled in my abdomen, heavy and dense. I was nearing the peak.

I paid no mind to the erratic sound of my breathing. Instead, my fantasy of him had eclipsed my sense of the present. All I felt, saw and heard was *him* – his finger pushing into me, his remaining hand expertly treating my throbbing bud to delicious friction.

"Ah," I gasped, and then held my breath. I was so close to reaching it that my instinct was to squeeze my thighs together, but I refused. I demanded to detonate first.

Focusing on my breathing, I rocked with the waves of pleasure that crashed against the shore of my mind. I was so aroused that keeping my breathing steady required conscious effort, but I knew the control would prove rewarding. Sure enough, which each deep inhalation, I climbed higher and higher.

My face twisted at the intensity. *Oh, my God.*

"Yes, *mon amour*," he said, and his French triggered me like nothing else. "Incinerate me."

All at once, everything unlocked. "Fuck!"

Gasping, my eyes sprang wide as a massive climax quaked through my body. Violent shudders raged throughout my entire system. Instantly, my thighs squeezed together on my hands. Between them, my vagina throbbed feverishly, begging for his intrusion.

Heaving for air, I collapsed into a daze. Wow.

The sound of a glass being placed on the table brought me back. Opening my eyes, I watched him stand with a proud look on his face. "Well done, darling. Consider me reduced to ashes."

A lazy chuckle slipped out of my mouth. "That performance warrants a reward."

"It surely does. Allow me to oblige," he said with a smirk and moved to join me on the sofa. Gripping my thighs, he spread my legs apart again to kneel between them. A gasp escaped my mouth when he suddenly jerked me towards him, but instead of lowering his head towards my folds, he leaned over me to stare into my eyes. His gaze felt as if it could suck the soul out of my body, and it was exactly what I wanted; I wanted him to possess me.

Reaching for my hand, he lifted it towards his mouth and brushed my fingertips across his lips. When he detected the finger that I had been pushing inside of me, he opened his mouth to suck it clean of my juices.

"Mm," he hummed appreciatively, and his erotic action led me to blush profusely. The vacuum of his suction sent tingles all across my body before it centred between my legs. He was so fucking arousing.

"You are absolutely stunning," he declared after removing my finger from his mouth. "I really am the luckiest man."

His amorous words reignited the colour in my cheeks. "Glad you appreciate me."

"That's an understatement."

"Prove it," I challenged teasingly.

"Your wish is my command," he chuckled, "but first, let's get you out of these confines." Grabbing my arms, he made me sit before he reached for my dress to remove it.

When I was entirely stripped, his gaze travelled across my skin to admire the view. "I stand for what I said the night we met," he said once the journey of his eyes ended on mine, "but with a minor modification. In *my* presence, you, and only you, should not be allowed to wear clothes. I no longer care for the beauty of other women. Let them be naked, or not. Your beauty is the only one I could ever notice anymore."

Reminiscences of our first night together made my heart throb. I recalled that I'd found him extraordinary even then. Now, he exceeded everything.

"I'll never agree to such terms," I replied, amused. "I'll wear what I like."

Placing his hand in the valley between my breasts, he pushed me down and pinned me to the sofa. "Then I'll rip it all off."

I laughed. "Then you should be prepared to pay for new clothes."

He grinned. "I refuse. I'll rip all your garments to shreds until you have nothing left to wear but my affection."

Pinkness spread across my face. "What a poet."

"Indeed. And now I shall make a poem out of your moans." With that, he placed his mouth on mine and kissed me like I was his sole chance at experiencing true passion in this life. While I felt the same way, it overwhelmed me. From the motion of his lips, it was apparent that he had been running out of strength earlier. His fervour was palpable, and it awakened the animal in me. Greedy for more of him, I took his T-shirt and dragged it towards his head. When it gathered under his arms, he released a noise of complaint into my mouth.

"I'm not finished kissing you," he insisted.

"I'm done with your demands," I grumbled and pushed harshly against him, but he remained unmovable. With zeal in my eyes, I glared up at him as I pushed the fabric further up, ultimately forcing him to remove it. The moment after he'd dragged the textile off his body, I discovered a grin on his mouth.

"I did that out of sympathy," he explained, amused, as I admired the impressive view of his powerful torso.

Laughing, I shook my head in comical despair. "Where's my reward, Will?"

"I'll show you," he purred before his lips targeted my pulse. After leaving hungry kisses on my neck, he journeyed lower, across my sternum. Reaching my collarbones, his lips traced across them both.

"I can't get over how beautiful you are."

"The feeling's mutual," I said, dragging my hands through the waves of his thick hair.

"These," he cooed, fingers following the shape of my breasts, "take my breath away. They're so firm."

"That's probably because they're smaller than average," I replied, amused. "Not much fat there."

"They are nothing short of perfect."

"My pecs probably add to their firmness."

Laughter burst from his mouth, tickling my skin. "The image in my head."

"I'm a hybrid," I continued to joke with a lopsided smile.

"Cara, with a shape like yours, there's no doubt you're a woman. And here's a fact for you – I've always preferred smaller tits."

"Really?" My eyes narrowed with suspicion even though I desperately wanted to believe him. After all, I wanted him to find my body perfectly designed – for him.

"Yes." There wasn't a trace of a lie in his eyes. "Personally, I find them prettier. Not that there's anything wrong with big tits, either. Anyway, I'm really more of an arse man. Can't you tell?" Wearing a lustful grin, he journeyed his hand beneath my body to cup my lower cheek.

"I suppose it's intuitive that an arsehole would prefer arses."

My joke made him laugh again, the air of it spreading across my skin.

"Fortunately," I continued, "I've got plenty of arse." I searched for a kiss.

"Indeed," he said just before he granted me his mouth.

Wrapping my legs around him, I began to grind against his crotch although I loved that we weren't rushing things. Instead, we were taking our sweet time, savouring each caress and the contact of our naked skin.

I'd been enjoying the dance of our tongues for a good while by the time he returned to my pulse. Closing my eyes, I relished the way he teased it. In fact, had I not disapproved of love bites, I would have begged him to continue for ages – the suction and flicks of his tongue felt so good against my throat.

Journeying down, he left tender kisses across the distance between my breasts until he granted my left nipple a harsh suck. "Ah," I groaned, treasuring the sharp feeling. His breath breezed across the now-wet bud, and it had a cooling effect. A beat later, he nibbled carefully on it, and the sensation drove me wild. It was just below the threshold of becoming painful.

"Honestly, Will," I panted and opened my eyes, "you read me

so well. It's like you know exactly how rough to be."

The cool air of his chuckle fanned across my sensitised nipple. "You make it easy for me. You're very expressive."

Wearing a smile, I watched the muscles of his shoulders and back ripple as he crawled backwards on the sofa. The view exacerbated my lust for him. Reaching forward, I smoothed my palms across the bumps and dents admiringly. Indeed, if I hadn't been an atheist, I would have mistaken him for a half-god. Either way, my atheism didn't prevent me from worshipping his body as though he were one, and I doubted it ever would.

When his lips trailed lower, my abdomen flexed under his gentle kisses, and he seemed to find the view amusing. "It's not every day that I sleep with a woman who's got well-trained abs," he commented and traced the vertical line between them with his fingers. "They're not *too* prominent, though."

"I like to eat," I said, amused.

He glanced at me with a playful smile. "So do I, and you're my favourite meal." To emphasise his point, he moved further back to drop a single kiss on my aching clit.

I gasped at once. Following my performance earlier, it was already hypersensitive. If he meant to make love to me with his mouth, I was sure I would be coming in no time.

Seeming to notice the same, he grinned. "Well, then. This should be quick."

I nodded vehemently. "I'm so ready for you."

"You always are," he replied smugly, but there was no lie within his statement.

Holding my eyes captive, he descended onto my drenched folds to clean up the mess I'd made some moments ago. Lapping his tongue across my slit, he hummed with delight.

"The taste of you is the ultimate aphrodisiac," he said with another grin before he proceeded to take my inner lips into his mouth. When he sucked on them, I gasped yet again. No one had done that before, but fuck did it feel amazing. The tingles travelled directly to my clit, as if the nerves were interconnected.

"Oh my God."

Hearing my appreciation, he did it several more times, which made my vagina ache for his penetration even more. Somehow, the attention he paid my inner lips enhanced the feeling of his absence.

"I need you inside me," I begged and tugged his hair in an attempt to bring his mouth back to mine, but he refused.

"Not yet," he replied with a chuckle.

"Please, Will."

He inserted his finger into me.

Oh my God. While it wasn't his shaft, it was sufficiently pleasurable, and now that his finger got between his mouth and my inner lips, he had to direct his tongue elsewhere.

A spasm rocked through my leg when he flicked it across my throbbing clit, and the sight amused him. "God, you're so sensitive."

"Make me come, Will," I whined and tugged his hair again. "You promised."

"All in good time, darling." The breath of his chuckle breezed my bundle of nerves, but before I could complain again, he sharpened his tongue to apply more pressure.

Immediately, my eyes sprang wide. Adhering to my plea, he was going straight for the main prize without a trace of mercy. "Shit!" I gnashed my teeth, my whole body tensing.

Squeezing my eyes shut, I held my breath while his tongue continued to taunt me, masterfully circling and then striking across.

Grabbing my breasts, I squeezed and tugged on my nipples as I neared the edge. My breathing grew ragged, the beats of my heart furious, as a formidable orgasm amassed within me. Eventually, my entire body was tensing under the sheer power of it. Every single one of my muscles flexed so hard that I finally started to shake. I ceased breathing then. All my focus was directed at enduring this forceful summoning.

Shocking me, he withdrew his finger from my vagina to push it gently into the hole below instead. At first, the tissues tightened around his digit as if to deny him but, since I had experience with this, I quickly forced them to relax. As soon as my body welcomed the intrusion, he began to pump his finger into me, back and forth, and the unmistakable sensation led me to cry out his name again. *Fuck*, that felt incredible.

My toes curled, and my fingers searched desperately for something to hold on to. Finding edges along his sofa, I gripped them harshly while I wailed his name. Realising that I was on the cusp of abandoning him for stupor, he withdrew his finger to lock his arms around my thighs instead. He must have anticipated my imminent shudders.

God. I was going to explode.

"I..." I uttered, high-pitched.

Responding, he increased the speed and pressure of his flicks, his tongue working my clit as though it was all he'd ever done. Spasms surged through me as my body begged for release, but he kept me captive in his grip.

"Ah!" A sharp breath, everything unleashed. Bliss commanded my entire system as I soared across an abstract state of life.

"Fuck," I cried out with abandon and collapsed.

As I recovered, he climbed over me to lavish my face with generous kisses.

"That was fantastic," I eventually croaked out over my laboured breathing. Opening my eyes, I looked up at his grin.

"Anal play take you off guard?"

I was certain my cheeks were flushed. "A bit," I admitted. "But it was a welcome surprise."

"I remember you said you enjoyed it, so I thought I ought to grab the opportunity." Suddenly, pure eroticism flared through his eyes. "Speaking of," he murmured and climbed out of the sofa. "I almost forgot."

Frowning, I sat up to follow his departure with my eyes. "Where are you going?"

"I'll be back in a sec," he said just as he entered his bedroom.

Upon his absence, I wondered what time it was. We had been going at it for ages, and at this rate, it didn't seem like we would finish anytime soon. The reality of that made me smile. I adored that we were able to treat sex as a fun, past-time activity. We'd explored each other's minds during our date earlier, and now we were exploring each other's bodies. I thought as I sat there that I wouldn't stop until there was nothing left of him to be explored, but upon second thought, I doubted I'd live long enough to see the day. He seemed endless.

In my peripheral vision, I noticed him return, so I turned my head to regard him. The sight that met me led me to gape. In his hands, he carried a bottle of lube and four different anal plugs of different shapes and sizes. All of them were black, which I supposed was for discretional reasons.

"I bought these the other day," he said. "I'd no idea which one you might prefer, but the lady in the shop recommended these ones."

Imagining the scene, I tittered. "While I appreciate this a lot, you're aware you could have bought them online, right?"

"I was worried they wouldn't arrive in time, so I threw discretion to the wind."

"Oh my God." I laughed. "People must have looked at you funny both when you entered and when you exited."

He smirked. "They did, but fuck them."

Rounding the sofa, he left each of the anal plugs in an organised line on the table – what a presentation.

"Which one?" he asked and folded his arms while he studied them. I couldn't stop sniggering.

"That one," I said and pointed to the one that was shaped like a penis, with veins and everything. However, it was thinner than the average penis and somewhat shorter. I had a similar one at home, which was how I knew which one to pick.

"Right." He reached for it. "This is actually a first for me," he said as he turned to face me with it.

The news surprised me. "Really?"

He looked absolutely thrilled. "Yes. I've done anal before, but I've never actually had sex with someone while they've had a butt plug inserted. I've done some research, though, so I promise I'll be careful. If you feel like I'm stretching you too far, we can proceed with a smaller one. Or, if the opposite is true, a bigger one."

I was amused. "Of course you've researched it." Without further ado, I snatched the item out of his hand with a rude expression on my face. "Before we start," I said, "I'd like to return the favour."

He looked bewildered. "What favour?"

Placing the butt plug aside, I reached for his jeans' belt loop and jerked him towards me. Glancing up at him through my long lashes, I unbuckled his black belt with resolve in my eyes. Realising what I intended to do, a slow smile crept across his kiss-swollen lips.

"I want to taste you," I said.

He moved his hand to my jaw. With wonder in his eyes, his thumb brushed across the line of it. "Be my guest, love."

He had no idea what he had in wait. Hopefully his cock wasn't the only thing I'd be blowing – his mind might become a casualty, too.

TIT FOR TAT

As soon as I had undone the button and zipper, I pulled down both his jeans and his boxers. His erection sprang free at once, pointing straight to my mouth, and the scent of it aroused me like no other. My eyes zoomed in on the head, and I noticed it was slightly wet. Precum? I hoped so.

Salivating, I gently brushed my fingertips across the length of him. My eyes were fixed on the bulging veins that branched towards the crest. Truly, he had the most flawless shaft I'd ever come across, and I intended to worship it completely.

I knew we had agreed to avoid using condoms from here on out, but I wanted to make sure that he hadn't changed his mind. I still hadn't taken a test, and although I was confident that Aaron hadn't given me any STIs since the last time I got checked, risking William's health wasn't my choice to make.

Glancing up at him, I asked, "Are you sure you wouldn't prefer to wear a condom for this?"

He frowned. "We've already been over this."

"Yes, I know, it's just—"

"Cara, if you've got something, I definitely do, too."

I stiffened. "What?"

"Yeah." He nodded. "In my throat. I've gone down on you several times. So, in the unlikely event that you've got anything, I'll probably need treatment as well."

Colour reduced in my face. He wasn't wrong. I shuddered at the possibility that he might have contracted an STI from me, but then I recalled what Aaron had told me on Tuesday – that awful night when I broke his heart.

Swallowing, I held William's gaze as I said, "If it helps, Aaron told me on Tuesday that he hasn't slept with anyone else in the past two years."

I thought I detected a flicker of compassion in William's eyes then, and it surprised me. Did he harbour sympathy for Aaron? "Well, I honestly believe him. Do you?"

"Yeah. He wouldn't lie about something like that."

"Then we're good to go."

Nodding, I directed my eyes back to his member. Excitement unfurled in my chest. I could hardly wait to sample the taste of him, feeling his skin on my tongue as I traced the veins of his erection with it. When my fingers reached the base of him, I brushed them across the surrounding and coarse strands of trimmed hair with a sinful smile on my mouth. "I love that you trim rather than shave," I said. "I've always preferred some hair on my men."

"I have the same preference when it comes to women, actually," he replied with some amusement. Knowing I had shaved away every hint of hair, I looked up.

"You do?"

"Yes."

"Oh. I'm sorry. I'll leave some behind for next time."

He grinned, thumb brushing lovingly across my cheek. "Cara, do whatever you're most comfortable with. I'll be thrilled to fuck you regardless."

"To be honest, I've only shaved or waxed it all off because I thought men preferred it bald."

He shrugged. "Some do, I suppose, but I don't."

"How come?"

"You just seem more…womanly with some hair there. Grown-up, if that makes sense."

I'd never thought of it that way. "That does make sense, actually." I grinned up at him as I gripped around his member. He was such a *man.*

Steering my eyes back to his impressive shaft, I realised it would pose a challenge to get all of him into my mouth. However, I'd had years of training when it came to controlling my gag reflex, so I would put it to good use.

Leaning forward, I planted generous but soft kisses along the crest of him. The same instant I made contact with his sensitive skin, the taste of his precum blessed my tongue. I smiled. It didn't taste bad at all. Though, judging by the presence of it, he had indeed been clinging to his self-control earlier.

The sound of a sharp breath made me look up. Back at me stared eyes that were suffused with arousal. His hand moved from my jaw to gather my hair instead, and he held it so firmly that my roots complained, but it was a sensation I relished.

His jaw clenched when I continued to tease him with tender kisses. After a while, I parted my lips, slightly, to suck carefully at the tip of him. Meanwhile, my hand tightened around the base of him, teasing.

Taking my sweet time, I continued to switch between kissing and sucking on the tip of his head to trigger his impatience. I wanted to drive him wild with lust. I wanted him to beg me to take him in completely, only so that he could spill every drop of his ejaculation onto my tongue. Simply, I wanted to drive him mad the same way he did me.

I wondered what his seeds would taste like. Some men's semen tasted fine, but others' could taste truly awful. However, judging by his precum, I had a feeling that the taste of him would be a positive experience. Either way, I was determined to milk him of every last drop and swallow it all.

"Cara," he growled under his breath as he brought his free hand to my jaw. I could hear the plea in his tone, and it made me smile again. "You're driving me mad."

"Tit for tat," I answered cheekily. To give him an impression of what he had in wait, I spread my mouth wider and took more of him in.

He groaned, hand tightening its grip of my hair. Tears surfaced in my eyes at once, but since I enjoyed it, I didn't protest.

Removing my hand from the base of him, I continued to take him in until the coarse strands of his pubic hairs grazed my lips. Once there, I swirled my tongue around him for some time, eager to tantalise. When he groaned again, I held my breath to create a vacuum. Hollowing my cheeks, I provided maximum suction while I slowly retreated, and the sound of his ensuing moan boosted my ego. As I retreated, I made sure to return my hand to his base to pump it.

"Mm," I vocalised just before I liberated his head from my mouth. "You taste *so* good."

Upon the liberation, his hand loosened its grip of my hair. His eyes hooded. "Again," he commanded.

Grinning, I planted a few more kisses on the crest of his erection before I spat a generous amount of saliva onto it. Sliding my hand away from his base, I spread it across his entire length to lubricate and prepare him for intense action. When it was sticky and wet, I gripped tightly around him again and began to pump him.

Remembering to not neglect his testicles, I angled my head to locate them below. Sticking out my tongue, I licked carefully across them while I assessed his sensitivity from the sound of his consequent groans. To test his limit, I increased the rapidness of my tongue's flicks and applied pressure until his hand fisted in my hair.

I'd found his threshold. Sticking with that pace and pressure, I continued to pump his member while I sucked and licked his balls. The sound of his groans exacerbated my arousal. *God,* I could hardly wait to feel him throbbing within me.

As soon as I thought it, I felt a drop of my fluids trail out.

Returning to his erection, I took all of him in and removed my hand to get to the base of him.

"Fuck, Cara," he hissed out. "Where you learnt this, I don't want to know, but please, don't stop."

Encouraged by his words, I hollowed my cheeks again to suck him hard as I pulled back. As I did, I simultaneously teased him with my tongue. When only his head remained within my mouth, I grabbed around the freed area to pump him. Inhaling deeply through my nose, I started bobbing my head, resolutely, and I made sure that my hand's labour was perfectly synchronised with my mouth's.

"Ah," he uttered, but it sounded strangely similar to a complaint. However, he made no move to stop me, nor did he ask me to, so I continued in spite of it. Deciding to deep-throat him, I took him in as far as he would go several times. Inevitably, I started gagging on him, which caused tears to well in my eyes before they trickled down my cheeks.

My cheeks had hardly started to ache by the time he suddenly stepped backwards to withdraw from my mouth. Worried I had done something wrong, I immediately looked up at him.

"Did I do something wrong?" I asked, concerned.

Using his grip of my hair, he tugged me up until I was standing in front of him. From his searing gaze, I got the impression he had stepped away for a different reason.

I was about to prompt him to answer when his mouth dived for mine, and his kiss was explosive. Overpowered by the heat of it, I mellowed against him and planted my palms on his chest for support.

Pulling away for a desperate pant, he growled, "You did everything right." Another famished kiss past, he alleged, "Your mouth is lethal."

Grinning, I demanded another kiss while I clawed into his chest, capsized by overwhelming lust for him.

"I need to be inside you," he professed, ravenous. "Skin to skin." He leaned against me, and it was obvious from his movement that he meant to force me to recline onto the sofa behind me, but I would have no such thing. This time, I wanted to be on top.

Grabbing his arms, I stepped sideways and guided him with me until it was *his* back that faced the sofa. Wearing a besotted smile, I parted from his mouth and discovered some confusion in his eyes. Seeing it, my smile took a mischievous shape before I placed my right hand on the centre of his chest. Exerting some force, I pushed against him until he overbalanced and dropped onto the sofa.

Before he could react to his new position, I grabbed his jaw and pressed my mouth on his as I descended onto him. Pouring all my passion into our kiss, I guided his body to turn along with mine until he was forced to lie down beneath me. Once I was straddling him, I pulled back from his spellbinding mouth to stare lustfully into his eyes.

When I saw him swallow, my confidence was further boosted. For the first time ever, William looked intimidated, and I relished the sight.

"This time," I purred and lowered my lips to search for the pulse that drummed in his throat, "*I* want to be in charge." When I found it, I greedily sucked and nibbled on it. Responding to the sensation, his hands roamed feverishly across my body, squeezing and clawing, until they settled on my bum. His nails dug into the flesh there, before he removed one hand to pay me a harsh spank.

Fuck. The sting of his palm burnt like fire. "You'll regret that," I stated after a hiss and lifted my head to glare into his eyes.

Challenge shone from their otherwise serene blue colour. Below, his familiar crooked smile emerged on his mouth, and the sight of its arrogant shape fuelled my determination. He had no idea how mercilessly I would obliterate its confident form. I wouldn't stop until I had extracted every ounce of the vulnerability that I knew it veiled.

"Careful, Cara," he warned. "You're not the only one ablaze anymore."

I released a mocking laugh before I ground my hips against him, sliding back and forth across his member to lubricate him with my dripping wetness. Clasping the nape of my neck, he groaned and brought my mouth back to his. His kiss was hard – forceful – as if he was trying to overpower me.

Retaliating, I angled my hips and pushed backwards, leaving him to slide right into me. The instant fulfilment led me to gasp into his mouth. I would never get over how far I stretched to accommodate him. It was just barely below the brink of being painful.

"Fuck," he hissed against my lips, nails clawing into my lower cheeks again.

I groaned. Now that there was no latex between us, everything felt much more intimate – raw. The friction was far more intense, heightening my awareness of him within me. He was warm, thick, and rock hard, while the veins of him rubbed deliciously across my tissues.

Tossing myself backwards, I sat up and fondled my breasts while I began to rock my hips against him, but I avoided grinding too much. Maintaining a motion of up and down was crucial if I meant to live up to my word and vanquish him.

"Oh," I moaned and closed my eyes. He felt so fucking good.

Fortunately, this position enabled me to control exactly where he struck, so it was unlikely that I'd lose control of my pleasure.

When I heard him groan beneath me, I opened my eyes to assess the efficiency of my motions, and I could tell he was struggling to contain himself. His abdominal muscles remained constantly flexed while I rocked against him, up and down. Biting my lower lip, I paid him an inveigling smile.

"Feel that, Will? How far I stretch to accommodate you?"

His response came as a moan, so my smile widened.

"How perfectly you fit into me?" I purred and clawed down across the bulging muscles of his torso.

"Cara, I swear to God—" Another groan cut him off.

"I wish you could stay inside me forever." I hummed seductively as I pinched and tugged on my nipples. Seemingly hypnotised, he gazed mesmerised up at me, but not a word escaped his mouth. Had I rendered him speechless?

Suddenly he rushed up after me, mouth claiming each of my nipples with ravenous sucks. Groaning with excitement, I dragged my hands through his hair. Our new position was powerfully intimate, and it made my heart run amok.

I loved having sex with him. I loved touching his naked skin, and I loved how high he made me feel. I'd never experienced anything like this. Our connection was palpable, and in the throes of passion, cosmic. Indeed, having sex with him transcended everything. It amounted to a state of total completion.

I was enjoying his body, but, somehow, it felt much deeper than that. It went beyond the shallow surface of the skin. I was experiencing his existence – every fragment of the stardust he was composed of, every whisper of his thoughts, and every heartbeat of his emotions. When our bodies moved as one, it was like our individual chemistry combined at a celestial level, and the result was a higher force that could never be undone.

"Mm." I tugged at the strands of his hair while I continued

to ride him.

"Fucking hell, Cara," he uttered. Trying to impede the motion of my hips, he gripped them firmly and pushed against them. "Show mercy," he pleaded when I grabbed his hands to shove them away.

Staring straight into his eyes, I nuzzled my nose against his and whispered an obstinate, "No." Gripping his shoulders, I pushed forward and pinned him to the sofa. Following his descent, I placed insatiable kisses all across his throat while I continued to bounce against him, and his subsequent moans were unlike anything else I'd ever heard.

I'd hardly moved like that for a minute, and already, he was producing the strangest, most arousing noises. "Ah-hah-ah," he uttered, and the sound was a strange blend between elation and despair. Amazement? I hadn't heard a more exciting sound all my life. From the noises he made, it was clear that I was succeeding in my quest. I was devastating him the same way he devastated me – leaving the other in splinters only to combine our pieces.

"Fuck, Cara," he hissed loudly. His hands found my hips again, and his grip was so hard that I struggled to move. "Cara, stop."

Stop? Was I hurting him? I slowed at once. "What's the matter?"

He shook his head, and he looked so lost. "I'll come if you keep this up. I mean it."

His answer only reinforced my determination. Grabbing his hands, I removed them from my hips and leaned forward to lock them on either side of his face. Holding them in place, I continued to rock against him.

"Ah." He grimaced, eyes pleading for mercy as they stared up into mine. "Cara, shit. How the hell are you doing this?"

I granted him a wet, lustful kiss. "Doing what?"

"When you're leaned forward like this," he panted desperately, "you're rubbing so precisely round my head. Seriously, you're gripping my cock so fucking hard." As I bounced down on him again, I extracted another beautiful moan from his mouth. "You're striking it too perfectly – I can't."

From his moans, I heard that he had absolutely lost control, and it excited me like nothing else. Fixed on sending him over the edge, I continued to charge down on him and ignored how much pleasure I derived from the friction myself.

"Cara, no. It feels too good," he protested and, shocking me, exerted real force to break my hold of his wrists. Intimidated, my breath hitched. He was much, much stronger than me, and it had never been more apparent. Witnessing it, I felt incredibly small and vulnerable. I never thought I'd see him utilise his true strength against me. I knew he wasn't the violent type – he'd never use it to hurt me, but it was still a humbling experience. I had clearly pushed him to his limit.

Scraping together what little I had left of courage, I dared to continue. Gripping my hips yet again, his hands pushed forcefully against my every movement to attenuate the impact.

"You need to stop," he insisted. "This position – *Stop*. Please," he begged, eyes beseeching. "I don't want to come yet."

"*I* want you to come," I replied fiercely and tried to shove his hands away. Ascending with some effort, I pushed down on him again, and he allowed me to repeat it another few times before he suddenly sat up. Wrapping his arms around me, he caged me in his hold so tightly that I couldn't move so much as an inch.

God, how I hated his physical superiority in that moment.

"William," I complained loudly, but was immediately silenced upon the fury that unleashed in his eyes. He was ablaze indeed.

"Riding is officially off-limits," he thundered and proceeded to throw his legs off the furniture so that I sat straddling him while facing the backrest behind him.

His fury seemed contagious, as it alighted in me too as soon as I processed his declaration.

"Like hell!"

Before I knew it, he'd shifted us around so that I was trapped beneath him on the sofa. Releasing me from his confining embrace, he propped his weight on his arms on either side of my head.

Hovering above, he glared menacingly into my eyes. "I dare you to try that again. I'll fuck you apart."

I released a whine. "This is so unfair!"

"Hardly."

"It really is! Why should you be allowed to make me come time and again, but when I want to do the same, you won't let me?"

"Because, unlike you, I can't come with mere seconds in between. I don't want to come this fast, Cara. I want to enjoy you for as long as possible."

I was about to suggest that even though he might not be able to get erect again immediately after ejaculating, we could do other things. However, hearing his explanation, I got the impression that he was specifically referring to penetration. Consequently, he managed to stir some sympathy in me, so, with a pout, I glanced up at him. "But I love riding," I complained through protruding lips.

"I can tell," he muttered before a sigh. "How about this then," he said, voice softening. "Whenever we've already had sex, you may ride me the following rounds that day. Just not the first. My endurance is always at its worst the first time."

His attempt to find a compromise amused me. "Okay. I can go along with that."

"Thank you," he said, and I could hear that his gratitude was profound. "But for now, *I'll* be the one fucking the other senseless."

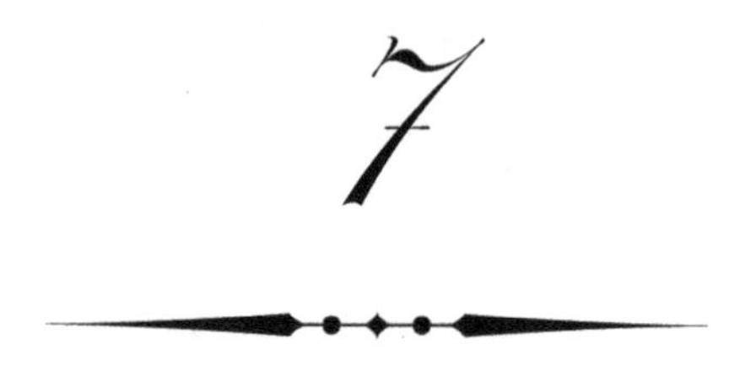

LET ME IN

INTIMIDATED, I GULPED. HOWEVER, WHEN HE PROCEEDED to withdraw from within me, I was rendered confused. Moving off the sofa, he reached for the butt plug I'd picked earlier. Seeing it, my sense of intimidation restored at once.

"Alas," he murmured while he reached for the bottle of lube, "you've already severely reduced my endurance, so I'll be cutting straight to the chase. Get on all fours for me, love."

My heart thundered in my chest as I moved to heed his command. Climbing up on all fours, anticipation simmered in my blood. The sound of lube spurting out of the bottle echoed in my ears. Awaiting the imminent intrusion, my fingers kneaded the leather of his sofa.

Suddenly, a cold drop of lube landed precisely on my anus. I tensed by instinct, but quickly reminded myself to relax. Soon enough, his warm finger spread the lubrication round my opening. I took a deep breath. This was bound to be a mind-blowing session.

Very gently, he pressed the tip of the object into me. It was cold, but I had expected it. Collapsing my lower body, I focused on my breathing to remain relaxed.

My action seemed to make him hesitant because he paused pushing it into me. "You okay?" he asked, voice tender.

"Mhm. I'm fine."

His patience was evident from how carefully he proceeded to shove the item into me. Now and then, he'd stop to let me adjust, and I lauded his intuition, or perhaps he had read this somewhere?

As soon as it reached a certain distance, my body proceeded to suck the rest of it in. *Fuck.*

"There we go. Well done, darling," he praised and caressed my back. "I'll be slow and gentle. Tell me to stop if it hurts."

Taking in a deep breath, I nodded my head and pushed my upper body back up to prepare for impact. Climbing onto the sofa, he knelt behind me and grabbed my hips to align my entrance with his erection.

Turning my head, I glanced out the windows. "What if someone sees us?" I asked as I stared straight through the window of the top floor in the neighbouring building. I couldn't deny it – the riskiness of our location was weirdly arousing. Then again, I'd always had a kink for relatively discreet exhibitionism.

"Fuck if I care," he replied, amused. "Do you?"

Blushing, I shook my head. "They can always shut the curtains."

"My thoughts exactly." The crest of him slid up and down my folds then, wallowing in my juices. "Ready?" he asked, and the low pitch of his voice right then sounded so seductive that I groaned.

"Yes."

Without further warning, he pushed into me. I gasped while my eyes widened. *Oh my God.* He was so fucking big, and now that the butt plug was stimulating the nerve-endings in my other hole, my awareness of his presence became all the more acute. This fulfilment was unlike any other I'd experienced before.

"Fuck," I whimpered and clawed the leather of his sofa.

He stopped at once, although he hadn't come all the way in yet. "Does it hurt?"

"No. It feels amazing."

"Good."

He groaned as he shoved further to reach the end of me. "Shit, Cara," he chuckled, "somehow, you feel even tighter than usual. I won't be able to last long."

"I'm going to come in record time. I know it," I reassured him, "so don't worry about it."

"If you don't, I'll make it up to you in other ways."

"That won't be necessary. I'll definitely come."

He was gentle upon his retreat, and his first few thrusts were gentle, too. I appreciated that, as I was somewhat struggling to accommodate him. However, the more aroused I became, the more my vaginal walls spread to welcome him. Noticing the same, he dared to increase the pace, and the friction of it blew my mind.

"Mm, yes. Just like that," I encouraged. "You fuck like a god, Will."

Spurred by my words, he leaned over me, arms coming around me to hold me intimately. "You're the divine power here," he alleged as his hands journeyed to my breasts, squeezing and fondling.

"I beg to differ," I replied with a smile and turned my head in search of his lips. Meeting them, he kissed me sweetly while he continued to drive into me, and the more he continued, the harder his thrusts became. With each shove, he struck the butt plug inside me, and the sensation bolted up my spine until it tingled in my nose.

After a while, his right hand let go of my breast to slide down my stomach instead, and then further to the apex between my thighs. Anticipating what came next, my heart skipped a beat.

A second later, his fingers were rubbing over my throbbing clit, and the combination of it all drove me senseless with pleasure. He was everywhere – both within and without. His hand on my breast, his lips on mine, his fingers on my clit, his shaft inside of me while it somehow stimulated both holes simultaneously – I couldn't take any more. It was too intense.

"Shit," I cried and pulled away from his mouth, needing air. The tension continued to heat up in my system, nearing its boiling point. Delicious chemicals amassed in my brain, drumming on the threshold as they threatened to burst past.

Reaching for his hands on my body, my palms wrapped over the back of his where I entwined our fingers. When he thrust again, I squeezed his hands so hard that my knuckles grew numb.

Air stormed out of my lungs. "Fuck," I mouthed.

"Mm, Cara," he purred sensually. "*J'aime être avec toi, et j'adore te faire l'amour. Tu es la femme de ma vie, Cara. Je n'aimerais que toi pour le restant de mes jours.*"

His French echoed in my mind as the most erotic thing I would ever hear. Instantly, my arousal escalated even further. I had no idea what he had said, but merely the sound set my libido aflame. I imagined it had contained dirty declarations, taking the shape of something sophisticated but passionate, all due to the beautiful language.

"Wow," I breathed out in my awe.

He continued masterfully, shaft striking precisely against my front wall while simultaneously pushing against the butt plug within me. I shook my head. This was entirely overwhelming. I'd never experienced such sexual intensity in my life.

"Will," I warned. My walls clamped down on him as if to reject him, and I sensed the butt plug slide out somewhat, but upon his next thrust, he shoved it straight back in.

Oh, my fucking God. "Ah!" Stars rained past my eyes. He was fucking me heavenly.

"Yes, Cara. Let me in." Releasing a loud groan, he gripped my jaw and turned my head. A heartbeat later, his mouth was on mine.

"Mph!" I whimpered into his kiss. A few desperate pants later, shudders spread throughout my body. Sensing that I was on the verge of surmounting the peak, he tightened his hold of me to prevent my escape.

And then it unlocked. "Ah!"

Sweet release eclipsed my mind, sending it into a state of utter delirium. Dissolving in his arms, faint whimpers escaped my mouth upon each of his thrusts as they increased in strength. He was nearing it.

"Ah," he groaned loudly for a final time and thrust so hard that it was somewhat painful. Stilling, he recovered above me with heavy breaths.

"Shit," he chuckled after a while. "I've never come that fast during sex."

"It was fucking intense," I said hoarsely. Wrinkles formed across my nose when he moved to pull out.

"Did it hurt at all?" he asked.

"Only the last thrust."

"Sorry."

"I survived," I chuckled and collapsed sideways.

"I'll bear it in mind for next time." He lay down next to me and cuddled me close. Smiling content, I nuzzled my nose against his naked skin and savoured his intoxicating scent. We rested there for quite some time, trading soft and chaste kisses while we surrendered to a peaceful silence. Whenever I lied next to him like this and shut my eyes, I felt capable of touching the sky. Indeed, these intimate moments were the closest I'd ever come to heaven.

Realising we were still on the sofa, a humoured smile crept over my lips. "The wall, the dining table, the bed, the sofa... Where next, Will?"

Batting my eyelids apart, I propped myself on my elbow beside him and saw a grin on his mouth, but his eyes remained closed.

"Let's make it a point to have sex on every available surface. We can start with the bathroom tomorrow morning," he proposed.

Smitten laughter escaped my mouth. Dropping a prolonged kiss to his chest, I felt his heart hammer beneath my lips. My smile soon widened into a grin.

"French seems to have a triggering effect on you," he murmured suddenly, and I could hear he was amused.

"It does."

"It's hilarious. You don't even know what I'm saying. I could be insulting you, and you'd just moan with pleasure."

I laughed at the truth of it. "Probably. What were you saying, though?"

His eyes remained closed, but another smile surfaced on his lips. "What do you think I said?"

I brushed my hand across his warm chest. "I really don't know."

His smile became a grin. "Take a guess."

"Will, come on. I'm seriously clueless."

Finally, his eyes opened, and the intensity of them took me off guard. For a moment, their blue colour read my face, but I couldn't gauge the emotion in them.

"I said I love being inside you and things like that."

A coy smile formed on my lips. "I see." Lowering my head, I kissed his shoulder. "I suspected they were crude declarations."

"Mm."

"Well, I love having you inside me, too."

"Good."

"Anyway, I need the loo," I murmured and climbed over him. Upon standing, I became hyperaware of the butt plug still within me. "This always feels so weird," I giggled and shielded my derrière with my hands as I approached his bedroom to escape further into the bathroom.

After sterilising the butt plug and cleaning up the mess he'd made between my legs, I returned to the living room. He hadn't moved an inch.

Grabbing my glass of wine, I was careful not to spill it as I climbed over him to squeeze in between his body and the backrest. Once I was comfortable, I released a contented sigh and took a sip.

We'd been basking in silence for quite some time when he suddenly asked, "So, have you taken a test yet?"

I stiffened at the reminder. "No. I'm sorry."

He sighed with disappointment.

"Honestly, Will, I forgot. It's just, after everything with Aaron, getting checked was the last thing on my mind."

The second Aaron's name rolled off my tongue, he tensed beneath me, and it made me look at him, but he refused to meet my gaze. All he offered was a single nod of his head.

"I'll do it next week." I tried to appease him, but he only nodded again. Scrutinising him, I wondered if his plummeting mood was due to my failure to take a test, or whether it was the mention of Aaron that had caused it. I considered asking, but would I appreciate knowing?

After swallowing a greedy mouthful of wine, I decided to ask. "What's the matter?"

His brows furrowed, and I could tell he was considering whether to indulge me or not. After a while, he finally said, "I don't exactly enjoy the idea of you two, and whenever you mention him, I'm forced to remember." He tucked his hand under his head. "Part of me finds it annoying that you care this much about what happened between you – enough to forget about things relating to me, such as getting tested. At the same time, I know he means a great deal to you, so I don't really expect anything else. I'm just sorry it's like that."

I pouted. I shouldn't have mentioned Aaron. We'd had such a wonderful day together, and now I had clumsily ruined a perfectly delightful moment by reminding him of my past partner again.

Still, I was grateful that he shared his thoughts with me, so I was about to reply that although I was upset about losing Aaron, I was ultimately happy with my choice, but a phone rang before I could. I was aware we had the same ringtone, but it couldn't be mine since it sounded close.

Reaching towards the floor, William grabbed his jeans to fish his phone out of the back pocket. When he brought his screen into our field of vision, I was immediately ripped out of my serene state.

John was calling.

"I should take this," William said, and his composure astounded me. Accepting the call, he raised the device to his ear and answered calmly, "Hi, Dad."

I held my breath. Meanwhile, William rubbed my back with his free hand as if he hadn't a concern in the world.

"No," he murmured, "I skipped today." Skipped what? "Just wasn't feeling in the mood for drinks – that's all." Oh. Right. It was Friday. Post-work drinks.

A few moments later, he groaned. "Really? Have I got to? Why not ask Jason? The twat's on summer holiday for crying out loud. He hasn't got anything but time."

His ensuing pout made me grin despite my anxiety. It was amusing to see him like this – in the role of someone's child.

"Yeah. Alright, fine. I'll attend." He released a loud breath that revealed his exasperation. "Jason's a tit for this."

I almost giggled, but wisely stifled the urge.

"The only reason I'm agreeing," William continued, "is because I know Alex and Andy are going to be there as well… Yes, I'll be on my best behaviour. Don't worry… Yes. Tell Mum I love her, too… Bye."

Stretching over to the table, he left his phone there and huffed out a loud breath.

Amused, I had another sip of wine. "What's turned you into

such a sulky teenager?" I teased.

He glanced at me before he looked away again. "Dad asked me to attend a charity event in a couple of weeks."

"And that's annoying?"

"Yes. I can't stand events like that. It's full of self-important people, and small talk is all you do the entire evening with god knows how many people. All those 'hello's, and 'how have you been?'s drive me mad."

I struggled to repress a chuckle. "Why won't Jason go?"

"Because the bastard told Dad that he's already made plans that day and that I am better suited since it's a chance to network. Plus, Andy and Alex will be there. Stephen and Jon aren't invited." He rolled his eyes. "He's got plans, my fucking arse. He can hardly plan further ahead than a week at a time."

I stood no chance at containing my laughter then, as what he had said was entirely true. Jason approached life one stride at a time and always had. He was a big dreamer, but he wasn't the best planner when it came to the mundane tasks of everyday life.

"Why won't John go himself?"

"He meant to, initially, but Mum's hospital is hosting an event for the staff that night, so they're double-booked. And, knowing him, he was eager to escape the event himself. He prefers to just transfer the assets directly to the charity instead of showing up to functions."

Laughter continued to roll out of me. "Like father, like sons, I suppose."

"Yeah," he grumbled.

"Is your attendance indispensable, though?"

"Yes. Someone needs to represent the family."

"I see. There's no way out of it, then." Laying down again, I rested my head on his shoulder and gave his skin a peck. "At least Alex and Andy will be there."

"Only reason I agreed."

Remembering that the office tended to go for drinks today,

I asked, "Do you think our colleagues will suspect, by the way? Since neither of us showed up today?"

Meeting my eyes, he looked sceptical. "Not in the slightest. They'll think it's a coincidence. Violet and Andy will cover for us if anyone asks – I'm sure."

"They're aware of our date?"

"Yeah."

I puffed out an anxious breath. "I hope no one else suspects. Ellie is worrying me a bit."

He tapped my back absentmindedly then. "Cara, you need to calm down about this whole dating-your-boss thing. Besides, as your supervisor, I'm the one at greatest risk. With greater power comes greater responsibility. I'm not saying this because I want you to stop fighting us. I'm sincerely trying to enlighten you of the status quo on this matter. Office romances are common. How we conduct one is the critical factor."

I wasn't convinced. If anything, his statement only made me worried for him. There wasn't a chance I would sit idly by while he, too, risked his career to explore our potential. "Perhaps we should draw up a contract that establishes mutual responsibility, Will. That way, if things turn sour between us, you won't be at any greater risk than me."

"Ever the pessimist," he muttered. "First of all, things won't turn sour. Second of all, what you're suggesting is known as a 'love contract'. It's commonplace in the US, but here in the UK, they don't tend to hold up in court."

I frowned. "Why not?"

"There are two reasons, mainly. First, an employee cannot be forced to sign away their right to protection against harassment in the workplace under UK law. Second, such a contract would contravene Article 8 of the European Convention on Human Rights."

I couldn't recall the precise content of Article 8. "What's that article again?"

His tone was patient. "Well, it's been incorporated into UK law under the Human Rights Act of 1998, which states that we are entitled to a private life. In other words, it's not illegal to have office romances in the UK. On the contrary, we are entitled to it, so long as we conduct it appropriately."

I turned my head to study him. "Have you actually looked into this?"

He nodded. "Right after you walked into my office the first time."

My eyes rolled into my skull while I groaned. "So, while I was reading through my contract, you were busy investigating whether you could legally still date me or not?"

"That's right."

"Christ. Was I that much of a foregone conclusion?"

"Not at all."

I shook my head when I added the pieces together. "So that was the work which required your 'immediate attention' back then."

"Yes."

"I'd have thought you were well-versed in this issue already, taking your past with Violet into account."

He shrugged. "I'm aware I can't be dismissed for having a sexual relationship with a colleague – all depending on how it's conducted, of course – but I wasn't sure if my role as your boss would change that fact. Plus, there was the romantic aspect to consider. Violet and I have never been in the same situation."

"Right." I sighed and averted my eyes. While I desperately wanted to trust him on this, I wasn't entirely convinced. "Have you got the handbook? If it's not illegal, I'm sure Day & Night has got a policy on this."

He eyed me, unimpressed. "You haven't read it?"

I shook my head. "Not that section. At the time, I didn't think it would be relevant."

He smirked. "Times change."

"Clearly."

"Right, hang on. I'll fetch it. It's in my office upstairs."

He had an office upstairs? I needed a tour of this place.

"What else is upstairs?"

From his expression, it was obvious that it had only just dawned on him that he hadn't shown me around the place. "Join me." He offered his hand. Taking it, I left my glass on the table to proceed with him up the stairs.

The first thing I noticed was the panoramic view, although it was interrupted by a few walls. Through the windows, I saw London's rooftops rest like a blanket beneath the sky. Mesmerised, I turned to gawk at him.

"Wow."

His attention remained on the view. "I love being here."

"I can see why."

From up here, it was like the city's vibrancy tempered beneath our feet. I was at the very heart of it, and yet, somehow, it seemed far removed. Watching it from a distance, a sense of tranquillity gripped me.

"This is another surface worth fucking on," he suddenly said, and his crudeness ultimately murdered my serene thoughts. Following the direction his hand pointed in, I spotted a huge sofa group in front of a massive television screen. To be fair, the whole thing looked like it belonged in a fancy cinema. Scenes of him and Jason shouting over a football match in here thrived in my imagination.

However, this place wasn't solely a home theatre. Rather, it struck me as a leisure room. Some feet away stood a pool table, as well as a table of brown wood, the edges and legs adorned with meticulous engravings. Atop it stood chess pieces.

"You've got an actual chess table?" I couldn't hide my amusement.

Youthful excitement shone from his eyes. "Care for a match?"

Though I hated to disappoint him, I said, "Perhaps some other time."

Browsing the rest of the room, I noticed that every wall was covered with bookshelves filled to the brim.

"Have you read all these?"

"Almost all of them."

"Christ. Avid reader, indeed."

"Yes."

I glanced at him. "Have you got a favourite genre?"

"Historical fiction. Definitely. But I read just about everything."

"Favourite author?"

His nose wrinkled. "Perhaps Ken Follett? I really can't say, but I've read every one of his."

With a nod, I allowed my eyes to continue their inspection. When I thought I noticed a fireplace, they narrowed. Below the TV, it formed a long horizontal line.

"You've got a fireplace?" I pointed to it.

"Yes. Hence why we absolutely need to have sex in here someday."

I laughed. "You're insatiable."

"When it comes to you, absolutely. Anyway, there's more." He tugged me towards a door behind us.

A king-size bed stood within the room behind it, as well as a desk and a contemporary wardrobe. "This is the guestroom. We can fuck here, too," he said, which made me laugh again.

Closing the door, he pointed to another one at the end of the corridor. "That's another bathroom."

He guided me in the direction of it but stopped when we encountered yet another door. "This is my office."

Walking in, he neglected to switch on the lights in the ceiling. Instead, he turned on his desk lamp, and I appreciated the soft illumination. This way, the night sky of summer was free to slide into the room.

Gazing around, I saw bookshelves here too, but the literature was exclusively law-related, unlike in the leisure room. Scanning the contents, William searched for the handbook we had come here for. Meanwhile, I enjoyed the old-fashioned atmosphere of the room. His desk chair was large and made of brown leather. Had it been centuries' years old, I wouldn't have been surprised. The dark brown desk was reminiscent of the chess table he had in his leisure room – the engravings were akin.

"There," he said. Looking over, I saw him withdraw the handbook from a shelf. I'd expected him to bring it over to me, but instead, he took a seat in his desk chair. Amused, I moseyed over to hover, but before I could manage the latter, he swept his arm around my waist and brought me onto his lap.

When his lips blessed my naked shoulder blade with a kiss, I smiled in his arms and turned my face to nuzzle my nose against his.

"Let's get to the root of this, shall we?" he asked as I pulled away.

"Yes."

He opened the handbook with his arms around me, index finger tracing the table of contents before he located the relevant page. He spread the book apart where the title was, "Personal Relationships at Work" and handed it to me before he booted his desktop Mac.

I gulped as I started reading the text. Skimming past the policy's scope and purpose, I headed towards the section outlining the employees' responsibilities and the potential consequences of failing to execute them. Soon later, I was reassured.

"Hm."

He kissed my shoulder again. "Told you so."

"Unfair dismissal is unlikely then, I suppose."

"It is." Nodding his head, he pointed to the screen. "Here, have a look."

Leaning closer, I saw that he had searched up *Niemietz v Germany (1992)* in the HUDOC database and opened the judgment. A smile surfaced on my lips. It was all coming back to me now.

"I think I remember this case."

Hearing that, he smiled as well, but his version was lopsided and fainter. "Do you remember what it says, then?"

I narrowed my eyes at him. "Something about us having a right to privacy even at work? It wasn't about romantic relationships at work, though."

Glancing at him, I could tell he was struggling not to poke fun at me. "No, you're right that the case doesn't go into detail about romantic relationships at work. However, the Court makes a general statement that covers it. This is where the ECtHR established that activities relevant to self-realisation and the development of personal relationships are entitled to protection in the workplace as well and may therefore also happen there." Steering the cursor to paragraph twenty-nine, he highlighted the relevant text. "Specifically, the Court reasons that, 'it is, after all, in the course of their working lives that the majority of people will have a significant, if not the greatest, opportunity of developing personal relationships with the outside world.' In conclusion, we are entitled to embark on a relationship even at work, Cara."

I pursed my lips. "Still, it says in the handbook that if a relationship exists between an employee and their line manager, it's both our responsibility to notify the HR department so that they can take steps to evaluate the situation and whether assigning alternative roles might be necessary, to avoid compromising the company's—"

"Yes, but until we're actually in a relationship, it doesn't apply to us."

I raised a brow. "It says 'personal relationship'. In the definitions, it is specified that a sexual relationship is included under that term."

He groaned. "Cara, they're just guidelines – not actual laws. We have every right to be doing this. I've already done it for a year with Violet. We'll be fine. Besides, you'll only be working under my leadership for three months. We can last that long without fucking up. All we need to do is remain professional while at work."

I tensed in his embrace. "We are walking on thin ice here."

"We're in the grey area."

"I don't feel comfortable breaking the guidelines. I studied law because I meant to abide by the rules, not break them. Seriously. I've inherent respect for rules like these."

"Cara, please. Be pragmatic, for once."

Uncertain, I chewed into my lower lip. Meanwhile, his eyes pleaded with me not to remain principled about this. Finally I released a sigh.

"No one else can know, Will. Only Violet and Andy."

He nodded. "Thank you. I just don't want you shadowing anyone else – I prefer to keep you to myself. Besides, we've already seen how well we work together. I swear this won't jeopardise that. We're a great team. It's in the company's best interest that we remain within our current roles."

Apart from his last statement, what he had said was true, but it was debatable whether this was really in the company's best interest. Regardless, I wasn't about to start it with him. Instead, I said, "If Ellie starts asking questions—"

"We'll tell her nothing."

"I'm relying on your discretion," I told him gravely.

Grabbing my jaw, he leaned in to place several kisses on my mouth. "And you are absolutely safe to do that."

I wasn't quite sure how I felt about this. "If I start to suspect that more people are aware of us, I'm going to notify the HR department," I warned him, "for pre-emptive measures."

"That's fair, but please give me a heads-up first."

"Of course."

He took my hand to shake it, and it made me grin. Then, he raised my hand to his mouth and brushed his lips across my pulse.

"Are you tired?" he asked softly.

"I'm knackered."
"Let's go to bed."
"Yes."

WILLIAM'S DOOM

THE FOLLOWING SUNDAY, OUR LOUD BREATHS ECHOED through my room in the aftermath of yet another passionate session. Earlier today, Jason and I had gone to the gym to train with William, and, afterwards, the three of us had headed back to the flat that I shared with Jason to have dinner together. Since I'd exhausted myself during today's workout, I hadn't thought I had any energy left to have sex, but when it neared midnight, William proved me wrong.

"Your sex drive is unbelievable," I remarked after some silence. Yesterday morning, I had woken up from the feel of his tongue between my thighs. We'd had sex two more times before I'd finally left when it became time for dinner. My vagina had never been so sore before, and yet I couldn't resist him. Whenever he laid his hands on me, his caress invoked lust too great to deny.

He chuckled, hand drawing lazy patterns across my waistline

while I cuddled his side. "Blame yourself," he said and tucked his remaining hand under his head.

"Me? I'm not the one initiating twenty-four-seven."

"No, but you're the one making me hard twenty-four-seven."

I blushed alongside a coy smile. "You'll ruin me if you keep this up."

He smirked, but his eyes remained shut. "Feeling sore?"

"Terribly."

"Can't say I'm upset."

I smacked his arm, playful, before I said, "I should invest in more lotion."

"Lotion?" His eyebrows furrowed. "Won't that upset your pH balance?"

I scoffed. "No more than you already are. Besides, there are lotions specifically designed for the vagina, Will."

"Right, then you absolutely should. I'm nowhere near having had my fill."

Suddenly, he opened his eyes and rolled onto me. Wearing a tender smile, he traced the bridge of my nose until he poked the tip. "Spend the night with me."

Blinking, I asked, "At yours?"

He nodded.

I wasn't sure. "Is that really necessary? It's almost midnight. I'll be seeing you in eight hours."

He groaned and rolled his eyes, despaired, I thought. "Stop being so practical all the time. I want to hold you in my sleep."

My heart fluttered at his sweet words. I truly adored that he never shied away from stating his true feelings. He wasn't remotely scared of being vulnerable with me, of revealing how much he liked me, and I admired that about him. I supposed it had to do with his genuine confidence.

I sighed. I couldn't deny that his offer was extremely tempting. However, for a moment, I considered suggesting that he could sleep here instead, but since I recalled he didn't have a change of clothes with him, I decided against it.

"Okay. I'll join you back at yours."

He looked surprised, and it amused me. I'd obviously managed his expectations well.

"Really?"

"Yes."

A winsome grin arrived on his mouth before he pressed it to mine. "Thank you," he mumbled into our kiss, but was quick to pull away. "We should get going, then. It's already quite late, and we need another shower."

I chuckled. "You go first. I can't move yet."

Sheer male arrogance shone from his eyes, and the smirk he gave intensified it. "As you wish."

Crawling out of bed, he approached the door and opened it. Poking his head out, he scouted for Jason's presence. Assuming it safe, he proceeded out and escaped into the bathroom.

I wasn't sure how long he'd been gone for when Jason called for me. "Cara!"

"Yeah!"

"Is it safe to come out?"

I giggled. Sitting up, I reached over to open the closest window before I hid under my duvet. "Yeah!"

His familiar footsteps drew closer and closer till he arrived in the doorway, and his nose immediately wrinkled. "Christ. Thank god you're airing the room."

An intense shade of red flourished in my cheeks. "Sorry. What's up?"

"Have you got any plans after work on Wednesday? Jon and Stephen want to have dinner with us."

"I'd love to."

"Cool. I'll let them know." He hesitated. "Do you think I should invite Livy as well?"

I smirked. While things hadn't escalated between them on Friday, Olivia had spent her entire evening with him, and, from what Jason had told me, they'd had great fun.

"Absolutely, Jason."

"Right."

"Have you told Will about her yet?"

He shook his head.

"Are you going to?"

"Yeah, when the time's right."

I nodded.

"Cara!" William suddenly shouted from the bathroom. "I'm finished. Hurry up and shower. We need to leave. It's already past twelve – and please tell me you've already packed."

My face instantly fell. Domineering William had returned. Gone was the tender lover I'd spent the weekend with. Jason burst out laughing upon the transition in my mood and pointed his finger at me.

"Tell me about it," I muttered and waved him away.

To give me privacy, he shut the door between us before I heard William say to him, "Cara and I are sleeping at mine."

"I gathered."

A moment later, William opened the door just as I was climbing out of bed. Upon the sight of me, he frowned, looked at his Rolex and shook his head.

"Tomorrow's going to be painful," he said. "I've got a meeting at half eight."

"I could always just stay—"

"Not up for debate," he interrupted and sent me a strict glare. "Just freshen up. I'll pack your clothes for the morning while I wait."

My nostrils widened at the idea. "I don't trust you to pick out an outfit for me."

"Tough luck. Besides, I've got a decent sense of style."

A valid point. "Sure. In *men's* clothes."

His lips twisted. "I don't see the problem?"

I blinked twice over. Grabbing my tits, I pressed them together and bounced them in front of him. Engrossed, his eyes followed the motion of my breasts.

"These look male to you?" I tilted my head.

Slowly, his lips spread into a wide grin, and his eyes glistened above it. "No, they certainly don't. They do look dreadfully good, though. And they're all mine."

I laughed. What an idiot. "They're *mine.* I only lend them to you once in a while, those few times you behave."

"But you're mine, so then those are, too," he argued as he approached. "All part of the package that is you," he purred and halted in front of me. It dawned on me at that moment that I was perhaps the only thing capable of distracting William's attention. Already, he'd forgotten about his earlier urgency.

He was about to reach for my breasts when I recoiled with a cheeky smile on my mouth. "I thought we had to leave?"

His eyes darkened. "You devil."

"All part of the package that is me," I fired back and went for the door.

"Bloody tease," I heard him mutter behind me, sulking.

§ § §

Although they were quiet, the sound of familiar footsteps entering the room stirred me awake the next morning. As my lashes fluttered apart, I turned over in the darkness and glimpsed a silhouette heading towards the bathroom. It took me a split second to remember that I was in William's bed rather than my own.

It smelled amazing in here. The scent of him was everywhere, drugging my senses and brightening my morning. Although I hadn't slept much, waking up to his intoxicating existence easily compensated for it.

"Will?" I called drowsily.

His silhouette froze at once. "Shit, sorry. I tried to be quiet."

Frowning, I switched on the night lamp attached to the wall on my side of the bed. The light hurt, but I managed to keep my eyes open despite it. When I looked back to him, I discovered him drenched in sweat, sporting training gear.

Bewildered, I asked, "What?" My mind was still too tired to construct a proper sentence.

"Went to the gym," he explained and wiped his moist forehead with his arm.

I gaped. He'd gone to the gym?

Glimpsing his alarm clock, I saw that it was seven in the morning. How early had he woken up?

"Are you being serious?"

He exhaled loudly. "Yeah. If I don't train before work, I'm less efficient."

I was astounded. Was there anything at all that could upset his self-imposed discipline? "Without proper sleep, you won't be efficient at all," I argued and pushed his colossal duvet aside.

He scoffed. "I'll be fine."

Awed, I shook my head. "Do you do this every day? Hit the gym before work?"

"Almost every day. Depends on whether it's a rest day or not."

"Good to know. Bedtime is eleven o'clock from now on, at the latest," I stated strictly. "I won't let you shorten your lifespan like that."

A blend of mirth and affection filled his eyes. "Don't worry, love. I'll be holding your hand right till the end."

My heart jolted at his unexpected display of devotion. Since I was incapable of stringing together a coherent response, he chuckled and continued, "Anyway, getting comfortable, are you? You're starting to sound like a girlfriend – making domestic rules like that."

I glared at him. "Or a mother."

He chuckled again. "I don't need a mother. I've already got one, and I like her." As he moved into his bathroom, he said, "In any case, I don't respond well to orders."

My eyebrows arched. "You like giving them!"

He popped his head out the door. "Indeed. For instance, you will shower with me. Now."

I grabbed his pillow and threw it at him, to which he responded with laughter.

"I don't respond well to orders, either!"

"No shit," he uttered through his laughter and kicked the pillow back at me, hitting me with notable precision – straight in the face. He must have been a deft and talented striker on the football field during his younger days, I thought. Either way, I had to laugh. Only William would think to kick a pillow in the face of the woman he was eager to woo. Sure, he'd give me flowers and bring me on amazing dates, but he definitely could not resist an opportunity like this, and I adored him for it. I loved that we could be playful like this.

"Unfortunately for you, love," he continued, "I'm still your boss."

"And fucking my boss gives me zero benefits whatsoever?" I countered, though I couldn't hide my grin.

"Apart from mind-blowing orgasms, zero, indeed."

I yearned to slap the smug smile off his mouth. "Then why am I doing this in the first place?" I taunted.

His eyes twinkled with his continuous mirth. "Repeat after me. Mind-blowing orgasms."

Nodding slowly at him, I emulated his tone and said, "You are obnoxious."

He chuckled. "Plus, you adore me."

I rolled my eyes and ignored how my heart pumped in agreement.

"Shower," he purred.

I folded my arms, stubborn. "No. You're going to try to fuck me in it."

"Absolutely. We've still got plenty of surfaces to cover."

This man. "I'm too sore, Will. I'll shower when you're done. In the meantime, I'll make us breakfast."

He pouted. "I'd been looking forward to hot sex in the shower."

I giggled at his ridiculous behaviour. "You're incurable. Insatiable!"

"And you're addictive," he declared with an alarmingly sensual tone.

"Will, my vagina is essentially inflamed after the weekend. Isn't your cock even a wee bit sore?"

Grabbing the top of the doorframe, he eyed me. The sight made me swallow. He was exquisitely masculine, and his current posture served as a painful reminder of it. Women hardly ever stood like that. Merely from how he carried himself, he oozed delicious testosterone. It wasn't fair. Drenched in sweat as he was, he was horribly tempting.

"No," he said flatly. "And I could always kiss your vagina – which is a lovely vagina, by the way – better. Besides, I'm sure an orgasm would make you forget all about the pain."

A wave of heat climbed up my neck and didn't stop till it crawled across my scalp. Had he just told me I had a lovely vagina? Regardless of how much I appreciated his carnal compliment, it was far too early in the morning to be dealing with his vulgar tongue.

"Right. I'm leaving before this escalates," I muttered and climbed out of his huge bed to head for the door. When I heard him lunge after me, my heart jumped. Squealing like a young girl, I sprinted out the door and hastily shut it. Behind it, his villainous laughter rang long and loud.

He was something else. An adrenaline rush at seven in the morning wasn't what I had expected, but he'd surely provided one hunting me like that. Shaking my head, I sauntered through his palatial flat towards his kitchen, where I glanced at the dark cupboards and the island that stood amidst the room, hosting a gas stove.

I went straight for his fridge to assess what I had to work

with. While rummaging through it, I noticed plenty of vegetables and fruits. It reminded me of Jason. Just like his brother, William was clearly preoccupied with maintaining a healthy diet. Well, I wasn't surprised. Taking his athletic physique into account, I'd already expected as much. No one could look like that at the ripe age of twenty-eight and be committed to rubbish food. However, knowing that, I was curious about the contents of his cupboards. Did he store any sweets in this place? Crisps?

Locating eggs and chives, I decided I'd make us omelettes. While they cooked in two separate pans I'd found, I inspected his cupboards. After having searched through every single one, I had only discovered one bar of dark chocolate, two packets of crisps, and a few packets of various nuts. He clearly hadn't lied when he'd said he didn't favour sweet things.

"What are you doing?" he suddenly queried, right behind me. Spinning around to face him, I blinked.

"Er, just analysing."

His left eyebrow curled upwards. "Analysing what?"

"Your diet."

Humour glinted in his eyes. "Odd."

"*You're* odd."

"What inspired you to do that?" he asked and grabbed a stool by his kitchen island. He had dressed, but he hadn't finished his attire. His light-grey waistcoat hadn't been buttoned up, and his bronze tie hung unfastened around his strong neck. The top buttons of his white shirt remained undone as well, but at least he'd put on his light-grey trousers properly.

He was such a vision, even now.

"Well, you're very athletic," I murmured while I admired his sense of style.

He smirked. "So?"

"Is it purely for aesthetic purposes?" I enquired and shoved the omelettes onto their respective plates.

"That's probably the last reason for it," he replied, amused. "I enjoy being healthy. I want to live a long life. Seems a bit self-destructive to ignore the obvious benefits of exercise, as well as stupid. I've always been this way. Jason's the same, so it shouldn't surprise you. And, in case you've forgotten, Mum's a doctor. She's been preaching a healthy diet and lifestyle since before I came out of her."

"I wasn't criticising." As I handed his plate to him, I watched him with a wry smile on my mouth. "And I wasn't complaining, either."

He grinned back. "Fancy what you see, Cara?"

"Yes," I admitted, unashamed. "Your appearance is remarkably beautiful. Your personality is too, but we weren't talking about that now."

He chuckled. "Good. If you're pleased, so am I. Besides, you're the only woman I'd bother to look good for." He wrapped his hand around the cutlery I extended to him.

Even though he'd said it with nonchalance, my chest tingled at his declaration.

Wearing nothing but knickers, I walked round the island to hop onto the stool beside him. He glanced at me from the corner of his eye and paused on my tits for half a second. Shaking his head, he smiled to himself.

"Speaking of remarkable beauty," he murmured.

I gave him a grin as I reached for my own cutlery, but froze when he suddenly leaned close.

His voice carried contagious lust when he said, "I'm dangerously close to abandoning my meal to eat you instead."

I gulped. "Are you?"

Dropping his knife, he lowered his hand to brush his fingertips across my thigh. The electric current that derived from his touch caused my lungs to malfunction – I stopped breathing. However, when his hand drew further in, sneaking its way up towards my slit, I was quick to restore my sensibility, so I recoiled.

I smacked his hand away. "You horny, insatiable twat," I said with an amused smile and shook my head. "Eat your eggs."

"I just happen to find yours more exciting."

As I processed his insinuation, my face felt to light on fire. "I can't believe you just said that. You're a total nutcase."

Reaching for his fork, he laughed. "I was half-joking."

Half-joking. I chortled. "You'd do best to shut up at this point, I think."

He left a swift and sweet kiss on my hot cheek before he reached for his iPad to read the news. The rest of breakfast we spent in comfortable silence. However, when I was about to get dressed after my shower, I broke it, and I was fuming.

"William! What the hell have you packed for me?" I shouted, aghast. I'd pulled my clothes out of my bag. Loose beige trousers and my ugliest red jumper. In this, I would look like a train-wreck with no shape at all. My paternal grandmother had gifted me the jumper for Christmas two years ago, and it had been so hideous that I had stored it in the darkest corner of my wardrobe ever since, only to be worn on those occasions when I reunited with her.

I heard him chuckle from within the bathroom, and it was a sardonic sound. "What?" His tone feigned innocence.

"Seriously!" Flustered, I walked to the doorway to show him the garments. "You have got to be joking!"

He studied me in the reflection of the mirror while he fastened his tie around his neck. A wry smile decorated his mouth. "You'll look lovely. You always do."

"You weren't kidding when you asked me to wear burlaps to the office, were you?" I roared and raised the textiles above my head in my frustration.

"Thanks to my genius, I'll be having a lovely day at the office with no sexual distractions to speak of," he replied, smug, and gave me a wink.

"This is outrageous! How dare you? I trusted you!"

"Your mistake."

"William Night!"

"That's me."

"I could strangle you!" I trembled in my anger.

"I'd like to see you try." He chuckled and folded his collar over his bronze tie.

"It's the middle of summer! I'll melt in this, you utter twat!"

He ignored me completely. Furious, I studied the red jumper.

"Give me one of your shirts," I commanded. "White. Anything that's not this."

He grinned. "That'll be the flag of a solid conquer, you know. I'd love to see you in my shirts."

"Fuck you." I charged towards his walk-in-closet. Hunting through the options, I found a simple white shirt that I could cut shorter and stuff into my trousers. While I wouldn't be showing much curve, at least I wouldn't be sweating, and I could undo the top buttons, as well as roll up the sleeves, for a more stylish appearance.

It wasn't that I was wildly preoccupied with dressing decently, but there wasn't a chance I could show up to work at a bloody law firm wearing what he'd packed for me. It would be strikingly unprofessional. That red jumper was a ridiculous piece with red roses of fabric poking out all across it, and those imitations of the flower looked dead – and it glittered, too!

As I salvaged my outfit from travesty, I hatched a plan of revenge. Tomorrow, I'd wear stockings to work. Over them, I'd wear a dress that I could lift to reveal them whenever he was nearby and it was appropriate. He might have a nice day today, but he surely wouldn't have one tomorrow. To make matters even worse for him, I would reject every single one of his potential advances.

Arriving in the doorway, he burst out laughing when he saw his redesigned shirt. "Points for creativity, darling."

"You're an arse!" I shouted back as I dressed into his shirt and stuffed it into the trousers I'd already pulled on.

§ § §

We were heading out on the street when he clasped my hand and dragged me towards the Starbucks on the ground floor of his building. We'd barely entered when I saw two female baristas peek up from behind the Mastrena espresso machines. They were both brunettes, looking to be in their early twenties, like me.

"Morning," one of them greeted.

"Morning," William replied, enthused, and sent me a glance.

"What can I get you, Will?" she asked and gave him an eager smile, clearly recognising him as her regular costumer.

"The regular," he said and withdrew his wallet from inside his jacket. Still horribly annoyed at what he'd done, I looked daggers into his broad back and folded my arms.

"And what shall I write on the flat white today?" she enquired, amused, and glanced in my direction. 'Tiffany', her nametag said.

William was about to speak when I interjected, "Please write 'inherent bastard' on his black coffee, and you can write 'William's doom' on the other."

I saw him stiffen in front of me, bordering on a cringe, while Tiffany pressed her lips together to stifle her urge to laugh.

"If you can," William murmured, "please make a heart in her latte."

Regardless of how angry I was about what he had packed for me, I found that charming.

"Abina, you got that?" Tiffany asked her colleague.

"A heart for William's doom," she replied with a nod. When she said it like that, I couldn't help my amusement. I giggled, which clearly infected Tiffany because she giggled with me.

"Rough morning, Will?" she teased him.

He cocked his head towards me. "Considering who's involved, nothing out of the ordinary."

"We'll see about that," I grumbled under my breath and approached the hand-off counter to wait for my coffee.

"Sorry. She's a fulltime job," William murmured to Tiffany whilst completing the transaction.

"I'm sure she's worth it," Tiffany replied, still amused, and looked over at me with a playful glint in her eye.

He sighed, nodding. "She is."

After offering William the receipt, Tiffany grabbed my cup and drew something else on it. Abina gave her a look of amusement when she saw it, but made no comment. Another minute passed and Abina handed over our beverages.

Once I saw mine, I couldn't fight the grin that caught my mouth. A major heart surrounded the text *William's doom*.

Meeting Tiffany's eyes, I winked, grateful for the moral support. "Have a nice shift, love," I told her and then turned my attention to William. He was analysing my cup with a suppressed smile on his mouth, but he said nothing.

"Thanks for the coffee, inherent bastard. To work, then," I said and walked proudly out of the shop while he trailed behind me.

9

SENSATIONAL STORY

On our way to work, I was growing increasingly worried about how we would tackle this. I'd never dreamt of finding myself in a similar situation, so I was clueless about how to proceed. William, however, had experience, and that reassured me somewhat.

"What do we do now?" I enquired, concerned, when we'd nearly reached the office building.

Frowning, he drained the rest of his coffee and tossed the empty cup into a litter bin we passed. "Since we're arriving together, do you mean?"

"Yes."

He smirked, but he didn't look at me. "So what if we are? Won't have to raise any suspicion unless we behave in a manner that warrants it."

My lips jutted while a crease formed between my brows. "I've never had a secret affair like this before, much less arrived at work with the person in question."

"We'll be fine." He hooked his arm around my neck to bring my head under his lips.

"I've been meaning to bring this up with you," I murmured. "I'd like to start working from the desk beside Ellie's."

Since he didn't immediately say anything, I sensed he could gauge my reasoning. Either way, I decided to elaborate, "I just think it's the wiser thing to do now that we're actually seeing each other, as it won't give people a reason to suspect that anything more is going on between us."

"I get it," he said, to my relief. "While I've enjoyed having you in my office, it is the wiser thing to do. Besides, you're clearly capable of managing your work independently these days."

"I'm glad you're under that impression. And, if ever you need anything, you can always just call my desk."

"You can be sure I will. Often."

I smiled. "That said, I'm a bit worried about Ellie. What if she picks up on it now that we're arriving together? Don't get me wrong, I like her in general, but I know she's prone to gossiping."

He cocked his head from side to side. "Talk to her about Aaron. Pretend you're still sleeping with him. That should divert her attention and remove any suspicion."

Amazed by his cunning mind, I lingered on a step. "That's brilliant, actually."

He shrugged.

As I considered his suggestion, I couldn't ignore the alarms that went off in my head. Whilst I admired William's ability to manipulate any situation into his favour, it also frightened me. Indeed, his flair for steering people onto the wrong course in terms of discovering the truth was a double-edged sword. If ever he used that ability against me, would I even notice? He'd fooled me before, when he made me believe he'd had sex with Francesca in his office, and that was precisely what troubled me. It was scary to rely on him to always do the decent thing and tell me the truth.

"Will, if ever you mislead me like that – which you have in the past – I will never forgive you."

He halted at once, and when I looked up, I saw a crease between his brows. "Cara, I swore I wouldn't do that again, and I meant it. That sort of behaviour isn't something I make a habit of. Last time I did that, I was absolutely desperate to get a read on you."

I wasn't reassured. "You might become that desperate again. Who knows?"

He sighed, and I could tell he was choosing his next words carefully. "Allow me to elaborate. I learnt my lesson last time. You made yourself abundantly clear – if I do something like that again, you're out. I wouldn't be so reckless as to ignore that warning. I want us to work. Besides, I'm sincerely ashamed of that whole thing. If I could rewind time, I'd have gone back and handled it differently."

"I appreciate hearing that. It's just," I shrugged, "sometimes, I get scared that it's an automatic response for you. You're so skilled at it."

He raised a brow. "It really isn't. Just because I'm skilled at it, it doesn't mean I do it frequently. I only do it when it's the only alternative I have to avoid chaos. Our colleagues finding out about us is an example of that."

"If you say so."

He cupped my cheeks and studied me intensely. "Cara, I will never abuse your trust like that again. I swear. What I've done in the past is not an answer for what I will do in the future. My only goal is to keep you, and I know that in order to do that, I must be honest about everything."

Finally, I was somewhat reassured, so I nodded and gave him a smile. "Thank you."

I'd expected him to release my head then, but, instead, he kept scrutinising me. After a moment, he drew in a deep breath. "Now that we're on the subject of trust, there's something I should say."

My blood stilled in my veins. "Go on," I urged, perturbed.

Sighing, he stepped even closer and brushed his thumbs across my temples. "Francesca messaged me on Saturday."

That was the last thing I'd expected to hear. Why on earth would she do that? Weren't they history? Or was she begging for yet another chance? I hoped she had enough integrity to avoid doing such a thing. "And? Didn't you already end things with her?"

He sighed again. "I did."

"Then what does she want?"

"She's got some stuff at my place – a designer dress that she left behind last time she was there. I wasn't aware of it. Had I been, I would have given it to her already."

"I see. Do you find it suspicious?" I asked, as I had no idea what to make of this. Was Francesca the cunning type? Would she have left it behind solely to have a reason to return?

He grimaced. "I'm not sure. She said she hadn't noticed that it was missing till she came back from Spain the other day, so I asked my maid who said it might be in my wardrobe, which it was."

So, he did have a maid. "Right. Well, thanks for telling me."

His lips blessed my forehead for a moment. When he pulled back, he said, "If you're uncomfortable about me seeing her, I can give it to Garrick – my porter – so that he can give it to her."

I smiled with gratitude. While I had no problem with him seeing Francesca for a final time, I appreciated that he consulted me first. It was a relief that it came so naturally to him to consider my feelings in this situation.

Placing my hands on his chest, I stretched up to give his mouth a peck. "I don't mind," I said as I sunk onto my heels again. "I trust you completely. Besides, the decent thing to do would be to hand it over yourself."

"That's what I thought as well, but I wanted to make sure you'd be alright with it."

"Well, I am," I assured him. "What will you do if she asks for another chance, though?"

He looked incredulous. "You know the answer to that."

"Will you tell her about me?" If he said yes, I'd advise him not to, because I considered it unnecessary.

"If it comes to that, yes. It might be just what she needs – to understand that it's time to move on."

I grimaced. Since I'd actually met her, I could imagine she would hate me for this. In her misery and potential envy, it wasn't unlikely that she would think I had been trying to seduce William under her nose all along. However, she would be wrong, and knowing that erased some of the guilt I experienced.

Either way, my heart still ached for her. William had definitely made her lovesick. Even though it wasn't my fault, I still felt responsible for some of the blame, because if it hadn't been for me, she could perhaps have had him for a while longer. Then again, the longer she would have had him for, the deeper in love she would have fallen, so perhaps I had spared her from some amount of grief.

I started walking again as I said, "If you think it's best."

"I do."

"And there's no way she'll tell anyone at the firm?" I glanced at him while he strode beside me. "She's not the vengeful type, is she?"

It was obvious from the arch of his brows that he hadn't considered that. "I hardly think she's that crazy, but now that you mention it, perhaps it's best to stay on the safe side. I'll just say I've met someone else."

"That's probably best. Either way, I feel really bad for her. She seemed like a sweet girl, so I'm sad to know she's miserable."

Suddenly, he halted in his tracks.

"You're very compassionate, Cara," he said, intrigued. "I noticed this about you very early on. Even when I had no right to be upset, *you* apologised for the scene I walked in on between you and Aaron. That trait of yours is fairly ironic, sharp-mouthed as you are, but I do adore you for it. You're complex." His thumbs teased the corners of my mouth while he continued to study me, engrossed.

"Complex," I echoed. "You're one to talk."

A crooked smile arrived on his lips. Above, his eyes twinkled with joy.

"For three years," he said, "you've been my brother's best friend. You've been so close. That reality has been fucking with my head ever since you walked into my office the first time. I cannot believe Jason's been hiding you away from me. The utter bastard."

I chuckled as I caressed his stubbly cheek. "I'm quite sure he wasn't trying to hide me. You were just too busy to have a look around."

He smiled. "Valid point."

I looked at his Rolex. "We need to get a move on, Will, or you'll be late for your meeting. You can drool over me later."

Shaking his head, he laughed wholeheartedly at my confident statement. His laughter was always such a bewitching sound, especially when I was the trigger, so I took a moment to savour it.

"Cara...My Cara," he said and leaned down to plant a firm kiss on my mouth. My heart fluttered at his phrasing, and then at the taste of his lips. *My Cara.* Surprisingly, it didn't scare me. On the contrary, it made my stomach tingle with myriad butterflies. I felt capable of soaring.

When he pulled away, he rubbed his nose against mine and smiled again. "I want to ask where you've been all my life, but, clearly, you've been kept safe by my brother in recent years."

"Safe," I quoted, amused.

"Safe indeed," he crooned and trailed his index finger along my jaw, down the slope of my neck, and continued till he reached the ribs protecting my heart. There, he halted, his sizzling stare burning into mine. "This won't be yours for much longer."

Knowing it was already his for the taking, my breath caught. Trapped in his magic, I gazed back at him, mesmerised.

"Silenced again," he teased and pecked my nose. "Because we

both know it's true."

I pulled out of his hold and gave him a wry look. "I'll be stealing yours first," I challenged. He merely looked at me, and his expression was unreadable. In his eyes, I detected conflict, but of what kind, I couldn't gauge.

"To work," he said and approached the building again.

§ § §

Upon exiting the lift on our floor, I was startled to find John waiting by Ellie's desk.

Shit. Not only was I late to work, but I was also arriving with none other than his progeny, whom I'd been sharing a bed with all night. I worried his piercing blue eyes could tell merely by a glance.

Panicking, I struggled to find a safe place to rest my gaze. It was weird to reencounter him in this formal setting whilst knowing I was dating his son. It made me wonder how William and I would tackle this situation if we fell in love with each other and decided to go official as a couple. Would we tell John everything about how our relationship had bloomed? Or would we keep the start of our romance a secret?

William would know best, I gathered, so I would leave it up to him to decide.

"Morning, John," William said, and his decision to address his father formally threw me off. I would definitely ask him about that under appropriate circumstances.

John's eyes flickered between his son and me before he glanced at his own Rolex. "Morning, Will. This must be the latest you've come to work since I hired you," he answered, bemused.

William shrugged. "Problem?"

John chuckled. "Not at all. Just unusual. What gives? You feeling alright?" His eyes narrowed for a brief second, and my heart clenched in horror. Could he tell? "You look far from ill."

I was a breath away from withering. Knowing how perceptive William could be, I dared not put it past John to be equally, if not more, adept at reading people.

"Yeah, I'm feeling great," William replied, and his composure astounded me. Thank god he was the one talking and not me. I was certain I'd perish if I were the target of John's scrutiny. "Just had a late night, so I went to the gym later than usual this morning. Since I knew I was coming in a bit late, I told Cara she didn't have to be here until half eight, either."

I stiffened at the mention of my name, as I hadn't seen it coming, but when I processed his statement, both gratitude and relief filled my system. He'd spared me from having to defend my tardiness.

John's inspecting gaze slid towards me then, and I didn't want to imagine how pale I looked. From the corner of my eye, I saw Elisabeth analyse me from head to toe, intrigued. Could she recognise William's shirt? I hoped not. It was a basic white garment. Even though it wasn't my style, it didn't stand out.

John's sudden laughter disconcerted me. "Cara, you're as white as a sheet."

"I'm sorry I'm late," I replied vehemently and looked at the floor since I was scared that he would discern the truth if I held his gaze.

"Oh, don't worry, love," he replied fondly. "Will's your superior, not me. There's no need to look so ashamed. If he says he won't need you until half eight, that's what you listen to."

I nodded feverishly and, with fleeting eyes, went straight for the desk next to Ellie's. I looked ashamed, did I? At that moment, I despised my open book of a face. Thankfully, he had assumed I looked ashamed only because I had arrived later than usual, and not because I'd been having sex with his son all weekend.

"You here for the meeting?" I heard Will ask behind me.

"Yes. I was hoping to have a word with you in private before then, but it'll have to wait until after since it starts in a few minutes. Nothing imminent, though."

"Right."

I stole a glance at Ellie while I pulled my chair out and reclined into it. With pursed lips, she was typing away on her MacBook. It was clear as day that she was dying to spill her questions, and I dreaded them already.

My face had been pale, but the instant my bum landed on the chair, a wave of intense heat crashed over my face. William might as well have been thrusting into me again. Could I get any sorer than this?

My gaze fastened on William's back when the two men journeyed towards his office, but all of a sudden, he turned his head to look at me. When he saw the new colour of my face, his eyes noticeably widened. Whether he grasped the reason behind my blush, I did not know, but his lips curved into a smug smile while he gave me a knowing wink. He must have gathered.

As soon as the door closed behind them, Ellie bent towards me. I'd barely had time to recover at all.

"Will's never late, Cara. Never," she whispered.

I didn't look at her. "He was today."

She chuckled. "I wonder why. Nice shirt, by the way. Did you find it in the men's section or someone's wardrobe?"

My blush intensified immediately. "I don't appreciate your insinuation, Ellie," I told her firmly. "The shirt is Aaron's," I continued. "I spent the night at his and forgot to bring a top."

Turning to face her, I saw her blinking, and the view satisfied me immensely. William's suggestion seemed to have worked. Suspicion was fading from her expression by the second. Instead, a rueful look crossed her face.

"Oh. I'm so sorry, Cara. I didn't mean to offend you."

"Don't worry about it."

She leaned away again. "Aaron. I'm embarrassed to admit that I'd forgotten about him."

"I can tell."

"How are things going between you?"

"I'm not sure, to be honest. He's been acting a bit different lately. More romantic."

She gasped with excitement. "I knew it. Friends-with-benefits arrangements never last. Someone *always* catches feelings."

I hated that she was right. "I'm not sure. He hasn't said anything."

"Would you want to try a relationship with him?"

For once, I was grateful for the presence of my blush, because it aided me in substantiating the deception. "I don't want to get my hopes up, Ellie. Can we talk about something else?"

"Aw, you sweet thing." Her maternal grin nearly triggered some guilt for lying to her. "If he's acting more romantic lately, I don't think you have anything to worry about."

"Will suggested I should work from here from now on. I hope you don't mind," I said, to make it clear that I wanted to change the subject. Deceiving her about this was difficult enough as it were, and I feared that she might discern my lies if we continued down the rabbit hole. I was not inclined to risk jeopardising my placement just to suffice her curiosity. Too much was at stake, so I was determined to keep her at arm's length.

"Of course not. I've been dying to have you next to me."

I gave her a fond grin. It truly was a shame that she was prone to gossiping because, aside from that trait, I really did like her a lot. Then again, I supposed everyone had their flaws, including me.

§ § §

William's day consisted of back-to-back meetings and conference calls, and it stirred my pity. He was having an intense day at work, and I knew he was running on spare battery after a night of scarce sleep. Elixerion Pharmaceuticals were also applying tremendous pressure on us in terms of deadlines. I was astounded by William's capacity; he worked as efficiently as ever. Indeed, as he had claimed this morning, he was evidently used to managing on little sleep.

Shortly before lunch, we attended a meeting with the rest of the team to brief each other on the progress we had made thus far, and to pinpoint any legal issues that had arisen, and which hadn't yet been resolved. After lunch, we were set to meet the lawyers from Porter BioScience, so when the team meeting concluded, Frederick asked William and Elisabeth to stay behind. My limited skills were no longer required.

I headed down to the canteen with Andy and Violet since Elisabeth and William had to skip lunch. Once I'd found a seat with my carrot soup and piece of focaccia, I sighed. William hadn't lied last night when he'd stated that today would be tough on him, and I regretted that I hadn't made it any simpler. I should have stayed at home last night or told him to leave earlier. That way, he would have caught some decent rest. At the same time, he was a grown man, so he was the only one in charge of himself. To be fair, I was confident he'd get cross if I treated him any differently.

Still, I felt partially at fault. While I wasn't familiar with the role of a girlfriend, I was positive that making his life easier was part of it. Rather than distract him, I was supposed to motivate him. Then I reminded myself that I wasn't his girlfriend. Ironically, that only made things worse.

"Well, this is a depressing lunch," Violet remarked while she dug her fork into her salad. Seated beside one another, Andy and I lifted our gazes simultaneously. Apparently, we'd both surrendered to contemplation without further ado.

"Sorry," we uttered in perfect unison before we turned to smile at each other.

"What's on your mind?" Violet asked, brown eyes flickering between us.

"You go first," Andy told me.

"It's nothing," I insisted. "I'm fine. Just tired."

Violet pressed her lips together, but it couldn't veil her amusement. "I bet you are."

Instantly, my face adopted the colour of a tomato.

"Yes," Andy said. I didn't need to see it to be aware of the taunting look on his face. "I heard Will was late this morning."

I tensed as I steered my eyes to my carrot soup. Where was William when I needed him? His two favourite colleagues were ganging up on me, grinning like mischievous vultures that were eager to pick at me, and I had no idea how to counter them.

"Yes," Violet joined, voice slightly hissing the way a snake would. "Can you believe that? Will. Late."

"Shocking," Andy emphasised theatrically. "We ought to tell the news."

"They'd be curious to know why," Violet purred with a lopsided smile.

"They would, indeed."

Violet rested her head between her hands, and I sensed her watch me with the grin of the Cheshire Cat while I feigned obliviousness and savoured a spoonful of soup.

"I heard he didn't arrive alone, though," she told Andy.

"So did I. Apparently, some lady was on his arm."

"Yes. I saw it with my own eyes. And he looked to be in a *very* good mood. John noticed, too."

Both turned to stare at me.

"Oh my God. Leave me alone!" I growled under my breath and glared between them.

"Sensational story," Andy continued without mercy. "William Night, the unattainable bachelor and incorrigible workaholic, has finally set his eyes on a woman. Rumour has it they've spent all weekend together. Sources close to Mr Night confirm that he hasn't treated any woman to that sort of attention in years."

"And that's today's breaking news," Violet cheered, delighted.

At this point, I was shielding my face with my hands. I hadn't been so embarrassed in a long time. "You guys are unbelievable. Remind me how old you actually are."

Laughter broke out of them both before Andy reached over to rub my back. "Calm down, love. Only taking the piss."

"Yeah. What we're really trying to say is that we're happy for you," Violet added.

Removing my hands, I gave them both a fond smile. "Thanks. Appreciate it."

"If ever he drives you mad, we'll be the ones to go to for sympathy," Andy told me sweetly. "Then again, you've got Jason, too."

Deciding to cut me some slack, Violet turned her attention to Andy. "What's up, Andy?"

He sighed. "I think I knocked Chloe up last night."

Air propelled out of my lungs while I depressed into my seat. That was one way to declare it. Mirroring my reaction, Violet stared at him, flabbergasted.

"Yeah."

"But I thought you were living at your parents' for the time being?" Violet probed.

He ran his hands through his dirty blonde hair, repeatedly, while he leaned back and looked at the ceiling. Panic was feasting on him, and it wasn't a pleasant sight. At that moment, I pitied him tremendously.

"I couldn't do it anymore," he said and fixed his sight on Violet again. "I don't feel like myself when I'm not with her, and don't you dare call that co-dependency, because it isn't. We're just not meant to be apart," he said, speaking so fast that the words were sprinting out of his mouth.

"Tell me. What happened?" Violet demanded.

"She called after work yesterday, crying her eyes out," he explained, "and asked if I could come over so that we could talk. When I did, she said it didn't matter anymore – that we don't need to have children. She just couldn't stand this distance between us anymore. And I know how irrational this sounds, but that changed everything for me. The fact that she's willing to put her baby idea to rest, just to be with me – that she's willing to let go of something she's wanted for so long, just to make me happy, and so that we can be together – well, it made me realise that I've been a fucking dick about all this.

"So, we ended up having sex – without a condom – and, this morning, I told her not to take the morning-after pill. And now I'm freaking out, but not in a bad way. I'm just," he paused, searching for the word, "shocked at myself. If she does get pregnant, I'm going to be a father. Can you imagine that? Me?" He pointed to himself and then shook his head, incredulous.

My lips had parted, and I struggled to close my mouth again. Even if William had called it, I hadn't seen this coming at all.

"I'm very happy on your behalf," Violet said. "I think you'll make an excellent father. Though, do you think she's listened to you?"

Visibly charmed by her reaction, he chuckled. "She's been texting me every fifteen minutes, asking if I'm sure, and saying that she's still got time to take the pill. But I'm not going to have a change of heart. I've had years to consider this, and, last night, I finally made up my mind. And, when I make up my mind about something, it's final – especially things of this nature." Well, I could relate to the latter completely. That was precisely how I felt about William. "Anyway," Andy continued, "don't tell anyone about this. Like the fact that William and Cara are finally having sex again, this is strictly between us."

I gasped, shocked again, as Violet cackled. I smacked Andy's shoulder. He turned towards me with poorly stifled laughter.

Determined to change the subject, I asked, "Have you told Will about Chloe yet?"

"No. I haven't had time. He was busy fucking you, and I was busy fucking her."

I smacked him again. Cheeky bastard.

His laughter roared. "Don't tell him," he said when it quieted in volume. "I want to be the one to do it."

Because I knew William would relish the news, a genuine grin bent my lips. After all, Will had been on Chloe's team since the start. "He's going to be happy."

"Yeah. Tell me about it. I can already hear his 'told you so'." When he shuddered, I smiled.

"I reckon Will's going to make a brilliant uncle," Violet chimed in.

"Without a doubt," Andy agreed. "Though, let's not jump the gun. She might not get pregnant."

"Would you try again if she doesn't?" Violet asked.

"Yeah. As I said, I've made up my mind. And honestly, feels great to sleep in my own bed again."

I rolled my eyes at how he managed to make light of this, but, since it was typical of him, I giggled regardless.

10

THEY'RE IN MY WAY

It was nearly five o'clock when I received a call from none other than my boss.

"Yes?" I answered professionally.

"Are you leaving at five?" Ever to-the-point.

"Yes?" I repeated. Did he need me to stay longer?

"Postpone that by twenty minutes. I'll be finished by then, so we can leave together."

Leave together? Did we have plans?

"Er, why?" I enquired, bewildered.

"Why, what?"

Knowing Ellie was seated right beside me, I had to choose my words carefully. "Why should I wait for that?"

"Get in here."

His impatience made me swallow. I wasn't used to being ordered around, and I didn't like it, either. "I'm going to the gym with Jason today," I said.

"Oh, you'll get a workout, Cara," he asserted, "but it won't be with Jason."

I blushed profusely and planted my hot face in the palm of my hand – this man. "One second," I said and rang off. There wasn't a chance I would have this conversation in front of Elisabeth. Pushing my seat out, I approached his office, rigidly. On my way there, I reminded myself to hold on to my strength. I knew full well that he was no man to underestimate.

Two knocks on the door and I turned the handle. Peeking inside, I found him buried behind piles of paper. Plenty of them lay scattered across the floor, and I realised he'd been working from it. He must have returned to his chair only to phone me. *Christ.*

I observed the chaos for another second before I directed my eyes to his. The sight made my heart plummet. While William was always a sight to behold, the look of him right then took my breath away for an entirely different reason to normal. Signs of sleep-deprivation were clear from his features. Pale-faced and battered, he studied me with a punctured drive in his eyes. It was striking, but for all the wrong reasons.

"Christ, Will. You need your bed." I closed the door behind me.

He tossed his head back, groaned, and spread his arms apart. "Come here, you."

A delicious current charged through my veins upon his sweet command. He sounded as though my company was the only thing capable of offering solace. With colour in my cheeks, I drew nearer until I stopped in front of him. It was obvious from the arch of his brow that he disapproved of the distance I maintained.

"Nearly there, darling," he said and, abruptly, launched forward to sweep his arms around my waist. He tugged me towards him with such force that I fell into his lap with a squeal. Caging me within his strong arms, he buried his nose in my hair and inhaled deep into his lungs.

"Mm. Thank you," he hummed and squeezed me against him. Blushing scarlet, I stared blankly ahead, unsure of what to do with myself.

Removing one arm from around me, he brushed my hair away from my neck and said, "Wait a few minutes, Cara. I've barely seen you today." His warm lips met with the area now exposed to him, but I remained stiff.

"Well, you've had a lot on your plate. I really don't think you should do anything other than sleep once you leave work."

He ran his nose along the slope of my neck. "I can sleep when I'm dead. Besides, you revive me."

I rolled my eyes. It really was astounding that he wanted to spend yet another day together. We'd seen each other constantly the past few days. Frankly, I was reaching my limit. "Will, as I said, I've got plans with your brother."

He sighed and reached for his phone on his desk. After dialling a number, he lifted it to his ear and studied me impassively. Meanwhile, I resorted to frowning at him. What was he doing? Dread caused me to gape the instant I realised his intentions.

"Hi, Jason, it's Will. Cara can't make it to the gym today."

"William!" I snapped, annoyed. He could be so bloody domineering. I was about to continue my protest when he lifted his hand to wrap it over my mouth.

"She's very sorry, but I'm not giving her much choice... Sure. I'll tell her. Bye." He put his phone back on his desk while I glared at him.

"Are you going to shout if I remove my hand?" he asked.

I slapped his arm and mumbled, "Fuck you!" into his palm, but it wasn't comprehensible even to my ears.

He sighed. "Right. Don't shout, yeah? Depending on the volume, someone might hear us." Though his hand did slide away from covering my mouth, he didn't remove it. Instead, he squeezed my cheeks together and grinned.

"You're adorable," he belittled me.

"You're infuriating!" I scolded through my jutting lips. Alas, that only made him laugh – hard, too.

"Sorry. There's no way I can take you seriously like that."

Grabbing his wrist, I jerked his hand away, but when I moved to escape his lap, he reacted by hooking both arms around me.

"Let me go!" I growled and fought against his arms. "You can't control me like that! I wanted to go to the gym!"

"That's not what you said. You said you had plans with Jason. I got them cancelled. You didn't argue that you wanted to go. If going to the gym was that important to you, why did you make Jason your excuse? You're only throwing a fit right now because you feel overruled."

He was maddening. It didn't matter that he was completely right. He should have asked for my consent before proceeding.

Spinning around, I glowered at him, but he shocked me when he leaned in and pressed his mouth to mine. Grabbing my head, he held me to him while he possessed my mouth the same way he possessed my heart. Rendered helpless against his power over me, I melted into his expert kiss and surrendered to his dominance.

The tip of his tongue teased the lining of my lower lip, seeking to explore what belonged so completely to him, though I hadn't admitted it to myself yet. Nevertheless, his kiss obliterated my good sense. Before long, I opened my mouth to welcome him and felt the delectable flavour of him explode within.

"Mm," I groaned and cupped his sharp jaw in my hands. While it moved against my palms, his stubble prickled my skin.

Eager to escalate the situation, his right hand dared its way down my waistline towards the apex of my thighs. Beneath me, his erection grew and strained against the material that separated our flesh. Feeling it, untameable arousal unleashed in my blood, urging me to take advantage. Knowing the extent of the pleasure he could provide, I groaned again while my face flushed. His lewd methods were entirely intoxicating.

The danger of our situation effectively vanished from my mind. Instead, desire implored me to take him in, as far as he would go, and never let him leave again.

At that moment, he had me completely spellbound. He could have had his way with me right then and there. Denying him simply didn't seem possible. However, a knock on the door bereaved him of the chance.

Leaping out of his embrace, I rushed to wipe my mouth and steady my erratic breaths. Meanwhile, William groaned and glared at the door.

"Yes?" he grumbled.

My pulse hit the roof when John stepped in. *Christ.* If he hadn't knocked, William and I would have been in tremendous trouble.

"Cara," he greeted through a delightful smile. "I'm glad I found you here. I meant to ask you this morning, but it slipped my mind – how is everything going for you?"

"Well, sir," I replied, composed. "I love it here."

His smile became a grin. "Excellent. And there's no need for 'sir's, Cara. In any case, I trust Will's been treating you well?"

Too well.

"Everyone has," I assured him with a nod.

"I'm happy to hear that. On another note, Jason's coming for dinner on Sunday. I told him to bring you along – if you're available and would like to come, of course."

"Right," William murmured. "I was just about to tell her that." He looked at me. "Jason told me over the phone just now."

I stared at William for a beat. Dinner with John and Daphné again? Would he be there as well?

Turning my attention to John, I said, "Yes, of course. I'd love to."

"Great. Looking forward to it." He smiled. "Anyway, would you mind if I borrowed my son for a minute?"

"Not at all. I was just leaving." I moved to the door.

"In twenty minutes," William called after me.

"Right," I confirmed. I wanted to turn and glare at him, but since I feared that it would pique John's curiosity, I refrained.

Once I'd shut the door after myself, I sucked in a deep breath and shook my head to myself. This wouldn't do. That had been too close a call. I dared not imagine John's reaction had he walked in on us. Wherever William found the foolish courage to behave that heedlessly was beyond me. Either he trusted our colleagues' ability to knock before entering implicitly, or there was something seriously wrong with his wiring.

I contemplated whether to return to my desk, but when I saw Elisabeth grinning at me, I decided not to. Restoring my equilibrium was crucial before I faced her again. I was much too rattled to be able to deal with her scrutiny. So, instead, I propped my back against the wall and resorted to waiting.

Sure enough, John exited five minutes later with a brooding look on his face. Had I not been so used to seeing his son wear the exact same one, I might have asked him if everything was alright. However, I'd learnt with time that it was merely the expression their faces found rest within.

As soon as he noticed me, his eyes lit up. "All yours," he said and paid me a wink, which ultimately unsettled me. Was he implying something, or was it an innocent wink?

Bemused, I replied, "Right. Thank you."

He chuckled. "I'll see you around, Cara."

"Yeah." I was still nodding my head when I poked it through the doorway, whereupon I saw William smiling to himself while he chewed on a pen.

"Why do you call him John?" I queried, puzzled.

He chuckled. "I only do that when we're surrounded by colleagues. We prefer not to remind people of our relationship. Easier to maintain professionalism that way."

Reasonable. "I see."

"Shut the door."

I swallowed, but I obeyed his command either way. Though, this time, I remained by the door. Here, the pull of his magnetism was weaker.

Nervous, I folded my arms across my chest. "That was a close call."

Removing his pen from his mouth, he dropped it on his desk with a chuckle. "It was. I'm sorry. I lost my mind for a sec."

I shook my head. "You're going to get us both sacked."

"I'll be more careful next time."

"Next time? You're not allowed to touch me here anymore."

His jaw fell. "What? What about my kiss for good morning and goodbye?"

I pressed my lips together. "If you behave well for a week, we can negotiate whether to resume the ritual."

He blew his cheeks out. "First you won't let us work from the same room, and now you won't let me touch you behind closed doors? I'm starting to think that dating is having the opposite effect of what I intended."

A laugh snuck out of me. "Are you implying that you'd prefer if we stopped seeing each other?"

"That's not even slightly funny."

Changing the subject, I asked, "Do you think John knows? About us? He winked at me just now."

The bridge of his nose contracted. "Hard to say. He's a bloody sharp man. I doubt it, though. If he suspected anything, I'm quite sure he would have confronted me about it."

I nodded. William would know best how to read his father, so if he wasn't concerned, I didn't think I had to be, either.

"What should we tell him if we ever get serious? Everything?"

His eyebrows twitched, and there was a flicker of a thought in his eyes that I couldn't decode. "If," he echoed.

Sensing his irritation, I looked at him guiltily.

"Ever the pessimist," he muttered to himself, eyes averting. "Anyway, I'd prefer to leave out the one-night stand bit. It would suffice to say that we met at Disrepute. He doesn't need details about our sex life."

"Right."

He sighed and gestured towards his desk. "Twenty minutes, yeah?"

Undecided, I studied him for a moment. "It's just, considering we've got another meeting with the team tomorrow morning, I'm not sure I can afford to spend an entire evening on you. I've still got a lot of work to do, and I planned to do it after going to the gym with Jason."

He frowned. "So do I. We can do it together, at my place. Besides, if we do, I'll be able to guide you through whatever challenges you might encounter."

Valid point.

"Cara," he lost his patience, "you'd make my day. Please."

"Fine."

§ § §

After work, a man with a funny-looking hat opened the door to William's building for us. With a slight bow of his head, he touched the brim of its twentieth-century appearance. This morning, it had been a younger man, but I'd been too busy being cross with William to mind him much.

"Mr Night," he greeted politely. He looked to be in his late fifties. A neatly groomed and white beard, in the form of a doughnut, surrounded his thin lips. Age had laid its mark on him. Wisdom and patience shone from his small brown eyes, which resided in a very round and constantly pink face.

I presumed he was another one of the building's porters since he wore the same hat that the man from this morning had. However, aside from their hat, they sported different clothes, so I supposed the hat was a mark to signal that they were on duty.

"Will, Garrick. For the last time," William replied, humoured, and gave his arm a friendly pat.

"Will," Garrick echoed, equally humoured. Hearing it, I suspected that this specific exchange of theirs was something that repeated itself perpetually.

His brown eyes darted in my direction, but when William's figure suddenly halted beside me, they quickly flickered back to him.

"You know," William said and waved his finger in the air. Directing it to me, he continued, "this is Cara Jane Darby. I expect you'll be seeing her a lot from now on. Could you write her name on the list of visitors allowed in without needing to request prior permission?"

Startled, I blinked twice over. That was a leap of faith – an affirmation that he believed we'd prosper together. This little scene, which could easily be mistaken for something insignificant in the grand scheme of things, warmed my heart rather a lot. Actions spoke louder than words, I supposed.

"Of course, sir." Walking towards the desk, Garrick unlocked a drawer and withdrew an iPad. He approached me with the device and asked me to spell my name for him. Afterwards, he raised it towards my face.

"He'll need to snap your photo," William explained and stepped away. "Smile for the camera, love."

I wanted to slap his sadistic grin off his face. Being told to smile on cue like that always made for the most awkward versions, but I made an attempt regardless.

"Beautiful," Garrick said and lowered the iPad again.

"She is, isn't she?" William agreed. His eyes squinted with his grin. I could hardly recognise him. He looked unlike himself – besotted. I struggled to reconcile this version of him with the domineering caveman he could present as at any time.

"Absolutely, sir." Garrick chuckled.

"I'm a lucky man."

"You are, indeed." Garrick extended the iPad to me then. "If I could have your email address and your signature, please, Ms Darby?"

Seeking an explanation, I looked at William, who said, "It's a matter of consent since we're storing personally identifiable information on you."

Of course. Had I cared to use my brain, I would have realised that. "Right."

After filling in my email address and drawing my signature on the screen, I handed the iPad back to Garrick, who responded with a courteous bow of his head again. It really was amusing that he insisted on behaving so formally. Had he always been this way? No wonder William favoured him so. He seemed impossible to dislike.

"Anyway," William said, "have a pleasant evening, Garrick. Give Rose my regards," William said fondly before he wrapped his arm around my waist to guide me to the lift.

"Thank you, sir. You as well," Garrick replied, delighted.

When the doors shut, I peered up at William, and I couldn't hide my amusement. "I've never seen you be that kind and welcoming to anyone before."

He scoffed. "Well, I like Garrick. He's a good man. Ex-military. Had a traumatic past, but he's recovered now. I fancy his outlook on the world. He's told me fascinating stories about his time in Afghanistan. It made him appreciate the smaller things in life, he said, which is why he's settled for the job of being a porter. These days, he fancies just watching normal life happen before his eyes."

Impressed with Garrick's history and outlook on life, my eyebrows arched as I rocked back and forth on my heels. Like Will, I found myself admiring him, too.

When the doors opened on his floor, I didn't wait for him to signal that I should step out first. By now, I had grown accustomed to his courteous tendencies in these aspects of life. For instance, he always held the door for me, pulled my seat out whenever we ate together, insisted on paying for me, and always ensured that he was walking closest to the street whenever we strolled along the pavement. Indeed, he had proved that he had adopted some gentleman customs, but in other areas of life, he paid them little regard.

Once I reached the door, I stepped aside to let him enter the code. The second he had, he grabbed my hand and dragged me inside, and his urgency took me aback. Dropping his bag onto the floor, he dragged mine off my shoulder and proceeded to slam the door shut. After he'd locked it, he gripped my hips and walked me backwards to pin me against the hard wood.

"I'm starving, Cara," he declared lustfully. A lump gathered in my throat under his smouldering stare. "And not for food," he continued huskily and lowered his mouth to mine.

Wherever he found his energy remained a mystery, but it was contagious in nature. The second his mouth blessed mine, he engaged my entire spirit, leaving my pulse to spike. Thrusting his knee between my legs, he spread them apart and pushed directly against my sex. The pressure surged up my spine and made me gape with pleasure.

Closing my eyes, I lost myself in his skilful kiss and wished for time to pause only so I could enjoy him for longer. I wanted to kiss him for a lifetime. He was just so damn good at it. Truly, he played the strings of my heart as though it were an instrument that he'd been meant to play all along – and he seemed the only one capable of mastering it.

"God, I've wanted you all day," he growled and lowered his hands to fondle my breasts. I groaned into his mouth and circled his neck with my arms, wanting to be even closer to him. The feeling of never getting close enough haunted me. Only when he was inside of me did the feeling abate.

"Then take me," I said and trailed my right hand down his firm torso, past each dent and protrusion of his abs, to reach for the bulk that strained against his grey trousers. When I found it, I gave it a gentle squeeze while my lascivious smile interfered with our kiss.

Groaning, he pressed his erection against my palm, eager for more. "I'd like to spend hours on you, but I'm too impatient." He parted from my lips to rest his forehead against mine. "Then again," he smirked, "I can compensate later. It's not like one round is the quota."

Without further ado, he reached between us to undo my trousers with haste. After he had pushed the material down, along with my knickers, his mouth reclaimed mine.

"This is my shirt," he mumbled into our kiss. "So, if you don't mind…"

He ripped it open. The buttons flew and scattered across the floor, the sound blending with my hitching breath.

"You've got a kink for shredding clothes, Will."

"When they're on you, yeah." He chuckled, and his smile flirted with his twinkling irises. "They're in my way." Planting his large hands under my thighs, he hoisted me up against the door and secured my limbs around his body.

"Remove your bra," he ordered.

Swallowing the lump in my throat, I reached behind me to obey his command. His eyes were glued to my breasts while I slowly revealed them to him. Courageously, I sent him a lewd smile and wrapped my bra around his neck to pull his mouth back to mine.

"Oh, Cara," he hummed appreciatively just before our lips reunited. Insatiably, his mouth devoured mine – taking possession of my body the way he had taken possession of my mind. I rejoiced in the taste of him, in the scent of him. Even the sounds he made aroused me senseless. He was the very embodiment of magic, and I was utterly enchanted by him.

For the first time in my life, I was truly on the cusp of falling in love, but part of me feared that it wouldn't be reversible. If my feelings for him transcended into the irrevocable, how was I supposed to focus on my career? Lately, all I could think about was him. In fact, I'd spent a considerable amount of today worrying about him, when I should have been focusing on work.

I frowned to myself while concern reigned my thoughts. This was escalating so fast. Our chemistry was of such a magnitude that I feared its power over me. A mere week ago, I had agreed to give things a chance, and already, I was utterly at his mercy.

Ever since then, I'd barely had time to catch my breath. I'd been in his audience for most hours of the day, so I hadn't had sufficient time in solitude to process what was happening, much less the changes in my behaviour. I hadn't even had time to recover from my heartache regarding Aaron.

Upon remembering him, I was upset, and I struggled to hide it. Here I was, worshipping the man who had been the catalyst of Aaron's heartbreak, without a single care. Was I truly so heartless? It seemed like a betrayal that I would recover from our broken friendship so fast when he'd been one of my closest companions for three years. I'd hardly given him a thought since Wednesday last week, because William had overshadowed everything else.

It dawned on me then that I required some space. Things were moving so fast that I was outrunning myself. I could hardly recognise who I was anymore, and it wasn't comfortable. I felt disconnected from who I had always been, and it was disconcerting. I was changing, and I wasn't sure I appreciated the version I was turning into.

"You're distracted," he said on a ragged breath. My eyes had closed, but I opened them upon his statement.

"What's the matter?" he probed and cupped my cheek to run his thumb across it. I shook my head.

"Cara, what's the matter?"

I averted my eyes. "I'm just a bit overwhelmed. I feel like we're moving very fast."

Processing what I'd said, he was silent for a beat. "I don't see the problem," he finally replied. "And look at me when you're talking to me, Cara."

Pouting, I met his eyes again even though it strained my heart to look at him right then. "There isn't a problem per se. As I said, I'm just a bit overwhelmed. This is totally unexplored terrain for me."

He was not impressed. "What – fucking a man you actually want?"

His bluntness made me glare at him. "Yes."

Sighing, he dropped his gaze to his erection between us. Following, I watched him push his trousers down. When I sensed him lift his gaze again, I swiftly met it. I'd expected him to look annoyed, but on the contrary, his eyes were soft as they trapped mine.

"Are you scared?" he asked quietly and studied my reaction.

"A bit," I mumbled and looked away again.

"What of?" he queried, and his tone was tender and patient.

Inhaling sharply, I chewed into my lower lip. After a few steadying breaths, I dared to confess it. "You."

When my eyes darted towards him, I caught him analysing me. His expression was unreadable, however, which frustrated me. I wished I could hear his thoughts.

"What do you think I'll do?" he asked. "I'm not going to hurt you if that's what you're thinking."

"No, it's not that." I grimaced and covered my face with my hands. His penetrative gaze was unbearable right now. "I'm not scared of what you'll do. I'm scared of how this whole thing might affect me. I'm very confused, Will. Everything's so intense. I'm in utter chemical imbalance here, and I know you're the cause of it. I don't feel like myself. My priorities haven't changed, but my focus *is*."

He groaned in despair. "Please, do continue to invent problems for yourself. You've surely got a knack for it."

His rude reaction provoked my temper. "I never said it was a problem. I was only stating a fact. You asked why I was distracted. Don't ask if you can't handle the answers," I said and folded my arms over my breasts. He was terribly exasperating. My blood boiled.

He raised a brow and took my wrists to force my arms apart again. "Just enjoy it, Cara. There's nothing else you can do about it, because I'm not going to stop chasing you."

My heart cried out at his affectionate declaration, but I couldn't understand what it was trying to say. "You don't get it, Will. It's like you've infected my brain. I can't think straight when you're in my life. Around you, it's like my head is talking in a language I don't speak."

He rolled his eyes. "Perhaps if you actually cared to listen for once, you wouldn't feel that way," he argued and reached between us to align his cock with my entrance.

"I am list—" A hiss interrupted my sentence when he thrust powerfully into me. *Fuck*. It hurt. I was still sore after last night, and he was so damned big. "Ah, gentle," I pleaded, high-pitched, and clawed into his shoulders.

"Just feel that," his voice was low, and it carried a soft bass that massaged my eardrums like a most sensual melody. "Listen to your body respond to this," he said and gently retreated. When he pushed in again, he was slow and tender. "Feel that, Cara? How much your body loves it?" He nuzzled his nose against mine. "Because I can. And you're dripping for me – clenching around me as though you never want me to leave."

I ground my teeth and rested the back of my head against the door. Buried within me, I savoured him. He felt unbelievably good. It never ceased to blow my mind. Finally, the burrowing desire to be closer to him was silenced. Rapture took its place instead.

He closed his strong arms around me, and I melted into his embrace, subdued. Conquered. While holding me so intimately, he pulled me away from the door and carried me towards his bedroom. The whole time, he remained within me, and I was already dreading his withdrawal. Like he'd said, I never wanted him to leave.

I clung to his frame as he descended onto his mattress, and groaned with delight when his lips found mine. Lying beneath him, I felt his hands roam across my skin, warm and soft, exploring every curve and angle of my wanting body. Meanwhile, the rhythm of his thrusts was careful but resolute, ravenous but controlled.

After a while, he propped his weight on his right arm, grabbed my jaw, and continued to kiss me into oblivion. Delicious endorphins released in my mind. This was different from every other time we'd had sex. Though he was always sensual, he was adding a new dimension to it this time around, and it wreaked mayhem across my emotions. His body spoke for him, conveying every ounce of his passion and transferring it into mine.

Before long, his thrusts changed altogether. Replacing the hard penetrations were slow and soft intrusions.

Was he making love to me?

"Look at me, Cara," he demanded, but I refused. I couldn't bear his intensity – I thought I would implode. His tender actions fuelled my confusion. My heart pounded in both agony and exultation simultaneously. If this continued, I'd go mad. I felt so divided.

Abandoning my mouth, he traced amorous kisses across my throat and jaw till he found my ear. "You've nothing to be scared of."

"Faster," I begged and thrust against him. I couldn't endure this pressure. Everything was too intense. Nothing I had experienced before could ever compare to this. It frightened me – intimidated me.

Between kisses on my neck, he said firmly, "No."

"Will, please." I tried to writhe away, but he lay down on top of me.

Taking my jaw again, he stared affectionately into my eyes, but the view only exacerbated my panic.

"Trust me, darling. I'll make you come this way," he said and thrust so deeply into me that it pushed the air out of my lungs.

Upon his steady retreat, I collected all my strength to tilt him over. After hurling us around, I proceeded to straddle him. Now seated on top, I was fully in control, so I let out a breath of relief.

He sighed and tucked his hands under his head. With an impassive expression on his face, he stared up at me, and I noticed that he didn't admire the view. Instead, his eyes were locked on mine.

"Go on, then," he said, and his voice was devoid of emotion. "Fuck me. Keep making this out to be nothing. Whatever you need."

I released a cry of frustration. Burying my hands in my hair, I tugged my head back, profoundly annoyed. At that moment, I realised that the fact that he could read me so accurately and so effortlessly was as much of a curse as it was a blessing.

Suddenly, he launched forward to clasp my wrists and lock them between us. Nose to nose, we glared at each other.

After reeling in a deep breath, I stated with a low voice, "I'm not making this out to be nothing. I'm just saying that it's moving very fast."

"So what if it's moving fast," he snapped back. "There isn't a universal recipe on how to tackle dynamics like these. Every relationship is different from the next, because people are different. And how the *fuck* is this 'fast'? We're not even in a relationship." His eyes spat furious fire. "So tell me, Cara. What do you want me to do? How the hell shall I slow this down when you've hardly allowed it to start?"

"Just stop talking!" I hissed and glared menacingly into his eyes.

"Fucking hell." He collapsed backwards at a total loss. "Jason warned me you were wrong in the head about attachment, but for fuck's sake. You're completely out of touch with your emotions."

"I'm not," I wailed and dragged my hands through my hair again. "I know I fancy you. I'm just trying to come to grips with it, but you keep charging forward before I can!"

His eyebrows furrowed with his frustration, and I felt him tense beneath me. I hadn't ever seen him so exasperated. "How am I charging forward!" he shouted and threw his arms apart. Glimpsing his torso, I saw that every muscle flexed upon his shout. "I've asked you out on *one* date! Not counting rounds, we've had sex – what – six times? Seven? And we've known each other for *months*!"

I met his eyes. "Yet four of them have happened in the past four days, Will. We *are* moving fast!"

He expelled a loud, long breath. "I have been patient as hell with you," he insisted. "And I am still trying to be patient, so help me God. What more do you want from me?"

It occurred to me at that moment that while he was pulling me forwards, I was pulling him backwards, and it amounted to a state of limbo. He was just as frustrated as I was. I wasn't the only one being pushed to my limit here. Our current dynamic was challenging us both, but for polar reasons.

I envied him intensely then. I envied his courage – his ability to embrace our potential so fearlessly. How did he do it? Wasn't he worried about the impact I might have on his life as well? Wasn't he scared of having his priorities changed? Facing the unknown, he was much braver than I was.

"I'm sorry. I just feel like you're not acknowledging how intimidated I'm feeling about all this," I quietly argued and looked away from him.

"Cara. I am. I really am. It's simply in my nature to take the initiative about things, and I'm sorry if that scares you. It's not my intention."

After a loud sigh, I dismounted him.

With a vigilant expression on his face, he watched as I collapsed onto my back beside him. "Not in the mood anymore?"

"No."

"Come here, you." He grabbed my arm to pull me towards him. Brushing my forehead free of hair, he placed a chaste kiss on it. "Are you angry with me?"

I laid my cheek on the bump of his shoulder, whereupon the masculine and unique scent of him drifted into my nose as a sore reminder of how irresistible he was.

"No. I'm just…knackered."

"Quick nap?"

"Yeah."

He set his alarm to wake us in two hours. Once he'd killed the lights, he brought his duvet over us both.

"Turn over," he commanded.

While rolling my eyes in the dark, I turned my back to him. Hooking his arm around my waist, he dragged me into a spooning position. There, he buried his nose in my hair, and I heard him take my scent deep into his lungs. His warm chest expanded against me, and I relished the feel of it.

"See you in a bit," he murmured and squeezed me against him.

"Yeah."

It took him about a minute to pass out. I could hear it in his changed breathing and feel it by his slackening hold. Obviously, he'd been running on spare battery earlier. Though I was tired as well, our argument had left me too rattled to fall asleep so fast.

I was still chasing slumber when I heard my phone ringing in the hall. I contemplated whether to ignore it, but since rest wasn't finding me, I decided that I might as well answer.

After sneaking out of William's embrace, I tiptoed out of his room, but before I closed the door between us, I cast a glance at his figure in the bed. Utterly at peace, he soundly slept, and he deserved it. He'd had a rough day, and I hadn't made it any better.

By the time I found my phone, it had stopped ringing. Olivia had tried to reach me. I was just about to call her back when her name occupied my screen again, and it alarmed me. It must be urgent.

"Hi, love," I answered.

"C-Cara," she sobbed, and my heart shattered at the dreadful sound. What had happened?

"Livy? What's going on?"

"It's...It's C-Colin," she replied through stifled sobs. "He's been calling...calling me all day, s-saying he wants me back, and I don't know what to do. I really need you."

Instantaneous fury unfurled within me. That bastard. He deserved to rot in hell for all I cared. "Shit. Don't answer if he calls again, alright? Where are you now?"

"O-on my way t-to yours."

I grimaced. "I'm not at home right now. I'm with Will. But Jason should be there. Just..." I closed my eyes, trying to think. "I'll be there as soon as I can, alright? I'll leave straight away."

"Thank you. I'm sorry if I'm ruining—"

"You're not. The twat's asleep," I answered with feigned cheerfulness. I was desperate to lighten her mood. "I'll see you in a bit, yeah? Stay strong."

"Y-yes," she snivelled. "Thanks, Cara."

"Of course, Livy. I love you." I rang off.

When I opened my eyes, I immediately searched for my clothes. Though William had ripped his shirt apart earlier – which I'd been wearing – I did still have my hideous red jumper in my bag. It would have to do. Since I was confident that I'd disturb William if I entered his bedroom, I didn't want to search for another shirt to borrow when he was finally catching some much-needed rest.

I dressed hastily. After collecting my things, I considered whether to inform William that I was leaving, but since I didn't want to wake him, I decided to send him a message on Instagram instead.

I had to leave, but I didn't want to wake you, hence this message. Livy needs me

Once I'd pressed Send, I put my phone in my bag and departed.

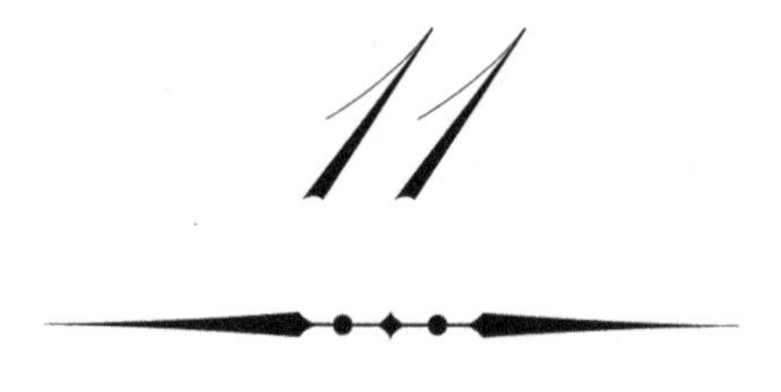

BIRTH OF A STAR

When I entered the flat, the first thing I heard was Olivia's snivels. Kicking off my shoes at record speed, I scurried into the living room to find her in Jason's company, hand clinging to a glass of red wine. They sat on the sofa, facing each other, but upon my arrival, Jason turned his head to acknowledge me.

The emotion in his eyes spoke for him. He was furious. Not only had he always resented Colin, but he was also seeing the woman that he had feelings for cry about the bastard.

"Hey, you," I cooed when Olivia directed her wet eyes to mine. Tears overflowed immediately.

"I told him to go do one," Jason said before she could utter so much as a word. "He called again just before you arrived. I answered. I don't think he'll be calling her again anytime soon. If he's wise, he never will."

"You should block him everywhere, Livy," I said.

She sniffed and nodded her head.

"Anyway, what did the devil have to say?"

She raised an unsteady hand to wipe her cheek. "He said he'd broken up with Alison because he missed me – that he made a mistake when he dumped me for her."

"Olivia," I used her given name, which I only did when I was utterly serious. "Please, don't tell me you're considering rekindling with him."

"No!" she asserted. "I told him to piss off," she continued proudly. "But it just reopened the wound, Cara. He's so manipulative. He wouldn't stop calling, and speaking to him made me remember all the mean things he's done."

"That's right, Livy," Jason chipped in. "He never deserved you. He's a total bellend."

"I know. I'm so over him."

Jason must have loved to hear that. However, when I glanced at him, sympathy was the only thing present in his features. There was no satisfaction whatsoever, and that only led me to adore him all the more. He could easily have given a thought to his ulterior motives with her, but instead, it was apparent that he was fully absorbed in empathy.

Olivia continued, "Honestly, it feels great that the tables have turned. I fancy him grovelling. I'm only upset because hearing from him took me off guard, and I'm angry with him for thinking I'd take him back. How weak does he think I am?" Flustered, she raised her glass and swallowed a greedy mouthful.

"So," I frowned, "there's nothing that really needs to be done. You're just here to cry and be angry?"

"Yes. I need moral support," she murmured. "Mum's got a date with her new boyfriend, and my flatmates are in Spain. I just didn't want to be alone right now."

"Right. Of course." I approached the sofa to grab a seat

beside Jason.

"Have you heard from Aaron since—"

"No."

She nodded. "Do you think you will?"

I stared blankly at her. "I'm not ready to talk about him, Livy. I've hardly had time to process any of my feelings. Will's been demanding my entire attention ever since it happened."

"I see. Speaking of Will, how was your date?"

Though I tried to hide it, a smitten smile surfaced on my lips upon the reminder of my date with William. He'd been so sweet to me. No man had ever treated me so well. And, during the span of it, he'd convinced me that we were indeed compatible. He seemed to understand my character completely – sometimes even better than I did.

Reminiscing made me regret our earlier argument. William had been right. Things might be moving fast between us, but why should we slow down? If things were right, there was no reason I should throw a spanner in the works and make them out to be wrong. It was silly, and it was immature.

Still, it was a fact that I struggled to come to grips with how much I already liked him. And the more I got to know him, the more obsessed I became – that was what scared me. My feelings were running miles ahead of my mind, and I hadn't yet caught up with them. As he'd done since day one, he divided me. His presence in my life had completely severed my mind from my heart, and now I was trying to weave them back together into a harmonious alliance again. However, that was proving mighty difficult now that they weren't speaking in the same language anymore.

I found myself lost in translation.

I sighed. So, as for how our date had gone, I supposed the answer was, "Too well."

Puzzled, Jason captured my gaze. "How does a date go 'too well'?"

"I don't want to talk about it."

He leaned closer, inspecting me. "Is it because you're falling in love with him?"

Intense heat crowded my face. "As I said, I don't want to talk about it."

Raising a brow, he scoffed. "Suit yourself."

"I think we both know the answer, Jason," Olivia murmured, amused, before she drained the rest of her wine.

To escape their scrutiny, I snatched the empty glass out of her hand and said, "I'll pour you another one."

Entering the kitchen, I placed the glass on the counter and opened a cupboard to grab one for myself. Whilst standing there, I wondered how Olivia was really feeling. She'd told us she was only angry, but I wasn't convinced. Part of me worried she wasn't being entirely honest with herself.

If she had truly moved on, it seemed unlikely that she would react so strongly to his attention. I was aware that, in matters of love, Colin had traumatised her somewhat, but still, her reaction was a tad extreme. Had she felt nothing for him, she would have blocked him already and treated him with indifference. Instead, he clearly still possessed the power to provoke her.

So I'd need to keep a strict eye on her from now on – damage control. There wasn't a chance I would let him lure her into his toxic web again.

When I heard them switch on the TV, I groaned. I wasn't in the mood to watch anything at all. Would Olivia get offended if I did some work instead? I still had a few documents relating to Porter BioScience's debt to go over, and it would make tomorrow much easier if I could finish it now.

Returning to the living room, I smiled at the sight of Olivia curled up against Jason's side, snuggling. However, everyone cuddled with Jason – even Jon and Stephen – so I reminded myself not to place too much meaning in it. He was everyone's teddy bear and always had been. Besides, Olivia would have told me if she fancied him. Of that, I was sure. Either way, it didn't prevent me from hoping that her feelings for him could transcend the platonic. Knowing Jason, there wasn't a doubt in my mind that he would treat her far better than any other man ever could.

"Here you go, love," I said as I placed her refill on the small table in front of the sofa.

"Thanks. We're going to watch *Titanic*," she said and patted the spot beside her as an invitation.

Titanic? Compassion stopped me from mocking her, as it was evident that she sought to be distracted from her thoughts of Colin. Seeing her like this wasn't remotely pleasant. It only reminded me of how terribly he had treated her. She looked so broken and fragile where she sat, with her heart of glass.

"*Titanic*?" I echoed. "Is that a wise choice right now?"

"Yes. I need to let it all out."

I looked at Jason. "Have you seen it?"

"No."

I pressed my lips together to stifle my urge to laugh. "Right. Well, Livy cries like there's no tomorrow whenever she watches that film."

He adjusted slightly to bring his arm around her before he gave me a firm nod. "I'm prepared. Would you recommend fetching some tissues?"

"A whole towel." I laughed.

Olivia giggled at my joke, and it was a lovely sound, all things considered.

Unsure of how to ask, I decided to put it plainly, "Right. Thing is, I've got a ton of documents to go over for an acquisition deal, so if you mean to watch a film, would you mind if I did some work instead? I would just be in my room, so I won't be far away if you need me. It's just, I've still got a lot of material to look over, and—"

"It's fine," she assured me with a smile. "I've forced you to watch this film with me a million times already. If you'd rather work, I'll understand. Jason's company is more than enough.

Besides, I mainly came over since I appreciate having you near, even if we aren't doing something together."

My shoulders sank with relief. "Thank you, Livy."

"It's alright. I know you love me."

"I really do."

"Besides, Jason's much better at consoling me than you are. Your approach is a bit too practical. No offence."

I chuckled. There was no lie in that statement. When it came to consoling people, I was at a loss. My instinct was always to remove them from the source that caused them injury, but when dealing with the emotional aspect that came in the aftermath, I was out of my depth. Still, it was something I strived to get better at.

"None taken. I'll be just over there if you need me, though," I said and gestured towards my bedroom door with my glass of wine. "I'll drop everything if you want to talk."

"Don't worry, Cara. I'll be fine. I'm not dying."

"Leo is," I said before turning for my bedroom.

"Leo dies?" I heard Jason question as I went.

"Christ, Jason." Olivia laughed. "Everyone knows that."

"I've been living under a rock, I suppose."

Taking my work laptop out of my bag, I placed it on my desk and took a seat. Once the screen lit up, I eyed the time and saw that it was nearly half seven. Instantly, my thoughts travelled to William, who was probably still asleep. Nevertheless, I checked my phone to see if he'd seen my message yet, but he hadn't. With a sigh, I put my phone aside and had a sip of wine before I opened the document I'd been working on earlier.

Neither Jason nor Olivia called for me even once. However I could tell they were nearing the end of the film when I needed my headset to drown out Olivia's sobs. Since my flow had effectively been interrupted, I rechecked my phone. This time, William had seen my message, but he hadn't responded.

Frowning, I stared at my screen for some time. Perhaps he

had just opened it and was contemplating what to reply. However, when an entire minute had passed, I began to doubt that he would respond at all. Was he giving me the silent treatment? For what reason? No, that couldn't be it. Perhaps he just didn't think there was anything to say. I found that a bit strange, though.

Shaking my head, I placed my phone aside and returned my focus to the document on my screen.

When it was nearly ten o'clock, I considered myself finished. My stomach was complaining now, which led me to remember that I hadn't eaten anything since lunch. It was typical of me. Whenever I lost myself in work, my appetite vanished, only to return with full force the minute I returned to the present. Shutting my computer, I grabbed my phone and pushed my seat out to hunt for some food.

Jason and Olivia were still lounging in front of the TV, but *Game of Thrones* was on the screen now.

"That's a contrast," I pointed out upon passing.

"Never gets old, though," Jason replied. He'd read all the books, and whilst he preferred them over the series, he still enjoyed HBO's adaptation rather a lot. I did, too, although I hadn't read the books.

Opening the fridge, I grabbed a can of strawberry yoghurt to blend with some protein powder and muesli. It wasn't an impressive dinner, but then I'd always been terrible at setting aside time to cook a proper meal. Aaron had always found that terribly amusing, but Dad did not, nor did Jason.

The thought of Aaron made me sigh to myself. Had he been here now, he would have made some joke about how I treated food as fuel rather than as a culinary experience, and he'd have been right. While I appreciated a well-cooked meal, I didn't see it as a useful investment of my precious time when I could instead opt for less time-consuming alternatives. In that, Dad and I were completely different. Mum, however, was exactly like me. So, during my upbringing, Dad had been the one to cook most of our meals.

I missed Aaron intensely at that moment, and it spurred me to unlock my phone to stalk him on social media. Opening Messenger, I saw that he had been active mere minutes ago, and the sight caused my heart to contract. I wondered whom he'd been interacting with and whether I was a subject of any of his conversations.

It was brutal to look at his name and know that sending him a message was off-limits. I hated this distance between us. It felt entirely wrong, even though it wasn't. If he truly had feelings for me, this was the only sensible course of action, and I knew that. However, I couldn't help but wonder if our friendship had been but an illusion. Still, while our bond's formation might have been motivated by different desires, there was no denying our chemistry. He might not want to be my friend, but our personalities were still compatible in some way.

I exited the app. I couldn't keep my eye on him like this – it wasn't the healthiest approach. I'd promised to give him space. To maintain it, staying away from him would make it much easier for me, because the more I thought about him, the more I missed him.

Opening Instagram, I saw that William still hadn't responded to my message, so I frowned with some concern. I considered whether to write him something else. It could, of course, wait till the morning. In the end, I'd be seeing him at work in less than twelve hours. However, there was something about his silence that provoked anxiety.

We'd argued right before I left, so it wasn't impossible that he was angry with me. In fact, perhaps our argument had inspired him to reconsider whether I was worth his investment. Was he getting cold feet?

The potential triggered dread to clench my heart. Without further ado, I searched for his name in my contact list to call him. The ringtone had lasted for a few seconds when it occurred to me that he might just have gone back to sleep. Had I been overthinking his lack of a reply? Worried I might wake him, I was just about to ring off when he suddenly picked up.

"Hi," he answered.

My breath hitched at the sound of his low voice. He didn't sound tired, so I doubted he'd been asleep. However, there was no affection in his tone, and he hadn't added any endearment like he usually did. He'd greeted me the same way he greeted his clients – polite but reserved.

"Hi," I murmured, and my voice betrayed my uncertainty. "Were you asleep?"

"No. I'm working."

Of course he was. "Right."

He was quiet for some time, waiting for me to continue. When I didn't, he prompted, "Was there a reason you called?"

I pursed my lips and folded my left arm across my chest. "You haven't replied to my message."

"Right, sorry. I wasn't sure what to say."

It was obvious from his voice that his guard was up, and it pained me to hear it.

I hesitated. "Are you angry with me?"

"No. What was the emergency, though?"

I couldn't seem to gauge his thoughts, and it disconcerted me. Something was clearly on his mind, but if not anger, what? "Livy's ex wants her back."

He groaned, and I could tell from the sound that he was not impressed. He found the drama silly and pathetic. "Right. Sounds like fun."

I didn't reply because I didn't know what to say. Silence drifted between us for a few seconds until I heard him sigh. "If there's nothing else, I'll see you tomorrow, Cara."

Panic seized my mind, leaving me to tense. I didn't want him to hang up. "Will, you sound a bit weird."

"Weird how?"

I shut my eyes to muster the necessary courage. It was difficult to allow myself to be so vulnerable with him. "Closed off."

"Well, what you said today wasn't exactly motivating. You made it clear that you'd appreciate some space, so here I am, giving it."

Sudden tears prickled my eyes, taking me aback. It was evident from his guarded tone and withdrawn behaviour that I had hurt him, and knowing that was hurting me, too.

"I'm sorry. I just panicked a bit."

He was quiet for another while. I wished I could hear his thoughts.

When he finally spoke again, he sounded dejected. "You keep trying to push me away, Cara. It's taxing."

A single tear of mine fell over, and I rushed to wipe it away. "I'm sorry. I don't mean to."

"You ask for space, but, when I give it, you want my attention. Honestly, I don't understand what I'm supposed to do at this point."

Before I dared to speak again, I cleared my throat in case my voice would expose how upset I was. "Well, I don't appreciate you giving me space right after we've had an argument. It's easy to misinterpret it then, like you're having second thoughts."

Another period of silence elapsed. "Right. That wasn't my intention, so I'm sorry if you experienced it that way. I just wasn't sure how to proceed. You're a difficult woman to understand sometimes."

I frowned. It felt wrong to hear him apologise when I had an apology of my own to give. "Don't...apologise. It's my own fault for not being clear enough. I'm sorry I'm so confusing." I swallowed the painful lump that upset my vocal cords. "I'm just a bit confused myself."

He didn't say anything. Was he distracted, or was he staring blankly around his home office, pondering our conversation? I could imagine him sitting in his desk chair, in the dark, his desktop Mac casting its blue light upon him, harshly illuminating his chiselled face and revealing the worry on his brow.

"Would you like to come over?" I asked. "I feel we should

talk, and I don't want to wait till the morning – not after how we left things."

I could hear his hesitation, and it hurt. "It's already quite late."

"Will, please."

Another sigh escaped him. "Alright, I'll come over. You're right – we should talk."

Instant relief unfolded in my chest. I thought I could soar. "Thank you," I said passionately.

"See you in a bit."

"Yes."

Hanging up, I sucked in a deep breath to compose myself. I hadn't expected that our conversation would rile such emotion, but it had. It wounded me to realise that I was hurting him with my actions. He didn't deserve it.

I stood there for another while, restoring my equilibrium. When the stinging pain in my chest had abated somewhat, I grabbed my bowl and spoon to head into the living room where I saw and heard Olivia's deep yawn.

"Will's coming over," I said to them. "Hope you don't mind."

Dreariness instantly faded from her features as her eyes widened with excitement. "Of course not!"

Was she drunk? Glancing at her glass, I saw that it was empty. "How much have you had to drink?"

"About a bottle, I think."

"Are you sleeping over?"

"Well, now that Will's coming, there's no place for me to sleep, is there? Or is he not spending the night?"

My lips twisted with my uncertainty. "I'm not sure. We didn't discuss it." Glimpsing Jason, an idea occurred to me. "If he does intend to stay the night, I'm sure Jason would let you sleep in his bed."

Olivia turned her attention to him. "Would you, Jase? I'd hate to sleep alone tonight."

Though it was barely visible, I thought I detected a hint of a blush in his cheeks. "Sure, of course."

I struggled to hide my smile when Olivia attacked him with a hug.

"Thank you," she cooed. "I promise I don't snore."

"She takes up a lot of space, though," I teased. "Don't be surprised if you end up on the floor throughout the night."

"I'll manage," he murmured, eyes fleeting.

§ § §

I worried as I waited for William to arrive. While our argument earlier had blown out of proportion, I knew I owed him an apology. However, I hadn't meant for it to turn out that way when I tried to explain my feelings to him. In hindsight, it must have hurt him to hear my concerns. I would have been, had I been in his shoes. I didn't want to hear him having doubts about us, so I should have returned the favour. Frankly, I owed it to him to express more confidence in us, as he went out of his way to ensure that I never had a reason to doubt his devotion. In that, he was a remarkable man.

When the doorbell suddenly chimed, I jumped.

"You get it," Jason said to me, but Olivia surprised us both when she launched out of the sofa and stormed towards the front door.

Standing, I blinked twice over before I followed her.

"Hello?" she spoke cheerfully into the intercom. Hearing her tone, he must have wondered if there were a child present.

Soon enough, she unlocked the door downstairs and opened the front door to wait for him. Amused, I watched her with my arms folded. Since William had always ignored the lift in our building, I was not surprised to see that he arrived by the stairs.

The instant he entered my field of vision, my breath caught in my throat. He was devastatingly lush, and he didn't even try. The most gorgeous man I'd ever seen, he made my heart tingle without any effort. He must have been designed just for me. In all fairness, he ticked every box, and even added a few of his own –

things I hadn't known I desired in a man until I met him.

Sure, he drove me mad in the blink of an eye, but he always knew when he was doing it. He just didn't always care, because he had integrity. When it truly mattered to him, he stood his ground irrespective of my own opinion. Frankly, I admired that about him, and I supposed I did because I was very much the same.

I couldn't have met a more kindred spirit. Hotheads that we were, our flames combined to keep us in our element, fuelling each other to become an even stronger, sizzling heat. And he was exactly that: in my element – my temperament.

I had always marvelled at how he could understand me so well, but when I gave pause to wonder, it wasn't really that astonishing. Like Jason had once said of us, we were similar. Only another fire would know how to read the dance of my flames, and he met them with force equal to my own. We balanced each other. Reinforced each other.

Smitten, I sighed at the dazzling look of him and wondered for a moment how the devil I had managed to capture his interest. My insecurities shouted that I was punching far above my weight, but my confidence yelled that I was entirely in his league. I decided to listen to the latter. Besides, William was not attracted to insecure girls.

Towering in front of Olivia's short person, he looked directly into my eyes over her head, and I saw lightning dance in his. I sensed no anger, but a challenge. A bag hung over his broad shoulder, and I hoped it meant he intended to stay the night.

"Oh my God, Will." Olivia groaned. "You're even more handsome than I remembered."

At first I was amused, but upon recalling Jason's presence and stated concerns about that fact, concern replaced it. Turning my head, I saw him standing a few feet behind me, and his expression was unreadable.

She might as well have punched him in the gut.

William's gaze lowered to meet Olivia's, and I watched as a self-assured smile claimed his mouth. "Good to see you again, Livy. And thanks, I suppose. Care to remind Cara of that every once in a while? I fear she's starting to take me for granted."

I frowned with some irritation. I was not.

"If she does," Olivia replied, "I'll personally deal with her." She turned to send me an icy glare that I hadn't seen coming.

"Hey!" I unfolded my arms. "Whose side are you on?"

"His. Definitely his." She pointed her thumb at him across her shoulder.

I looked at the ceiling in my despair.

"Marry him," she crooned and essentially liquefied where she stood, visibly charmed. I rolled my eyes at her.

"She's drunk out of her mind," Jason commented behind me and chuckled to himself.

Hearing him justify her behaviour intensified my compassion for him. I felt so bad for him then. Olivia was practically drooling all over his brother. That had to hurt.

"Absolutely," I said before I continued to joke, "Nothing else could explain why she'd ever want me to marry Will, of all men."

He was not amused. "Bitch," he muttered and passed Olivia to enter the flat.

"All yours," I teased.

"Ever the challenge," he grumbled and kicked off his shoes. When he approached me afterwards, it was with an intimidating resolve in his stride and eyes. He halted a mere foot away, and as I turned my gaze up to regard him, I swallowed nervously. In the light-blue and piercing colour of his eyes, I saw impatience dwell.

"Livy, would you mind if I borrowed Cara for a minute?" he asked, staring at me.

"Not at all," she replied supportively.

"It's not going to be a minute," Jason warned her. "More like hours. We might as well go to bed. We won't see her till the morning."

William smirked as he shot his brother a mischievous look. "If you actually need us, you may knock."

Reaching forward, I hooked my index fingers into his trouser pockets and tugged him closer with a smile.

"Yes. Will and I need to talk," I said, my tone amorous to avoid perturbing him.

Cupping my cheeks in his hands, he gave me a half-hearted smile. "We do." He placed a peck on the tip of my nose before he took my hand to guide me to my room.

"See you in the morning, then," Jason called after us.

"Yeah," I replied.

"Wait, Cara," Olivia called.

Pausing in my tracks, I glanced at her over my shoulder. "Yes?"

"Could you wake me up before you leave for work tomorrow? I've got a lunch date with Mum."

"Of course."

"Thanks."

After giving her a reassuring smile, William and I continued towards my bedroom.

"They're so cute together," I heard Olivia state dreamily.

"You wouldn't be saying that if you'd heard them have sex. Nothing cute about that," Jason muttered.

Once we had entered my bedroom, I shut the door and locked it. After collecting a deep breath, I turned and admired him as he approached my bed. He took a seat on the edge of it and crossed his legs at the ankles. While tucking his hands into his pockets, he watched me with a guarded expression on his face. His defences were up, and it hurt to see.

Sighing, I folded my arms and wondered where to start. As I fought to weave my thoughts together, I strode towards him and moved to straddle his lap before I circled his neck with my arms. His familiar crooked smile surfaced on his mouth, and I adored the view. Withdrawing his hands from his pockets, he smoothed them across my bum.

I stared deep into his eyes for a long while, merely savouring my circumstance. Life had thrown me the treat of a lifetime, and I wasn't about to waste it.

"I'm sorry for what I said," I started and played with the hair at the nape of his neck. Curling it around my fingers, I studied the complexion of his gorgeous face. His gaze was softer now.

"I didn't mean for it to come out the way it did," I continued. "I'm not having doubts about us, or the direction we're headed in. It's just that you intimidate me, and I'm not used to this. This is my first experience with dating and – you know – feelings of this kind. I'm not drilled in how to handle them, but I'm trying.

"Truth is, they scare me. Intense feelings stress me out because I rarely experience them. Whenever I do, I tend to remove myself from the source, and this time around, that happens to be you. But I won't fall victim to old habits, because, William, I actually trust you. So, I'm genuinely sorry. You didn't deserve to hear that. Ever since we agreed to give this a chance, you've been nothing but perfect towards me. Had I been in your shoes, I would have reacted far worse than you did. Frankly, I think I'd have slapped you."

He chuckled and shook his head. "Trust me, Cara, part of me definitely wanted to spank you."

Colour spread across my face while I lowered my head to nuzzle my nose against his. "Forgive me?"

"Of course." He placed a chaste kiss on my mouth. "And I'm sorry as well. I should have expressed more sympathy towards your feelings in all this. I realise you're intimidated, so I should have handled it better. I didn't mean to disrespect you. I got caught up in my own opinion and hurt, frustrated feelings – failed to be empathic – and I'm sorry for it. I was minding my own stakes in this when, really, I should have been tending to yours. But, Cara..." He clasped my head and stared deep into my eyes. When he continued, his voice was attentive and loving.

"You mustn't forget that you're not alone in this. Sometimes, I think you do. As though I am a threat, you're making me your enemy, when I'm truly fighting alongside you in this. I'm right there with you. We're supposed to be a team, darling. If there's one thing I promise you, it's that I'll be with you every step of the way. I won't make you go it alone. We'll deal with potential problems as they arise. And from now on, I'll try to pace myself to your preferred speed, alright? I know I can be a bit aggressive, but I'm working on it. I just get so eager – very impatient, because I see such potential for us, and I don't want to stall embracing it."

My heart hammered. He never ceased to astound me. There was such remarkable depth to him – so many layers that I couldn't wait to peel away. Sometimes, when his core shone through, the beauty of it blinded me.

When I first met him, I hadn't been prepared to fall in love at all. My mind had been far removed from the sheer concept of it. Now, however, I was starting to face it.

I was falling in love with him, and, for the first time since I'd realised it, it didn't scare me anymore. His faith in us powered my courage. He uplifted me – made me stronger. With him, I was maturing. He was teaching me that daring to admit weakness actually implied strength.

"I'm not scared anymore," I said, though it bordered on a whisper, and traced tender kisses across his sharp cheekbone.

His hands trailed down my sides until they settled on my bum again, squeezing and stroking. "Good, because you have no reason to be. This isn't trivial, Cara. This is profound. I'm serious about you."

Quietly, I dared to confess, "I'm serious about you, too."

His responding smile took my breath away. Elated, his eyes roamed across my face. "How about some reconciliation sex, my love? It's supposed to be great, but then again, sex with you always is."

My love. The endearment echoed in my mind while my chest

tightened. A dense emotion engulfed it, imprinting in my heart, but it felt entirely right. I wanted to be his love. Not just a love, but his love. It had only been two words, but they'd sounded like a declaration of devotion.

My inhalation was slow and careful – apprehensive, but expectant. Sex with him right now was precisely what I wanted. No, it was what I needed. I needed to feel close to him – to be consumed by his passion. I needed him to remind me of why I felt so cold and desolated whenever his hands weren't touching me – when he wasn't blessing me with his attention.

I hadn't known it before, but, before I'd met him, my world had been dark, bleak, and idle. Amidst the black sky of it, he'd arrived like the birth of a star – my personal sun, charging my world with life and wonder.

I craved him. Merely the thought of feeling him within me again caused excitement to lace with my blood. Though I was calm on the surface, the yearning for his flesh stormed beneath my skin, urging me to touch him, to take him in – to *let* him in. Then, I would finally know peace, the chaos settling into a most magnificent, unfathomable creation.

Releasing a nervous breath, I grazed his lips with my own and whispered, "Get inside me, Will. Claim what's yours."

His eyes glowed, and I saw his jaw shut, tightly. Struck by my words, his fingers clawed into my bottom.

"Fuck, Cara, you've no idea how much that turned me on," he stated huskily before he pinned me to the mattress.

My breath caught in my throat upon the extreme force of my emotions. They celebrated in my chest, and the sensation of it extended all the way to my toes and fingertips. I felt electric.

While trailing the tip of his index finger down my cheek, he warned, "This is going to be slow and intense, darling."

I swallowed. I knew he would consume me absolutely now. He was going to rip out my heart and claim it as his own, to have and to hold. Finally, I was brave enough to allow him.

I was ready.

ONLY A NAME

William

She was right. The red jumper I'd packed for her last night, which she was currently wearing, was perhaps the most hideous piece of clothing I'd seen all my life. Nevertheless, she still managed to take my breath away. A beauty like her could turn heads wearing anything, especially if she wore nothing. But I'd tried to tell her that once, and she'd shut me down immediately.

Cara was a difficult woman to pay compliments. More than annoy me, it fascinated me, and it did because – unbeknownst to her – it revealed her vulnerabilities. She was constantly scouting for a way to read negatives in the positives between us, constantly searching for a way to fend off any effort at earning her affections and attachment. Relentlessly, she looked for excuses to dislike me, for reasons to deny the palpable chemistry we shared.

Never did she turn a blind eye to the many ways a simple

sentence could be misinterpreted. If I provided the tiniest of gaps in my statements, she would dive straight into it and obliterate it from within. By doing so, she deliberately derailed from what I had truly meant to say, and I knew it was because she wasn't yet brave enough to face the truth. She wasn't ready to acknowledge the true depth of my feelings for her.

While Cara was inarguably a stunningly beautiful woman, her beauty hadn't ensnared me the very first time we met – a time that seemed so long ago now. There were plenty of beautiful women on the planet, and I tended to find beauty even in the ugly. Imperfections were the true mark of beauty, the way I saw it, because they made it real – genuine.

Instead, it was the precise moment she'd opened her mouth that had sealed my fate. In the span of the mere seconds that it had taken her to insult my very existence, the remaining seconds of my life had been decided. I was going to have her, or I was going to die trying. I'd never wanted another person more in my life. The rest of our conversation that night had converted what was initially a want into a pure, ruthless need.

Though it had taken me a few weeks to realise that I was in love with her, the perfect clarity following my revelation had been astounding. It was either going to be her, or no one. I would never want anyone else as much as I would always crave Cara. And never lightly did I use the word 'always'. I was a man to choose my words carefully. They had to harmonise with what I truly thought and felt at the moment I spoke them. Simply, they had to be true – not universally, but subjectively. So, naturally, 'always' meant precisely that. It was an absolute, just as my desire for her was.

If I hadn't managed to capture her, other women might have been able to entertain me for brief intervals during the remainder of my life. Still, I knew without a doubt that for the rest of my days, Cara would be the only woman I thought of before I fell asleep, just as she would be the first that I thought of in the morning.

That had become crystal clear to me when she had abandoned me the morning after we'd first met. Hopeful she would change her mind and show up at my doorstep, I had waited for her in the week leading up to our coincidental reunion. Each time I had stood in my lift, the ghost of her presence had haunted my thoughts, and each time I had gone to bed, the memory of her touch had echoed across my skin.

Hope had still been dwelling in me that fateful day when she walked into my office, but she crushed it completely when she had declared that she would rather pretend like we'd never known each other more intimately than most. It had occurred to me then that she had never intended to see me again. Our reunion had been a strike of sheer luck, not intention, and I had resented her for that. I hated the idea that it was the arbitrariness of life that I had to thank for encountering her again rather than a desire in her to see me again. What I inferred from it was that she hadn't been as affected as me. I'd been just another man to her – a fun night. Nothing about me had stirred any sentiment of affection in her. I hadn't been exceptional the same way she had been, to me.

When I'd no longer dared to hope that I would ever know her so intimately again, I had wanted to exorcise her from my mind, but since it would require that I consigned the memory of us to oblivion, I couldn't. Such terms demanded too much. The sacrifice would be too great. Even if it would cost me my happiness, I wanted to remember her – what she had felt like beneath my touch, how captivating her mind was, and how all-consuming our chemistry was.

It had taken me one night to fall madly and irrevocably in love with her, and I hadn't even known her true name. That disclosure had been an earth-shattering experience. I'd fallen head over heels for the first time in my life with a woman I knew nothing about.

But that wasn't exactly true, was it? A name was only a name. It wasn't an implication of her character the same way the flight of her hands was, or each gesture and tug of her lips. It didn't whisper of the thoughts her bewitching mind contained the same way the sound of her laughter did, or the way she phrased herself. It was only a name.

I'd been rendered defenceless when she gave me a specific look – a look that I would come to know as unique to her character – later that evening. By now, I knew I would never grow immune to it.

Cara's eyes carried a gleam that drove me mad with desire. I wasn't quite sure how to describe it. It was easier to describe the effects because they were quite similar to symptoms. Still, if I had to try, there was a certain mischief about that look of hers that blended with unquestionable confidence and a ruthless drive much like my own. Quite simply, it told me she was not going to surrender her dignity or integrity for anyone. She was going to meet every challenge I tossed her way, and words would be rendered devoid of sufficient meaning when trying to convey how much I loved that part of her.

That look of hers was gone now. Trepidation had replaced it. With blue eyes wide, she stared up at me as though I were a predator about to seal her fate. In certain ways, I supposed I was. I would do everything within my power to ensure that our futures would be forever entwined.

"Thought you said you weren't scared anymore," I teased and lowered my head to stare deeper into her eyes. I hoped mine expressed the intensity of my feelings – how profoundly I desired her and wanted her to be mine. Absolutely mine.

Although I had suspected it for some time, she had only dared to admit it mere moments ago – she was intimidated by her feelings for me. While it was a progression, things were moving much slower than I preferred. Had it been up to me, she would be my girlfriend right now, not just my lover.

I hated that I had to keep us a version of a secret. I wanted to tell my parents of her, and I wanted to be able to dote upon her at the office. Simply, I was eager to officially mark her as my territory, but until she was ready to enter a relationship with me, it would have to wait.

I'd mainly appreciated the fact that I could see through her pretence so easily, but, sometimes, my ability to do that frustrated me more than anything else. Her feelings for me were obvious. She loved me, even if she refused to admit it, and it demanded every sense of restraint I had to respect her reluctance to confess it just yet. It was extremely tempting to try and force the truth out of her, only so that we could embark on our fantastic potential. But, more than that, it was tempting because it was agonising to have to keep my mouth sealed about my extreme feelings for her.

I wanted to tell her I loved her, and I wanted to tell her until she was sick of hearing it.

My feelings were bottling up to the extent that I often felt about to burst. In fact, I already had, though in French. Last Friday, she thought I'd been sharing dirty declarations, but what I'd actually done was tell her exactly how much I loved her. The relief, however, had only been temporary. As I stared into her eyes now, I desperately wanted to extract the truth from her and dispel her silly fears, only so I could be relieved of the pain of having to conceal the extremity of my feelings for her.

However, as opposed to me, intense feelings frightened Cara. It was obvious that she was scared to lose her head, caught in the whirlwind of her emotions. We attacked that matter differently. Intense feelings didn't frighten me at all. On the contrary, I enjoyed them. They seldom arose in me, but, whenever they did, I felt acutely alive. Gone was the humdrum, and present was the sheer marvel of life. In that, Cara was the ultimate catalyst.

While the same couldn't be said for her, intense feelings didn't confuse me, nor did they make me feel like I was losing my head or my sensibility. Rather, they served as clear indications of which path I was supposed to take.

Very few things scared me, but I knew that there was one thing which frightened me above all, and that was to be powerless. Being powerless in any given situation paralysed me with agony. Especially, that pertained to the inability to help someone I held dear or being unable to prevent the loss of someone I cherished.

Losing Cara, and being unable to change that fact, was a perfect example of something I feared intensely, and that was the only reason as to why I kept my mouth shut about my feelings for her. If I pushed her too far, I worried she'd leave me.

It was quite evident that it hadn't crossed her mind that this was as much of a novelty to me as it was to her. I'd never been this obsessively in love in my life. Sure, I'd lusted after my fair share of women, but never had it felt as crucial to my existence as my lust for Cara. This time was different, because love had been added to the mixture.

I had never loved before – not like this. She had become an irreplaceable part of me. If she left, she would take that piece of me with her, and I would never be able to recover it. She was part of my history now, and thereby part of my identity.

"Everything's just a bit intense," she murmured and ran her hands down my sides to tug my shirt out of my trousers.

"That's how it's supposed to be, Cara. Doesn't it feel good?" I dipped down to steal a kiss. Her soft, warm mouth moulded against my own, and still, the sensation of it wasn't something I had grown familiar with. I yearned for the time it would – when the form of her lips would welcome mine as though I had just come home – a home which contained years of history, as well as security and love.

"It doesn't feel wrong," she said as she pulled away for a breath. I wanted to roll my eyes at her, but resisted. She had an irritating tendency to understate her true feelings. I was looking away from her in my annoyance when she grabbed my jaw. As I captured her deep blue eyes, I saw a soft smile on her plump lips.

"I'm glad you're here, Will. Waiting till tomorrow to see each other again would have been a mistake."

Further progression. Excellent. She was warming up to me, wasn't she? Little by little, I was tearing down her defence.

"I'm grateful you see it that way. I agree." After stealing another kiss, I reached for her hideous jumper to remove it from her mouth-watering anatomy. As the soft skin of her flat stomach revealed itself, I savoured the view while grinding my teeth together. The urge to take her was vicious. I wanted to claw down her skin and watch the red lanes surface, as marks of my presence, after my nails had abandoned her.

So I did.

Dragging my nails down her firm torso, I watched the redness emerge with a sense of satisfaction. It was physical evidence of my exclusive place in her life. As of now, no other man had the right to do this. If only the marks would remain. Should she decide that she wanted nothing to do with me, I wanted my successor to see the evidence of my existence and past role in her life on her skin. I wanted them to glare at him, and I wanted them to kill his desire for her.

It was my inherent jealousy that was to blame for that wicked desire of mine, as well as my feverish urge to possess her. If I couldn't have her, I didn't want anyone else to have her either. One might argue that if I had truly loved her, her happiness was something I would have prized above all, whether provided by me or someone else.

I would never agree with that.

If provided by someone else, I would not appreciate her happiness at all, and if anyone dared tell me that I did not truly love her because of that, they lacked the experience to truly understand. Nobody would ever love Cara as intensely as I did. I was rarely completely sure about things, but about that, I was. So long as we were together, and so long as it was a mutual practice, I would do everything within my power to meet her every desire and need.

Had it been platonic love, perhaps I would have appreciated it, but this wasn't as pure and innocent as that. This was romantic love, and that changed the entire dynamic. Romantic love was intricate and – for me – reserved for one person only. Cara I loved romantically, and I wanted to be the only man she would ever love romantically as well. Anything else would be my ruin. If she replaced me with another lover, I'd never be happy. I'd be desolated and despaired, regardless of whether she was happy with someone else.

Still, I'd never force her to be with me. My conviction was simply that I could never be happy without her just because she could be happy without me. Quite honestly, I would hate her for being happy without me. If I was going to suffer, I wanted her to suffer with me.

In the end, her happiness with someone else would not be a contagious thing that would ultimately infect me as well. Our joy was not linked. I would be an isolated case.

Without her, I'd be miserable and lonely. It was as simple as that.

So, while I would never force her to be with me, I would never forgive her for leaving, either.

After staring at the marks for a brief moment, I steered my eyes to her face, where I saw that hers were shut. Even though she had robbed me of the chance to read the emotion in them, her expression made it abundantly clear – she was savouring the feel of my hands on her body. Her teeth were chewing on her lower lip while the rest of her fair face looked serene.

I marvelled at the view. Witnessing the effect that I had on her boosted my ego. It also instilled a sense of security in me that this passion I contained was very much mutual. From the look of her, it touched her, too. I hoped it wasn't only an illusion, but, even if it were, I wouldn't want to break out of it.

Lifting the garment higher, I was pleasantly surprised that

she had neglected to put a bra on when she'd left my flat earlier. The less clothing in my way, the better. Her small pink nipples were erect, and I wondered if it was because she was already aroused, or whether it was due to the room's temperature. Either way, I was going to have my share of them.

Lowering my head, I trailed my nose across the tip of her right nipple and smiled to myself when she locked her legs around my waist. Collecting her left breast, I gave it a gentle squeeze and silently appreciated how soft, and yet firm, it was within my palm. The nipple of it I gathered between two of my digits and tugged, just as I moved to engulf her right with my mouth.

I heard her sharp inhalation before her back arched to plant her breasts deeper within my possession. This was something I loved about making love to Cara. She was abnormally sensitive, and I relished the responses of her body. I knew without a doubt that most of them were impulsive and subconsciously performed, which further convinced me of her desire for me.

Her hands gathered in my hair, tugging at the strands, while I took my sweet time with her. I was in no rush. Making love to her was my favourite activity. Watching her shudder and twist in the throes of passion was something I could do for a lifetime without growing bored.

But that wasn't what I loved the most about it. What I cherished most was how united we felt. Only when I was within her did she seem to let her guard down. It was only when I physically entered her that she seemed to let me enter her heart as well. That was what motivated my incessant need to pleasure her, because when I was within her, I felt loved by her. That was also why I refused to let our sessions of lovemaking be brief moments. I wanted to extend her moments of love for me for as long as I physically could manage. In the end, feeling loved by her was all I wanted.

Moreover, the look of ecstasy on her face when she reached her peak was unlike anything else, because when it grabbed her, I knew that I was the cause of it. No other man. Only me. *I* was at the root of her pleasure, and I wanted to bear witness to it time and again. Knowing I could bring her such bliss made me feel like I'd succeeded, even if only for the brief moment it lasted.

Dragging my right hand down the curve of her waist, I felt my cock strain against my boxers and trousers. The shape of her was testing my patience. Already, I wanted to delve into her, but I wouldn't. Not yet. Not until she was writhing beneath me, mad with a craving for my flesh.

Her fingers abandoned my hair when I trailed my hand towards the apex of her thighs to rub her. She started tugging on my shirt, clearly eager to remove it, but not yet. I wanted to rub her more. Friction, friction, I reminded myself, but not too much. Just enough to tantalise.

Women were sensual creatures. So much of arousal was in their head. Unlike men, they weren't as easily triggered by a fine vision. They needed to be teased, caressed and worshipped, and for that, I'd always been grateful, because there was little I enjoyed more than praising the female anatomy. It was such an intricate design, like a complicated maze I could never seem to map out entirely. Every time I explored it, I discovered something new – a hidden pathway leading to her imminent arousal.

"Mm, Will," she complained when she'd managed to gather my shirt under my arms. Feverishly, her hands roamed across the bare skin of my back, then to the front to caress my abdominal muscles, and then back again to claw down my shoulder blades.

Sighing, I stretched up to undo my sleeves and drag my shirt over my head. After tossing it away, I looked back to find her smiling at me with a lascivious twinkle in her eyes. I stared. I couldn't help myself.

"You are fucking breathtaking, Cara," I declared and placed my index finger in the middle of the valley between her breasts. While holding her gaze, I dragged it down to her navel, feeling her muscles flex beneath my touch, responding. After circling it once, my finger trailed further down until I reached the spot where I assumed her clit was beckoning my attention just beneath her trousers.

With her eyes trapped by mine, I applied pressure. Her lips parted, and her eyebrows furrowed – bull's eye.

"You like that?" I teased and reduced the pressure again.

I was surprised when sudden determination emerged in her eyes. With swift motions, she shoved my hand away and reached up to grab my trousers. I watched her undo both the button and the zipper with a look of amusement on my face. She was surely impatient.

With some force, she pushed both my trousers and my boxers down to liberate my erection, and, once she had, she didn't hesitate to wrap her warm hand around the base of it. Her mouth had nearly reached me when I buried my hand in her hair and tugged her head back, denying her the satisfaction.

I fucking loved Cara's blowjobs, but there was a reason as to why I wouldn't allow her to perform fellatio on me. She was too good at it. Since I never felt quite so loved by her as I did when we made love, I was determined to last as long as I possibly could whenever we did. Because of that, I – paradoxical as it may seem – hated it when she gave me blowjobs. By doing it, she severely diminished my endurance.

"I want to taste you," she whined, annoyed, and glared up at me. "It's not fair! I always let you go down on me."

Didn't matter. "Life's not fair."

She stared up at me for a while, hesitant. "Is it because I'm bad at it? I thought you liked it last time," she brought herself to ask. "If I am, you can tell me. I'd like to get better, so some feedback would be nice."

A groan escaped me. "No, Cara. You're amazing at it, which is why I don't like it when you do it. Men need to reload. You're a woman. You wouldn't understand because you can have multiple orgasms during one round. We've already been over this."

Baffled, she held my gaze. "That's it? That's your reason?"

I was confused. "You sound disappointed."

"Well, I am. I find it mean. Riding is apparently off-limits, and now blowjobs are as well? You're always giving me several amazing orgasms, and I'd like to return the favour, Will. Giving you pleasure brings me pleasure."

"Well, you're giving me pleasure by letting me be in charge of yours," I countered. "Different kind of pleasure, sure, but pleasure nevertheless."

She folded her arms. "You're ridiculous."

When she behaved like that, this overwhelming urge to dominate her possessed me. Grabbing hold of her shoulders, I planted her flat against the mattress and glared into her eyes. Frankly, I was irritated she tried to rob me, to some degree, of the one moment I felt loved by her, which was when I was inside of her.

"I don't care. Let me have this," I quietly demanded, my voice low.

She swallowed, I saw, and stared vulnerably at me. "Fine."

I don't know how long I tortured her for until I reached the limit of my patience, but if someone had told me an hour, I wouldn't have been surprised. By the time I finally entered her, I had watched that beautiful look of ecstasy claim her face several times. That ecstasy blended with a sense of serene euphoria when I pushed past her soaked, tight walls to reach the end of her.

Holding her eyes under arrest, I stared fixated at her while I pushed into her as far as possible. I only halted when I saw a faint trace of pain flicker across her face. There, I lingered for a beat, struck by relief. When she looked at me now, I saw nothing but affection in her eyes. Her guard was down. Right now, she felt safe to love me, as I had trapped her in the moment, rendering her incapable of thinking further than her current pleasure.

"Pleased?" I teased and ran my nose across her smaller one.

"Yes," she admitted, and as I leaned up again, I saw that a

wide smile had taken over her mouth. "You fuck better than anyone else, Will."

I knew she hadn't meant to hurt my feelings. These were her defensive mechanisms speaking, trying to make light of an otherwise intense situation, which was the only reason as to why I didn't snap at her, regardless of how much I wanted to set her straight. This wasn't fucking. This wasn't some trivial exchange or mutual agreement to let our bodies be used by the other to quench primitive urges. This was far beyond that. This was profound.

Instead of replying to her ridiculous statement, I confessed, "This is my favourite place, Cara." After gently retreating, I thrust inside her again, and I pushed far. Some pain crossed her face again. Suppose I did tend to push her to her limit, in every way. "Right here," I specified and pushed slightly further as I dropped another kiss on her lips. Barely a groan escaped her mouth when I lingered at the very end of her. Was she holding her breath?

I kept penetrating her, gentle in my thrusts this time around, mindful of the fact that she had complained about her soreness all day. Besides, I wanted to make love to her – not fuck her. Fucking was meaningless – pleasurable, but still meaningless. This wasn't. This was anything but. This was my silent way of telling her that I loved her – my wordless way of reminding her that she loved me, too.

I wanted to experience her, savour each groan leaping off her tongue, each contortion of her pretty face, and each scrape of her nails down my back while her legs shoved me towards her to bury me deeper within. I'd never get over how perfectly I fit into her, how her warm walls would clench around me, soaked with her arousal, while they tried to prevent my retreats as if they begged for me to remain within her, precisely where I belonged. Merely the pressure of her was better than any other woman I'd slept with.

I'd never felt so at home in another body before.

There was no denying that I wanted to charge savagely into her, that I wanted to possess every tissue of her body, inside and out, that I wanted to devour her until there was nothing left of her for anyone else to enjoy. However, I could do that any other day. Besides, we'd done rough, and rough wasn't appropriate now. This moment was unmistakably delicate.

When her eyebrows furrowed deeper than usual, I could tell I'd struck the right spot within her. Repeating my pattern, I watched, fascinated, as her lips formed a small circle beneath my hovering figure. Removing my right hand from her hair, I directed the thumb of it to her throbbing clit and began to rub. Meanwhile, I focused on hitting that same spot within her with each of my thrusts, fixated.

Her walls started quivering around me, squeezing. She was getting there, fast. Indeed, she was exquisitely sensitive, and I doubted I'd ever stop appreciating it.

"Mm, fuck!" she cried. Her back arched off the mattress, neck bending backwards until I could hardly see her face anymore while she clawed into the sheets.

The view drove me mad. Fuck slow. I couldn't do it.

Charging fast and hard into her, I heard her whimper just as her shivers started. Her hands abandoned the bed sheets so that her arms could hook around my neck instead, and when her head whipped forward again, she stared up at me as though in a frenzy.

"Will," she pleaded, or perhaps it was a warning. I swear, whenever my name rolled off her lips in precisely that fashion, it demanded all my strength not to fuck her into ruins.

"Yes, love. Let it loose," I ordered and wrapped my arm around her back to hold her against me. Forehead to forehead, I stared into her eyes and saw how they hooded with her climb.

"Give in to me, Cara," I commanded through grinding teeth and shoved harshly into her. She removed one arm from around my neck to try and push my hand away – the hand that was rubbing her clit – but I would have no such thing. I was determined to craft an agonising orgasm within her, a most bittersweet sensation, just like she was to me.

She tossed her head back just as her limbs tensed around me, and although she was rigid with her pleasure, every muscle of her body quivered, robbing her of any control. My lips dived for her exposed throat to ravish it with kisses, particularly along her pulse where I knew she was especially susceptible.

"Will!" she wailed, and I knew from the sound of it, as well as her quivers, that she climaxed. I tightened my embrace of her as she had an irritating tendency to try and push me away right after she came, as if she couldn't stand my nearness because it overwhelmed her.

Well, fuck that. Overwhelming her was one of my favourite pastimes.

However, the pressure her vagina applied in the wake of her orgasm made me stress a bit. I had to slow down, or perhaps even withdraw, if I meant to last as long as I wanted. My cock was throbbing within her – almost painfully – as it begged for release, but I couldn't allow it. Not yet. I'd hardly had my fill of her love.

Deciding upon withdrawal, I rolled us around and caressed her back while she recovered atop me, seemingly spent.

"Did you come?" she eventually asked, eyes closed. There was a tone of surprise to her hoarse voice. I brushed her hair away from her face and smirked.

"No. But we've got all the time in the world."

I thought I heard her sob tearlessly the once, and it made me shake beneath her with stifled laughter.

After a few steadying breaths, she propped herself on her arms on either side of my frame and gave me a lazy smile that only reminded me of why I'd fallen so madly in love with her. She was easily a femme fatale, and even though I had sensed as much from the start, it hadn't intimidated me. She might be the end of me, but if she were, I'd die a happy man.

"Could I be on top?" she asked, and the eagerness in her eyes was irresistible.

However, knowing how fantastically she performed while on top, I hesitated. Then again, she was rather sore, so perhaps I ought to make an exception to the rule.

Studying her, I remembered how she had behaved in my flat earlier, after she had hurled us over and demanded to straddle me. It wasn't until she'd been seated atop me that she had relaxed. It occurred to me that it must have been due to the control such a position entailed. On top of me, she could choose the pace, the depth. It was also easier to maintain more distance between our bodies.

The more I considered it, the less I wanted to oblige. Riding was clearly something she opted for whenever she experienced the intimacy of a moment as too powerful. I wasn't about to let her do that again.

"That depends," I said. "Are you going to be a dick about it again?"

She frowned. "Dick about it?"

"Are you going to make this out to be nothing? As though I could as well have been anyone?"

She froze atop me, eyes widening. "What – no. You could never be just anyone." Her eyebrows furrowed as if she were annoyed with the mere idea.

I swallowed. How terribly I wanted to believe her, and yet I couldn't. Not yet. "Prove it to me, then. I dare you."

Her eyes narrowed. Grabbing my jaw, she leaned so close that the tip of her nose poked mine. "You don't think I can?"

Fuck, how I wanted her. She was such a challenge, and it aroused me like nothing else. When she stared at me like that, everything but her ceased to exist for me.

"Not really," I said, nonchalant in my tone. I was hiding bitterness. "Not when it comes to this. This – admitting that I'm special to you – is your Achilles' heel, and for that, I quite often think that you're pathetic," I admitted. "Pitiful."

A furious fire ignited in her eyes. "Well, I loathe you quite often. Perhaps that's why."

I sighed. "You're so determined to disguise your affection in abomination," I argued impassively and gently patted her bum. "It's not working, Cara. Look at me. I'm naked in your bed, about to make love to you time and again, and I'm not going anywhere. Surely, you must see that your efforts are futile?"

"I've said I fancy you," she grumbled.

I couldn't have been less impressed. "What are you – ten?"

"Fuck you."

"Perhaps I didn't make myself clear enough. That's what you should try to avoid – no fucking."

She flushed bright red and moved to sit upright atop me. My jaw clenched hard. She was unfairly gorgeous. Gravity hadn't interfered with her breasts yet, but even when it inevitably would, I would still find her stunning.

"William, I don't know how!" she confessed, flustered, her eyes fleeting. I rarely saw her so ashamed.

So, I'd been right after all. She couldn't prove to me that I was special to her. She didn't know how – just like I'd said. She only knew how to fuck.

For a few seconds, I was sure my disbelief was palpable. It was disconcerting to witness her behaviour, ashamed and upset as she was. Like a parent to a child, a strange urge to console and comfort her gripped me, so with haste, I rushed up after her until we were nose to nose.

"Hey, it's alright," I soothed.

"I'm sorry," she said, and when she met my eyes, I saw that hers were wet. Christ, she was such a novice. It was rather enlightening to see how deeply this affected her.

"Don't be silly. I'll just have to teach you." I hadn't ever done this myself, but my intuition was urging me to follow it into the unknown, with promises that it would guide me through it.

She looked nervous. "What do I do, then? Move slowly?"

I chuckled. "For example. And some eye contact might be a good idea, I think. However, it's not really about the physical aspect as much. Just try to relax. Don't focus on how to get me off. Instead, focus on what you're feeling. Whatever you feel, just enjoy it. Don't try to control it. And, perhaps most importantly, don't shut me out."

Her blush magnified until she was the colour of a tomato. Fascinating.

Visibly intimidated, she gulped. "Okay," she mumbled, although it sounded to be to herself.

After ascending somewhat, she grabbed my shoulder with her left hand and used the other to align me with her entrance. Upon her descent, my lips parted with my groan. I couldn't stop myself from digging my fingers into the flesh of her hips. She felt unbelievably good. Her body was a fucking temple – a place to worship the divine.

When she had hooked both her arms around my neck, she rested her nose mere inches from my own and stared vulnerably into my eyes, if not even susceptibly.

After enjoying her delicious movements for a while, I queried softly, "How does this feel?"

"I…Profound," she admitted coyly. "But good."

"Only good?"

"Tremendous," she clarified and lowered her head to hide her face in the crook of my neck. Although I wanted to prompt contact with her eyes again, I resisted. I was already pushing her to her limit. Then, to my satisfaction, she lifted her head again, seeming to remember. I appreciated that more than I would be able to tell her. It was a clear sign that she was determined to battle her demons for me.

"Cara, you're incredible," I said passionately and moved to leave a kiss on her mouth.

Staring into her eyes, I saw her walls crumble. During that

brief moment, which wasn't even a breathing space in the span of time, I was secure in her love for me. For as short as it lasted, she sincerely loved me back, and I hadn't before felt so completed.

By the time she cried my name in abandonment for the final time, her long brown hair spread around her head like a vision of the divine, I was drenched in sweat. To a certain degree, I was also satiated. No matter how briefly, she had dared to love me back.

The powerful orgasm that grabbed me felt as if it was shooting out of my gut as I spilled myself inside of her, rather than in dreadful latex. I had hated the condoms that had separated our flesh from making contact. Irrational as it was, it felt like they had prevented me from enjoying the entirety of her.

I kissed her with all I had as I climaxed, but when my mind eventually succumbed to stupor, I collapsed beside her and draped my arm over my eyes to surrender to the blissful dark. I must have lain like that for many minutes because, when I finally removed my arm and turned my head, I discovered her fast asleep beside me, seemingly comatose. Not even an earthquake looked capable of stirring her awake. It made me pity her. Like me, she hadn't caught much sleep last night, and since Olivia had required her support earlier, she hadn't been able to enjoy the same nap that I had.

When I'd discovered her gone, I had despaired. Finding her message hadn't appeased me. She hadn't mentioned our argument at all, nor suggested a time to reconcile. I'd inferred from it that our argument wasn't a priority to her – that she wouldn't care if things went south. Rather, she'd consider it a relief. I had hated that idea. She might have had a legitimate excuse to leave, but she could at least have expressed some concern about our fight.

Then again, time had shown that I had been overthinking her message. In the end, it was she who had initiated our reconciliation tonight. What I deduced from it was that, rather than us, it was her feelings that were moving fast. So, I supposed I was getting closer. One day soon, I hoped I would make her burst. Then, at last, would I be able to tell her how much I loved her, how truly senselessly I loved her.

I hoped I wouldn't burst first.

MILESTONE

William

I dropped a kiss on her naked chest, then her forehead, and tucked her in before I climbed out of bed to have a shower. Even if I experienced the drowsiness that almost always ensued after an orgasm, I didn't feel tired enough to fall asleep. I blamed my earlier nap for that.

Was Jason still awake?

After switching off the lights to let Cara sleep in peace, I dressed into my boxers and exited her room. As my eyes scouted the living area, I saw only Jason. Headphones covered his ears, so I gathered he was listening to music whilst he sipped on what looked like his fourth bottle of beer, sprawled on the sofa.

Bloody summer holidays. I envied the bastard. I couldn't recall the last time I'd been on a proper holiday. Must have been two years ago, when I'd gone to the Bahamas with Alex, Andy and Chloe. That holiday hadn't been particularly pleasant either, seeing as Nathan – Alex's father – had died of a spontaneous heart attack.

Jason didn't notice me, so I headed down the hall to make a quick process of a shower. Seeing as his eyes were shut upon my return, he didn't notice me now either, so I walked straight to the kitchen to grab myself a bottle of beer as well. It was only when I halted beside his figure in the sofa and bent until my face was inches from his that he sensed my presence.

"Fuck!" he squealed, much like a young girl would, and at deafening volume. He recoiled against the backrest of the sofa like a frightened animal, blue eyes wide with panic. Soon enough, anger replaced it. I wondered with some concern if he'd managed to wake Cara.

"Ah, shit, Will! Why have you got to be such an intolerable dick!" he chided as he clung to the cushions.

I leaned away. "Well, since you're such a twat, someone's got to be the dick." After a beat, I continued, "Be quiet. Cara's asleep."

"You should have thought of that before you decided to scare the living shit out of me."

"You're right. I should absolutely have anticipated a reaction like that from a twat like you."

He groaned, but said nothing. Gazing around again, I wondered where Olivia was. Had she gone home?

"Where's Olivia gone?" I asked and directed my eyes to him again.

"She went to bed."

Taking his headphones off, he folded them together and leaned forward to place them – very carefully – into their case. Jason had always been odd like that. Like myself, he'd always been tidy, but there were certain things he added a particular order to. For instance, his wardrobe had always been labelled: shirts here, trousers there, and boxers over there. During our youth, I had tended to bring the napkin holder to the table whenever I ate, and he had always put it back to the spot next to the coffee machine afterwards. That had amused me terribly, so, sometimes, I'd moved it just to take the piss out of him – to be a nuisance the way a sibling should.

Another idiosyncrasy of his was how he had treated the bathroom we'd shared. He could never seem to sterilise and scrub it enough, and the same applied to the kitchen. In areas of the house where germs typically flourished, he was compulsive about cleaning. He really took things to the extreme.

I remembered how much fun I'd derived from that. Even our nanny – Lydia – had joked that he would put her out of a job. Of course, neither Mum nor Dad would allow that, so with time, Jason had become Lydia's favourite. Together, they exchanged tips on how to remove stains from clothes, how to remove grime from the trickiest corners, and which solvents were best when trying to remove as much bacteria as possible. Jason was particularly fond of how Lydia organised the groceries.

The memory made me smile.

"Here?" I asked.

"Yes."

I stared at him. "In your bed?"

"No, in the kitchen, Will." He frowned. "Yes, of course in my bed."

It was all fairly ironic. Women frequented his bed without pause, and yet he hadn't had sex with anyone for quite a while. I found it both hilarious and upsetting.

Like me, Jason had always been fastidious about whom he granted his sexual attention. However, I supposed what made us different boiled down to confidence and perceptiveness. Jason was clueless about women and always had been. Even when women were blatantly interested, he remained entirely oblivious to that fact, which ultimately led him to miss his chance once they got too impatient with his passivity. I, on the other hand, tended to pick up on the signs rather quickly, and if I returned their interest, I didn't hesitate to act on it.

I said, "I thought you were going to bed as well?"

"I am. I'm just waiting for her to fall asleep first."

That confounded me. "Er, why?"

"Because she's drunk."

I failed to understand his reasoning. "So?" Grabbing a seat beside him, I sipped my beer.

"And emotional," he added, as if that was enough of an elaboration.

"So? Aren't you friends?"

He groaned and glanced at me from the corner of his eye. "Well, yeah, but Livy gets silly when she's drunk and emotional. She needs comfort, and I don't want to seem like a source for her to get it – not like that."

Humour emitted from my expression. "In other words, you're scared she'll try to use you as a rebound?"

He looked annoyed. "Well, sort of. I'm just saying that *if* she tries anything, I'd rather avoid it."

I leaned back. "How risk-averse. I take it you aren't interested in having sex with her, then."

His hand clenched around his bottle while he looked away, and I saw it as a tell. Something was clearly on his mind, but what?

As my eyes inspected him closely, I tilted my head. "Is there something you're not telling me?"

The sound of the breath he released betrayed his inner conflict. Instantly, my intuition overruled everything else. "Have you got feelings for her or something?"

"What? No." His incredulity was obviously fake and discerning that only exacerbated my suspicion. It wasn't like him to lie to me, so why was he now?

"I can tell you're lying," I said, "but suit yourself."

Finally, his gaze met mine, and he sighed. "I might fancy her a bit."

Fancy. There it was again – that poor and pathetic word. Cara used it too. I couldn't stand it. Up against the extent of my emotions, it seemed so shallow. Were their emotions truly so destitute of depth?

Either way, this was news. I had often wondered whether Jason was sexually keener on Cara than he let on, so this contradiction was something I welcomed. Then again, perhaps he had merely given up on the idea of her now that I had laid my claim on her.

"Do you?" I probed, mildly shocked. While I didn't know Olivia at all, she didn't strike me as his type. Harper – his past flame who also happened to be my dear friend – was very different from Olivia, or at least that was my impression. Harper was reserved, sometimes a bit socially awkward, and hyper-intelligent in academic matters. She had a sense of humour too, but it was painfully dry and rather quirky, which I had used to make fun of during our days as classmates. I could, of course, be wrong, but Olivia seemed more bubbly, slightly less astute and – overall – more stereotypically feminine, which there was nothing wrong with. I just hadn't thought it was Jason's taste.

He looked embarrassed. "Yeah."

At first I was a bit offended to be learning about this now, but, upon second thought, I gathered there had to be a reason why he hadn't shared it with me sooner. Had it only just dawned on him? "Why haven't you told me?"

"Well, she's been in a relationship for the past three years."

"You've fancied her for the past three years?" I was astounded.

"No, not three years. More like one."

"Then I don't understand how that's supposed to explain why you haven't told me sooner."

He sighed and bent his neck over the sofa's backrest to study the ceiling. "Because, Will, you would have been an annoying tit about it."

I frowned. "Why do you say that?"

"You would have urged me to pursue her despite her relationship with Colin."

That was indeed my general philosophy when it came to romance. Had it not been, I would probably have respected Cara's arrangement with Aaron and left her alone entirely. Thank god I hadn't.

"You're right. I absolutely would," I confirmed with a smirk before I took another sip of my beer.

"Yeah, so, that's why I haven't said anything. I couldn't be bothered to listen to your nagging. I already knew what you would have said."

I chuckled. "Fair enough. She's single now, though. Here's your chance. Don't let it slip away."

He swallowed a mouthful. "I envy you for that, you know," he eventually murmured. "People can say what they want about your methods, but you've always chased after what you want with a ruthless drive, completely unapologetic. And more often than not, it gets you where you want. Even Cara, you've managed to get, and I honestly doubted any man ever would."

I raised my brow at him. "Cara's not admitted to anything yet. All she's said is that she fancies me, so I would hardly say that I've managed my objective. And in any case, you should listen to yourself right now. You're essentially saying you're not assertive enough. Why not do something about it? You clearly know what your problem is. So, ask her out on date. Sure, she'll be surprised, but the worst thing that can happen is that she rejects you. If she does, she probably would have done it either way, be it now or later."

He was quiet for a long while, contemplating. "I'll give it a thought."

"Give it a go."

He rolled his eyes. "I might. Anyway, what do you mean you don't have Cara where you want yet? She's completely in love with you."

Had she told him that? If she had, I was closer to my goal than I'd initially thought. If she'd confessed it to him, it was only a matter of time before that would escalate into confessing to me.

"Has she told you that?" I couldn't help the hope that poured from my tone.

He shook his head, and my heart sank in my chest with my disappointment.

"She doesn't need to. She's my best friend, Will. I know her like the back of my hand."

"You'll forgive me if that argument doesn't serve as sufficient reassurance," I replied with a shake of my head. "She might be in love with me." Pausing, I searched for the right words to explain my concerns. "However, that doesn't mean she's willing to accept it. She's got walls, Jason. Fucking massive walls."

"I told you she struggles with attachment."

"It's both fascinating and infuriating at the same time. Her independence is so extreme."

"Well, if you consider it logically, there's no reason why she should try to be less independent. Not growing attached gives her more freedom and there's less chance of her getting hurt, though I doubt she's like that chiefly because she's scared to get hurt. It's just an easier way of life, to be honest. At least from a logical perspective."

I had reached the same conclusion in my analysis of her, so I nodded. "It's definitely innate."

He chuckled. "Yeah. And bear in mind that Cara's never been in love before. Smitten, maybe, but never in love, so I'm sure she's just shocked at herself. You arrived at an inconvenient point in her life – she's preoccupied with her ambition."

I groaned. He was only telling me things I already knew.

He sighed before he elaborated, "She's not…She's not a feeling type of girl, Will. She hasn't got much experience in dealing with feelings. She's always been quite placid that way."

"It's fucking irritating."

He laughed. I didn't see the humour. There was nothing laughable about our situation, much less my feelings for her.

"In case you need your memory jogged, you used to be just like her," he reminded me, amused. "Even with Kate, you were emotionally distant."

My cheeks expanded with my breath while I nodded repeatedly. "Yes, I know. Sometimes I think that's why I get so impatient. Since I've been where she's at, I know how far she can come. She just needs to mature a bit more."

He chuckled. "I won't disagree with that, but it's still a process she has to go through on her own, Will. She'll come around, though – I'm sure. Just stay patient."

"See, I'm trying, but it's difficult. I love her, Jason. I love her to bits, and I yearn to tell her."

"I know." His tone held sympathy that I absolutely despised. I didn't want his pity. It made me feel pathetic.

"Do you think I could tell her first? Or would that scare her off?"

He eyed me strictly. "Maybe wait a bit, Will. You haven't been dating for very long, and you need to bear in mind that she's only just ended things with Aaron. He meant a great deal to her. She told me before you arrived today that she hasn't had time to process that fact at all since you've been demanding her entire attention ever since it happened. She needs to be allowed some room to come to grips with everything."

Horribly annoyed, I frowned. I hated the fact that even though Aaron was physically out of the picture, he still managed to stall our progress. I wished she would forget him already. I wished she would put him out of her mind for good, right now. In my head, Aaron was irrelevant. He was old news. He wasn't part of our lives anymore.

My blood boiled at the notion that she still cared for him. It stirred my demons, my jealousy. I hated the idea of them.

For three years, he'd had her. Less than two weeks ago, he'd been about to have her again, and that despite the intimate night she and I had shared just hours before. That spoke volumes. She'd been able to push thoughts of me aside so easily when it came to him. It was glaringly apparent that she harboured a great love for him, even if it hadn't outmatched the feelings she seemed to harbour for me.

But how small was that margin? Had I prevailed over him easily superior, or had I won by a slim chance?

I'd told her I was sorry for how I'd behaved that dreadful night, and, in almost every way, I was. But I wasn't remotely sorry that he was out of the picture, hopefully for good, and I wasn't remotely sorry that I'd cock-blocked him. In fact, I had bloody celebrated it. Only over my dead body would I have let him have her that night, or on any night onward.

If he so much as dared to approach her again, it was not unlikely that I, under duress, would resort to questionable methods, all depending on how she would respond to him. Should she welcome him back susceptibly – or display even the faintest trace of the same affection she once held for him – she would be the target of my anger.

I'd never get violent, but I would resort to other means capable of keeping them apart. If that meant stirring her guilt by revealing how much hurt her actions inflicted upon me, so be it.

This was where some people might disagree with me again. Some might think that since I claimed to love her, my intention should never be to cause her pain. Well, what about my pain? Shouldn't that matter, too? Who were they to tell me how to love?

There is no such thing as a universally correct way to love and to be loved. To believe anything else would be delusional. Everybody is different, and their needs with them. Thus far, my way of love was the closest to the ideal when it came to meeting Cara's needs. Why else would she want to be my lover?

My own needs were quite simple: Cara had to be mine alone. Sharing her with Aaron – a past lover – was out of the question. To meet that need of mine, I expected her to abandon him. If she refused, why the hell should I bother to meet hers like some selfless fool without any self-respect to speak of?

So yes, I loved her, but that did not mean that she had me wrapped around her finger. I bowed to no one when they did not deserve it. If she couldn't discard Aaron for me, then she most certainly did not deserve it. I would, without hesitation, return her own medicine and refuse to meet her needs.

I would prioritise my own joy to the same extent that I would prioritise Cara's, and I expected her to treat me just the same. If she proved unable to do that, and instead prioritised only herself, she and I were going to have a problem.

It wasn't that I was unwilling to sacrifice certain needs of mine to meet hers. On the contrary, I was willing to sacrifice plenty so long as it was a mutual practice. However, Aaron was a hard limit for me. Should she be unwilling to sacrifice him for the sake of us, especially when she knew how important it was to me, I would be forced to leave her out of respect for myself, and I would never forgive her for making me do that. I would hate her for bereaving our potential, and I would hate her for daring to offer me only scraps of her rather than the entirety of her. Simply, I would loathe her for not valuing us as much as I did.

It was a fact I couldn't ignore that Cara was weak for him. If I believed anything else, I'd be naïve. And that weakness of hers scared me. It fed my insecurities. If I fucked up, even just a little, would she return to him? Would that be it for us?

She'd told me several times what a comfort he was, that he never bothered her, that he might as well 'be air' to her. She'd led me to believe that she appreciated his stability and predictability. He was a source of security, and I knew she favoured that about him. Down the road, I worried my character might inspire her to miss that. If I came up short, would she dump me for him and return to old ways?

That would fucking break me.

I reminded myself to answer Jason's counsel about waiting a while longer before I confessed my love to her. "Yeah, I get why you'd advise that. Still, I can't help how clear things are to me. It blows that she's not on my level."

"I'm sure she is, Will. She just happens to express it differently," he argued. "Cut her some slack, would you? I know it's hard for you to see it because you don't know her like Livy and I do, but we've seen immense changes in her. She's really warming up to you. She wants it to work out just as much as you do."

When I didn't immediately answer, he sighed before continuing, "You need to understand that the Cara you know is different from the Cara I know. I knew her before you were part of her life, so you've got to trust me when I say that the progress she's made is tremendous, and it's all for you."

I knew his points were valid, but I didn't want to listen to him. Eager to embrace our potential, anything that stood in the way of that was difficult to respect. But since he was talking sense, I would force myself to listen.

"I'll give her a month. That's all I can manage."

He groaned, head dropping in despair of me. "Then don't expect her to reciprocate straight away."

"As long as she doesn't leave me, I'll be fine."

"She won't."

I wanted to be as certain as he was, but I couldn't be. Not until she told me herself.

"Do you think he'll reach out to her? Aaron, I mean?" I asked and looked away from him since I feared he'd sense my anger and tailor his reply accordingly.

"It's not unlikely," he said, and I noticed his hesitation. "They were best friends, Will, and they'll be studying together again next term, for their LPCs. They've also got a lot of mutual friends. They're bound to bump into each other now and then."

I stiffened. The very idea of them interacting again sent my heart racing at a perturbing speed. The hard beats were something I recognised as a manifestation of intimidation. Ill with fear, I felt quite nauseous all of a sudden, as if I were about to vomit.

That urge intensified when revolting images of him trying to claim her physically marched into my mind. I couldn't stand them, much less him.

I hated that he knew what she looked like when she orgasmed. I hated that the sound of her moans was a familiar melody to him, and I hated that her response to his caress had fed his delusion that he somehow mattered more to her than all the rest.

Since I knew perfectly well what she looked like stripped and glistening with passion, I hoped more than anything that Aaron had never seen her quite as senseless with pleasure and desire as I had. I hoped he hadn't looked into her eyes and seen her mind transcend into an immeasurable space the way I had. The mere thought of him in my place, trying to convey his love for her each time he immersed himself into her beautiful body, truly made me nauseous.

I'd always appreciated that Cara was experienced. The fact that she'd slept with several men before I entered her life had never bothered me at all. I'd rather have a woman who knew what she liked and didn't like than a woman who had yet to find out. Sex was simply better that way from the start.

However, her past with Aaron bothered me because I knew it rooted deeper. He wasn't just another bed partner. It hadn't only been sex between them. Cara could deny it all she wanted, but she'd be lying to both herself and to me. They'd been sleeping together for three entire years.

What made it truly intolerable, however, was the fact that he had feelings for her. He was in love with her, too. Even though I knew that no one could love her as intensely as I did, he still loved her.

If he were anything like myself and claimed to love her as ardently as I did, I reckoned there was a slim chance that he would let her go without a fight. Had I been in his shoes, I'd constantly scout for a way to persuade her to choose me over him. It was perfectly plausible that he was lying in his bed right now, reassessing his tactics, while wishing Cara were there beside him.

While part of me hoped the silence of her absence was screaming at him to remind him of his defeat, another hoped for the opposite. The less he yearned for her presence, the better my chances.

"He intimidates me," I confessed. "Or rather, the idea of them, I should say."

Jason sighed, slouched on the sofa. "You're overthinking. Cara doesn't want him like that. If she did, they would have been a couple years ago."

I was about to argue that he couldn't be sure she wouldn't change her mind when the door to her bedroom opened. My head spun to acknowledge her, and, as I did, I searched for any evidence that she might have overheard our conversation. Though, judging by the groggy look of her, I highly doubted it.

"Hey," I said, and even I could hear that my voice was drenched with affection. "Did we wake you?"

She shook her head. "No. I need the loo." She turned for the bathroom.

When the door closed between us, I faced Jason again. "Have you told her about Livy?"

"Yeah."

Again, I was somewhat offended – he had chosen to confide in her before me. "What does she make of it?"

"She's supportive."

"But Livy hasn't told her anything? Anything that could imply you might have a solid chance?"

He looked dispirited. "No."

That wasn't promising, but it wasn't final, either. "Perhaps she just hasn't entertained the thought since you seem disinterested. Or, better yet, perhaps she hasn't said anything because you're her best friend's flatmate. She might be worried it could make things awkward for Cara."

"That's a lot of maybes." He shrugged. "I'd prefer not to speculate. I'll find out sooner or later."

"If she's got any taste, she'll be overjoyed to have a chance with you."

That made him grin, and it was a version I recognised all too well. When we'd been younger, he would always flash it to me before he said, "Will, you truly are my best mate, above all the rest. You know that, right?" The brotherly affection that poured from his eyes after each time he professed it never failed to resonate with me. It was obvious that he sought my validation – yearned for me to requite his statement, and, each time I confirmed it, he'd look so proud and pleased with himself. How happy it had made him when he was only a boy, to be adored to the same extent by his elder brother.

"Yeah," I said, responding to his thoughts, "you're my best mate, too – even if I do annoy you half the time."

"All the time," he playfully corrected.

"Half the time," I repeated. "Don't get cheeky with me."

When Cara exited the bathroom, she turned her back to her bedroom door to approach us instead, and she didn't stop till she had reached the end of the sofa where we sat. The black robe she wore, made of satin, triggered my fantasies. She looked like the gift of a lifetime, just waiting to be unwrapped under my hands.

In all fairness, she looked like a gift offered to me by the God I had never believed in, as if He was trying to mock my lack of faith by granting me her to serve as blatant evidence of His existence, because oftentimes, I found it hard to believe that a masterpiece like her hadn't been designed by divine intervention. I'd never felt closer to religion than when I found myself captivated by her, ceaselessly fascinated.

"Livy gone to bed?" she asked Jason.

"Yeah."

"What time is it?"

"Half-past midnight."

Hearing that, she handed me her undivided attention. "Will, shouldn't you get some rest? You've hardly slept the past few days."

She could be surprisingly attentive. My heart throbbed, if only for a split second, so after necking the remainder of my beer, I asked, "Want me to hold you, do you, love?" I hoped my playful tone would disguise, or at least excuse, how I'd actually fished for reassurance.

A grin formed on my mouth as I – transfixed – watched her face turn crimson. There was nothing I enjoyed more than witnessing the effect I had on her. At that moment, while she contended with the brightest of reds, I wondered what her exact thoughts were, and I wished desperately that I could have heard them.

After a composing breath, she muttered, "Are you coming to bed or not?"

There was no denying that I wanted to poke fun at the new colour of her face, but since I was enduring a moment of deep adoration for her, I managed to resist. My brother, on the other hand, did not.

"Damn, Will, you turned her into a proper tomato." While looking over at me, Jason spilled his laughter and pointed at her.

She whirled around immediately, seemingly mortified, and headed straight for her bedroom.

Since her reaction only made Jason laugh louder, I pushed his shoulder somewhat harshly to shut him up and called after her, "Cara, I'm sorry. I didn't mean to embarrass you. I'll join you in a moment, but I've got to brush my teeth first. Have you kept my toothbrush?"

Halfway through the door, she stalled. "Your toothbrush?" She turned to look at me, puzzled.

"The one I used last I slept over?"

"If she hasn't tossed it away, it should be there," Jason murmured. "I haven't touched it."

"I wasn't even aware you had a toothbrush here," she said, and I could tell from her demeanour that she was uncertain of how to react to the reality.

Was this a step too far for her?

"It's my brother's place as well," I said, because I didn't want to trigger her panic. "It's not weird I'd have a toothbrush here. Anyway, he had a spare, so I made use of it that night you got plastered at the club. If it makes you uncomfortable, you can throw it in the bin tomorrow."

She studied me, and again, I wanted so badly to hear her thoughts.

Soon enough, the filtered version of them came out, "No, it's fine. I don't mind. I'd rather you kissed me with a fresh breath."

Of course, her reply was devoid of any sentiment of affection. True to her character, she focused on the practical aspect, just like she did with everything else.

The subsequent disappointment I experienced was something I worked hard to disguise. I wished she would have expressed more excitement. So yes, it was only a toothbrush, and thereby a trivial concern. However, in the grand scheme of things, it also served a symbolic purpose – represented a sort of milestone. Keeping a toothbrush here was physical proof of the direction we were heading in. It meant that my visits would be a frequent and recurring event. By that, it symbolised the manifestation of our relationship.

However, as I processed the rest of her statement, I sensed my insecurity about our relationship – or whatever I was supposed to call it – diminish somewhat. Like Jason had said, she was progressing. I knew the fact that I was allowed to keep a toothbrush here was a much bigger step for her than it was for me.

While wandering along that lane of thought, I wondered whether Aaron had been allowed to keep one here. I found myself divided, because while I wanted to ask, I was reluctant to remind her of him. I didn't want her even thinking about him.

With our eyes locked, I said, "If you're sure you don't mind, I'd like to keep it."

Suddenly, I thought I saw genuine adoration in the form of a smile on her face. However, since I hadn't seen her wear quite that version before, I failed to recognise the true feeling behind it in its entirety. Even so, a whisper in my mind dared me to believe that it might have been love.

A delicious shade of pink resurfaced in her cheeks just as she replied, "Do". Then, with a fleeting gaze, she continued, "See you in a bit," and closed the door after herself.

Had my eyes deceived me just then, or had I really glimpsed the true depth of her feelings for me?

After entertaining the possibility in silence for some time, I turned to Jason again. "Suppose I'll see you in the morning."

"Yeah."

"Why not try and spoon Olivia tonight? Just to get a feel of it."

"Dickhead," he muttered.

"It might be a nice change to spooning my soon-to-be girlfriend. Not that I mind, weird as that is," and I meant it. Now that I was certain he'd never harboured feelings for her, the fact that they frequently cuddled and slept in the same bed no longer bothered me. Like Cara had insisted, their bond was similar to that between siblings, but I hadn't been able to trust it until now.

He scoffed. "That's because you know as well as I do that I've never harboured sexual interest in Cara."

"I've never been more grateful you're blind and deaf, Jason."

He laughed. "Go to bed, you utter clown."

After brushing my teeth, I placed my toothbrush beside Cara's and smiled to myself. Milestone, indeed.

By the time I got into bed again, she was nearly asleep. It still reeked of sex in here, but she'd opened the window, for which I was grateful. Grabbing around her slender waist, I tugged her soft frame into the spoon of my embrace and placed a kiss on her naked shoulder. Responding, she snuggled deeper into my hold of her. It was quite a simple action, and yet it stirred immense feelings.

"So you do want me to hold you," I teased.

"All the time, Will," she professed, and her smitten tone took me aback. In the dark, a look of disbelief occupied my face. I surely hadn't expected to hear that.

"Good," I said, "because I won't let go."

14

SWEET VENGEANCE

CARA

WILLIAM WOKE ME UP BY GENTLY SHAKING MY shoulder. My eyelids fluttered apart, and while I adjusted to the light, I studied him through squinted eyes. Drops of sweat crowded his temple, and I saw that the rest of his hairline was also saturated with the bodily fluid. Had he been working out again? Judging from his attire, he wasn't fresh out of a shower.

Puzzled, I sat up. "Will? Why are you covered in sweat?" Since my voice was hoarse, I cleared my throat.

"I wanked bloody hard to the thought of you just now. Surprised you didn't wake."

Oh my God – this man. I hadn't thought I could blush so soon after waking up, but he proved me wrong.

"William, you've got a serious mental health problem," I whined in despair and collapsed.

Reduced to a fit of laughter, he doubled over beside my bed. That man never overlooked an opportunity to pull my leg. Despite it, the elating melody of his laughter made a sincere smile bend my lips.

"I couldn't resist. You should have seen your face. Priceless," he excused himself once his laughter ceased. "I was training in the living room. Borrowed Jason's weights. Anyway, I'm about to have a shower. Care to join me?"

"No. You jinxed it. You may wank bloody hard to the thought of me instead."

"Come on. It'll be quick."

I turned my head to eye him in my scepticism.

"I promise," he said.

I stared at him for a beat, still waking up. My groggy mind struggled to latch onto reality and dull routine after my adventurous dream, where I'd been chased by pirates. "I'm sorry, but no. I'm just not in the mood. Later, yeah?"

Underwhelmed, he gazed back. "Fine."

Surprising me, he removed his shirt and flung it onto the floor as if to show me what I was missing out on. The view made me salivate. I was positive his action had been deliberate. He wasn't playing fair. For a moment, I regretted having told him of how attractive I found him to be, because he seemed determined to use it against me. His abs glistened with fresh sweat as he approached. When his fists landed on my mattress, he leaned forward to reach me, and I saw the muscles of his shoulders and arms ripple, serving as a sore reminder of his tantalising masculinity. He was horribly tempting.

He placed a chaste kiss on my mouth and, as he pulled away, said, "Your loss."

When he pushed away, I stared after his beautiful backside. My fingers tingled upon the sight, begging me to claw into the slabs of muscle on it. *Ugh.* That view was going to haunt me all day, and I knew he'd done it on purpose. I was incorrigibly susceptible to his allures. It didn't matter if my vagina was terribly sore. It still ached for his presence. Were his insatiable tendencies starting to rub off on me?

Still, recalling what he had made me wear to work yesterday, I forced myself to resist him. Today, I was determined to take his sexual frustration to new heights – sweet vengeance.

§ § §

Later, while we dressed, I feigned obliviousness as I grabbed a pair of black low-denier stockings and a black dress appropriate for work. Indeed, I was dressing for William's funeral.

Mentally, he appeared to be miles away from the present, doing the buttons of his sleeves whilst standing in front of my desk. Work was probably on his mind.

In my black lace underwear, I took a seat on my bed, and while stealing glances at him, slowly slid one stocking up my right calf. By the time he looked in my direction, I'd reached my knee.

The following scene was rather comical. After that initial glimpse, he looked back to the buttons of his white shirt as if he hadn't seen a thing. Then, his entire figure froze. Slowly, his head turned to register the view. I pretended not to notice his gawk and continued to dress as if I were the most innocent creature on the planet.

"Cara," he said, and his voice was flat.

I didn't look at him. "Yes?"

"What are you doing?"

"I'm getting dressed. What does it look like I'm doing?"

"It looks like you're trying to kill me." He sounded as menacing as a predatory animal that was weighing whether to attack.

I couldn't resist meeting his eyes then, and the heat of them was scorching. He looked barely reined. Still, I pretended to be unaffected. "Kill you? What – no. I'd never."

From his clenched jaw and the slight movement of his lips, I could tell he was gnashing his teeth.

"I don't deserve this," he declared.

"Oh, yes you do," I replied aloofly and got started on my left stocking. I was quicker with that one. "After what you made me wear yesterday, you really fucking do. You brought this upon yourself. You should think twice before you mess with me, Will. I'll have my revenge in the ways available to me."

He actually sobbed, albeit tearlessly. "Cara, no. Please don't. I'm sorry. It was only meant to be a joke. It was just a jumper. It's not like I'm going to tell you what to wear, just please don't wear that. I'm begging you. For my cock's sake – my sanity's sake."

Amusing how he said that as though they were interlinked.

I scoffed. "What sanity? You've never been sane."

Stretching up, I pulled the dress over my head and smiled cheekily at him while I brushed it off. "Do you know what I love about this dress, Will?" I turned my back to him. "When I bend over, even just a little, and lift it like this," I grabbed the hem of the somewhat loose skirt and raised it only a little as I curved forward, "I leave just enough to the imagination."

I eyed him over my shoulder. A speechless William was a rare sight. He looked about to lunge for me.

Stretching up again, I faced him. "Enjoy your day, darling. I'll make sure to pay you a few visits. Though, you may only look – not touch."

I wasn't sure if it was a whimper or a groan that came out of his mouth – a combination, perhaps. Either way, the noise amused me, so I was wearing a grin as I went for the door to wake Olivia. His footsteps charged after me, the sound prompting apprehension, so I increased my pace. Jason's bedroom was mere feet from my reach when he finally launched forward to wrap his arms around my waist.

Worried he was going to have his way with me again, I squeaked and writhed in his hold, but his hand was quick to cover my mouth.

"What are you doing?" he whispered, and by his tone, I realised he hadn't meant to have sex with me at all. Since my confusion silenced me, he saw it safe to remove his hand.

"I'm going to wake Livy," I answered, baffled.

His eyes flickered to Jason's door. "Why?"

"Because Livy told me to wake her. She's got a lunch date with Dawn, her mum."

"What if they're naked?" he whispered back. My heart raced while my eyes widened. Had Jason told him?

"Jason told you?" My voice was no louder than his.

He nodded. "Last night."

Unsure of how to proceed, I sighed and glanced at the door. "I don't think they would've had sex."

"She was quite drunk last night."

"That's just all the more reason. Jason would never touch her in such a state."

The corners of his mouth curled downwards while he cocked his head. "Fair point."

I turned for the door.

"Wait," he said and shoved my hand away from the handle. "If we're going to do this, allow me."

Puzzled, I gazed up at his profile and heard him clear his throat. As quietly as possible, he opened the door. Glimpsing through the darkness, his chest expanded with his deep inhalation, and he called, "Jason Night!"

For a second, I sincerely thought John was present. It made me gasp, but Jason's ensuing squeal drowned out the sound. I'd never heard him so frightened before.

"Fuck!" Jason roared. William guffawed beside me and bent to grab his knees. Spurred by hilarity, I joined him immediately.

Seeing as William had abandoned it, the door slid further open, and the view only made me laugh harder. Jason had jumped out of the bed while Olivia lay shocked amidst the tousled duvet, their eyes wide as they stared at us.

"Seriously, Will! You need to stop doing that. You're going to give me a heart attack. For fuck's sake – I thought you were Dad!" Jason chastised.

"That was the point!" William cackled. A tear leaked from his eye. "Ah, this gets me every time." He shook his head.

Like a bull, Jason stampeded to the door and slammed it shut. Turning towards each other, William and I resembled two young brats while we both cried of laughter.

"That was incredible," I said. "I had no idea you could do that."

It hadn't occurred to me that dating Jason's brother would provide an irreplaceable chance at seeing sides of my flatmate that I otherwise would not.

"Ah…I always used to do that when we were still living in the same house and I found him snoozing round the place. Never failed. Dad waking him up during his teenage years has traumatised him, and the sadist in me can't resist triggering it. But he's got himself to thank. If he'd woken up when he was supposed to, he wouldn't be liable to this."

"Brilliant. That was just brilliant." After a chuckle, I realised I'd have to check my makeup since I'd actually cried. "How's my makeup?"

He scanned my face. "I'm tempted to say that you don't need it since you really don't, but it's fine."

"Aw. You can be surprisingly sweet, Will."

He frowned. "I'm always sweet to you. Well, I try to be."

"Try is the key word," I teased. "I'm sorry to say it, but you're not 'always' sweet. Sometimes you're vulgar and direct instead, but I forgive you for it because I fancy you vulgar and direct. I quite like you just the way you are."

Seemingly moved, he merely stared at me, and I found it curious.

"What's with your face?" I asked.

"What?"

"You look funny. Did you expect anything else?"

"No, I'm just... That was sweet of you to say."

I chuckled and faced Jason's door. "Jason, I'm sorry I laughed."

"Honestly," Jason answered, "the two of you together is a lethal combination! I fear for humanity!"

I ignored his ridiculous comment and called, "Livy, are you up?"

"Yeah," came her reply. "Thanks for waking me. Nearly pissed myself, but I'm up."

I nodded. After what had happened with Colin, I was keen to keep a strict eye on her, just to make sure she wouldn't do anything stupid and self-destructive, so I decided to ask, "Are you free to hang out later?"

"Yeah."

"Come over around six, then?"

"Sure."

"Okay, see you then. Will and I are leaving for work now."

"I hope you'll have a shite day, Will!" Jason yelled.

"I'll tell Dad you said hello," William replied wittily, still amused, and stuffed his hands in his pockets. Looking towards me, he said, "He loves me."

I smirked. "Of course he does."

He studied me, but I couldn't gauge his thoughts. "Do you ever tease your sister?"

I chuckled. "Of course, but not like this. I don't sound similar enough to Mum, but I've pulled her leg a lot."

"I feel it's our duty as the elder sibling."

I laughed, but he appeared to be too absorbed in his current thoughts to find it contagious.

His head tilted. "Speaking of Phoebe, how is she?"

"She's well, I think."

"You think?"

I smiled. "Well, we've got that sort of bond where we don't tend to speak all that often. Last we spoke, she was doing fine, though."

"I see. So you haven't told her about me yet?" He looked slightly disappointed.

I frowned. "I've told her about our first and second encounter, but since I haven't spoken to her in about a month, she's not aware we're dating. Now that you mention it, I should probably give her a bell."

"What will you say?" he probed, grossly curious.

"Er, that we're dating?"

He turned his profile to me. I wished he hadn't done that, because I wanted to read the emotion in his eyes. "I'd like to meet her," he said, but his tone was quiet.

"Sure. She's coming over in late August. If you're still around by then, you'll see your chance."

When he faced me again, he looked so elated that I took a moment to appreciate it. It was obvious that the fact that I was willing to introduce him to a family member pleased him, and that filled me with glee. However, I had to admit that I was slightly surprised by how much it seemed to mean to him, especially so soon.

"You know I'm not going anywhere, Cara," he professed firmly. My heart throbbed. He could never say that a time too many.

"What's she like? Anything like you?" he asked then. "Does Jason know her?"

Phoebe had surely piqued his interest. "She's great. Very sweet, but quite introverted. Not shy, but reserved. She can be quite uncompromising when it comes to her values, though. She's also very artistic. Likes to draw a lot. I'm sure she'll adore you. She's always appreciated authentic individuals. And yes, Jason does know her. Quite well, actually. Phoebe loves him, but then again, who doesn't love your brother?"

He smiled crookedly. "Yes, I've always envied him for that. He's good with people. Much better than I am. I just don't have the same patience."

"Well, William…" I sighed. "You have a way of mattering deeply to those you do manage to charm. You're the type one either hates or loves. And those who hate you simply don't understand you. I wouldn't care about it if I were you."

"Oh, I don't," he assured me, and his smile turned smug.

"You're so unapologetically you," I remarked with a tilt of my head. As I admired him, I couldn't help the smitten smile on my face, because I truly loved that part of him. It earned my respect.

"You're not so different, you know." He withdrew his hand from his pocket to ruffle my hair.

"Now, why'd you have to do that? Now I've got to redo my ponytail."

"Couldn't resist."

"Can you ever?"

"Oh, Cara, you've no idea how good I am at resistance." His eyes gleamed while he said it, and it made me frown.

"What's that supposed to mean?"

"That it's relative. Anyway, let's leave for work, or we'll be late." He turned on his heel.

"You don't get to decide when a conversation is over," I grumbled after him.

"Watch me."

"Fuck you, Mr Ambiguous."

§ § §

One thing the Tube was great for, aside from being the most efficient means of transportation in a city like London, was zoning out into daydreams. Today, my favourite daydream was standing opposite me, reading the news on his iPhone amidst the densely crowded train. Even though people surrounded us from every angle, I only saw him.

Last night with him had been dreamlike – fantastically surreal. I'd never experienced such intense sex in my life. It was as though he'd added a whole new dimension to it, beyond that of the physical aspect. He had suggested more eye contact, and now I could understand why. Staring into his piercing eyes, I'd felt as if our minds had connected, not just our bodies. Everything had been intimate and extreme. Plain old sex seemed empty in comparison, if not even bleak. It had been unlike anything else. Uncanny. Out of this world.

It had struck me as a revelation. I'd never been able to distinguish sex from making love, but William had made the difference crystal clear. While sex with him had been fantastic from the very start, he had surely raised the bar yesterday. I'd thought our earlier sessions had been remarkable enough, but after last night, he had shown me the very definition of mind-blowing sex. My thoughts had been completely obliterated. I'd only felt, and what I'd felt was pure ecstasy – exultation, even. Compared to it, my past three years with Aaron appeared trivial and even bland.

William remained oblivious to his surroundings while I continued to stare at him. Flashing images of last night showed no mercy to my mind. I was staring at him, but I didn't really see him – not in the present tense, anyhow. His clothes were gone, and a faint layer of sweat glistened on his powerful chest in the dim light of my bedroom. Around me were his arms, caging me to him as he met each of my descents, all while his gaze burrowed into mine.

Slowly, heat climbed to my face and prickled across my scalp. I was taken aback when acute arousal flooded my head to the extent that I felt about to burst. Truly, I'd never felt so close to bursting. I could hardly breathe. Tensing, I dug my nails into my palms and released a loud, tormented breath.

Hearing it, William's eyes dashed anxiously to mine. Reading the look on my face, his eyebrows knitted. "You alright?"

I couldn't answer. The aggressive urge to jump on him and rip his clothes off was stronger than any other I'd endured. I'd never wanted him this badly, or any other person for that matter. It was ridiculous. Had we been alone in here, I'd be a lost cause.

My eyes widened when a drop of lubrication slid down my inner thigh. *Oh my God.* I was going to perish. This was it. I was going to combust at the hands of unbearable lust.

"Cara," William prompted and stowed his phone in the inner pocket of his suit jacket. Had I not been so momentarily overwhelmed by my extreme desire for him, I would have offered a thought of pity to the fact that he was wearing a full suit in this hot weather. It especially couldn't be comfortable here on the train, where it was so humid that it might as well have been a moving steam room.

"I'm fine," I wheezed out and tore my eyes away from him. But I wasn't remotely fine. I was barely holding it together.

When he grabbed my jaw to make me look at him again, I actually hissed. His action evoked the fresh memory of when he'd done that while we made love last night, and the intensity of his eyes had looked exactly the same.

After gauging the frenzied emotion that spun in my eyes, he gaped. "Are you…?" It was almost a whisper.

I huffed out another loud breath and tried to ignore my pounding heart. His lips were so close. If I leaned in just slightly, I could kiss him. Responding to impulse, I tried, but his grip on my jaw prevented me. Sadistic humour swirled in his eyes while a wolfish grin dominated his mouth.

"Oh, you just turned the tables against your favour, darling," he whispered, eyes flickering around us to see if anyone were eavesdropping. "So much for trying to tease me with your dress today, eh?"

A quiet whimper flew out of my mouth. He was driving me crazy, and he wasn't even doing anything. *God*, I had it bad. There was no doubting it anymore: for the first time in my life, I was in love.

Mirth clouded his irises as he laughed. "You should see your face."

Suddenly, the train stopped to let passengers off and on, and

I grabbed the opportunity to add some distance between us. I couldn't bear his proximity right now because, in his presence, I felt high. As I snuck away, I glanced at him over my shoulder. He was laughing to himself while shaking his head.

"See you later, then," he called after me. I pretended not to have heard him, but since the surrounding crowd looked puzzled at me, my blush intensified.

By the time I got off the train, I'd regained my equilibrium. To manage it, I had forced myself to think of my dead cat from childhood, Lizzie – anything depressing, basically. However, when I felt the familiar electricity of our skin making contact, I lost it again.

I'd nearly reached the stairs now, and when I turned to acknowledge him, his grip tightened around my hand.

His amusement had not passed. "Ladies first," he said, and gestured towards the steps.

As I moved to climb them, his gaze dropped to the skirt of my dress. His jaw drew shut. Glancing over his shoulder, he observed the queue of people behind him, particularly the men, before he moved closer to me. We were almost the same height now, albeit he was slightly taller.

Leaning next to my ear, he quietly stated, "Bit too revealing that dress, in settings like these."

Heat accumulated in my face while I hurried to hold my dress firmly around my thighs. I hadn't thought of that. From this angle, the people below could probably see more than I'd intended.

Seeing my reaction, he smirked. "I've got you covered, love," he purred. "Literally."

"Thanks," I replied, embarrassed.

"Yeah, gratitude is actually warranted. I'm not doing this for me at all. You see, personally, I don't mind people admiring what's mine. I revel in their envy. Boosts my ego. I love the idea that they can look, but not touch. I can, however." For emphasis, he placed his hands on my hips.

He could be so odd. Truly, his way of giving compliments was remarkably eccentric.

"Clown," I muttered, which earned me a laugh. "You are so odd sometimes."

"Aren't we all?"

I scoffed. "Compared to you, I'm ordinary."

"Ordinary, standard, normal…I tend to see those words as synonyms of boring."

A giggle snuck out of me. "That doesn't surprise me in the least."

"And you're not boring, Cara. You're anything but."

That was a much better compliment. "Thanks," I said, and I meant it. "Neither are you."

"Could we be more compatible?" His tone was playful.

I shook my head. "I don't think so."

"Neither do I."

15

THE CURSE OF RED JUMPERS

AS WE EXITED THE CONFERENCE ROOM AFTER OUR meeting with the team, William suddenly stopped.

"I don't know about you, but I'm in desperate need of a coffee," he said. Had he read my mind?

"Same. I'll go get some from the breakroom."

Just as I was about to walk away, he gripped my elbow. "No, I'll do it. I'd like some fresh air to clear my head—" his eyes scanned my stockings—"so I thought I'd step out."

I smirked. My attire was clearly bothering him. "If you insist."

"I do. Continue your work on the DD in the meantime."

"Alright. See you soon."

Forgetting our surroundings, he leaned closer, intending to give me a kiss, but the fear in my eyes quickly reminded him that he'd receive a slap if he moved an inch further. Jerking backwards, he straightened himself while gazing down at me with wide eyes.

I glanced around us immediately, but no one seemed to be paying us attention, thankfully.

"I'm so sorry," he said very quietly. "I'm so tired, I—"

"It's fine."

He swallowed. "It won't happen again. I'm on autopilot today."

"Your autopilot sucks," I muttered.

He nodded. "Yeah. A coffee should fix it."

"Then go get one. Quickly."

With that, he handed his laptop over to me and turned around to approach the lifts.

§ § §

It was nearly time for lunch when my boss – who was also my lover – returned from his errand. What an odd combination. I'd never thought I had it in me to sleep with my superior. Seen from the outside, it must have made me appear like a gold digger. It didn't help my case that William came from a wealthy background.

In his hands, I saw two cups of Starbucks coffee. A smile stretched my lips as I tried to read the ink on the side, but his fingers were covering it.

"As ordered," he said and placed the smallest cup on my desk. Still smiling, I wrapped my hand around the warm material and turned it to read the writing.

Spare me from the curse of red jumpers, it said, and it made me chuckle. He was clearly seeking to earn my forgiveness for the clothes he'd made me wear yesterday, and I had an inkling as to why. I knew my attire was bothering him today, so he was probably trying to inspire my mercy. Knowing him, he was hopeful that a display of mercy would include tending to his insatiable libido.

"And this one's for you," he said and put the other one on Elisabeth's desk. "Soya latte is your regular order, right?"

Elisabeth's eyebrows curved with her surprise, and the sight made me giggle. I doubted William had ever fetched her coffee before. "It is," she confirmed. "Thanks, Will. This was actually sorely needed."

"You mentioned you'd had a bad night's sleep."

Amused, she raised the beverage to take a sip. "What's got you into such a benevolent mood?"

He shrugged. "I've read somewhere that kindness can be contagious," he said and glanced at me. I smirked at his insinuation. He was indeed trying to inspire mercy in me.

"Have you adopted the religion of Dalai Lama?" she asked, humoured. "Be kind whenever it's possible. It is always possible," she quoted the wise Tibetan Buddhist.

"I may have come across some of his teachings lately."

"Striving for inner peace, Will?" I teased after a sip.

"It speaks!" he replied, and his eyes darted to the cup I was holding. Anxiety swirled in his eyes for a moment, and I relished the sight. Though, I did detect some relief as well. Was it because I was drinking it? Did he perceive it as apology accepted? Probably. But it wasn't quite right. Not yet.

"It?" I echoed. "Are you referring to my divine status?"

Ellie burst out laughing at my joke. It was blasphemy, but, yes, I had just compared myself to heavenly power. While I wasn't religious, I didn't usually take pleasure in making light of religion. Generally, I was one for respecting religious beliefs. My personal persuasion was that respect and tolerance was the cure to all cultural arrogance and ignorance across the globe. Live and let live, simply. However, when I was up against William, I would resort to any means capable of challenging him. I demanded the last word.

"I call narcissist," William countered with a twinkle in his eyes.

"Bow at my feet, you useless mortal," I taunted and took another sip.

"Useless?" He barely managed to suppress a chuckle. His lips were another story. They formed a breathtaking grin, and it made my heart tingle to know that I had put it there. I adored a smiling William. When it wasn't at the expense of other people, he was enchanting whenever he smiled.

"You heard me." I showed him the writing on my cup. Useless, indeed.

His smile faded immediately before he cleared his throat. "Right. About that, could I have a word with you in my office?"

"Mm, let me check," I replied with a tone of scepticism and opened the window of his virtual calendar. "Looks like you've still got some paperwork to do at the moment, so it will have to wait. The transaction between Elixerion Pharmaceuticals and Porter BioScience isn't going to complete itself. Artificial intelligence just isn't quite there yet. You're a few generations too early, I'm afraid. Tough luck."

"Cara." He sounded despairing.

"Yes, dear human?"

Ellie pressed her lips together and focused on her screen, clearly eager to hand us a version of privacy.

"I'll stay after hours," he argued.

"I'm afraid god's busy right now. You'll have to manage without me for a while." I showed him my to-do list.

He raised a brow. "As my legal assistant, it's in your job description to aid me with my work to the best of your ability. That, right now, is seeing me in my office. If you don't obey," *obey*, "it will ultimately affect my work, so if you'd *please*—" He gestured towards his door.

"I hear your prayers, my mortal subject, when you put it like that," I muttered and pushed my seat out. "I shall do god's work." I grabbed my cup of coffee to bring it with me.

"Good luck," Ellie said to me.

"Thank you," William replied before I could, as though she'd been speaking to him. A confounded expression crossed my face when I looked at him. Soon enough, laughter spilled out of my mouth. He was certainly on edge today, wasn't he?

Groaning, he gripped my elbow to guide me away, and, behind us, Ellie's snorts echoed through the office.

After opening the door, he dragged me into his office and locked it behind us. High on my horse, I strode towards his white leather sofa and reclined, leisurely. As I crossed my legs, I made sure that the top of my stockings was on full display. Meanwhile, I rested my left arm on the sofa's backrest and passed him a confident smile.

"So..." I feigned obliviousness. "I should warn you, I'm not a certified psychologist, but I do make a hobby out of it. I'm also very expensive, but I'm sure we can come to an agreement on the price. With that out of the way, what can I do for you?"

He started shaking his head to himself, and, all of a sudden, laughter rumbled from the depth of his lungs. A huge grin split his face apart while he tossed his head back and surrendered to his fit. Startled, I watched him in awe. Was I truly that hilarious to him?

"My God, Cara," he uttered and wiped a fallen tear away. "You're something else."

Since I was fighting back a grin, it turned into a crooked version. "Glad you recognise it."

He stalked towards me then, but I raised my foot before he could proceed too far. With the sole of my stiletto pressed flat against his crotch, I angled my heel, gently, to poke his evident erection.

"William," I scolded theatrically. "I can't fuck a client."

Remaining still, arousal flared through his eyes while his Adam's apple ascended and fell. A breath later, his jaw clenched. "You're torturing me."

A wicked smile stretched my lips. "It's called divine retribution."

His jaw flexed again, hands twitching by his sides before he raised his right to wrap it around my ankle. "Cara, please. I can't concentrate on work."

My eyes drank him in. He was such a vision – what a beautiful man.

I took another sip of coffee while I watched his expression beg for my carnal attention. I couldn't believe I was even considering doing something like this – it would be incredibly unprofessional

– but he was so damned tempting. Perhaps I could make an exception, just for today?

Growing impatient, he said, "Please. Let me worship you."

I pursed my lips. Mild punishment was surely in order, so I was dragging things along because I fancied him grovelling.

"You are asking me to commit gross misconduct, Will," I reminded him soberly. While I couldn't deny how desperately my body ached for his sexual treatment, part of me was reluctant to act on it for fear of getting caught. I knew the odds were small, but it wasn't impossible. Either way, the idea of doing something as risky as this launched adrenaline into my bloodstream, and somehow, it only intensified my lust for him.

"In other words," I continued after a beat, "you're asking me to risk my job for you. We both know what the consequence might be if we follow through with this."

"We won't get caught," he insisted. "I swear. Everyone's heading for lunch in a minute. And, if we do get caught, I'll claim full responsibility."

It didn't work quite like that. Either way, I said, "On your knees, please." I knew he wasn't going to do it. He was much too proud, which was why it brought me such joy to tease him about it.

"Cara."

I raised a brow and pointed to myself. "Hello? God?"

"You've got to be kidding me." He groaned and ran his hands through his hair. I envied them. I wanted to do that, too.

I tilted my head and stared challengingly into his eyes. "Worship, you said."

He blew his cheeks out before he puffed out the air with some frustration. Next, he shocked me by dropping straight onto his knees. I was sure my eyes had never been wider, nor my mouth, for that matter. William Night was kneeling in front of me, just for a chance to ravish me. I would never forget this moment. My heart was beating so fast that it could be mistaken for something static.

Placing my coffee on the table, I stood up with a complacent smile while he remained on his knees, eyes entreating me to indulge him. Stepping forward, I reached for my dress to lift it just a little. Raising one leg, I let it rest over his shoulder while I clasped the nape of his neck to bring his face closer to the beckoning wetness between my legs.

"Was this what you had in mind for lunch?" I asked teasingly.

His nose skimmed my underwear, and I heard him inhale my scent deep into his lungs. "Yes," he said, ravenous, and dared to let a hand trace my stocking. Sliding it across the back of my calf, he made his way towards my inner thigh. My skin tingled beneath his gentle, warm touch.

"Devour me, then."

I gasped at his subsequent swiftness. At lightning speed, he brought my leg over his free shoulder and proceeded to stand. Afraid of falling, I squealed as I crouched over him to maintain my balance. Meanwhile, he rushed towards the sofa behind me.

He launched us onto it, and my heart had barely managed two beats by the time he climbed atop me, hovering. When his eyes arrested mine, the lust that swam in them rendered me momentarily frozen. He was a force I couldn't defeat.

"Are we actually going to do this?" I asked when some panic seized me.

"Oh, absolutely, darling," he purred and dived for my neck, lips stroking my pulse with clinical precision. I'd never thought how well he read my body was going to be a cause for concern. Were these walls soundproof?

As I melted beneath his touch, my hands journeyed through the soft strands of his dark brown hair. His lips climbed higher, towards the line of my jaw, then grazed across it until he found my mouth.

Damn him and his wonderful mouth. I was helpless against it. He used it so well, kissing me into oblivion. Pushing his tongue past my lips, he teased mine masterfully while his large, warm hands roamed across my body, caressing and squeezing. The rapid stream of my blood rushed to the space between my legs, making it throb – already preparing me for his intrusion. Truly, it was uncanny how quickly and how effortlessly he managed to excite me.

When his hand slid under my dress, his fingers – light as a feather – skimmed the bare skin between my stockings and my lace underwear. His appreciative groan pushed into my mouth and, startling me, he shoved the bulk of his erection right against my entrance. *Oh my God*, the friction.

Breaking away from his enchanting kiss, I turned my head to stare blankly at his desk. "Will," I panted. "What if someone catches us?"

He gripped my jaw to make me look at him. I nearly sobbed. He was much too tempting. How was I supposed to resist him?

"I locked the door, Cara."

"Are the walls soundproof?"

He grinned. "Yes. We'll be fine. In your own words, you brought this upon yourself," he said, and from the breathiness of his voice, his arousal seemed substantial. *Christ,* his libido was unlike any other I'd encountered. We'd had so much sex lately, and yet it was apparent that he was still nowhere near satiated.

"I've proved I can do quick," he reminded me and pushed my dress upwards until it gathered around my waist. "We'll be quick."

"You're going to be my ruin," I complained and closed my eyes to spare myself from the gorgeous sight of him.

"I wouldn't have it any other way," he said resolutely and gripped my knickers to tug them down my legs. "Fuck me, Cara," he uttered through a loud exhalation. "These stockings are lethal."

I should never have worn them. I'd overestimated myself, severely, and now I was paying the price. Worse was it that the aching desire to connect with him only abated when he entered me. When he wasn't inside of me, the urge to be closer to him was a merciless constant. I hoped for the life of me that this was only a phase, because if I was going to endure it for the rest of my life, I might as well wave my sanity goodbye. I'd never wanted someone so desperately. I craved him more than anything else.

I soon realised that there was little use in trying to resist him. The desire to feel him within me was simply too extreme. Denying him was so painful a thought that I didn't even consider it a reasonable option.

Surrendering to temptation, I pushed against him until he obliged and leaned back. Without wasting a second, I lunged for his trousers. If this relationship pulled through, I would break records with how swiftly I could undo trousers. Practice makes perfect.

"That's the spirit," he said appreciatively and twirled the length of my ponytail around his wrist. By now, I knew him too well not to realise why he did exactly that. He was ensuring that I wouldn't manage to blow him, and I hated it. One day soon, I would demand to perform fellatio on him. Though, I expected I'd have to handcuff him first if I was going to manage it.

That idea made a cunning smile nest on my mouth. As the plan formed in my head, I looked up at him with a gleam in my eye. If only he knew what he had in wait.

Suddenly, he tugged my head back, and the pain of it made me whimper. Lowering his face to mine, he stared intensely into my eyes. "When you have that look in your eye, I'm reluctant to be quick about this," he warned.

I almost said "sorry", but bit my tongue to avoid surrendering my pride.

"You've got five minutes," I replied instead. "That's all you get."

His eyes glinted – the challenge aroused him. "Five minutes to make you come? *Mon amour*, I only need one."

I wanted to tear his self-assured smirk off his mouth, but, before I could, he placed his hand at the centre of my chest and pushed me down to lie flat across the sofa. Tucking my thighs over his shoulders, he gave me a lecherous smile while he slowly lowered his head towards my slit. When his breath breezed across it, I realised just how wet I was.

I closed my eyes and prayed to the god I didn't believe in that no one would knock on his door within the next couple of minutes. After that attempt at religion, I brought my arm over my mouth to help me quiet the whimpers that were soon to battle against my lips.

When he pushed his tongue out to draw a circle around my clit, my whole body tensed. The nerves were overly sensitive after all the sex we'd had, and it made me realise that he was going to prove himself right. Considering how sensitive I was at normal, and how dangerously skilled he was with his tongue, this would take no time at all. Liberation, in the form of delicious chemicals, was already lurking around the corner. I doubted I'd require more than a minute.

To my relief, he'd meant it when he said he would be quick. He did not waste his time triggering my climax. He'd barely completed three circles before his pitiless tongue targeted my clit with perfect precision, flicking up and down and sometimes sideways.

My breath was on lockdown in my lungs. Afraid that anyone would hear us, I fought to contain even the smallest sound, but the lack of oxygen seemed to speed up the process. The tension rallied in my gut, radiating from where his merciless tongue pleasured my nerves. Every fibre of my being seemed to contract while I squeezed my eyes shut to withstand the tormenting build.

Relentlessly, he continued, until I truly thought I was going to faint since I didn't dare to breathe. When my quivers started, I tugged his hair and felt him tighten his hold of thighs to keep me in place. Desperate for release, my back arched off the sofa while I shook my head to myself, about to implode.

At last, spots rained past my eyes as the acute force of a blissful orgasm raged through my veins, mollifying me. I'd never climaxed so quietly before, and judging from the magnitude of it, I deserved a standing ovation.

I'd barely been allowed thirty seconds to recover by the time I felt the crest of his shaft gliding across my saturated folds.

"That wasn't even a minute." He smirked above me, his lips glistening with my fluids. "I commend your silence, though. Very impressive."

"Sometimes, I don't know whether to slap or kiss you," I replied on a ragged breath. The sound of his chuckle made my chest tingle. In the light-blue colour of his eyes, pure affection danced.

"Why worry about that when we can have sex instead?" he said and, upon that note, thrust into me.

Oh my God. Nothing would ever compare to the sensation of the first thrust. It felt so fucking good.

When a groan escaped me, I rushed to cover my mouth. Even though the walls were soundproof, I dared not trust them.

"You look like you could use some help with that," he teased and removed my hand to silence me with his mouth instead. I could taste myself on his lips, and the presence of my own flavour – on and within his mouth – heightened my arousal. I loved the idea of him being covered in traces of me.

He'd kissed me for a while when he suddenly pushed himself up and withdrew from within me. What was he doing?

I was about to ask when he moved off the sofa to grab my hips. Flipping me around, he pulled me towards him until my bum pointed straight at him while I remained on all fours atop the furniture.

"Since you demanded quick, this position is better," he said and, at once, pushed into me again. From this angle, his thick shaft rubbed right across my front wall, causing me to clench and tremble around him. Lowering my head, I bit into my hand. *Fuck*, this was going to be intense.

"Don't be too rough," I pleaded. "I'm very sore."

"Don't worry, love. I'll give you the best massage you've ever had," he purred and gently retreated. The motion he started was staggering. While it wasn't rough, it was certainly fast.

I realised he was holding back. Instead of burying himself

entirely within me with each thrust, he focused on stimulating the head of his length instead, all while remaining acutely aware of that sweet spot inside of me. Was there anything sexual he couldn't do to perfection? His erotic prowess was invincible. Indeed, he was massaging my walls in the most pleasurable way.

When my own hand muffled a relatively loud whimper, he grabbed my ponytail to drag my head back. Soon after, his large palm covered my mouth to help me keep quiet, and I appreciated it more than I was able to express. Like this, I was free just to enjoy him.

After a single, harsh shove, he whispered in my ear, "You feel so fucking good, Cara. I will never have enough of this – of you."

I moaned into his hand, my breath condensing on it. Closing my eyes, I marvelled at how lovely it felt to have him within me again, even if I was much sorer than ideal. But what I found was that my soreness only increased my awareness of him inside of me, and I was thankful for that. It served as a reminder of how apparent it was that he belonged there.

As his shaft continued to strike that susceptible spot, my muscles flexed to respond to the tension that amassed within me. I was climbing again.

"Come on, Cara," he commanded and used his free hand to rub my clit. The sensation was extreme. Pleasure surged up my spine, causing me to arch again. Holding my breath, my face contorted as I focused only on how close I was to finding bliss.

But upon a particularly precise thrust, he provoked my quivers. My toes curled in my stilettos. Before I knew it, I collapsed beneath him, but he followed my descent. In and out, he continued to plough into me. I thought I would explode. How I could produce such pleasure, and endure it, was beyond my comprehension. Before I'd met him, I wouldn't have thought it was possible to experience something as immense as this – that I could physically contain something so great.

"Mph!" I whimpered into his hand. My walls squeezed him –

a warning of my imminent climax.

"Ah, fuck," he groaned. "Keep that pressure, darling. Come for me," he demanded and continued to shove himself into me with that mind-blowing pattern.

I stopped breathing again, and it triggered my peak. It was like my mind detonated when I was finally liberated of the torment. Overwhelmed, my back charged up against him while I cried my sweet release into his palm.

"Shit," he groaned again, grinding his teeth. From the sound, I knew he was close. "Cara, I'm reaching it."

"Yes." I pushed back against him, hoping to help him get there faster. After shoving harshly into me four more times, he suddenly pulled out. A moment later, the low pitch of his groans echoed in my ears as he spilled his warm release on my cheeks.

I hadn't expected that, so I turned my head to look at him. "Why did you pull out?"

Studying my bum, he bit his lower lip, smiling. "You have no idea how hot you look right now."

A wave of heat slapped my face. "William," I whined.

He laughed. "That said, I definitely prefer creampies."

"Then why did you pull out?"

Grinning, he approached his desk. "Thought you'd appreciate it."

I frowned. "Why? So I can wear your sperm on my dress?"

"It's not on your dress."

"No, but it will be as soon as I pull it down. Seriously, Will. How am I supposed to clean this up?"

He laughed again as he grabbed his blue suit jacket from his desk chair. Reaching into the front pocket, he withdrew a white handkerchief. Since I hadn't expected it, I smiled at how considerate he was being, cleaning up after himself. This was even better than if he'd emptied himself within me. I'd hardly want to walk out with his sperm trickling down my thighs until I found a toilet.

"Thanks," I said as he returned to my figure in the sofa.

Wearing a smile, he dried me off.

"Next time," I continued, "you're welcome to come in my mouth instead."

His eyes drizzled of erotic thoughts when they met mine, but he said nothing. Dropping the handkerchief on the floor, he joined me on the sofa, though he reclined towards the other end. Sprawled over each other, we lay there for a few minutes, recovering.

Finally, I rolled onto my side and studied him lazily. His eyes were closed, and his neck was curled over the sofa's edge.

"Will?"

"Yeah?" He sounded perfectly content and didn't so much as stir.

"Do you think this will ever end?"

He tensed. "What?"

"Wanting each other?"

Lifting his head, he opened his eyes and stared at me for some time. "While I can't speak for you, I doubt it."

I sighed. "Then I'm fucked."

"Literally." He smirked. "Why do you say that, though?"

"Because I never thought I had it in me to do something like this. Three weeks ago, I was telling Ellie about how unprofessional I thought it was to fuck someone while at work. Now I feel like the world's biggest hypocrite."

"That's my fault. I've corrupted you." He didn't look remotely unhappy with that.

I glanced away. "That's precisely my point. Well, it's not your fault per se. I mean it's not your fault I react like this. But…you're making me change as a person."

When I looked at him, his expression was tender. "Cara, don't worry," he said. "While I doubt it'll end – the wanting each other – it's likely to change. Takes a different form after a while."

I sometimes forgot what a deep man he was at heart. If I ever introduced him to Dad, the two of them were likely to appreciate one another rather a lot. Like Dad, William relished conceptual and philosophical ideas. I could already hear them discussing different beliefs, energetically and enthusiastically, their dinner getting cold on the table between them. Dad would absolutely adore him, and so would Mum.

"What sort of form?"

He shrugged. "An abstract one. Instead of wanting me only physically, you'll want me in other ways."

My heart throbbed. It knew precisely what he meant. I'd want his love more than anything else. But the truth was, I was there already.

Staring at him, I wondered if he felt the same. I knew he had feelings for me, but I didn't trust that they had transitioned into love yet. Part of me wanted to ask out of curiosity, but the larger part didn't, as I didn't think I'd appreciate knowing the answer just yet.

If I asked him now only to learn that he didn't feel the same way, I would definitely be hurt. I doubted I'd become insecure, as that wasn't in my nature, but I would feel discouraged. Indeed, at this point, I was likely to become somewhat withdrawn if he rejected me, at least for a while. When considering that we had only just begun to explore where things could lead, that wouldn't be ideal.

And, if he was in love with me, hearing it could make me feel obligated to requite it. Since I was still unsure about whether my feelings for him were momentary or lasting, I didn't want that. After all, I had only just realised it myself. Now, my feelings had to stand the test of time. I had to be sure that they were solid – that they weren't flimsy – before I confessed to him. If I still felt this way in a few months, I would tell him regardless of whether I thought he felt the same way or not.

I was also inclined to remain cautious because of the red flags I'd detected, and I was still scouting for more. Confessing that I was in love with him right now would be far too soon. While I had feelings for him, I wasn't sure he was *the one* – that he would be worth my devotion and that a relationship would succeed. From my understanding, feelings were only one part of the puzzle. For a relationship to work out, there were several other things which had to be in place; many other factors had to be considered. Were our goals compatible, for instance? Our views on marriage? Children? What about our temperaments? Could I tolerate his flaws for years to come? Could he tolerate mine? As I pondered it, I recognised that it boiled down to one very simple question: would we be destructive or constructive together?

Thus far, we'd been both. However, ever since I'd agreed to date him, I thought it was fair to say that we'd been on the constructive end of the spectrum. It helped to remember how attentive William had been when I'd explained my concerns to him after that dreadful night when I'd brought Aaron home with me and William had been there. Instead of getting defensive, William had listened to everything I had to say and had accepted blame where it was due. Since then, he'd worked hard to show me that he intended to mend his ways, and I wasn't blind to it. Even after we'd argued yesterday, we'd been able to communicate and reconcile within a few hours. Both of us had spent that time trying to understand the other's perspective, which had enabled us to identify our own mistakes. What I took from it was that William was indeed a constructive person. His reaction and approach to criticism was a healthy one, and that gave me hope for a future between us.

However, to be sure of it, I required more time.

"Anyway," he glanced at his Rolex, "seeing as it's time for lunch, thanks for giving me the best meal I've ever had."

I smiled. "Same."

"On another note, are you busy this Saturday?"

Sensing where he was going, my smile widened. "No."

"Well, how about another date? My place this time. I'll cook dinner for you."

Drool accumulated in my mouth instantaneously. Having tasted the fruits of his culinary skills before, I was confident it would be quite the experience.

I dragged myself towards him. Cuddling his chest, I collected his scent in my lungs and listened as his heart hammered against my ear. From its beats, I could tell he was more anxious than he let on, and I had an inkling as to why. During the scene in his penthouse yesterday, I'd told him that the pace we were moving at intimidated me. So, he was probably worried he was pushing his luck right now.

But he wasn't. I knew there were plenty of women out there who complained about their men not taking enough initiative or making their interest clear enough, and here was I, moaning about the opposite. Well, I was done with it.

"I'd love to," I said and hugged him tightly. "But until then, let's take a break when it comes to sex, alright? My vagina is destroyed. I mean it."

"Fine."

"Thank god," I groaned.

He chuckled. "Make the most of your brief holiday."

"I will. Your sexual appetite is that of a rabbit."

Tucking a lock of my hair behind my ear, he said, "Only when it comes to you."

Flattered, I beamed at him. "At what time on Saturday?"

"I've got plans with Alex and Andy earlier in the day, so perhaps around seven?"

The mention of Alex made me frown. "Right. That mysterious Alex. Who is he? Jason's mentioned him a few times."

He nodded. "He's one of my best friends. Him, Andy and I are a bit of a trio. Been that way for as long as I can remember."

"I see. And what does Alex do for a living? He a lawyer as well?"

He shook his head and was quiet for a beat. "Does Winton Properties ring a bell?"

Winton Properties? I could have sworn I'd heard that name somewhere. Racking my brain, I frowned to myself until a shocked expression obliterated it. "Alexander Winton? *Millionaire* Alexander Winton is your best friend?" I asked, astonished, and propped myself on my arms to stare down at him.

He looked hesitant, one eyebrow furrowing somewhat. "You're aware I'm a millionaire too, right?"

Shocked at the disclosure, I gawked in total disbelief. It felt like something was sucking the air out of my body. I was dating a millionaire? What the hell? I wouldn't tell that to a living soul. "Are you?"

It was obvious from the way his eyes smiled that my reaction charmed him. "Yeah. Not as rich as Alex, though, but then that's hard to manage. Still, I'm so glad you're not a gold digger. And in any case, he's not single. He's got a dreadful girlfriend named Abigail."

Majorly offended that he could even think along those lines, I smacked his chest, which earned me a huff.

"Don't be daft," I scolded. "How can you think like that? I'm offended."

He glared back. "Christ. I specifically said you aren't like that, and I was only joking. Well, about most of it. Abigail *is* awful. Regardless, you know I get territorial about you. I can't help it. It's out of my control, even if I do try to keep a tight rein on it."

I rolled my eyes. "You're such a caveman. How your genes have survived extinction – actually, that's probably *how* your genes have survived extinction."

"Exactly." He sounded so complacent that I rolled my eyes again, but I gave him a puzzled look upon remembering a certain detail about Alexander.

"Isn't Alexander a year older than you?"

Nonchalant, he supported his head by entwining his fingers behind it. After a shrug, he said, "So is Andy." He was?

"Did you attend the same school? Since you say you've been friends for as long as you can remember?"

"Yeah. I've known them ever since nursery school, and we

also went to the same prep school and Westminster together."

My jaw fell. "You went to *Westminster?*"

"House Ashburnham. Definitely helped me get into Cambridge."

"Wow. That's amazing. What was it like? I thought it was a boarding school?"

"Not exclusively, and it was brilliant. Definitely sending my kids there."

"Wait, hang on. So you were in a year above your own? Or did you just happen to play with Andy and Alex one day and boom, your friendship bloomed?"

He smirked. "Bit of both, really. We played together in nursery school, but I was also in a year above my own."

Impressed, I averted my eyes and shook my head to myself. There was no denying it – the man was exceptionally intelligent, and it excited me in ways only he could manage.

"Clever fellow, I know." I could hear from his tone that he wasn't being serious. "But it was Dad's initiative. I learnt to read fluently when I was four, so he kicked me into school as fast as he could to maintain my momentum."

Leaning up again, I gaped at him. I'd learnt to read when I was five. Though, fluently? I was at least six, and I had thought that was enough of an achievement. How intelligent was he, really?

"That's outstanding. Are you joking?"

He shook his head. "Learnt to read upside down first, actually. Was quite odd. Dad would always read the newspaper at the kitchen table in the mornings, but he never held it. It was just lying flat across the table, and since I always sat opposite him, it just happened that way. I'd study the letters every morning, wishing I knew how to decipher them like Dad did, and then, one day, it just clicked. I was three then. After that, my parents hired a tutor to help me learn how to read fluently. By age four, I'd managed."

My grin was both amused and astonished, and I covered it

with my hand, disbelieving. "You're joking. You're so joking!"

He laughed. "I'm really not. You can ask Dad next time you see him. The first word I read was 'apple', and I remember it vividly. I pointed to it in the newspaper, demanding his attention from across the table, and read it out loud. You should've seen his face. I've not seen it like that since. Gutted that I set the bar for myself so early on."

"That's insane!" I couldn't stop my laughter. I was completely flabbergasted. Caught by my giggles, he shook beneath me.

"Fun fact."

"Incredible. Are you a genius?"

He frowned. "I don't care for labels like that. I only care about what I produce."

"How noble," I teased and patted his chest. "Your brain turns me on."

"I thought you said you were sore."

"I am, and now I'm depressed because of it."

He burst out laughing.

I looked bashfully away from him and grabbed his wrist to check the time. "We need to get back to work."

"We need to get lunch. I'm starving, and for food this time."

"After you," I said and climbed off him.

Once I'd pulled on my underwear again and brushed off my dress, I said, "Well then. I'll leave the bill for my service on your desk by the end of the day. I hope you found my therapeutic expertise worthwhile."

A chuckle escaped him as he loosened his tie to redo it. "Best shrink in London, without a doubt. After this, I guarantee I'll be the most efficient I've ever been."

"Good." Smiling, I moved towards him to help him refasten his tie. I sensed him study me, but I resisted meeting his gaze.

"I might need to schedule in daily appointments, though," he said, and when I glanced up, his eyes were examining the fresh colour of my face in detail.

Completing his tie, I patted his chest with a raised brow. "You wish."

"Make it come true."

I laughed. "No. This was an exception to the rule. Now, back to work."

"Lunch first."

"Right."

HARD LIMIT

THE FOLLOWING SATURDAY, I STUDIED MYSELF IN THE full-length mirror of my bedroom. Swivelling round to study my backside, I grinned. "He'll swoon," I told myself and dropped my gaze to my bum – a bum he'd often told me he found "enticing". Well, tonight, I was going to use it against him.

I was wearing the whole package – a black lace bustier which my black stockings were attached to, as well as a very, very skimpy thong. If he'd found my bum enticing before, this was going to blow his mind. He had no idea what he had in wait.

Three knocks interrupted my narcissistic ogling. "Yes?"

Opening the door, Jason was quick to slam it shut again. "For fuck's sake, Cara! Give a poor man fair warning next time, yeah! Jesus Christ!"

"Do I look alright?" I asked, indifferent, and glanced at myself in the mirror again.

I loved lingerie. Wearing it, I felt capable of seducing the world – the ultimate physical power. The deadliest weapon. Never mind men's superior strength. When used correctly, women's femininity would render them into harmless puppets. Indeed, I loved the power of femininity. I had worshipped it for as long as I could remember. Why wish to be a man when you could have just as much fun as a woman? If not even more. Multiple orgasms? Yes, please, thank you very much. I also appreciated being ruled by only one head.

"Do you look 'alright'?" Jason echoed, dumbfounded. "I mean fucking hell, I might be a version of a brother to you, but I'm not your gay best friend. Show mercy, yeah?"

And there Jason proved my point. He didn't stand a chance.

"Sorry. I wanted to test the effect. I'm hoping I'll make William swoon."

"Swoon, explode, perish, eat you – depends on how you look at it, really. I almost feel sorry for him, but I've got a feeling he's going to retaliate. Are you sure you want to do this to yourself? You might be setting your own trap, Cara."

My jaw clenched. That was a valid point. Femininity was great, but so was masculinity, and especially when it was in the shape of William Night. In the end, I was no less susceptible to his allure than he was mine, and he had an aptitude for turning the tables whenever I tried to torment him sexually.

Jason was right. I should not underestimate his brother's sexual prowess.

"Yeah, maybe. Anyway, what's up? Aside from your dick?" I asked.

"Ha-ha. Very funny."

I laughed as I grabbed my grey dress to pull it on. I was positive William wouldn't suspect a thing as to what I was wearing beneath it. He might notice the stockings, but surely not the bustier.

Jason continued, "I was going to say that I'm about to head

off to meet Livy, Jon, Stephen and Giselle."

Smoothing my hands down my dress, I said, "You can come in now. I've dressed."

Hesitant, he opened the door and barely dared to peek inside. Once he had established that it was safe, he pushed the door wide open. Releasing the handle, he folded his strong arms and sized me up.

"You trying to kill him? Has he done anything wrong, beyond that of the usual?"

I chuckled. "No. I'm in the mood for some teasing."

His lips moved into a shrewd smile. "I've made up my mind. I feel sorry for him."

I gave him a confident look and fetched my handcuffs off the bed. "How do you reckon I'd stand the best chance at getting him into these without too much protesting? He *is* stronger than me." I dangled them in front of my face.

Jason's smile faded instantaneously. I wasn't sure I'd ever seen his eyes quite so wide. "You've got to be kidding me."

I sighed. Was I taking it too far? "He never lets me give him blowjobs. Says it messes with his endurance. Sorry if that's more than what you wanted to hear, but I've had enough. This is the only way."

Clearing his throat, Jason shook his head to himself as if to shake out sinful thoughts that the sight of the handcuffs had evoked. "No way. You're on your own. I'm not going to help you torture my brother. He might be a dick, but I love him."

"Love dicks, do you?"

His nose wrinkled. "You're so funny."

"Don't worry, Jase. We're in the same boat."

"Cara." He rolled his eyes.

"I'm only teasing you," I laughed. "I know you're not into men, Jason. You're into hands, aren't you?" I continued to taunt, referring to his committed relationship with his right hand.

Laughing at my joke, he waved his partner in the air. "Been

my loyal companion ever since I was eleven."

"Eleven!" I gasped in horror. "That's so early!"

He smirked. "What can I say?"

"You're no better than your brother!"

He scoffed. "Oh, I so am."

"Not sexually, you're not. You're only on hiatus – a beast in hibernation!"

His laughter roared. "You're killing me!"

"May God bestow mercy upon the poor, unsuspecting woman you first sleep with once you crawl out of your cave."

He flashed me a grin to die for and a truly unfair wink. "I'll treat her well, Cara. You know I will."

My heart throbbed. He was such a sweet man. "Jason, the woman you bless with your affection will be the luckiest woman alive, and I mean that. Hopefully, Livy will recognise that too."

"You're making me blush," he joked. "Anyway, I've got to go. I'm meeting Livy in fifteen minutes." He glanced at his Rolex, which was identical to the one William and John always wore. Perhaps it was a family thing? "We're going to the cinema before finding a pub to grab a few pints. Let me know if you and Will would like to join us." He met my eyes. "I'm not expecting it, though. Knowing you, you'll probably fuck each other into a coma."

Air poured out of my mouth. He could be just as vulgar as his brother. "Brutal."

"Only calling a spade a spade." Turning on his heel, he gave me a lazy wave.

"Take care of Livy for me," I called after him. "I'm still worried about her, even if she says that Colin hasn't reached out to her again."

He froze in the doorway. Turning his head, I saw anger swirling in his eyes at the mention of Colin. "Yeah. I'll take care of her."

I sighed, my shoulders sinking with relief. It was reassuring that

I wasn't alone in looking after Olivia. "Thanks, Jason. I love you."

"I love you right back. Now, *you* take care of my brother. Don't kill him. He's the only one I've got."

I grinned. "No promises."

I heard him chuckle as he sauntered down the hall. "Tell him I said hello, and that I'm with him in spirit."

"I'll say hello. Nothing else."

§ § §

"Hello, Garrick," I greeted with a smile when I passed him in the lobby of William's apartment building.

Touching the brim of his hat, he bowed his head at me. "Miss Darby."

"Cara," I corrected him, amused. I remembered he had insisted on calling William "Mr Night", and I wondered if his time in the military was to blame for it.

"Cara," he echoed after me. Next time I saw him, I knew he would address me as "Miss Darby" again. The thought made me chuckle to myself. Some things never changed.

After ringing William's doorbell, I took a step back as I waited for him to open the door. When he did, I rushed to cover my mouth with my hand to muffle my laughter. The man was wearing an apron!

Seeming to realise what I found hilarious, he motioned towards himself. "What? Can't have the fat splattering on my shirt. It's expensive. I might be wealthy, but I don't squander my money if I can avoid it."

He had a knack for finance, did he? Hot. While I was no gold digger, I still found people with a healthy understanding of pecuniary matters attractive. Then again, as an M&A lawyer, of course he was no stranger to such things. He had to have some aptitude for business, finance and economics to succeed within that field of law.

Him and Mum would have lots to talk about. Phoebe, too,

was likely to appreciate William's interest in the business world. The more I thought about it, the more I realised how well William would get on with my family.

"Very sexy," I purred and walked past him while I trailed my hand across the textile of his black apron.

After I'd dropped my purse on the chest of drawers, I looked around. I hadn't recalled it before, but on this very floor, I'd left my shredded knickers behind after our first encounter.

"You know, I just recalled – what did you do with my knickers?" I asked.

"Drenched them indirectly merely by existing," he teased as he locked the door behind me.

"Ha-ha. I meant after we first met. You tore them apart, and I don't remember seeing them the next morning."

He turned to look at me, and his expression was sharp. "Oh, those. Yes, I kept them. They're in my nightstand. I sniff them just before I go to bed every night. Helps me sleep."

I smacked his arm, though gently. "Stop pulling my leg. I'm curious!"

He laughed, eyes sparkling of mirth. "What do you think I did? I tossed them in the bin. I'm not crazy." Debatable. "Anyway, feel free to leave your knickers behind any time you like. This time, I promise I'll keep them." He reached for my waist. Since I was worried that he'd feel my bustier, I rushed to entwine our fingers before he could. Unsuspecting, a smile formed on his sinful mouth before he placed it on mine.

"What are you cooking?" I mumbled into our kiss.

"Lamb. Mum's recipe."

"Mm, can't wait," I cooed and pecked him repeatedly.

"Speaking of that, I need to check on it," he murmured and released me to go into his kitchen. I trailed after him with a smirk. Surely he was husband material.

Hopping onto a stool by his kitchen island, I watched him

scurry about, seemingly in control. "Anything I can do?"

He shook his head. "Would you like a glass of wine while you wait? It should be ready in a few minutes."

"Sure."

As I watched him fetch a bottle from his fancy wine fridge, I wondered if he'd ever treated any of his previous lovers to the same attention. Had he cooked for any of them? As I thought about it, I was spontaneously reminded of a certain question that had haunted me all week. However, he hadn't mentioned it at all since Monday morning, so I hadn't wanted to ask for fear of seeming insecure. Either way, I gathered now was a good time to air it. So, while I watched him pour me a glass, I enquired, "So... Have you met Francesca yet?"

He looked shocked at himself. "Shit, I'm so sorry. I was going to tell you, but I completely forgot. I met her last night."

"No worries." I smiled. "How did it go?"

He sighed, and his behaviour was elusive. "As expected."

"That means?"

"She cried like a fucking newborn."

Upset on her behalf, my lips jutted out. "I'm sorry," I mumbled. "Did she ask you for another chance?"

He nodded. "I was quite gentle if I can say so much myself," he said and searched my eyes for judgement. I believed he'd been as gentle as he – as William Night – could manage, but really, that had probably made it all the more painful for her. She must have seen a trace of his tender side, of the potential it contained, which I was blessed enough to experience every single day.

"Where did you do it?"

"At the hotel she's staying at. I wanted to be able to leave when I found it appropriate. Having her here would stall things."

I nodded to myself, unsurprised by the fact that he had thought of things like that beforehand.

"Used to breaking up with people, are you?" I muttered and

raised my glass to my mouth.

He leaned across the island to stare into my eyes. "You'll never have to find out."

My whole body froze. He could be unbelievably sweet when he wanted to. I was trying to calm the rising heat of my face, feigning nonchalance, as I said, "Smooth." But truthfully, his words had struck straight through my heart.

He chuckled and leaned away again. "Thanks."

"So she doesn't live in London? Since she's staying at a hotel?"

He shook his head. "She resides in Southampton, but most of her work is in London, so she's looking for a new place here. Has been for a few months. Until she finds one, she's staying with friends or at a hotel. But she's often abroad, so she's not really in a rush to find a place."

"Did she ever stay with you?"

He frowned. "No."

"Did you offer her to?"

His frown intensified. "What are you getting at? No."

I chuckled. "Damn. There's no need to get so defensive. I'm only curious."

"If you're trying to gauge whether there was ever anything romantic between us, I'll let you know there wasn't. At least not on my account. It was just sex, Cara, and I wanted to keep it that way. Hence why I never offered her to stay here for longer than a night." He turned for the counter.

"As I said, I was only curious," I replied, which was the truth. I wasn't worried about him and Francesca. Rather, I was worried about *her.* If she had asked for another chance yet again, she seemed a bit desperate, and desperate people shouldn't be underestimated. "Regardless, I suppose she's totally out of the picture now?"

With his back towards me, he nodded his head. "Third time's the charm, hopefully."

"Hopefully," I echoed and took another sip. "I hope she isn't going to be a problem."

"She won't be," he insisted. "I won't let her."

I shrugged. "If you say so."

"Now that we're on the subject of past bed partners, there's something I've been meaning to say," he murmured and glanced at me over his shoulder. The look on his face told me I ought to prepare for something unpleasant.

"Wait," I said and raised my glass again. After an inappropriately large mouthful, I lowered it onto the island and exhaled loudly. "Okay, I'm ready."

Since he wasn't amused, I gathered it was something truly serious.

"Aaron," he said, and it prompted my loud, long groan. Tossing my head back, my eyes rolled into my skull as I despaired.

I didn't want to ask but, "What about him?"

"Has he reached out to you since he confessed to having feelings for you?"

Leaning forward again, I tried my hardest to refrain from pouting. Truthfully, I did hope Aaron would reach out to me. I hoped he would get over me sooner rather than later, and I hoped we could enjoy a platonic friendship in the wake of that. I missed him terribly. It felt like a limb of mine had been cut off now that we weren't speaking anymore. He knew all my secrets. I trusted him implicitly, and whilst I still had Jason and Olivia for that, there was a gaping absence of Aaron.

He hadn't been my boyfriend, but he'd surely been a version of a partner. We'd studied together, slept together, and shared a profound, irreplaceable friendship as well as mutual friends. Quite frankly, we'd shared every aspect of life apart from romantic love. He'd even met my family on several occasions, and I was certainly no stranger to his mother, Mary-Anne.

God, I missed Mary-Anne.

"No," I finally answered.

He turned to face me entirely, and the heat of his glare was sizzling. From it, I could tell that I was not going to enjoy where he was going with this. Couldn't he have postponed this fight till after we'd had sex?

"Do we have to discuss this now?" I enquired with a pleading look.

"Yes," he said resolutely and switched off the oven behind him, presumably to let the lamb rest before serving.

"It won't take long – hopefully." He folded his arms and continued to hold my eyes under arrest. Meanwhile, he gnashed his teeth. "My demand is quite simple." *Demand.* "I don't want you anywhere near him."

My heart slowed as I tried to process the magnitude of his "demand". I hadn't been prepared for its ruthlessness at all. "Will, what?"

"I understand you might be studying together for your LPCs, so I get that you can't avoid him there, but in any circumstance where you can avoid him, I expect you to."

My jaw fell. This was outrageous. He wouldn't even accept us remaining friends? "Are you actually being serious?"

His body language radiated obstinacy. "Cara, he's got feelings for you. That makes him a hard limit for me. You know I'm territorial. I don't trust him not to try and take you away from me. If I were in his place, I would have done just about anything to persuade you to pick me over him. In fact, I've essentially already proved that. You used to be his, for lack of a better word, before you agreed to go on a date with me. And I know you're weak for him."

Air stormed out of my mouth while my face paled. "Will, I'm not!"

Anger swelled in his features, and alongside it was impatience. "Don't even dare try to deny it. He's special to you, Cara. There's a reason you've shared beds with him for three bloody years. You might not have loved him romantically, but some love is undoubtedly present. You are definitely weaker for him than I find acceptable, and after you nearly slept with him again two weeks ago, and furthermore *lied* to me about it, I don't trust you at all when it comes to him."

A lump had gathered in my throat, and I struggled to swallow it. Hearing his concerns was paining me. My chest tightened. Stung.

"William, I've apologised for that. I wasn't thinking straight."

He shook his head. "It's not enough, Cara. The damage has been done. If there's one thing you've made clear, it's the fact that you're extremely fickle about these things. For fuck's sake, it's been three months of back and forth between us. It's done my head in."

I was struggling to remain calm. Strong emotions were scratching beneath my skin, threatening to escape the confinements of my body. I had to remind myself not to get too defensive. It was paramount that I handled this constructively. So, instead of attacking him, I said, "I'm sorry."

Looking away from me, he sighed. A period of silence elapsed before he said, "Knowing how fickle you can be, I don't trust you not to run into his arms the instant we come across a rough patch. And I can't stand the idea of that. I really can't." His jaw clenched, and he closed his eyes for a moment. "It makes me nauseous, and honestly, fucking furious. And I especially can't stand it when I know he'll just be waiting for it to happen, patiently anticipating the moment when I might fuck up. Strategically, that's when he's going to strike – when we're at our most vulnerable.

"You can try to convince me that you aren't going to do that all you like, but I am never going to believe you. Your prior behaviour has made it crystal clear that you're extremely indecisive, and I will not build a relationship with you on such a shaky foundation. I fucking refuse. Either you're in, or you're out. If you're in, Aaron isn't included. I mean it. I do not feel secure in you yet, and I certainly won't feel secure in you if Aaron is around."

Speechless, I could only stare at him. Was that the impression

I'd given him? That I wasn't fully invested in this? Sure, I knew I could be indecisive, but once I made up my mind, I always saw it through. In fact, that was the very reason as to why I could be indecisive about things. I didn't want to commit to something without doing it fully. So, obviously I would be fastidious about my choices. I needed to be absolutely certain before I decided.

Finally, my brain connected with my mouth. "William, I'm not going to—"

"I don't believe you, and I've explained why," he cut me off uncompromisingly. "You haven't done anything to prove yourself worthy of my trust. I mean, bloody hell, Cara. You were about to fuck him right after our night out together. You slept in my arms that night and essentially woke up beside me. Before then, you agreed to consider giving me a chance. And yet you *still* managed to invite him home with you, and you fucking went and lied to me about it."

Tears surfaced in my eyes. I only looked at him, lost for words.

Realising that I couldn't speak, he continued, "So easily, you abandoned even the thought of me. You fucked up when you did that – monumentally."

"William!" I yelled, horribly frustrated. "You and I weren't together back then!"

"We still aren't," he reminded me, and my mouth immediately drew shut. Hearing that hurt more than I'd expected.

"See my point?" His brow arched. "You should have thought of this before you decided to lie to me, and before you dragged him home with you. It was a severe mistake on your end, and now you'll have to deal with the consequence, which is that I do not trust you with him. You're clearly capable of pushing thoughts of me aside when it comes to him. I'm sorry that I'm upsetting you, but as I said, he's a hard limit for me. I can't build anything with you if he's going to be part of your life. It will drive me mad with jealousy and worry, and I will not subject myself to that. I don't deserve it."

I chewed into my lower lip. This felt extremely unfair. "Will, I understand your concerns, but you and I weren't exclusive then the way we are now. This is different. And how would you feel if I told you that you couldn't be friends with Violet?"

Evidently underwhelmed, he replied, "First of all, Violet has never had feelings for me. Secondly, Violet was the one to end our arrangement. I meant to end it with her, but she beat me to it; the moment I told her about you, she insisted we should stop sleeping together. Aaron, on the other hand, went on to ask you for an exclusive relationship. Thirdly, had you wanted me to quit being friends with her, I would have done it out of respect for you, and Violet would have understood."

This piece of information took me by complete surprise. While I knew Violet was supportive of Will and me, I hadn't thought it went this far.

Unsure of what to say, I closed my mouth and averted my eyes.

After some silence, William continued, "Violet isn't a threat to you at all. No one is. And don't forget the fact that I intended to end my arrangement with her as early as April. By contrast, you kept fucking Aaron even though you knew I hated it. And you admitted that you fancied me at that point, even if you refused to act on it. Cara, that speaks volumes as to what you're capable of with him. Clearly, your feelings for me do not prevent you from sleeping with him, and I don't trust that that's changed, and least of all when you're angry with me."

He ran a hand through his hair, and from his fleeting gaze, I could tell he was trying to string his next argument together. "And let's face it," he continued, "you're going to get angry with me now and then. To think anything else would be naïve. We're both hotheads. Already, we argue like it's our livelihood, even if it's just part of who we are. I need to be able to have a fight with you without having to fear that you're going to seek shelter in another man's bed. It's about trust. All of this is about trust, and you do not have mine.

"What's more, you're not a jealous person. It's both silly and unrealistic of you to think that we should treat this as if our needs are identical when they clearly aren't. I'm a jealous man, and we're going to have to work around it. It's part of the package. Everyone's got flaws, and that's probably my biggest. I'm sorry if that seems unfair to you, but, realistically, my jealousy is an actual concern of ours. I'm constantly working on it, but – fuck me – Aaron isn't something I can overlook. That's asking too much of me."

He blew his cheeks out before he captured my gaze. "Let me say it like this. Had you been the jealous lover in this scenario, I would have cut him out in a heartbeat for you. And you know I would. I could easily still have been friends with Kate, Cara, but I chose to cut her out because I didn't want her to be a matter of concern in my future relationships. She was my best friend, too. I know how hard it is, but it's necessary pain."

He was being perfectly rational, and I hated it. I hated his damned solicitor mind. All his arguments were unbearably solid. It exasperated me to the extent that tears leaked from my eyes. He was giving me an ultimatum. I already knew who I was going to choose, but I truly hated the fact that he was forcing me to do it – that I couldn't even keep Aaron as my friend.

The choice was made a little easier when I considered that Aaron probably wouldn't reach out to me again anytime soon. And, as time dragged on, losing him was going to hurt less and less. Besides, I had the opportunity to build something profound with a man I was in love with now. I wasn't about to cast it aside.

And, frankly, I could understand where William was coming from. What I had done in the past didn't merit his trust. It didn't matter if I knew in my heart that I'd never choose Aaron over him. That was an irrational argument. I couldn't back it up. William had rational arguments based on concrete evidence. I stood no chance in this trial. I could do nothing but rest my case.

"Okay," I said meekly, though it was almost a whisper. In all fairness, I sounded utterly defeated. Dropping my gaze to my hands in my lap, I nodded vaguely. "Okay, I get it. No Aaron."

He released a breath that was so loud that my eyes shot towards him. I hadn't seen him this relieved since I'd agreed to go on a date with him. "That was much easier than I'd expected," he stated, slightly shocked.

"Yeah, well, forgive me if my mood is shit for the next hour or week," I countered and looked away from him while I reached for my glass of wine.

"Take all the time you need, darling. I know I'm asking a lot from you. Nevertheless, I'm extremely grateful. Truly, you have no idea how much I appreciate this. With him out of the way, I don't really have any concerns."

I glowered at him, still petty. "Worst date ever."

"Oh, Cara. Don't be nasty with me. You're being mean." He frowned, visibly irritated. "I get that it isn't ideal, but at least you've still got me."

"I'm making a huge sacrifice for you right now, so you'd better be worth it."

He flashed me a gorgeous grin, as if to remind me. "I am." He turned to open the oven. "On another note, Alex wants to meet you."

I stiffened. I'd almost forgotten he had been spending the day with him. "What?"

"Yeah, I've mentioned you. He's impatient about it, really." After placing the lamb dish onto the counter, he faced me. "I said I couldn't make any promises, but I'd definitely like to introduce you to him. He's a great man. Incredibly intelligent and remarkably patient, as well as placid and mild." That was quite a detailed description. It made me smile against my will. He was obviously very fond of him. "I think you'll like him rather a lot. Though, hopefully not too much."

I rolled my eyes. That jealousy of his was seriously getting on my nerves.

"What have you told him?" I asked.

"That we're seeing each other."

"And he's that impatient to meet me already?"

He faced the counter again, and I wondered if it was because he didn't want to look me in the eyes. "I might have told him about you a couple of months ago," he muttered and reached for a knife to slice up the lamb.

"After our first encounter?"

He nodded. "Will you meet him?"

I smiled and rested my head in the palm of my hand while I admired his backside. "Sure."

He tensed, head slowly lifting. Turning, he watched me, surprised. "Really?"

"Sure," I repeated with a nod. "I've already met both your parents, your brother, and Andy. What's one more going to hurt?"

He pointed at me with the knife he was holding. "Do you see the blatant imbalance?"

I was positive my responding smile matched that of the Cheshire Cat. "Yes."

His eyebrows drew towards the middle of his face. "And what are you going to do about it?"

"I said I'd consider introducing you to my parents if you make it to ten dates, Will. This is our second – and counting."

He groaned and faced the lamb again. "So slow," I thought I heard him complain, but I wasn't sure.

"When do you want to introduce me to Alex?"

"Friday. Remember that charity event which I've got to attend?"

"Er, yes?"

"Well, as you know, Alex is going, and so are Andy and Chloe. I'd like it if you were my plus one."

I whined, "Ugh. Couldn't we make it a regular dinner instead? I've never fancied the idea of prestigious balls. I don't belong there."

"Cara, I'd really appreciate your company. I'll be suffering enough already, and your presence would make it tolerable."

I remembered something important then. "But going out in public like that, where people we might know will see us, could mean drawing attention to our sexual relationship, Will. Word could spread to the office. Is it really worth that risk?"

He snorted. "You're my assistant. It's perfectly common for single men and women to bring their assistants to events like these. Alex is bringing his as well. Besides, several important people will be there. It's an excellent chance for you to network."

I remained hesitant. "If I agree to this, you've got to promise that you won't touch me intimately where others might see us. Considering that these people are part of John and Daphné's circle, I'm genuinely worried that word will spread to them, or the office."

He gave me a grin. "It's a deal. Thank you."

I couldn't help it – I pouted. "You're welcome. Can't believe I'm agreeing to this."

"I appreciate it. Anyway, speaking of Alex, I think he's in love."

A ridiculing laugh leapt out of my mouth while my eyebrows climbed up my forehead. "I'd hope so, since he's got a girlfriend."

He cringed. "Yeah, it's not with his girlfriend."

Appalled, I leaned backwards. "What? What a bastard!"

A nervous chuckle escaped him. "Don't be so quick to pass judgement, love. There's a long story to this. His girlfriend, Abigail, is an actual psycho. I'm certain."

I was intrigued. "How so?"

He sighed. "I'm not going to go into too much detail because I'm not in the habit of sharing secrets, but he was never in love with her. A few complications along the way have made Alex feel forced to remain with her. He's experiencing a lot of guilt. Just trust me when I say the complications I mentioned are legitimate concerns."

"Shit."

"Yeah. I warned him about her from the very start, but he

didn't listen to me. We actually fell out at a certain point because of her. First proper fight we've ever had. I was a bit too blunt with a very serious allegation regarding her, and he lost his patience with me. He's forgiven me now though, mainly because he started to see what I was already seeing."

I wanted to know more about this, but I refused to pry. "Will you tell me one day?"

"I'll have to ask for his permission."

His loyalty and reliability turned me on. His jealousy might be a serious flaw, but he surely compensated in other departments.

"I respect that," I replied and had another sip of wine. "Whom do you suspect him of being in love with then?"

"A lovely girl named Ivy. He's known her all his life, but she's always been in a relationship – till now."

"Have you met her?"

"Yes, but only a couple of times, though. She's a family friend of his."

"I see. What's she like?"

"She's a bit like Livy with her cheerfulness, only she's much quirkier. I think you'll adore her. I find her delightful, and she's very humble. Extremely shy, though."

"Really? Is she posh?"

He snorted. "Not at all."

I applauded. "How old is she? Do you know?"

"Twenty-five, so Jason's age."

"Nice. And what does Ivy do?"

He stole a glance at me, and his smile was impish. "Alex's personal assistant is on maternity leave, so Ivy's stepped in to take over for the time being."

That was underwhelming. "In other words, she's his assistant?"

"Yes."

Despairing, I shook my head. "You guys are unbelievable."

He laughed. "I don't know what you're on about. In case you

need your memory jogged, the woman I thought I'd hired was a completely different person from the apparent med student I had slept with some weeks earlier."

I sniggered. "True."

"Anyway," he shook his head, evidently still amused, "she'll be Alexander's date on Friday, so you'll get to meet her then."

"Right. I'm actually looking forward to that. I'll make sure to invite her and Chloe over for tea one day, so that we may bitch and moan about our men together," I teased.

He chuckled. While he scoured the cupboards, I examined him in detail. He hadn't so much as stirred when I'd mentioned Chloe, and he hadn't expressed signs of knowing about her potential pregnancy when he'd mentioned her himself, either.

"Have you had a heart to heart with Andy lately?" I asked, although I stressed sounding nonchalant.

"What, about the fact that I might become an uncle soon?"

I grinned. So he had told him. "Yes. Are you excited?"

He faced me with a dashing smile. "I'm happy he's finally made up his mind, but I saw it coming. As for being an uncle, yes, I'm looking forward to it. I've always liked children. Though, she might not get pregnant straight away, if at all, so I don't want to celebrate that yet."

Determined to stay on the subject, I ignored his comment about children. "You did see it coming. That why you haven't spoken to me about it yet?"

He frowned. "I wouldn't have been able to speak to you about it sooner. He told me today, when we were hanging out with Alex."

"Oh."

His head tilted. "How long have you known?"

"Since Monday."

"You're good at keeping secrets," he remarked, but he didn't sound impressed. On the contrary, he sounded alarmed. "I haven't sensed a thing."

"I'm not going to have sex with anyone else, Will," I grumbled, seeing straight through him. "I'll have nothing to hide."

"If you're wise, you won't."

Again, I rolled my eyes. He could be so suspicious, and intolerably so.

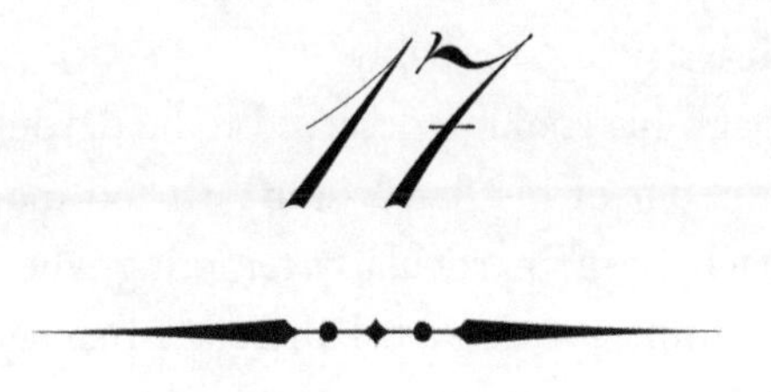

ALL MY FANTASIES

The red Bordeaux he had chosen to complement the dish was outstanding. As I filled my mouth with my last bite, the flavour of it exploded in my mouth. Overall, I was greatly impressed by what he'd managed. Daphné would have been proud.

On the table between us stood a bouquet of white flowers that I didn't know the name of, but they were big and reminded me of lilies. Earlier, when I'd seen the serviettes that he had artistically folded, I hadn't been able to stop my laughter. He did nothing halfway, did he?

Steering my eyes to his comely face, I smiled to myself. Sometimes, I had to just savour the view of him. He was, without a doubt, the most handsome man I'd ever seen, and he was exclusively mine for the time being.

His square jaw clenched and unclenched as he chewed, and I

was puzzled by the fact that I found the sight arousing. Did I find everything he did arousing? Could he so much as breathe without inadvertently dampening my underwear? I honestly doubted it now and then.

I groaned inwardly and rolled my eyes in despair of myself, but he didn't notice. Clearly, he was preoccupied with his thoughts. I wondered if it was work. Probably.

Even though his cooking deserved to be devoured until he'd have to roll me out of his flat, I didn't eat too much. Having a bloated stomach wasn't particularly tempting when considering what I had in mind for dessert. I therefore managed to resist a second serving.

"You're a wonderful cook, Will."

He smiled on his mouthful. "I'll cook you the scrambled eggs you love so much for breakfast in the morning."

I stared at him, smitten. I would never get enough of his attentive side. "I wasn't wrong when I said you're boyfriend material the night we met. Go, intuition," I said and patted my own shoulder.

He raised a brow at me, seemingly not flattered. "I find it strange that you consider me 'boyfriend material', and yet you're so difficult about committing to me. What a paradox you are." Reaching for his glass of wine, he had a sip while I pondered over what he'd said.

"I'm not that difficult now, am I? I'll agree I was difficult to begin with," I said, "but I had valid reasons for that, and I wasn't looking for anything serious when you barged into my life."

"Barged," he echoed, amused. "Is that what I did?"

"I'd say so. How long did we stay at Disrepute before you essentially dragged me home with you? An hour?"

"About," he confirmed with a slight nod of his head. "And how about now then, Cara? Are you looking for anything serious now?"

My stomach fluttered with the myriad butterflies that suddenly found a home in it. I looked coyly away from him when heat dominated my cheeks. "I've already told you I'm serious about you."

"You'll forgive me if I can't hear that enough," he said affectionately and put his glass back on the table between us. "And you're still difficult, but you're getting there," he added. "I'm aware this is your first experience with dating someone, so I'm smearing myself in with patience. I know I can be demanding, but I'd say we're doing rather well at communicating."

"You tend to interrupt me whenever we're arguing, though."

"I prefer monologues to dialogues," he jested.

"No shit, Narcissus."

He laughed at what I called him. "I'm sorry if that's a habit of mine. I'll bear it in mind for next time."

"Thanks."

"I'm not very impressed with your appetite, by the way." He pointed to my plate. "You hardly ate. Were you lying when you said you enjoyed my cooking?"

I shook my head. "No, it was delicious. I just wasn't very hungry."

His stare was scrutinising. "Please tell me you've got a healthy relationship with food."

I chuckled. "Yes, Will." I reached for my glass of wine. "I have a healthy approach to these things in general. I used to count calories when I first started lifting weights, so I've got an intuitive understanding of how much I need to eat to stay in this exact shape. I also tend to eat healthy, and I have a healthy relationship with alcohol, too."

He pursed his lips. Although he was visibly amused, I detected some doubtfulness in his features. "Have you forgotten that I held your hair while you vomited the other day?"

I cringed at the unpleasant memory. "You can't hold that against me. That was the exception to the rule. You can ask Jason about this. He'll back me up."

Reclining in his seat, he nodded. "Yes, now that you mention it, I recall him stating that night that he'd rarely seen you that drunk."

"See? And don't forget that I'm still in my early twenties. For people my age, excessive consumption on a night out is rather normal in this country. This isn't France or Italy. We don't treat alcohol like they do."

"You sound ridiculous. We should treat it like they do," he argued, annoyed. "I've always despised that part of our culture. It's pathetic and unbecoming. Embarrassing, even. Are you aware that the external social expense of alcohol costs England approximately twenty-one billion pounds a year? That's fucking abhorrent."

"Wow."

He nodded vehemently. "Imagine what we could have spent those resources on if people weren't such bleeding idiots. We could have countered actual, serious crime – organised crime, but instead, the police have got to bring Billy to the station because he's so sloshed he doesn't remember where he lives. Angela over there has managed to drink herself unconscious, so the ambulance just arrived for her. Oh, and after that, they've got to respond to a pub brawl, because Ned just had to punch Jimmy in the face."

I chuckled. I loved William's flair for sarcasm. It was incredibly sharp, just like the rest of him.

"When do I cast my vote, Mr Politician? William Night for prime minister."

His expression became condescending. "Since when did criticising society make people politicians? Caring for how the country is managed seems like a fair concern to me. And you know I'm opinionated."

"I agree with this. I wasn't defending that part of our culture. I was only saying. The point of this is that I don't drink much very often. But now I'm curious. From the sound of it, you didn't experiment with alcohol during your teens."

He reached for his glass of wine again, only to stir it. While staring at the spiralling red liquid, he said, "I did experiment, but I wasn't reckless. Smoked some spliff on occasion, and attended a few parties, but, like you, my education was sacred to me. I was also preoccupied with sports, particularly football. Didn't want to sacrifice my stamina, or my marks, for rubbish like drugs. You know I've always been driven."

My eyes were slightly wide. I hadn't expected this at all. "You've smoked marijuana?"

He chuckled. "Yeah. I smoked marijuana much more than I drank alcohol. Was my favourite drug. Still is, but I don't do it anymore, seeing as it's illegal. I remember I used to be scared shitless – paranoid, actually – whenever I got some in since I worried the police would catch me." Well, we had that in common. "I was at my most rebellious when I experimented with it. I was fifteen, sixteen? Quit after about a year when I realised it was making me lazier about school. I had straight A's at that time, so I was actually getting closer to getting into Cambridge. Because of that, I realised I had to quit, since it could affect my marks."

Amused, I brushed my hair behind my ear, crossed my forearms on the table and leaned forward to smile at him. "And I suppose you still had straight A's when you graduated from college?"

He chuckled. "Yeah."

"I am so surprised."

"Anyway, I do find marijuana more rewarding than alcohol."

"How come?"

He shrugged. "Well, I enjoy reflection, and marijuana incites that. It's also much safer than alcohol. When you're high, you're still relatively in control of yourself compared to when you're drunk. You only laugh, eat and think a lot. Either way, it's probably the stupidest thing I've ever done in my life, all things considered. But I wouldn't change it for the world. Taught me a lesson or two."

My amusement didn't seem about to subside anytime soon. "Did Alex and Andy do it with you?"

He laughed wholeheartedly. "If they did? We used to sit in the attic of Andy's parents' house, high as a fucking kite, listening to old vinyl records while we discussed everything between heaven and earth. We've got some seriously great memories from that time. We quit together, actually. Sort of a pact."

"You three are a really good influence on each other it sounds like."

The grin that claimed his mouth was so pure that I had to take a moment to admire it. Above, his mesmerising eyes sparkled with glee. "Yeah, we are. Always have been."

"How did you get involved with it?"

He studied his plate absentmindedly, reminiscing. "Alex lost his virginity with this girl named Scarlet, who was in the year above ours. They were regular bed partners for about a year, so she hung out with us a lot. Cool girl. I really liked her. She handled my banter with grace and retaliated without mercy. Anyway, she smoked *a lot*, so she was sort of our dealer, for lack of a better word. Her parents are renowned artists, and they smoked a lot as well. She stole their stash quite often but was never punished. Poor role models, I suppose."

"She sounds intriguing." A femme fatale, I supposed, luring the three chaps onto such an unlawful path.

"She was brilliant. Very clever and unconventional. I remember I was a bit dismayed when she left for university to study psychology. I haven't spoken to her since."

"So Alex is weak for mischievous girls, is he?" I couldn't help my crooked smile.

"Back then, yeah, I guess. She was thrilling to him. Brought an element of suspense into his otherwise humdrum life. He's been weak for idealists ever since, though. He's always been quite idealistic himself. But more than anything, he's weak for stability and reliability in his women. Ironic that he's in a relationship with Abigail, seeing as she is anything but that. She's neurotic."

Fisting my hand, I rested my cheek on it. "I see. And Ivy is an idealist, then?"

"That's my impression, yes."

I nodded to myself while thoughts of my sister came to mind. Phoebe was also assuredly an idealist. "Idealists are charming."

"They're quite adorable, indeed."

His tone made me curve a brow. "You sound degrading."

Chuckling, he rubbed the back of his head. "Well, I tend to find them a bit naïve, but when they aren't, they're crucial for the world. In the end, they're the ones that implore us to move in a constructive direction. Without them, this world would be hell on earth, I'm sure."

Intrigued by the stories of his adolescence, I gave pause to wonder for a moment.

"When did you first have sex, then?" I asked bluntly and studied him, engrossed. He didn't so much as stir.

"I was fifteen."

We'd been the same age then. "Of course."

Glancing sideways for a moment, he frowned to himself. "Been sexually active for nearly half my life now. Odd to think of."

"Ever been inactive?" My tone was dry, but I was genuinely curious.

He met my eyes again. "Are you asking if I've had any dry spells?"

"Mhm."

He shook his head and focused on his dish again. "Never."

Why wasn't I surprised? "No wonder you're so good in bed."

His responding smile was smug. "I like sex."

"I'm shocked."

"And I like it with you the most."

I beamed at him. If he'd been sexually active for thirteen years of his life, I gathered that was an achievement on my part. "Who was your first, then?"

As he swallowed a mouthful, he frowned again. "Girl named Blaire. I was her first as well. She was in my class. I broke her heart eventually – still feel awful about that. Though, it wasn't like

I played with her feelings. I made my intentions clear from the start, but she was infatuated with me, so I suppose she was blind to reason. She didn't listen, and, foolish as I was, I decided to treat her like a rational being, meaning I expected her to know what was best for herself."

"You're such a dick, Will," I chuckled. "I feel terrible for all the women you've left behind. You're a heartbreaker. Blaire, Kate, Francesca. How long is the list? Honestly?"

He lifted his gaze to glower at me. "You don't want to know. And it's never been on purpose. You know as well as I do that you can't choose whom to fall in love with."

I swallowed a lump in my throat when I realised that this piece of information was actually alarming. Clearly he had a knack for seducing women and leaving them in ruins.

Was I going to be a number in that row?

"Your brother is a saint compared to you," I alleged. "Instead of seducing susceptible women to get his fill – ultimately leaving a trail of broken hearts behind him – he rubs one out."

He sneered. "Like you're not guilty of 'leaving a trail of broken hearts behind' you as well."

I pursed my lips. "Touché."

"When did you lose your virginity?"

"I was thirteen."

He froze at once, colour fading from his face while he gaped at me in blatant horror. "That's really fucking young. Who with?"

Grinning, I raised my hand and showed him my index finger and my middle finger. "These two."

For a second, he merely continued to look at me, then he guffawed so heartfully that I had to join him.

I said, "You asked when I lost my supposed 'virginity'. That's my honest answer. I took it myself when I was thirteen."

"That," he pointed his knife at me, "was a good one."

"To answer what you actually meant to ask, I had sex for the first time when I was fifteen as well."

"With?"

"My best male friend, Scott."

He shook his head. "Of course. And let me guess, he developed feelings for you and now you're no longer friends."

Escaping his gaze, I sighed and rubbed my hands together. "Yeah."

"Classic Cara."

I groaned. "I guess it might be a pattern. Either way, you've never been primarily my friend, so you're safe."

"Yeah, I couldn't bear the friend-zone."

"It's not really your natural habitat." I smiled, amused. "You know how some people just can't be friend-zoned? And then some are nearly always friend-zoned?"

He laughed. "Yeah."

"Well, you're in the former category."

"Thanks, I think. And I suppose Jason would be in the latter."

I grimaced. "Since he fancies Livy, I really hope not."

"Me too." After swallowing another mouthful, he exhaled in what I thought was despair of his brother. "He's hopeless. You were wrong when you said he just rubs one out instead of breaking hearts."

I studied him with some confusion. "Why do you say that?"

"Well, there are two reasons why he's giving that impression, but I'm not sure I should burst your bubble."

I frowned. "Then don't. Why would you try to paint a bad picture of your poor, lovely brother anyway?"

Bemused, he arched a brow at me. "I'm trying to paint a true picture. Yours is flawed. Terribly flawed."

My lips moved into a pout at the thought of Jason being anything other the innocent angel I imagined him to be. "Enlighten me, then. What are the reasons he's rarely involved with women?"

William sighed again. "Well, unlike what you seem to believe, it's not due to fear of breaking any hearts. Rather, it's because he doesn't intuitively understand how to approach and seduce women. He's certainly not avoiding sex because he prefers being without it. In other words, reason number one is that he's never been any good at reading women. He's shit, actually, and that's putting it mildly. Secondly, and perhaps most importantly, he seriously lacks the necessary courage that is required to approach them. In the end, most women expect men to make the first move, so, when he won't, his chance usually slips away. He always just assumes women aren't interested in him."

"Are you trying to say that Jason just walks around presuming he's undesirable?"

"One hundred per cent."

"Oh, for fuck's sake. That's pathetic. Come on, Jason."

He laughed at my audible despair. "That's what I'm saying."

"You ought to teach him, Will."

"Like I haven't tried," he replied with sarcasm. "I've helped him out several times in the past. In fact, I almost helped him into a relationship a few years back, with a friend of mine named Harper."

Now that he mentioned it, I vaguely recalled Jason revealing sometime in the past that he'd been on the verge of embarking on a relationship a few years back. "Right, he's told me something like that. What happened between them again?"

He grimaced and dropped his gaze to his plate. "Just didn't work out. It was while he was living in Mumbai, working for Alexander's charity. They had a brief fling, but since he was moving back to England after the summer, neither of them communicated whether they'd like to pursue something more serious." After clearing his throat, he frowned to himself and proceeded to change the subject, "Speaking of Jason, what's he doing tonight?"

Since he was clearly uncomfortable discussing Jason's private life, I would allow this change of course. "He's going to the cinema with Giselle, Jon, Stephen and Livy. Asked whether we'd fancy joining them for a few pints afterwards."

"Yeah, that's not going to happen. I haven't had my dessert yet," he purred and gave me a sizzling glance.

"What, you haven't made me a cake?"

He chuckled. "Why, is it your birthday? Thought that was December twenty-first."

"Good memory."

"I have actually got dessert prepared, but I was lazy, so it's only ice cream."

I found it amusing that he labelled himself "lazy" after serving me this incredible dinner. "You haven't got a lazy bone in your body, Will."

He leaned forward to stare deep into my eyes. "You must be right, seeing as my bones are currently aching for you to undress."

My jaw dropped. I hadn't seen that one coming. Would I ever grow used to how blunt he was? I doubted it.

"Let's clean the table first," I said and looked away from him as panic seized me. I'd have to figure out how to get him into those handcuffs fast, because I knew perfectly well that I could only stall his lust for so long.

Pushing my seat out, I grabbed my plate and stood to head into the kitchen with it. By the time he joined me there, I'd finished rinsing my plate and had stowed it away in his dishwasher. As I was about to pass him, an invisible and electric charge surged between us, begging me to draw nearer to him, preferably into his arms.

But I didn't. Instead, I maintained a safe distance, which piqued his curiosity.

"I've got something for you," I said in order to satisfy it.

"Do you?"

Glimpsing him, I saw that he was both surprised and puzzled. Oh, he had no idea, the clueless fool.

"Yes. Wait here," I told him and felt his stare burrow into my back till I turned around the corner to fetch my purse from the hall. As I came back to the kitchen, my heart raced. Peeking around the corner, I found him leaning against the counter with his hands in his pockets.

"Turn round," I ordered, deciding to improvise.

Wearing a frown, he faced the counter.

Nervous, I said, "Don't look. If you do, I'll chop off your dick."

Soft laughter drifted out of him. "Love my cock that much, do you? Keen on having it all to yourself?"

"Maybe."

"It's already all yours, Cara, and I can assure you that it's most useful when attached to my body. You wouldn't know what to do with it as well as I do."

I chuckled. He had a point. "Fine, you get to keep it. I'll take your balls instead."

Fishing out the handcuffs, I dumped my purse on the floor and hid them behind my back. The noise of the silver metal jingling echoed in my ears, alarming me. Hopefully, he hadn't identified the sound. My heart pounded against my ribs while I vigilantly approached.

"If you're wearing nothing but lingerie when I turn around, you're in for a long night, Cara," he warned. My breath caught in my throat. He must have noted my stockings. Damn him and his bloody intuition. He was ruining the surprise.

However, I hadn't undressed yet. I would wait with that until I had made him come solely with my mouth. Since men needed to – in his own words – "reload", I wagered the sight of a woman in lingerie would speed up the process.

"I'm not. Is that a fantasy of yours?" I hoped it was.

He cocked his head from side to side. "One of many." My prayers were heard.

I smiled behind him. "Is role-play one of them?"

He shuddered. "No. Can't stand that."

"Good to know. I can't either."

"I should add that all my fantasies include you."

I was blushing when I halted two feet behind him and silently inhaled deep into my lungs, mustering courage. "Give me your hands, but don't turn round. It's a present."

Please, let this work.

His head tilted, but he didn't turn. Very slowly, he withdrew his hands from his pockets and reached behind him. My heart stopped beating when I brought forth the metal and rushed to cuff his wrists together simultaneously. He stiffened completely first. Then, suddenly, he jerked against his confines.

Squealing in fear, I jumped several feet backwards. *Oh, my God.* I had actually done it. I had managed to subdue William fucking Night.

He spun around to face me, and his eyes were smouldering. "What's the meaning of this?"

Regaining control over myself, I dared to approach again. While smoothing my hands across his powerful chest, I leered up at him. The Adam's apple of his throat ascended and dropped with his swallow, and I saw his pupils dilate.

"You just said your cock was mine. I'm about to take advantage of it," I purred and stretched up on my toes to whisper in his ear, "with my mouth."

A whimper poured out of him as I leaned back. Holding his gaze, I gave him a lascivious and confident smile while I slowly descended onto my knees.

With eyes wide, he uttered, "Fuck."

LET'S BEGIN, SHALL WE?

While I hurried to undo his trousers, I replied cheekily, "Yeah, well, desperate times, desperate measures." Watching the promising bulk of his erection, I wetted my lips with my tongue. "You brought this upon yourself. I've given you plenty of opportunities to let me have my way."

"Cara," he snapped and stepped sideways. Trying to escape, was he? Over my dead body. "Take them off this instant!" he ordered feverishly and glared down at me. I heard him rattle the handcuffs behind him, desperate for liberation.

A sadistic laugh slipped out of my mouth while I followed him, eventually trapping him in the corner of his kitchen. If we'd had spectators, this scene must have looked comical. I was literally chasing his dick.

"Lean back and relax, Will," I said, and my amusement didn't waver. "I'll make you feel good. I promise."

With some force, I dragged both his trousers and boxers down, leaving them to pool around his ankles. Now liberated, his erection pointed straight at me, exposing how aroused he was. He could pretend all he wanted that he didn't appreciate being controlled like this. His cock told me otherwise.

"I hope you're ready for the consequence, Cara," he growled under his breath while he glowered down at me. "I'm going to fuck you senseless. So hard, in fact, that you won't be able to walk for the next few hours."

Reclining onto my heels, I felt my vagina tingle upon his threat. Hammering in my chest was my heart, pumping blood through my veins at a frenzied speed. Behind my ears, I could hear my pulse thump.

Seeing his erection in such bright lights made me swallow. I was slightly intimidated by the view. I could hardly fathom that it fit into me, much less my mouth. Would I be able to deep-throat him? I knew I'd managed to in the past, but not without spilling a few tears, so I was wearing waterproof mascara today for that reason alone, as I was determined to bring it to the finish line this time. Remembering how I'd gagged on him the only time I'd performed fellatio on him before, I'd now labelled it my "blowjob-mascara".

"Mm, Will, you know exactly what to say to turn me on," I teased and pushed my tongue past my lips to lap it gently across the tip of his impressive length. I barely touched him, and yet he recoiled quite dramatically.

"Fucking hell," he complained, eyes turning to the ceiling. "I'd no idea you were this adamant about doing this."

Wrapping my hand around the base of him, I gazed up the length of his body with a look of mischief. When he saw it, his eyes hooded.

"Don't you dare look at me like that. Get me out of these. I'm going to fuck your brains out."

The breath of my arrogant chuckle tickled his erection as I leisurely trailed my tongue down the length of it towards my hand. The smell of him was driving me mad with desire. Finally I would have my way, and I would take my sweet time with it. I would torment him just like he insisted on tormenting me every time we joined heat.

"Cara," he purred softly, seemingly changing tactics. "Let me out of these and I promise I'll let you blow me before I do anything else." His tone was patient, almost pedagogical.

I managed to suppress a sardonic laugh. "Really?" I cooed innocently instead.

Hope shone from his eyes as he stared intensely into mine. Nodding vehemently, he said, "Yes."

"Do you think I'm stupid, William?"

Instantly, the hope in his eyes was slaughtered by frustration. "You're going to kill me." He threw his head back, broad shoulders sinking. "I want to fuck you so badly – I'm going to explode."

"Aw. Explode in my mouth, yeah?"

I spread my mouth over the crest of his member. Closing my eyes, I devoured the taste of his precum. I was looking forward to sampling more of the flavour this time, as I would make sure to bring things to the finish line. I wondered if it would taste foul. Some men had awful-tasting sperm, and I was about to find out if William was one of them, though I surely hoped he wasn't. Aaron's had been just fine.

At that moment, it dawned on me that this might be the one thing William could prove worse than Aaron in.

The suspense.

I clenched my fist around his length as I took him deeper into my mouth. My lips stretched to accommodate him, but I was careful to sheathe my teeth with them while I flicked my tongue across the head of his shaft. As I did, a beautiful groan of pleasure drifted out of his mouth, and it prompted me to look up at him.

He looked high. His lips had parted only slightly, and his eyes were faded. *God*, how that look on his face turned me on. It motivated me like nothing else.

"Fuck, Cara," he said through his teeth and shoved himself deeper into my mouth. "That tongue of yours is seriously lethal."

I smiled, encouraged. Knowing the vibrations of my voice could leave tingling sensations in his member, I hummed against him in my mouth while I slowly bobbed my head. Releasing his shaft from my grip, I spread both my hands across his muscular thighs while I pleasured him solely with my mouth. I was collecting courage to take all of him in.

After a few more gentle bobs of my head, I pushed forward and squeezed my eyes shut when I felt him reach the back of my throat. Tears were triggered at once. I'd always wished I were one of those women who didn't have a gag reflex, as I truly loved giving blowjobs, but alas, I'd had to learn how to control it instead.

When I reached the base of him, I lost it. Gagging on him, I immediately retreated and focused instead on the long and appreciative groan that escaped him. As I returned to the tip of him, I heard him rattle his confines again.

"You're driving me mad!" he cried.

"Yeah? Good," I purred and grabbed around him again to expose his sac. Lowering my head, I lapped my tongue carefully across it and felt his thigh flex against my left hand. While tending to his balls, I made sure to pump him with my hand.

A whimper slipped out of him. When I looked up, I saw that he had closed his eyes and dropped his head forward. He shook it to himself, clearly tortured, which made me smile.

Moving back to his shaft, I took him into my mouth again and increased my pace somewhat. While drawing in on him, I met each of my sucks with my hand, careful with the amount of force I exerted. Hard, but not too hard. Just enough to drive him crazy.

I continued for minutes on end and ignored the fact that my

jaw was starting to ache from having to hold my mouth so wide apart for so long. It was definitely painful, but the pleasure it gave him easily compensated for it.

When I was nearing my limit, I bobbed my head, breathlessly, at feverish rapidness, only to be shocked when he started thrusting into my mouth, perfectly synchronised with my movements. Again, I squeezed my eyes shut and welcomed his eager shoves. Since he was abnormally large, tears trailed down my cheeks, but I would not stop. I refused. I would make him come.

"Ah, shit," he panted and fought against the handcuffs again. "Let me out of them. Bloody let me out of them," he begged.

I ignored him completely.

"Cara, darling, I'm going to come," he warned and slowed his thrusts. Responding, I increased my own pace instead, pumping him hard and fast with my hand while my sore mouth continued to indulge him.

"Cara, I mean it. Unless you want it in your mouth, you need to stop." He sounded alarmed. I wanted to scoff at him, but refrained. Instead, I reacted by deep-throating him yet again, and, just as I was about to pull back, his warm release spilled into my mouth.

"Ah," he moaned and pushed harshly into my mouth to pump out the rest of himself. I nearly choked on the amount, but thankfully managed not to. Only after I'd swallowed every last drop of him did I pull away for air, and as I did, I was positively surprised by the flavour of him.

Not bad at all. In fact, it was remarkable. His release hardly tasted like anything. It was quite a neutral flavour. I could tell it was sperm, but it wasn't remotely distasteful. He must have been made for this – the embodiment of erotica. He seemed created for the purpose of indulging sensual pleasures.

I found it incredibly relieving. Knowing this, performing fellatio on him wasn't ever going to be something I'd shy away from. Truly, what a relief. It served as a lovely reminder of how compatible we were. I relished performing fellatio, and his sperm was optimal for it.

Breathless, I looked up at him and gave him a wry smile as I cleaned the corner of my mouth with the pad of my index finger. Trapped in bliss, he gazed lazily back at me, large lungs heaving for air.

"Show me," he said. Kinky.

Opening my mouth, I proudly revealed that I'd swallowed every drop of him. A crooked smile nested on his mouth.

"You're wicked, Cara."

Chuckling, I climbed up on my legs and smoothed my hands across his chest. "You taste quite good. I was pleasantly surprised."

He frowned. "So I've been told, actually. Had me worried in the beginning, so I researched it. Apparently, it doesn't correlate with sperm quality. Just how some men are designed."

I burst out laughing. "You've researched it?"

"Yeah. I want children one day. I got worried."

I continued to laugh, endlessly charmed, and patted his chest. "Good for you, Will."

Affection danced in his alluring eyes. "Yeah. And you, I suppose, since you're so determined to give blowjobs that you're willing to go to the extreme measure of confining me."

"Was the only way."

"Let me out of them, Cara," he commanded. Was I finally growing immune to his authoritative tone with me? "You've had your way now."

I shook my head. "No, not yet. I think I'll hang on to my power for a bit longer," I taunted and began to unbutton his shirt.

"You're being unfair," he protested. Giving him a smirk, I dropped my gaze to the view I slowly exposed beneath my hands. It made me salivate. I'd never stop appreciating how fit he was.

"You're so sexy, William," I purred once I'd finished undoing the last button. Spreading his shirt apart, I admired him in all his glory. With his physique, he could easily have been mistaken for a Greek god. Biting on my lower lip, I clawed down his muscular chest and watched the red marks emerge after my nails. "Appetising," I added and shot him a lustful glance.

"Right now, I really wish I wasn't," he replied sulkily and turned his profile to me.

I giggled as I gripped his shirt to bring him with me into his living room. He stalled me for a moment, struggling out of the pool of his trousers, before he glared in my direction.

"I'm not your pet," he grumbled.

"You're my sexual servant."

"So high on your horse. You're going to regret this, Cara."

I pressed my lips together when I realised he might be right. I was essentially taunting a wild beast in captivity right now. "I'm a bit scared to release you now. Maybe I'll have you sleep in those."

"Oh, I will have your fucking head if you do!"

I laughed and laughed as I dragged him along. Once we reached one of his sofas, I planted my hands on his strong shoulders and shoved him onto it. He was staring up at me with a pout on his face when I grabbed the hem of my dress to peel it off slowly. It was really quite comical, because before the garment covered my face, he'd been pouting hard, but after I'd pulled it over my head, he was gawking instead. The floor appeared to have summoned his jaw.

Leering at him, I dropped my dress to the wood below our feet. "You've always appreciated my bum, Will," I said and turned one-hundred-and-eighty degrees to eye him over my shoulder. "How do you find it now?" I caressed my buttocks, seductively.

I'd never seen him ogle me quite so blatantly and extensively before. Unashamed, his eyes roamed up and down my body, repeatedly. After a long and deep inhalation, he shut his mouth and steered his gaze to mine.

"Let. Me. Out!"

"Ah-ah," I scolded and faced him again. "Don't think so," I crooned and moved to straddle his lap. Hooking my arms around his neck, I rested my breasts just beneath his jaw. His stubbly chin fit perfectly into my cleavage, and I grinned as I felt the coarse strands of it graze my skin. "Don't they look good, Will?"

He closed his eyes while a grimace crossed his chiselled face. "Cara, I'm in pain. Please."

Chuckling, I cupped his jaw in my hands, aligned my mouth with his, and leaned forward until not even an inch separated them. Meanwhile, I started grinding against him. "Pain, you said?"

The groan he released was almost a sob, the breath of it breezing my mouth. "Please, let me out. I'll be gentle. I promise."

When I persisted despite his plea, he continued, "Cara, I'm begging you. Just let me touch you. I want to make love to you. Sweet, intense love to you."

My heart throbbed at his phrasing, rendering me frozen. He'd made it sound like a dying wish. What's more, it evoked the memory of the last time he'd said something similar. It had been right before he'd introduced me to a whole new dimension of sex, and it had been more profound than anything I'd ever experienced before.

Surrendering to temptation, I sighed. I wanted to feel that again. "Fine."

He tensed beneath me, but only for a few seconds. "Thanks," he eventually said and mellowed under my body.

Abandoning him, I went for my purse to recover the keys for the handcuffs. It wasn't until I turned around again that I realised he was staring after me, and the sight of him was staggering. He resembled a man who had found his salvation.

Unnerved by the intense emotion in his gaze, I avoided it bashfully as I made my return. "Lean forward," I mumbled as I took a stand behind the sofa and faced his broad back.

Obeying, he bent to expose his wrists to me and patiently

waited while my trembling hands relieved him of his shackles. Just when I had managed, he spun around and reached for me, but my reflexes were too swift. Jumping backwards, I stared wide-eyed at him, and the rapacious look in his eyes made me acutely aware of the fact that I'd been deceived. He did not intend to make love to me at all. On the contrary, he looked about to deliver punishment.

For a few seconds, we merely stared at each other, anticipating a movement, predator and prey.

Finally, I squeaked, and the sound of it triggered his lunge. Squealing and screaming, I ran towards the dining table. "William! You promised!"

"Well, I fucking lied," he snapped and chased after me. My heart was in my throat when I rounded the square table and turned to look at him. Pure adrenaline enhanced my senses, alarming me of looming danger. I was so fucked.

"You bastard!" I said when he crouched by the table, observing which direction I might run. When he pretended to step to my left, I gasped and rushed towards my right, but thankfully brought myself to stop when I saw that he had.

"I am going to fuck you till you can no longer breathe, Cara," he growled and glared at me across the table.

His savage words caused arousal to soak my underwear. I held my breath as I felt it slide out of me. What on earth? Was my vagina an idiot? I should not be reacting like that.

"William, I'm sorry. I only meant to tease you a bit."

His eyes widened with incredulity. "Tease me? That was nothing short of torture! Get yourself over here before I climb over the table," he threatened. "I will catch you. You're only postponing the inevitable."

Just when I looked to the heavens for aid, he lunged onto the table. *Oh my God.* I'd turned him into an actual animal.

Squealing again, I turned for the kitchen, but, before I got far enough, his fingers managed to twirl into my long hair. Using his grip, he tugged me harshly backwards until my lower back collided with the table. I whimpered and angled my face to catch a look of him, and, as I did, I found him grinning at me. He looked radiant.

"Cara, I swear, I fucking—" He cut himself off by pressing his lips together. After a composing breath, he continued, "I find you endearing."

I hadn't thought I could blush in a scenario such as this – hair being pulled by a ruthless savage about to fuck me into ruins. Then again, suppose the fact that I was in love with him made me overlook it.

"Thanks, Will. Enough to let go of my hair?"

He smirked and hopped off the table to land beside me. "Definitely not," he stated and bent over to heave me across his shoulder. Daunted, I stared at the floor beneath my head. What had I done?

We'd nearly passed his sofa group when he suddenly stopped. Bending sideways, he fetched the handcuffs out of it. My eyes widened. *Oh no.*

"Let's see how you like your own medicine, shall we?" he said and spanked my bum.

"Will!"

"Object all you like, *mon amour*. I'm insusceptible for the moment."

Charging towards his bedroom, he was a determined man. Kicking the door open, he headed towards his bed and dropped me onto it. I was about to run for it again when he clasped my shoulders and manhandled me onto my stomach beneath him. After a short battle, he had secured both my wrists behind my back and locked them in the handcuffs.

Satisfied, he pulled back to admire his craft. "Now then," he eventually said. "Let's begin, shall we?"

19

ANY YOUTH IN THE WORLD

Vigilant, I turned my head when I heard him shift behind me. He was approaching his nightstand, and, from it, he withdrew a shiny rose-gold object that I recognised all too well.

My eyes sprang wide. It was a vibrator. I was dying tonight.

"William, no!" I both pleaded and protested.

I nearly mistook him for the Devil when he flashed me a sadistic grin, blue eyes gleaming above. "Have you got any idea how sexy you look? I reckon adding your cum-face to this is going to make it a masterpiece, if it isn't already."

My mouth dried upon my sharp inhalation. Within me, my heart threatened to pulverise my ribs. This was not going to end anytime soon.

While holding my gaze under arrest, he undid the sleeves of his shirt and shrugged out of the white material to discard it on the floor. As he climbed into the bed again, I swallowed.

"What's your record, Cara?" he asked and directed his attention to my buttocks. Appearing to admire them, he ran his hand across and squeezed.

"My-my record?"

His eyes darted back to mine, and the sexual twinkle in them indexed my doom. "Yes. What's the highest number of orgasms you've had during one round with a partner?"

Blood sprinted to my cheeks. "I don't know."

Underwhelmed, he stared back. "You don't know?"

I shook my head. "I lost count. Well, to be honest, I stopped counting. My brain crashed."

Nonplussed, he knitted his brows. "Who holds the record, then?"

I looked back at him, confused. "Do you mean who was I sleeping with when it happened?"

He nodded, which led my blush to worsen. Bashful, I glanced away. "You," I barely mumbled.

The responding grin that tugged on his lips was bewitching. He looked ten years younger while he appeared to soar across cloud nine. "Really? When was this?"

Still coy, I said meekly, "After I agreed to go on a date with you." That session had been animalistic. He'd left no doubt in my mind that – to him – it had been a matter of reclaiming what was rightfully his.

His eyes glinted with elation. "You have no idea how happy I am to hear that. Though, let's make it ten tonight, at the very least, shall we? I'm sure we could do more, but we've got to start somewhere, right?" Upon that note, he switched on the vibrator.

Oh my God.

His voice was saturated with thrill when he continued, "I'll have you count them out loud this time around, just to be sure you don't forget. Ready?"

"No," I whimpered and buried my face in the mattress while

my whole body stiffened to prepare for impact. The familiar sound of the vibrator warned of imminent torment.

Grabbing my hip, he flipped me around, and as soon as I was on my back, he spread my legs apart to kneel between them. Intimidated, I stared up at him and swallowed once more.

He placed the vibrator in the concavity between my collarbones while a crooked smile formed on his tempting mouth. Slowly, he dragged it to my cleavage where he allowed it to rest. Then, his eyes abandoned mine to admire the view of me.

"Cara, honestly, you will always be the most beautiful woman to me," he stated soberly. "When we're fifty, I'm going to remember this, and even if lines have creased your pretty face by then, I'll see the years in them that I've spent with you, and that will forever be more beautiful to me than any youth in the world."

Astounded by his sweet declaration, I gaped up at him. I'd never heard anything more romantic in my entire life. The extreme emotion that engulfed my chest made me feel like I was about to explode.

"William," I uttered feebly, and my face contorted at the immense love that I had for him at that moment. Caught up in the intensity of my feelings for him, I nearly spilled three words that I shouldn't. Not yet. It was far too soon. I had to be sure that I truly loved him – that my feelings for him weren't wavering – before I brought myself to declare something so momentous, because once I said it, I couldn't take it back.

Chuckling, he leaned over me to stare deep into my eyes. "I'm all yours, darling," he assured me and lowered his mouth to leave a kiss in the corner of my mouth. Yearning to embrace him, I rattled my handcuffs, but it proved futile. It made me sympathise with the amount of frustration he must have endured earlier. Nothing tempted more than to smother him right now.

"Annoying, aren't they?" he teased and ran his mouth down my throat to trade gentle kisses with my thumping artery. It felt so good that I shut my eyes to savour the sensation. He knew all the weakest spots on my body.

My eyes were still closed when he shoved down the bra of my bustier to reveal my breasts. Soon after, his warm mouth covered my left nipple, sucking and nibbling. The acute pleasure of it surged into my core, leaving me to arch to grant him full possession. Down my sides his hands ran, repeatedly tracing the curve of my waist, all while the vibrator remained between my breasts.

After a long minute, he fetched the device out of my cleavage and abandoned my left breast to tend to my right. Just as his mouth closed around my nipple, he placed the vibrator to my sensitised left. The delicious vibrations made me writhe against my confines again. He was driving me mad, and he had only just begun.

"Will," I moaned and opened my eyes, hopeful the plea in them would inspire his mercy, but he glanced up at me with a cheeky smile on his mouth.

"Insusceptible, Cara. Insusceptible," he reminded me. Gathering his digits around my right nipple, he tugged it.

"Ah." I shut my eyes again. Ever slowly, he dragged the vibrator down the centre of my stomach towards the apex of my thighs. When he halted just above my clit, my heart skipped a beat.

"Fuck," I complained and shook my head to myself, mentally preparing.

"Fuck indeed." As he stretched up again, I opened my eyes to observe him, ever on alert. Staring into my eyes, he hooked his fingers into my thong to drag them to the side. Then, he lowered his gaze to have a greedy look at the view. A smug smile dominated his lips when his eyes returned to mine. "You're glistening, Cara. Soaked. And I haven't even touched you there yet."

The heat in my cheeks increased. "William!"

"I'm grateful you've left some hair behind this time."

"Had I known you'd do this I'd have shaved it all off."

Chuckling, he slid his finger between my folds. A breath later, he raised the same finger to his mouth to sample my taste. My lips parted. Engrossed, I watched him suck on it, devouring my flavour.

"Speaking of appetising, I fucking love the taste of you, Cara."

My blush was constant. Speechless, I observed him lower his head to place a single kiss on my aching bud. I jerked backwards immediately.

"Oh, that's charming," he commented. "You think you stand a chance?" His laughter was pitiless when he lifted the vibrator between our faces. With eyes wide, I heaved for air. But to my surprise, he switched it off.

"My pride insists that I should make you come with my mouth first," he explained and put it aside. As he grabbed my thighs to tuck them over his shoulders, I squealed inwardly. To secure me in place, he locked his arms around my legs and didn't waste so much as a breath before he circled my clit with his warm tongue.

I gasped and bent my neck, shocked by how ready I was. He wasn't striking me directly, and yet the delicious friction of his licks spread towards the centre of my nerves, pleasuring me slowly towards my peak.

"Shit," I hissed and writhed against him. The breath of his laughter breezed my wetness. Soon, the sadist in him impelled him to flick his tongue across my clit only once, simply for the sake of torment.

Responding to the pleasure, my eyebrows furrowed as I groaned. When he swept across that particularly sensitive spot along my left side, I thrust against him and gnashed my teeth. *Shit*, that felt too good. Seeming to notice, he focused his point of impact on that precise place.

"Ah!" I cried out as the tension rallied within me, merciless in its magnitude. It was charging at such speed that I was momentarily shocked by it. How could this be possible when he wasn't even hitting me directly?

"Will," I gasped as every muscle of my body flexed in an

attempt to counter the tremendous force of my looming orgasm. *God*, I wished I could tug his hair, claw down his back – something, anything – to relieve this paralysing tension that raged within me.

Responding to my cry, he increased the rapidness and pressure of his licks, and it made me gape. *Fucking hell*, I was going to explode. I shook my head and squeezed my eyes shut. Just when my toes curled, I held my breath and concentrated only on withstanding the tormenting amount of pleasure he provided.

I wasn't sure how long I held my breath for, but, by the time my quivers started, I was dizzy. Really, it felt as though my head was about to blow off. I wasn't going to last. This was agonising.

Then, all at once, I was released from the unbearable tension.

"Ah!" I wailed, back arching as euphoria stole me away. Dissolving, I heaved for air as I tried to restore my equilibrium. Through the obscureness of oblivion, I vaguely heard him switch on the vibrator again. I'd barely been allowed ten seconds to recover by the time he placed it to my throbbing clit.

Gasping, I tried to thrash away, but his grip on my hip prevented me. Opening my eyes, I found him watching me, seemingly riveted.

"Shit!" I wailed again. This was so overwhelming that it bordered on torture. Already, I started to climb again. Above the static noise of the vibrator, I heard my own erratic breath.

"Count, Cara," he commanded and stared fixedly into my eyes.

"One," I moaned and struggled to breathe through the fantastic friction that the device delivered.

He chuckled. "Nine to go."

I bit into my lower lip and shut my eyes. All sorts of weird things happened behind my eyelids. While I couldn't see a thing, I could have sworn I saw stars – tiny little explosions that were growing larger and larger by the second. They blended with various shades of red.

Digging my nails into my palms, I bent my neck again and

felt my body convulse away from the mattress. Desperate to escape the agonising pleasure, I tried to turn onto my side, but he denied me the satisfaction with his grip on my hip.

"William, please," I begged and shuddered somewhat violently. It was growing so fast. I was seconds away from coming again.

"But I am pleasing you," he cooed and dipped his head down to tantalise my left nipple with his mouth. *Fuck.* He sucked it harshly, and the sensation rippled through my veins until it tingled within my sex. My legs acted of their own accord when they wrapped around him, squeezing him so hard that I lifted myself off from the mattress.

"Wow, Cara," he uttered, impressed. Opening my eyes, I stared straight into his striking pair. The sight actually pained me. He was perfect. Just perfect. From the look in his eyes, I could tell he was entirely captivated by this intense moment between us. Truly, the mere view of him triggered me like nothing else.

"I'm…coming," I gasped before I locked the air in my lungs, paralysed.

He pushed the vibrator harder against me, causing my eyes to widen. Even if I tried, I could not utter so much as a sound anymore. My brain had disconnected from my mouth. All I could focus on was the tremendous force that swelled within me.

Higher, higher. It was like a bomb went off within me when I finally came. The acuteness of my orgasm was so intense that I cried out my release at the top of my lungs.

"Count, Cara," he commanded again when I collapsed beneath him. Thankfully, he removed the vibrator to allow me some room to compose myself.

"T-two."

"Well done. Now, let's escalate things." He trailed his index finger down my stomach, slowly, towards my soaked slit. My heart missed a beat. Escalate things?

When he pushed a single finger into me to gently massage

my front wall, I groaned in delight. *God*, it felt good. I wanted him within me. My craving for his flesh was extreme. I wanted to feel him fill me up, stretching me to my limit, and pleasure me into the celestial.

"Will, please. Get inside of me already."

His smirk murdered my hope. "Not until we've reached at least five." With that, he placed the vibrator back on my overly sensitive clit and continued to finger me.

"Oh, God," I whimpered, my face contorting. "Shit!"

"I quite like these handcuffs, Cara. Good thinking, even if it wasn't part of your plan to be the one put in them."

"Fuck you," I growled. I was sure I resembled a wild animal when I bared my teeth to him as I hissed. To punish my courageous outrage, he pushed a button on the vibrator, leaving it to intensify in its vibrations. Meanwhile, he pushed his finger precisely against that susceptible spot within me.

"Fuck!"

"Soon, darling. Soon." He descended to place a belittling kiss on my forehead.

Inserting another digit, he fingered me without a trace of pity as the vibrator continued to torture my clit. The friction tending to my bundle of nerves, as well as his long fingers inside me, was driving me insane.

I was reaching it in record time. Yet again, my toes curled, and my walls clamped down on his digits within me.

"No. I'm coming again," I whined and fought against my confines. All I wanted was to touch him. The desire to do it was maddening. I wanted to cup his sharp jaw, feel the spiky strands of it scrape my palms while I stared into his captivating eyes. I wanted to caress his beautiful, broad shoulders while I clung to him as he made love to me.

I fucking hated handcuffs. I would throw them in the bin first thing tomorrow.

"This is remarkably fascinating. I seriously envy your gender for this," he said while keenly observing each response of my body. "Then again, even for a woman, you're exceptionally sensitive."

I wanted to tell him to shut up and let me focus on this agonising build, but since I couldn't breathe anymore, I was unable.

My jaw drew shut as the tension stretched out to my fingertips and toes, rendering me immobile. Then, finally, it released. Air stormed out of my lungs while I finally softened. At that moment, it was as though dopamine was all I consisted of.

"Ah, stop, Will. I need to recover or I'm going to die," I warned hoarsely. Adhering to my plea, he removed the vibrator and studied me, transfixed, while I recovered below him. He didn't withdraw his fingers, however, but he did stop thrusting them into me.

"How many, Cara?" he reminded me.

"Three," I replied breathlessly.

"So we still have seven to go. You ought to muster your strength. I'm nowhere near finished with you."

I forced my eyelids apart to look at him in my laziness. "Will, make love to me. Please," I begged. "I want to feel you inside me."

He chuckled. "And you will, but not yet. I'm not an idiot, Cara. I won't fall into a trap that I designed myself." I realised he was referring to his deceit earlier.

"I will never fall for that again," I grumbled, annoyed. "Hope you're happy you used your ace already. How dare you exploit my weakness like that?"

Seemingly charmed, his eyes twinkled. "I'm glad to hear that the idea of making love to me has become a weakness of yours. But in any case, I'll find other ways. By now, you should know I've always got an ace hidden up my sleeve."

I looked away from him, annoyed by his superiority, even though a small – big, actually – part of me did fancy that he was able to defeat me. It earned my respect, and it set my libido on fire.

I whimpered when he returned the vibrator to my pulsating bud. Shifting my gaze back to his, I regarded him vulnerably, trying to stir his compassion.

"Insusceptible," he reminded me flatly and directed his attention to my breasts. A lovely smile covered his mouth then. "You know, I never really understood the fascination with tits. I've always found them attractive, obviously, but I've never been able to fathom some men's obsession with them. But seeing yours like this, I finally do. I am definitely obsessed with your tits – and the rest of you."

Had he just declared himself obsessed with me? This man was nothing short of staggering. Worse was it that he hadn't expressed even a trace of shame while he was at it. Per usual, he was totally unapologetic. Overwhelmed by both his words and his treatments, I blushed profusely and looked at the ceiling in my hopeless state.

"William. Now is not the time to be pondering over tits. I am in agony here," I snapped.

He chuckled. "Now you know how I feel."

What?

"What?" I frowned at him, but instead of replying, he pushed his fingers deeply into me, successfully distracting me as the pleasure annihilated any chance at coherent thoughts.

"Mm," I groaned and closed my eyes to yield to the moment.

By the time I reached my fifth orgasm, I was hardly anything but a sack of meat and blood. Exhausted, I couldn't minister so much as a muscle. By contrast, William's energy was off the charts. I'd hardly whispered the word "Five" by the time he gripped my hips and flipped me onto my front beneath him. Lifting only my bottom, he swiftly proceeded to unfasten my stockings.

From his practised speed, I surmised that this was not the first time he had undressed a woman wearing relatively complicated lingerie, and it made me experience a flash of green emotion. The idea of him undressing another female like he was currently undressing me was uninviting. It made me feel less special, and I didn't enjoy it in the least. I wanted to be the only woman William lusted after.

"Done this before, have you?" I asked, tone disguised in nonchalance, but behind it, I was hiding bitterness.

"I may have," he admitted, amused. "Though, never with a woman I've wanted as much as I want you. Honestly, Cara, it pales in comparison."

My heart ached as a bullet of affection for him charged through it. While he could certainly be trying at times, I could always count on him to reassure me when I needed it most.

"You always know what to say, Will," I replied fondly and turned my head as I hoped to convey my adoration for him with my eyes.

His smile made him look a bit shy. "I mean it, though."

I believed him, and I did because he wasn't in the habit of saying things he didn't mean. In the end, his honesty was one of his most admirable traits, albeit brutal at certain times. But even when it was, it was always necessary evil. Tough love, simply.

I was returning his smile when he hooked his fingers into my thong to drag it down my thighs, over my stockings. When he suddenly lowered his head, my eyes widened.

"No, don—" I objected, but I cut myself off with a groan when his soft mouth met with my pulsating clit. "Fuck," I hissed and faced the headboard of his bed as I fisted my hands behind my back.

"This is going to get rough, Cara. Fortunately, you're more than ready," he warned breathily and stretched up behind me. After grabbing my left hip, he aligned his erection with my folds and then proceeded to lubricate himself in my arousal. As he slid up and down repeatedly, I clenched my jaw to prepare for impact. He hadn't even entered me, and yet my slit still tingled intensely upon the attention he was granting it.

"I am so fucked," I whispered to myself and planted my face on the mattress.

"Not yet, you're not," he replied, seeming to have heard me. Without further warning, he thrust hard and deep into me.

Oh, my God. "Ah!"

Just like he always did, he stretched me to my limit, and he didn't stop until his crest poked the very end of me. There, he lingered, savouring the feel of me clenching around him.

"Now you are truly fucked," he stated with a groan and crouched over me, strong arms landing on either side of my frame to support his weight. Withdrawing, he shocked me with his next thrust. The strength he applied was ferocious. It was nearly just painful, but not quite. It was at the stage just before it, on the bliss-point.

I held my breath as I was pushed forward across the mattress with each of his savage thrusts. Only when I reached the headboard of his bed did he pause them. Curling his large hands over my shoulders, he lifted my upper body and moved us forward until I was smothered between the headboard and his powerful body. My chest was planted flat across the dark wood. As he smoothed his hands down to my hips, he jerked my lower body backwards to better align himself with me.

"I badly want to rip off your underwear," he growled under his breath, and his statement made me giggle.

"That is seriously a kink of yours, Will."

"You look so enticing, and yet, ironically, I just want to get rid of it. It's driving me mad."

I glanced at him over my shoulder. "Which is it, Will? Underwear or no underwear?"

He smirked. "I think I'll make you come both with and without. In that order. I'm greedy like that."

Reminded that I still had five orgasms to go, I let out another whimper. Another followed the instant he shoved into me again. Immediately, he recreated his aggressive pattern. As he continued to plough into me, my chest bounced on the headboard of his bed. Since my nipples were erect, they were susceptible to the friction of it. It was like tiny bites every time I was pushed against the wall.

"Oh," I moaned and tossed my head back upon a particularly perfect thrust. Resting it on his broad shoulder, I closed my eyes and revelled in the sensation. There was nothing I loved more than when William demanded possession of my body. His proclivity for dominance wasn't something I would ever stop appreciating.

"Hear that, Cara?" he whispered in my ear and gave my temple an extended, tender kiss. Focusing on my hearing, heat soon flooded my face. Indeed, I could hear it. Below the flapping noises of our flesh parting and meeting was the subtle sound of my audible arousal, blending with the noise of our bodies making contact. I was completely drenched. Now acutely aware of it, I realised my fluids had trailed down my inner thighs. For all I knew, I was soaking his bed as well.

"I love how wet I can make you," he purred and wrapped his strong arms around me to hug me against his warm chest. "But..." he murmured and suddenly withdrew.

He abandoned me entirely, so I turned my head. Confused, I watched him lean over the edge of his bed to recover his shirt from the floor. Bent over as he was, the sight of his muscular back made me swallow the drool in my mouth. He was so fucking attractive. My heart contracted as I ogled the view of his rippling slabs of muscle.

Once he returned, he met my eyes and smiled, amused, upon noticing my puzzled expression. "That much lubricant is ruining the friction," he explained and gently dried me off. Impressed, I observed his action from the corner of my eye.

"Have you studied sex, William? Who knows things like that?"

"It doesn't require a Sherlock to understand that, Cara. Anyway, looks like we'll have to change the sheets before we settle for sleep tonight. You still have five orgasms to go."

I exhaled long and loud and looked to the heavens for aid.

"I'm going to be severely dehydrated by the end of this."

His ensuing laughter was wholehearted. "Dehydrated," he echoed.

When his laughter ceased, he wrapped his hand around the chain between my handcuffs and reclined to lie on his back, successfully dragging me with him. "Now then," he said, satisfied, when I lay atop his chest. Running his hands down my body, he didn't stop until he reached my thighs. When he did, he spread them apart, bucked his hips up, and guided the head of his erection towards my entrance.

After a single, deep thrust, he rolled us over, withdrew, and shoved harshly into me again, leaving my buttocks to be pushed up towards my back.

"Oh my God," I wheezed. Like this, he was sliding straight across my front wall. And he had been right. Now that he'd dried off some of my natural lubricant, I could feel him much better.

"God won't be helping you tonight, *chérie*," he responded playfully. "In fact, I'll make sure to grant you divine pleasures in His stead."

I planted my face on the mattress and moaned to myself, knowing full well that he wasn't lying. I should have listened to Jason. Teasing William had not turned out the way I'd had in mind – at all.

While supporting himself on his elbows on either side of me, he started a different rhythm entirely. This time he was slow, but still, he reached so fucking deep. Grinding my teeth together, I focused on my breathing while I tried to stabilise the growing tension within me. That mission was fruitless. Amassing in my lower abdomen was a vicious climax that was certain to blow my mind.

"Will," I moaned pleadingly.

A deep groan escaped his mouth. Suddenly, he pushed up. Gripping the chain between my handcuffs again, he dragged me with him and swiftly locked my body between his arms. I revelled in his embrace. No other embrace had ever stirred such immense emotion in me – not like this. In his arms, I felt like I belonged.

"I love being inside of you, Cara," he confessed, and it triggered my heart to race at dramatic speed. I was hyperaware of his word choice. He *loved* being inside of me.

"And I love having you within me, Will," I bravely said and rested my head on his shoulder. If only he knew I'd meant that I loved having him within my heart as well.

As if provoked by my response, he tightened his embrace of me to such a degree that I could hardly breathe. Suddenly, he dropped his mouth to my shoulder and bit gently into it. His action puzzled me. It was the way he did it that made it odd, because it lasted for many seconds while he continued to smother me against him. What made it particularly conspicuous was the fact that he stopped thrusting altogether. It didn't appear to be part of his sensual designs. On the contrary, it seemed part of resistance.

"You alright?" I queried breathlessly.

He released my shoulder and leaned out of my line of sight. "Yeah. Why?" His voice was devoid of emotion.

"You stopped."

Promptly, he thrust into me again. "Just trying to control my urge to come," he insisted, but his tone didn't convince me. However, he provided no opportunity to continue my interrogation when he resumed his earlier rhythm. Clasping my breasts, he squeezed and tugged on my nipples.

"Ah," I groaned appreciatively. The tension assembled again. "Oh, I seriously wish we could do this forever," I admitted in my ecstatic state.

His soft chuckle massaged my ears before he nuzzled the crook of my neck with his nose. After planting a soft kiss on the skin of it, he said with affection, "You and me both, Cara."

Responding, I jerked against him, and gasped as the movement only shoved him deeper into me. Instantly, I began to quiver. My impending orgasm had been looming closer than I thought.

"Fuck," I whined as my walls closed around him.

"Ah. That's it, Cara."

"Mm!" I shuddered in his hold of me, wanting to escape from the unbearable tension that consumed my entire person.

"Come on," he growled under his breath and ploughed harshly into me. At once, my thoughts scattered into oblivion as bliss stole me away from him.

Only vaguely did I hear him say, "Four more to go."

20

BON APPÉTIT

I WAS BARELY ALIVE AFTER MY EIGHTH ORGASM. DURING ACT number seven, he had inserted a butt plug into me, and its presence had triggered orgasms more formidable than any other I'd experienced before.

Pulling out of me, he wiped a layer of sweat off his forehead with his arm. "How many, Cara?"

I couldn't recall the last time I'd been this physically exhausted. This was nothing short of a bloody fuck-marathon. I couldn't string so much as a word together anymore. All thoughts had abandoned me while I concentrated solely on enduring this.

Grabbing my hips, he turned me onto my stomach and spanked my arse. A yelp poured out of my mouth. The sting of it burnt into my flesh. Judging by the force he had exerted, I was positive that the print of his hand remained.

"How many, Cara?"

Collecting my strength for another two breaths, I barely managed to croak out, "E-eight."

"Indeed, eight. Two left," he purred and smoothed his hand across the area he'd struck a mere moment ago. "But before we get to it..." He reached for the back of my bustier to undress me. I was completely limp while he removed every article of clothing covering my skin. Once he'd finished – after unfastening and refastening my handcuffs – I was lying on my back again.

It demanded some willpower to open my eyes. He was sitting on his heels, eyes devouring the view of me.

"While I fancy you in lingerie, nothing beats the view of you naked," he said and trailed his index finger, light as a feather, around my breasts. Closing my eyes again, I felt my vagina pulsate. My heart might as well have relocated to it. I dreaded sitting tomorrow, and even walking. I was going to be terribly sore after this, and I still had two more to go. The mere thought made me utter a sound that resembled a sob.

"I'll be right back," he said and hopped out of the bed, not nearly as a drained of energy as I was. I didn't bother asking him what he was doing. I was merely grateful for a break, and I hoped it wouldn't be too quick.

Alas, I was made aware of his return only a minute later from his weight on the mattress. That awareness was intensified when I felt something ice cold land on my left nipple. Gasping, I opened my eyes and watched him drag a spoonful of raspberry sorbet across my breasts.

"Time for dessert," he said and scooped up another spoonful from the box before he guided it to my mouth. Since I was already gaping, he inserted it without trouble, and the bittersweet taste of it blasted in my mouth.

"You look like your blood sugar is running low," he teased with a wink. "I hope you don't mind – I didn't bring a bowl. It's been a fantasy of mine to use your body as a plate for quite some time. And I'm in the habit of making my fantasies a reality."

"You're kidding," I whispered, astounded.

"No," he chuckled. "I wasn't sure which flavour you'd prefer, but raspberry sorbet is my personal favourite. It's not too sweet, and perfectly savoury, kind of like you. Though, I've got dark chocolate, too, if you'd rather have that. Then again, since I'll be doing most of the eating – or licking – it's only fair I get to choose the flavour."

The extent of his eroticism was infinite. I was sure. I'd never done anything so erotic and carnal my whole life. He was remarkably creative in bed.

Fascinated by his own design, he watched, transfixed, as he left a trail of sorbet down the centre of my torso. It flexed beneath the cold spoon that heightened the sensitivity of my skin. It was so chilled that it gave the illusion of burning. When he reached my navel, he dropped another spoonful within it before leaving behind yet another line that stopped just above my clit.

Engrossed, I observed him cover even my calves in the sticky dessert. The only place he left alone was my slit, and I gathered there was a reason for it. Knowing him, he probably knew exactly what should and should not interfere with my vagina.

After placing the sorbet and spoon on his nightstand, he moved to hover above me. While staring deep into my eyes, a wicked smile ruled his mouth. "*Bon appétit*, the French would say," he said and then descended to collect the trail of sorbet that he'd left on my throat earlier. His warm tongue spread across my thumping pulse. Overawed by the sensation, I shuddered.

"Mm. Cara and raspberry is easily my new favourite flavour," he cooed and lifted his head to leave a chaste kiss on my closed mouth.

"You're unreal, Will." I met his eyes with adoration shining from mine. Chuckling, he pinched my left nipple.

"Ah," I complained.

"Quite real, it would seem," he teased. "In the end, I exist to make your dreams come true."

I rolled my eyes at his comment, but was distracted when he replaced his fingers with his mouth to lick away the melted sorbet which coated my breasts.

He took his – quite literally – sweet time with me, leisurely licking me clean. All the while, he made sure to leave my slit for last. It was only when he was licking his way up my calf, towards my knee, that I prepared for what was coming. Kneeling in front of me, he supported my ankle with his hands while his merciless tongue slid further and further along my leg. When he reached my inner thigh, it tickled.

"Mm!" I giggled and tried to jerk away. At once, his eyes trapped mine, and what I discovered in them didn't look too well for me.

"Ticklish?"

"No," I lied.

Narrowing his eyes at me, he flicked his tongue across my sensitive skin again and effectively extracted another giggle from my mouth.

"Oh, Cara." He smiled against my flesh. As he ran the tip of his nose across it, I saw his smile transition into a devilish grin. "Duly noted."

Damn him.

His laughter was villainous as he continued to slide his tongue closer and closer to my folds. Just when he was about to tend to them, the wind of his breath spread across me first, and it was cool.

"Let's make it a delectable nine, shall we?" With that, he flicked his tongue across my most sensitive area.

"Mm," I groaned and gritted my teeth. And then he hit me with expert precision. Having his dessert, he blew my mind.

My hips bucked up in an attempt to escape, but, with his grip on my hips, he slammed me back down on the mattress. I battled against his hold of me, which in turn forced him to dig his fingers into my hips so hard that I was certain I would bruise.

Whimpering, I grimaced as the agonising tension simmered within me, spreading through my veins and making my body tense. I did not give a single thought to how I must have looked when I finally cried out his name with abandon.

Rendered immobile, I savoured the blissful orgasm that stormed through my system. Nothing else mattered. I couldn't even dedicate a thought to his existence, and that spoke volumes. But he forced me to remember him when he suddenly penetrated me again.

Gasping at the fulfilment, I was ripped back to reality. I was lying on my stomach again, beneath him. After lingering within me for a beat, he twirled my hair around his fist and dragged us up until I was on my knees in front of him. He did not release my hair when he reached for the vibrator lying beside us and switched it on. My heart paused beating.

"I say we go all in for number ten, darling," he said before a chuckle and brought his arm around me to place the vibrator directly on my clit.

"Ah, no!" I wailed and recoiled backwards, momentarily forgetting that it would only push him deeper into me. Jerking forwards again, I was stopped by his grip on my hair. I was shackled to him. There was no escape. He was everywhere, inside and out.

"You're not going anywhere." His voice was low. Withdrawing, he proceeded to shove powerfully into me again, starting a punishing rhythm that summoned my final climax. This was fucking unbearable. The friction of the vibrator blended with the agonising pleasure of his precise thrusts, and each time he ploughed into me, the butt plug moved to stimulate the nerve endings in my other hole.

I couldn't breathe anymore.

Not a sound made its way out of my mouth while he panted behind me. Tugging my head back, he bent my neck backwards and covered the slope of it with ravenous kisses. Overwhelmed, I started shuddering as I climbed higher and higher.

In and out, he went, on repeat. And he reached so deep. When my walls pressed down on him, he released my hair to circle my waist with his arm.

"Come for me, Cara. I'm right there with you," he commanded and tugged my nipple. Since I had stopped breathing, the lack of oxygen induced my orgasm.

I'd never trembled so violently before.

Dropping the vibrator, he caged me in his arms and secured me in place while I turned rigid, overcome by the magnitude of my incredible orgasm.

"Fuck!" I cried out and saw tiny spots of silver shoot past my closed eyes.

"Ah," he groaned and pushed so hard into me that I wailed out his name. After another merciless thrust, he spilled himself within me and finally let go of me, leaving me to collapse against the mattress, utterly spent.

"That was intense," he stated on a ragged breath and gently withdrew. My vagina was totally beaten. Following his departure, it ached and seemed oddly hollow. Grabbing the end of the butt plug, he pulled it out and dropped it on the floor. Next, he finally undid my handcuffs and rolled onto his back beside me.

For minutes on end, we lay there, restoring our equilibrium. I, for one, was also restoring my sanity.

Eventually, he reached out for me, but his fingertips had hardly skimmed my skin when I hoarsely said, "Don't touch me. I'm dead."

Disobeying, he chuckled as he ran his entire palm lovingly down my damp back. "We need a wash."

"I am *not* moving. This bed shall be my coffin."

Sighing, he climbed out of bed and walked into his bathroom where I heard him start to run a bath. Returning, he walked around the bed to clasp my ankles. After tugging me towards him, he snuck his arms under my knees and back to lift me across his chest. Completely limp, I opened my eyes to look up at him. He stared straight back with a tender expression in his eyes, and it made my heart throb.

He said nothing, however.

Once he had lowered me into the bath, he turned for the door and exited. I basked in the hot water. It was exactly what I needed. The heat of it soothed my battered body and restored a portion of my strength.

From the corner of my eye, I caught a movement through the open door. Turning my attention to it, I discovered him changing the sheets of his bed, and the sight warmed my heart. I loved that he was so familiar with domestic chores. I truly loved that he didn't adhere to traditional gender roles by avoiding tasks like cleaning and cooking. I thought to myself that the day I found him sweeping floors would be the day I demanded to be his girlfriend.

I smiled to myself as I watched him put on a fresh sheet with meticulous attention. He didn't allow so much as a crease to disturb the fabric of it. In that, he was strikingly similar to his brother.

I was still admiring him when he suddenly looked towards me, catching me in my spying. A crooked smile shaped his mouth as he stretched away from the bed.

"I was worried you'd fall asleep and drown," he said. "Glad you're still remotely alive. I wouldn't know what to do with your corpse."

Chuckling, I faced away as I closed my eyes.

"Much less what to do without you," he added after a beat.

My heart jolted and my eyes reopened. Pure love coursed through my chest while his winsome words echoed in my mind. Turning towards him again, I pleaded, "Come join me. The temperature's lovely."

"In a moment."

Impatiently, I waited for him to finish up. When he finally had, he sauntered towards my figure in the bath and climbed in to recline behind me. He closed the tap while he was at it and then brought his arms around me to drag me towards his chest. With my legs between his beneath the surface of the water, I snuggled deeper into his embrace and exhaled, content.

"We have the craziest dates, Will. I'm not looking forward to the sex after date number three," I murmured and closed my eyes. Against the back of my head, I felt his heart pound, but the sensation of it was soon disturbed when his chest shook with his laughter.

"Don't worry, Cara. This won't be the standard we set for ourselves. Next time, we'll have lazy sex."

"Mm, that sounds lovely."

"As in five minutes from now."

I tensed at first, but then I realised he was only pulling my leg. "Ha-ha."

"Nearly got you there," he chuckled.

Reaching for the showerhead, he proceeded to wash my hair. As he did, he covered my eyes with his hand to ensure that no water bothered them. When he eventually rubbed shampoo into my hair, I nearly fell asleep, because he added a scalp massage to the mixture. Drool gathered in my mouth.

"That feels so good," I whispered drowsily and struggled to remain conscious.

"I aspire to make you feel good."

"You're succeeding."

Since I was still robbed of all strength by the time we'd washed up, he wrapped me into a towel and carried me back to bed. The clean sheets he tucked me into were like a meeting with paradise. My head had barely rested on my pillow for five seconds by the time I passed out. I didn't even notice that he snuggled up to spoon me.

§ § §

Revived, I woke up the next morning to the sound of a phone ringing, but it wasn't mine. Opening my eyes, the first thing I saw was William's irritated frown, even if his eyes were still shut. I realised he was holding me only when he let go to fetch his phone from his nightstand. Groaning, he opened his eyes to read the name on his screen. His frown intensified.

Sitting, he eyed the screen and accepted the call. "Yeah?" He sounded groggy.

Suddenly, his whole figure tensed. "You did what?" Pushing his duvet aside, he stepped out of bed and went straight into his wardrobe. Smitten, I stared after his beautiful backside with a contented smile on my face. I could never ogle him enough.

"Alex, I'm honestly delighted to hear that. You did the right thing."

Alex was the one calling him? Turning my gaze to William's alarm clock, I saw that it was nine in the morning. What on earth was he calling William for at this ungodly hour? Nine in the morning on a Sunday? Was he daft?

No way. I was going back to sleep. Turning my back to him, I snuggled into the duvet and tried to ignore their conversation, but it proved impossible when I heard him say, "Yeah, it's no bother. I'll be there in half an hour."

What? He was leaving? Whirling around, I searched for contact with his eyes through the open door, but he was too busy dressing to notice me.

"See you soon," he murmured and rang off.

"You're leaving?" I immediately asked.

Wearing nothing but a pair of navy-blue trousers, he turned to face me from within his wardrobe with a sombre look on his face. "Alex broke up with Abigail last night. I've got to be there for him. And I'm worried he'll change his mind. This is a critical time. I'm determined to convince him to let this be a permanent decision. It's not the first time they've hit a bump in the road."

My eyes widened. I surely hadn't expected that. Vaguely, I noted his changed mission. With Andy, he'd been adamant about guiding him back to Chloe. With Alex, he seemed motivated to sever his tie to Abigail completely.

"You really do not like her."

He raised a brow. "To be perfectly honest with you, I hate her. I've never met a woman I find more disagreeable. She's toxic, and she's ruining Alex. He got a bit depressed after his father died, and Abbie hasn't done anything to ease his suffering. She's only made it worse. So yes, I actually hate her for that. I don't want her anywhere near him."

I wasn't aware Alexander's father had died. "His father died?"

He nodded as he took a light-blue shirt off a hanger. "Yeah, two years ago. Spontaneous heart attack. His father was here, but Alex and I, as well as Chloe and Andy, were in the Bahamas together when it happened."

"Christ," I breathed out. "That's awful."

"It is, and Abbie's only made his life worse ever since. But, regarding their split, I suspect Ivy's part of the reason. Well, I hope she is, because if that's the case, she might be just what he needs to stick with his decision. He can't be pursuing her while he's got a girlfriend."

"I wish there were something I could do," I mumbled with a sympathetic pout.

Charmed, he gave me a smile as he swiftly fastened the buttons of his shirt. "I'm sorry I can't make you breakfast, but I trust you'll manage on your own."

I sighed. "I will."

He headed into the bathroom to brush his teeth and groom his hair, and, once he'd finished, I admired his graceful deportment as he approached. Simply the way he carried himself oozed attractive confidence. When he had rounded the bed to reach my side, he took a seat on it and cupped my cheek in his hand. The tenderness that his irises contained made my heart smile. I was dreadfully susceptible to that look of his.

"Get some more rest. I did a number on you last night."

"Ten, Will. You did ten numbers on me last night."

"I love myself." He smirked.

"At least someone does."

He whistled. "Brutal."

"Only teasing you. Now, leave me alone with my dreams. Alex needs you."

His thumb brushed across my cheek. "Don't you?"

I scoffed. "Not now, I don't."

"Nonsense. You hate that I'm leaving," he argued conceitedly. Well, it wasn't so conceited in the end, as it was indeed true.

"Get over yourself."

"Admit it."

"Fine! I'm really disappointed I'm not getting scrambled eggs for breakfast!"

He burst out laughing. "Just admit it already! It's perfectly alright to be disappointed that I'm leaving unexpectedly."

I moaned and shielded my blushing face with my pillow. Like myself, he could be impossibly stubborn. Speaking into it, I said, "Yes, Will, I'm disappointed you're leaving, and I can't wait to see you again for dinner later."

"That wasn't so hard, was it?"

"No."

"Good. Next time, try to upgrade it to a 'Will, I can't manage without you'."

I dragged the pillow away to scowl at him. "Take your banter and shove it up your arse, you utter bellend."

Laughing again, he lowered his head to kiss me right on the tip of my nose. "So close. I was so close."

"Not by a long chalk. You should know better than to question my independence."

His grin was contagious as he stretched up. "Oh, I encourage your independence. It's one of my favourite things about you. Anyway, see you soon."

"Yes. Go save your friend."

"I shall."

BULLETPROOF

DURING THE WHOLE TRIP HOME, I WAS ACUTELY AWARE of my soreness. The dense crowd of people on the train had no idea of the fuck-marathon I'd been subjected to last night, and it made me smile to myself. I wondered how many sinful secrets the man next to me kept veiled, and then the woman beside him. It was odd to think of how innocent people looked at first glance when they could be hiding all manner of crimes for all I knew. Appearances were so deceptive. They revealed so much, and yet so little at the same time.

When I strolled along the familiar pavement towards my flat, I was confident that I resembled a penguin with my strides. My entire body ached after William's merciless treatment last night. Thinking about it, an abundance of heat streamed into my face. Vivid scenes from our sensual session flashed in my mind. I remembered standing in his shower this morning, where I'd seen the bruises he'd left on my hips. Oddly enough, I loved them. They were a delicious reminder of how perfectly he pleasured my body.

As I entered the flat, I was confused by how quiet it was. Was Jason still asleep, or had he gone to attend some plans he hadn't informed me of? It wasn't like him to be absent without notice. Frowning, I dumped my purse in the hall and ambled past my bedroom, both the dining room and the kitchen, through the living room, until I finally rounded the corner to come upon his bedroom door. Since it was closed, I surmised he was still asleep.

After paying the door two knocks, I turned the handle and peeked inside. My mood plummeted upon the sight. I'd seen Jason hungover quite a few times before, so I was certain that this wasn't it.

Lying on his torso, his long legs were spread slightly. He was only wearing a pair of grey Calvin Klein boxers. With his hands tucked under the pillow that supported his head, he stared blankly out the windows of his private balcony doors overlooking Pembridge Square Garden. Looking out, I saw the green leaves of the trees rustling in the wind. Next to the gravel trail that went through the long, narrow garden, an old man sat on a bench, reading a newspaper. I just barely saw him behind all the colourful vegetation.

Steering my gaze back to Jason, I realised he was morose.

"Jason?" I called, concerned, and walked in to climb into his bed. He didn't reply until I rested flat across his back and hugged him against me. From the clean scent of him, as well as his damp hair, I gathered he must have showered shortly before I arrived.

"Hey," he mumbled and glanced at me from the corner of his eye when I poked my head to the side to get a better look at him.

"What's wrong?"

He sank beneath me with his long sigh. "Rough night."

"What happened?"

He was quiet for so long that it exacerbated my anxiety.

"Jason, I don't like seeing you like this."

He closed his eyes and frowned. "I did something stupid."

"Everyone does something stupid from time to time when they're drunk."

"No, Cara, it's not that kind of stupid."

"What did you do, then?" I feared the worst. Had something happened between him and Olivia?

He swallowed a lump in his throat. His eyes were still closed when I saw his lips twitch as he struggled to phrase himself. After huffing loudly, he finally brought himself to say, "I asked Livy out on a date last night, and she said no."

I froze as I processed his statement, and I could have sworn my heart broke for him. "Oh, no. Jason, I'm so sorry."

Despairing, another sigh poured out of his mouth. "This was what I feared – that I would make things awkward for you, seeing as she's one of your best friends. So, if she acts weird if I'm around you both or if ever I'm mentioned, you'll know why."

"Jason." I rolled onto my side so that we lay nose to nose. Upset, I watched him open his eyes to gaze into mine. "I really am so sorry," I said. "You don't deserve this. She's obviously blind, but you know as well as I do that she's got rubbish taste in men."

"Yeah, well, she and I have got that in common. I'm always chasing the unattainable," he murmured, and I could hear he was annoyed with himself.

Still trying to comprehend the truth of things, I stared at him. "What did she say? How did you...?"

"I'd had a couple of beers. Was reasonably tipsy when another lad started chatting her up, and she didn't approve of the attention, so I pretended to be her boyfriend to make him go away. At a certain point she thanked me for it, and I said that if she wanted, I could take her on an actual date and maybe be her real boyfriend someday." He shuddered. "You should have seen her face. It was awful. Took her a good minute before she started the whole speech about how she's always regarded me as a brother, and that even though she thinks I'm lush and sweet and whatever, she doesn't think she can grow that sort of feelings for me."

Sympathy made my chest ache. I wanted to slap Olivia for being so incurably blind. She had terrible taste in men. If she didn't want to have her heart broken, she ought to reconsider her targets. Unlike Colin, Jason would have treated her well. But then again, if Olivia wasn't interested, they simply weren't compatible. It was as William had said: we couldn't choose whom we fell in love with. So, Olivia couldn't force herself to fall in love with Jason even if she wanted to.

"She'll probably ring you about it," he mumbled before he closed his eyes and frowned to himself again.

"Jason, I'm so sorry. Really, I am. I hate seeing you like this. And I know you don't want to hear it, but she's clearly not worth your attention. If she doesn't realise your value, that's honestly her loss." Dismayed, I cupped his cheek in my hand to stroke it with my thumb.

"Yeah, I know. Still blows though, but I'll get over it soon enough. On the bright side, it's good to have a clear answer. I've been torturing myself with 'what if's for the past year, so it's nice to know I don't have to wonder anymore. It was actually Will who convinced me to do something about it. So, while I wish this wasn't the outcome, I'm glad I listened to him. I'd hate to waste more time on her."

My pout intensified. "I wish I could give you the world. That's what you really deserve."

The first genuine smile since I'd come home claimed his mouth then. "I love you, Cara."

"I love you too, Jason. I'm here for you if you want to talk about anything at all."

He squeezed me against him and planted a kiss on the top of my head. "I honestly don't know what I'd do without you. Along with Will, you really are my very best friend. I'm grateful you're not cross with me for placing you in such an awkward situation."

Against my will, I smiled, amused. "Well, it would hardly be fair if I got upset with you for that after everything with Will."

He chuckled. "Yeah, I guess I earned myself a few karma points there."

"Oh, for sure. You've handled it with grace. I wouldn't have held it against you had you disowned me."

He scoffed. "I'd never. How are things going between you, though? Is he still alive after your stunt?"

My face lacked emotion as I stared back at him. "Er, you were right. He retaliated. If anyone were close to dying last night, it was me. He made me come ten times, Jason. Ten! It was vicious!"

He gaped. "Ten?" he whispered, astonished.

"Bloody ten!"

"That man's a legend."

"No, don't you ever do that to anyone. It was torture. I have banned handcuffs from the bedroom after last night."

He giggled. "That's hilarious. We can always trust Will to turn the tables, can't we?"

"Unfortunately," I muttered and rolled onto my back to stare up at the ceiling. After a deep breath for courage, I blurted out, "Other than that, I'm in love with him."

There. I finally confessed it out loud. *God*, it felt alien. But so good. Liberating, actually. I could hardly believe I'd said it. Out loud. Me. I hadn't thought I'd declare something like this for at least another ten years.

Since Jason turned mute, I felt compelled to turn my head to gauge his reaction. Gobsmacked, he gazed wide-eyed back at me. Nodding vehemently, my face matched the colour of a crimson rose.

"Yes. I said it." A face-splitting grin tugged my lips apart while I laughed. "I am so in love with your brother, Jason, you've no idea. He's everything I could have wished for, and more. And I just love the fact that he can handle me. I fire so many shots, but he's bulletproof! What makes it even better is that he fires right back at me! And he just gets me, you know? It's like he knows exactly what to say, and I just love our banter. He teases me better than anyone else, and I just adore it.

"And I love his sense of humour and his flair for sarcasm. And his intellect, his wisdom. Not to mention his reliability, his loyalty, and his…everything. I even love how blunt he is. Well, his flaws are a bit bothersome, because he is insanely jealous and territorial, but I think I can manage. Besides, odd as it is, I almost like those traits, too, because they're part of him. And the fact that he takes such good care of his friends, and you, is seriously endearing. Do I sound like an idiot? Oh my God, I sound like a clown. I'll shut up now."

He whistled through his teeth. "Wow. You're actually full-on fangirling over him. This is radical."

"I know. I'm so smitten. He's all I can think about, Jason. What's worse, I saw him just a few moments ago, and yet I already miss him! It's pathetic!"

"It's beautiful, is what it is. Have you told him?"

I shook my head. "No. I need more time. I feel it's a bit too soon. I need to be absolutely certain he's the one I want before I confess it. In the end, he's prone to doing things that make me question whether we stand a chance."

"Like what?"

I sighed and set my gaze on the ceiling again. "Well, last night, for instance, he insisted that I can't even be friends with Aaron if I want to keep seeing him. He doesn't trust me at all when it comes to him, and while I get where he's coming from, it honestly hurts my feelings a bit. It blows that I've got to sacrifice one of my best friends just because Will doesn't trust me. I find it very upsetting, and I also find it controlling. I wouldn't dream of doing anything with Aaron again – not like that. But Will made it crystal clear that it's useless to try and tell him that, because he doesn't believe me – not after how I behaved in the beginning.

"But see, I also find that very unfair, because I only behaved like that because I honestly didn't think it was appropriate for me to be with him when he's both my boss and your brother. More than that, I wasn't looking for anything serious, which Will obviously was and still is. That's why I was so difficult about things, and it's also why I behaved the way I did. But he doesn't seem to get that."

He blew his cheeks out and shifted onto his back beside me. After shoving his hands under his head, he shared my fascination with the ceiling. "Will can be a bit uncompromising. I'm genuinely sorry to hear that he's unwilling to bend when it comes to Aaron. Personally, I know you'd never do anything with him now that you're with Will. But you have to try and see it from Will's perspective. He feels threatened by Aaron and how close you are."

"I know. It's just annoying since Aaron isn't actually a threat."

"Well, you also need to bear in mind that Will doesn't know you like I do. He hasn't seen how you and Aaron were together for the past three years the way that I have. I can try to speak some sense to him, if you want, but I doubt it would be effective. He's very 'my way or the highway' sometimes."

I rubbed my eyes. "Yeah, you can try to tell him if you want, but I've no expectations. Besides, I gather I'll just worry about that bridge when I get there. For now, Aaron hasn't shown any sign of wanting to link up again, so I won't worry about it unless he does. If he does reach out, I'll bring it up with Will again. If he doesn't, there's nothing to worry about."

"Sounds like a decent plan."

"Mm. But do you know what's weird?"

"What?"

"That I'm not scared of confessing because I fear he won't reciprocate. All I'm scared of is telling him too soon, because once I do, I've got to really mean it. I can't take it back. Isn't that odd?

I mean, don't people tend to be scared of dropping the L-bomb because they're worried it might not be requited?"

He scratched his cheek while he contemplated what I'd said. "It is a little odd, actually. I suppose he's done well with reassuring you about his interest."

"He really has," I confirmed, besotted. "I'm not sure if he loves me back yet, but the way he treats me has made it clear that even if I tell him, it won't scare him off."

Jason wrapped his arm and leg over me to smother me against his chest. Then, he treated my hair to repeated kisses. "I'm really happy for you, Cara. I've always had a feeling you and Will were compatible."

"Yeah. Since you and I weren't meant to be, I'm glad I could secure at least one man of the Night genes."

His chest shook against me. "Sounds like you wish you could have loved me romantically."

"Oh, there was certainly a time when I did wish that," I revealed without a trace of shame, hoping it would lift his spirits somewhat. "You've no idea how perfect you are, Jason. One day, some woman is going to realise that, and even if it isn't Livy, that woman will make you forget all about her."

"I hope so. Anyway, have you got plans before dinner?"

"No. I've reserved the entire weekend for work."

"Christ."

"It's alright. I was already prepared for this when I started studying law. After all, corporate law is notorious for its inhumane work hours."

"Yeah. Same with medicine, I suppose."

"Yeah. We're fucked."

"We are. Anyway, should we cuddle up and watch TV together?"

"Yes."

22

I'D RATHER HAVE THE HONOUR

In the grand foyer of their home in Chelsea, Jason and I were greeted by Daphné and John. A delectable scent wafted through, deriving from the kitchen, and I detected a loud presence of garlic. Saliva accumulated in my mouth.

"It smells amazing," I commented and was just about to shut the front door when familiar fingers folded over the edge to stop me. That hand was one I recognised at once. The mere sight made me blush and freeze. All I could think of was how those long and beautiful digits had fingered me several times last night.

I was completely crazy about him.

When he pushed against the door, I stepped aside, ending up at an angle beyond his line of sight. The first thing he saw was his parents. Striding in, he journeyed the very same hand that had been inside me all night to greet them. The thought intensified my high colour.

"Mum, Dad." After kissing Daphné on the cheek, he turned to Jason and me. "Useless waste of space," he greeted his brother before focusing on me.

Had it been any other day, Jason would have laughed at that, but, following last night's regrettable turn of events, playfulness had deserted him. Seeming to notice, William stole another glance at Jason while he reached for my hand. After completing a visual sweep, the elder brother frowned to himself, puzzled, and then offered me his full attention.

His large and warm hand closed around mine. Staring at him, my pupils dilated. That weird electricity, which had yet to become familiar to me, charged into my hand and surged through my veins till it bolted straight through my heart. Myriad butterflies fluttered within me.

I wanted to jump on him, kiss him, ravish him.

But I couldn't.

Looking into his eyes, I realised the actual extent of how much I'd missed him since this morning. It was ridiculous and, frankly, pathetic. I'd seen him mere hours ago, and yet I had experienced each one as separate infinities.

His hypnotic gaze kept me entranced. "Cara. It's always nice to see you outside the office."

My lips parted at his surreptitious statement. He was bold. I would never have dared to make a furtive joke like that right under his parents' noses. "Nice to see you too, Will."

His characteristic crooked smile took over his mouth. "I'm glad you decided to *come*."

The urge to slap him was vicious. As he teased me in front of his blindsided parents, his amusement was palpable.

"Yeah," Jason chimed in, "she's got to be home by ten, though."

I just barely managed to suppress the urge to laugh. His sense of humour had returned in the nick of time. I seldom saw William taken aback, but if anyone could manage it, it was Jason. He spoke

William's language fluently, and I found it hilarious.

Rediscovering his tongue, William echoed, "Ten, you said?"

Ever smooth, Jason covered his tracks with, "Yeah, she's got a FaceTime date with Phoebe, her sister."

"She's the one living in New York, isn't she?" Daphné asked me then.

"Yes."

"It was business she studied, right? At Columbia?"

It charmed me that she remembered so much of what I'd shared last we met, which was back in April. "Yes." I grinned.

"Clever girl," John commented. "Like her sister."

"Like her sister, indeed," William said and tucked his hands into his pockets.

John inspected my face. "Yes, Will keeps bragging about your performance, Cara. Says you've exceeded all expectations."

Had he? I frowned to myself as I wondered if William's opinion was entirely biased or relatively objective.

"I'm doing my best, at least."

"Always so humble," John chuckled.

William said, "I believe she'd prefer knowing that Fred is impressed with her work."

"Why do you say that?"

"Well, I suspect that, unless it contains criticism, my opinion of her work doesn't matter to her anymore. We're too familiar with each other, so no amount of praise seems to reach her. She probably thinks I'm biased," he looked at me, "which is insulting, by the way."

I had no idea the man could read minds. Either way, his last statement made me laugh. "Sorry. I don't doubt your ability to be objective."

"You shouldn't."

John's smile revealed his amusement. "Well, Cara, I'll let you know that Fred is very impressed as well."

I grinned. Was it true? Seeing as Frederick was a senior

associate, that was rather uplifting. "Really?"

"Really."

"Well, Will's a brilliant mentor, and he's quick to notice whenever I'm confused about something, so I think the main reason I'm managing alright is because of that."

A proud look crossed John's face before he glanced at his eldest son. "I'm glad to hear that, though I expected no less of him. Anyway, how would you like a glass of wine, dear?"

"I'd love one."

"Right this way." He turned towards the living room. As he guided the way, he said, "Regarding work, there's something I've been meaning to discuss with you, Cara."

Instantly, apprehension seized my body while I dared a glance in William's direction. Our eyes met, but his composure released me from some rigidity. He wasn't at all worried, so it seemed unlikely that John had picked up on our romance and intended to confront us about it.

"Oh?"

"Yes." John looked at me over his shoulder. "How do you find corporate law so far?"

"Riveting, to be honest."

He grinned. "Wonderful." Entering the living room, he gestured towards one of the cream-coloured sofas. Jason took a seat beside me while Daphné and William settled on the sofa right across from us. Between us stood a low coffee table of wood, and its rough texture and light colour made it seem rather vintage – and expensive. Atop it stood a silver bucket containing ice and a chilled bottle of rosé wine.

"What's your plan after the summer?" John asked me while he pulled the bottle out of the bucket.

My heart raced upon his question. Hope urged me to believe that he was about to discuss career-options with me. Was that why William hadn't been alarmed earlier? Had he anticipated this?

Could he and John have discussed this without my knowledge? The possibility drove me to glance at William again. He hadn't mentioned a thing, but then perhaps he'd wanted to keep it as a surprise.

"Well, I intend to start my LPC," I said. "Although the plan is to combine it with an LLM."

John nodded as he opened the bottle. "That's what Will did. He mentioned you wanted to do the same. Is the University of Law where you mean to complete it?"

Wearing a smile, I looked at William again. "Yes."

As he poured a glass, John said, "So you're staying in London, then. Have you applied for a training contract yet?"

It was impossible to stop grinning. "Yeah. I've applied to Day & Night, among others."

John's piercing eyes met mine then. Grabbing the stem of the glass he had just poured, he walked to hand it over to me. "I was hoping you would say that."

"Really?"

"Yes, so Will and I have had a chat with Theresa." Working for the HR department, Theresa Ainsley had been the one to interview me when I had first applied to Day & Night LLP for a vacation scheme. "Once you complete your work experience placement," John continued, "she'd like to discuss a training contract with you, to be completed after your LPC LLM."

It was difficult to sit still. I wanted to jump and scream with glee. "Are you being serious?"

"Utterly."

"Oh my God! John!"

He laughed, and as I glanced around, I saw that everyone else were grinning, too.

"Thank you!" My excitement was so extreme that my hand trembled as it held my glass of wine, leaving the liquid to swash within the solid material. I turned to Jason. "Did you know about this?"

Elation emitted from his features. "We all did."

Turning my gaze to William, I hoped he could sense my gratitude. His expression was tender, and I detected some pride in his eyes, too. A vague smile stretched his lips. Had our situation been different, I would have stormed over kiss him – every single part of him. I hadn't expected him to assist my career like this. Sure, I knew he was doing everything within his power to train me well, but to actively help me with acquiring a training contract? That was above and beyond.

"John, I cannot ever thank you enough," I said and directed my attention to him again. "I'm overwhelmed. I swear I won't give you a reason to regret it."

"I don't doubt it for a second, love." After giving me a wink, he cast a glance at William. "It's difficult to impress Will, so you must be doing something right." I thought I detected some suspicion in his tone, so when he focused on me again, I stiffened. Dropping my gaze to the glass of wine in my hand, I slowly raised it to my mouth.

Around John, I couldn't help my fleeting eyes. I hadn't thought anyone could be more intimidating than William, but his father was. His light-blue eyes were remarkably intense. It was as though he could read my entire soul in the span of a mere glimpse, so I hardly dared to hold his gaze. The few times I did, I could have sworn that if I lingered for a second too long, he would see my carnal sessions with his son through my eyes.

There was shrewdness about John that challenged even William's. Simply, he was William times two. Knowing that, I refused to underestimate him under any circumstance.

That I saw so much of John in William made me wonder about Daphné and John's relationship. Here they were, married for thirty-one years. Steering my eyes to Daphné, I watched her study William's profile while maternal affection oozed from her expression.

I'd always liked Daphné – tremendously, in fact. While she was generally a quiet woman, she wasn't shy. She was patient and wise, but I'd witnessed first-hand that she could snap if she disagreed with something being said or done. When I considered how much figurative room charismatic John took up, I gathered it was only natural that they would complement each other in that department. He talked, she listened. Not all the time, of course, but that was the gist of it, I reckoned.

Suddenly, her gaze dashed in my direction, catching me staring. Though I was quick to avert my eyes, I wasn't quick enough. During the brief collision of our eyes, I saw hers narrow somewhat. Soon later, they flickered between William and me.

Unsure of whether my expression had revealed anything, I panicked. Thankfully, William diverted her attention by saying, "I saw Alex today."

"Oh, Alex." Daphné's smile was fond. "How is he?"

"He's...Well, he broke up with Abbie last night. Told Andy and me over breakfast this morning."

"He did what?" Jason questioned, astonished. "He broke up with Abbie?"

William nodded. "Told me to tell you since you hadn't answered your phone this morning."

Jason grimaced. "Yeah, sorry. I was busy." *Busy brooding over Olivia,* I thought to myself with sympathy. "Anyway, at last."

"That's what I said."

"At last," Daphné echoed with a scoff. "Don't be rude, you two. Is Alexander alright?"

As if he hadn't heard his wife, John said, "Thank fucking god."

Shocked by his candid reaction, I observed him with arched brows while utter silence ensued. I sensed both William and Jason study me, anticipating a reaction. Then, all of a sudden, John burst out laughing and gave me a smile so winsome I'd have thought he was years younger. There was no doubting which parent Jason and William had to thank for their inherent charisma. I could see the evidence in John's grin.

"Pardon my French, Cara," he excused himself while Daphné

shielded her face with her palm. "I can be a bit blunt."

A snigger leapt out of my mouth. Finally, I knew where Jason and William found their inspiration. John was the source, and though I'd suspected it, it was hilarious to witness it in action. What a unique style of parenting.

"Oh, don't worry, John," I said with a lazy wave of my hand. "I've grown used to blunt people after living with your son and having your other as my boss. Just another day, this."

He joined my laughter, and I realised from the sound that he was slightly embarrassed and appreciated how forgiving I was. "I try to put on a filter, but whenever I'm in my own home, I tend to forget. We prize honesty here, and sometimes, I confuse that with transparency."

"As you might understand," Jason said and wrapped his arm over the sofa's backrest behind my shoulders, "Abbie isn't a popular person in this household."

I'd heard so much about Abigail since last night that I honestly wished I'd met her. Perhaps then, I would have understood what was so dreadful about her.

"Allow me to explain," John said. Lowering his hand to just above his knee, he looked directly into my eyes. "I've known Alex since he was this big – or small, I should say. I forget, huge man that he is now. Six-foot-six, is he?" He glanced at William.

"Yeah."

"Huge fellow. Anyway, that chap has grown into one of the most benevolent and intelligent men I know, and his aptitude for business is remarkable. When he took over after his father, he propelled the company – Winton Properties – into a global success. I'm in awe of his achievements. And yet, he hasn't let his success get to his head at all.

"But, you see, Alex took it quite hard when his father died – my good friend Nathan. Then, only a few months after his passing, Abbie made advances, and before we knew it, she and

Alex had embarked on a relationship."

He stretched back up with a sigh. "Now, I've known Abbie since she was around sixteen, which was when she started socialising with William's circle, and my impression of her was never a good one. Frankly, she's always struck me as a spoiled brat who only thinks about herself. If you combine a personality like that with a selfless one like Alexander's, it doesn't tend to end well for the selfless party. I love that chap, and it's clear to everyone who knows him that his relationship with Abbie hasn't been healthy for him." He focused on William. "So, if it's true what you say and he's finally ended things, I couldn't be prouder of him."

"Cheers to that," Jason said and raised his glass.

"And they say women gossip," Daphné commented, underwhelmed. Still, she raised her glass.

Wearing a crooked smile, I said to her, "They say that because they don't truly know, or bother to understand, that every woman differs from the next."

When she met my eyes, the gleam in hers spoke louder than words. She approved; I could tell I had pleased her by sharing my feministic view. Had there been any room for doubting that, her ensuing grin erased it.

"Just to clarify—" William's eyes flickered between us—"who are 'they'?"

Giving him my undivided attention, I struggled to disguise my affection when I replied, "Since you have to ask, the concept of stereotyping women is clearly foreign to you, so you're not included under that term."

A complacent smile arrived on his mouth as he nodded to himself. "Happy to hear that."

"I've raised him well," Daphné told me with a wink.

"Indeed. You've raised them both well," I emphasised and gave Jason's thigh a friendly pat.

"I'd like to remind everyone that I've played a part in raising them as well," John said then, earning himself a laugh from us all.

"You surely have, darling," Daphné replied. "They prove that every time they act like idiots."

Her wit extracted a giggle from my mouth. As products of John and Daphné's combined forces, there was no wonder William and Jason whipped their tongues around with little mercy.

"Hah!" Jason pointed to John. "She got you there!"

"In case you didn't notice, she insulted you too, Jason," John muttered.

"All three of us in the same go." William nodded, impressed. "Well done, Mum. *Touché*, I should say."

"Anyway," John grabbed the bottle to pour the remaining four glasses, "I suppose Abbie won't be Alexander's date for Lakewood's charity event on Friday, then?"

William shook his head as he reached for the glass John offered him. "She's invited, though, so she might still show up."

"For Alexander's sake, I hope she doesn't."

"How about you, Will?" Jason asked then. "Are you bringing a date?"

His question nearly made me gape. Since I had already told him, he was well aware that I was going with William. It was obvious that he was only looking to pull his brother's leg, but he was risking that I could become collateral damage.

Anticipating an answer, Daphné and John watched William with the eyes of a hawk. However, he appeared entirely unaffected as he leisurely sipped on his glass of wine. After he had savoured the aftertaste for an extended while, Daphné groaned.

"Oh, William. Must you be so annoying?"

I giggled. I relished the dynamics of this family. It was refreshing to witness their interactions. More than that, I appreciated that they seemed to let their guard down around me.

John muttered, "He was born annoying, dear. Took him nearly thirty hours to get out of you."

What a comedy show. I'd pay money to see this, and I was getting it for free. The only downside was that I wasn't sure whether it was appropriate to laugh.

"What's it to you?" William finally brought himself to reply, and I silently commended that his eyes hadn't so much as flickered in my direction.

"Oh, you know what," Daphné grumbled. "We never hear about anyone you're involved with."

He shrugged. "I value my privacy."

"He still hasn't denied it," Jason pointed out. "And I know for a fact that he's bringing someone."

At that moment, I wished I could vanish at a snap of my fingers. What was Jason doing, putting us on the spot like this?

Looking at his younger brother, William furrowed his brows. "Don't be fooled, Mum. Jason's just amused because of who I'm bringing."

Mirroring William, John frowned as well. "Who is it, then? There's no use in hiding it, Will. Several of our friends will be there. We're going to find out one way or another."

Hearing that, I realised why Jason wasn't being overly cautious. He knew his parents would find out either way. The more I considered it, the more I appreciated it. Rather than let John and Daphné find out through external sources, he was providing us with the opportunity to tell them ourselves. Ultimately, that gave us more control over how it would be perceived.

William smirked. "I'm honestly just dragging things out because I find it funny."

"God, you're so annoying," John grumbled. Despite my anxiety, I barely managed to contain my laughter.

"Like father, like son," Daphné joked, triggering my laughter to surge out despite my effort to suppress it. Immediately, I rushed to cover my mouth.

"I'm so sorry," I said hurriedly.

Charmed, John smiled at me. "Don't worry, Cara."

"Shall I tell them?" Jason teased William.

William chuckled and shook his head. "I'd rather have the honour." Turning to his father, he said, "I'm bringing Cara."

I nearly choked on my sip. It demanded all my willpower to lower my glass and feign nonchalance because, within me, my heart wreaked havoc.

All eyes turned to me, and the attention caused my face to grow hotter than I could recall it having been before. I dared not meet a single gaze. I relied entirely on Will to get us out of this clinch.

Before the ensuing silence could become awkward, William continued, "Thanks to Jason, Cara and I have been friends for a good while now, and since I didn't have anyone to bring, I thought it might be a good chance for her to network." It was during times like these that I appreciated his quick mind and silver tongue the most. He'd made it sound like inviting me was the most sensible thing to do.

"Right," John said, and his tone took me by complete surprise. I hadn't heard a trace of disapproval. On the contrary, he seemed supportive. "That's a wonderful idea, Will."

"I thought so, too."

The relief I experienced was considerable. Really, I thought I could soar. Finally, I dared to glance around, but what I discovered immediately restored a portion of my anxiety. While both Daphné and John looked unfazed on the surface, it was evident from their forced behaviour that they were suspicious after all. They were a bit too stiff and their eyes a tad too fleeting.

But of course they weren't so easily convinced. In the end, no one had more experience than them in dealing with William's eloquent and persuasive character. Moreover, they weren't gullible, nor were they stupid or naïve. What remained to be answered was whether their suspicion indexed trouble.

"If you think it's inappropriate," I murmured and looked

straight at John, "please let me know."

The moment his gaze met mine, I was trapped – arrested on the spot. It was impossible to look away. In an instant, his eyes pierced mine, carefully inspecting and extracting every single one of my secrets. After a slight twitch of his brow, he broke the spell to focus on his eldest son instead. As soon as he looked away, I was confident he knew.

Fuck.

"No, don't worry, Cara," he said whilst scrutinising William, but William's behaviour gave nothing away. It was impossible to decipher his thoughts. Seeing it, I finally understood how my lover had mastered such an impressive level of self-control. In light of how deeply he valued privacy, he must have practised maintaining his composure all his life to prevent his perceptive father from discovering things which he would rather keep to himself.

It occurred to me then that if John was actually suspicious, it was my reactions that were to blame. If I hadn't been here for John to examine, William might have been able to convince him that nothing was happening behind the scenes. However, I wasn't equipped to handle a force like John. I was hardly even equipped to handle his son.

"As Will said, it's an amazing opportunity for you to network, Cara," John continued. "So if Will deems it appropriate, I've no problem with it. I trust his judgement implicitly."

"What about mine?" Jason joked, and I appreciated that he was trying to lighten the atmosphere.

"With my life, Jason."

"Nice one. Since I'm a med student, right?"

"You ruin the joke when you explain it, idiot."

I laughed, but it was a nervous sound, as there was no denying the tension in the air. John and Daphné definitely suspected, and it made me scared. William and I needed to discuss how to proceed, and it was urgent.

23

OPEN BOOK

THROUGHOUT DINNER, WE WERE KEPT COMPANY BY AN invisible guest that, if tangible, would have taken the shape of a giant elephant. It stomped around the room, demanding to be acknowledged, but none of us obliged. Instead, we all turned a blind eye to it while discussing work, news, politics and just about everything between heaven and earth. That was something I adored about the Night family. They were a band of bright minds, so there was no shortage of intellectually stimulating conversations. That also made ignoring the uninvited guest much easier.

After dessert, we'd settled for tea on the roof terrace, and on our way there, Jason had pointed to a door and whispered in my ear that it was William's childhood bedroom. I had just exited the bathroom, so now that I was about to pass it again, I couldn't resist the opportunity to have a look.

Sneaking towards the door, I turned the handle and peeked inside, curious as to what memories and clues it might contain with respects to his childhood. Unsurprisingly, all sorts of prizes and awards, ranging from sports to academic achievements, decorated a shelf above a large white desk. Upon closer inspection, I saw he'd won several chess prizes. Well, I should have anticipated as much.

It was quite a spacious and tidy bedroom, hosting a small sofa and a big TV. But, weirdly, it was so neatly put together that it looked almost sterile. Apart from the shelf above his desk and the posters on his walls, every surface area was free of any objects. Perhaps he'd removed them when he'd moved out? Or had it always looked like this?

Not even the edge of his desk had a dent or mark in the wood. It made me wonder if he'd had a desk before which had been replaced with this one, but after a visual sweep of the frame of his king-sized bed, and even the windowsills, I could tell it wasn't the case. William was, and always had been, in the habit of taking excellent care of the things in his possession. Supposed that included me.

Tracing my fingers across the smooth, white paint of the windowsill, I gazed around and tried to picture him as a child. It wasn't too difficult to imagine him seated by his desk, revising. It was a little harder to imagine him seducing Blaire, his first sexual partner. As I looked at his bed, my nose wrinkled. Had they done it there?

Looking around again, I studied the decorations on the walls. Apart from one poster of Pink Floyd, all of it consisted of Chelsea FC posters. There was even a Chelsea FC shirt hanging on the wall above the headboard of his bed. Leaning closer, I saw that it was signed, but I wasn't sure about the name. Was it Frank Lampard's autograph?

Just barely not a hooligan, I thought to myself. Well, at least I had a clear idea of a date I could take him on. I could buy us tickets for a match.

"She said no?" I suddenly heard William question from the corridor outside. I tensed. I could not be caught in here. It would render me into a creep.

"Flat out 'no'. Said I'm like a brother to her," Jason replied.

"She really said 'brother'?" William sounded appalled.

"Yeah."

"Fuck me. That's brutal."

"It was."

"Christ. I'm sorry it turned out this way, Jase – especially when you finally grew the balls to do it. Though, from what Cara's told me, I'm under the impression she's got poor taste in men."

"Yeah, I'll get over it. Anyway, I'm grateful you motivated me to ask. Nice not having to wonder anymore."

They were drawing nearer, so I panicked. Rushing forwards, I ducked under William's desk and held my breath.

"To be perfectly honest with you, J, I don't think Olivia's the right type of girl for you. I obviously don't know her that well, but she doesn't come across as particularly interesting. I think the perfect girl for you is some beautifully strange individual, like Harper."

"Please, Will. Harper still lives in Mumbai, and she hasn't given me any reason to believe she'll move back to London anytime soon. I stopped waiting for her years ago, and you know that."

"So you've said. Still, every time she visits, you sleep together."

"That's just friendly at this point. Casual sex. I've told you this a million times."

"I can't believe she's the last girl you've had sex with. Seriously, haven't you slept with anyone since Christmas?"

Jason groaned. "Leave me alone."

"You really ought to do something about that."

"Well, I only just tried, didn't I? And got rejected."

"Right. In that light, I'd like to retract my statement."

Jason chuckled. "Thought you might. Anyway, have you spoken to her lately?"

"To Harper? Yeah. I think it was in May. I remember I told her about Cara, so it was definitely after April. Have you?"

"Yeah. Two days ago, as it happens, on Instagram."

"How did that go?"

"Well, I told her about Livy."

"Did you? How did she react?"

"I'm not sure. I only told her because she gave me the impression that she had met someone, so I wanted her to know that I had as well."

"Really? Has she? I wasn't aware of that. I should probably give her a bell – hear how she's doing."

"I think she'd like that."

They paused just outside the door. My heart thundered. Were they coming in?

"Think Cara's lost?" Jason asked then.

"It's a big house."

"Maybe she's just taking a shit."

Oh, my God. No. He had not just said that. Not to the sole man I had ever fallen in love with. I could kill him. Beneath William's desk, I cringed about ten times over as Jason's words echoed in my mind. My hands itched to strangle him.

William moaned. "See, this is why I'm a dick to you. You're no better yourself. Why'd you have to say that?"

Jason's loud laughter travelled through the corridor. "Oh, did I burst your bubble? You thought girls don't drop a load? You thought Cara hasn't even got an anus?"

Could this get any worse?

"That's not what I said, and that's not what I thought. I've had sex with her, Jason. I'm aware she's got an anus. I'm only saying that your sense of humour is shit."

"Nice pun."

That made William laugh.

"Jason!" Daphné called before she continued to speak in

French. Although I hadn't the faintest idea of what she was saying, she sounded impatient.

Soon enough, Jason replied in the same language, and after a brief conversation, I heard both brothers ambling for the stairs.

As soon as their footsteps were out of hearing range, I rushed out of William's room. I'd just climbed the stairs leading to the terrace when I abruptly halted. Through the door, I saw only John and Daphné's backs, but the sight was one of those beautiful things I would never forget – a scene between people where intimacy was at its purest.

Cradling her shoulders with his arm, John held Daphné close and trailed the tip of his nose up and down her temple while he appeared to whisper in her ear. Welcoming the words, Daphné mellowed in his embrace and turned her pretty face to kiss him on the lips.

I stared. I couldn't help myself. My heart contracted at the sheer beauty of their union. They were clearly happily married. When I saw things like these, it genuinely touched me. Not only that, but their happiness also seemed infectious. Merely after witnessing it, I felt happy as well.

Looking at John and Daphné, I was reminded that one of my primary desires in life was to have a marriage like that – when the time was right, of course. I was confident they'd had their awful fights and serious pitfalls, as most marriages were guilty of, but knowing that this was the result made those fights pale and, frankly, seem trivial in comparison. Marriage was about overcoming obstacles together. It was about being a partner, not just a lover. If ever I married, I'd want that – a husband I could fight with because we were equals and because we wanted to grow together, not apart.

Content, I sighed to myself. They were the very definition of a thriving partnership, and they were beautiful. Inspiring.

The exact moment that a pair of strong hands gripped my

hips from behind, a voice uttered in my ear, "Boo!"

Squealing inwardly, I recoiled into a familiar embrace while my heart jumped to my throat. Whirling around, I looked up at William.

"What are you doing?" I growled under my breath and shoved his hands away.

Amusement swam in the serene ocean of his eyes. "What are *you* doing? Ogling my parents?"

I frowned. "I didn't want to interrupt."

"They're not into swinging partners, Cara. Sorry."

I feigned a compassionate pout. "That must be rough on your Oedipus complex."

A titter of amazement slipped out of him while his eyebrows jumped. "God, your mouth."

Grinning back, I reached for the door.

"Hey, hey, wait." He grabbed my wrist. While turning me towards him, he glanced at his parents. Determining it unsafe, he pulled me down the stairs with him, where he descended onto my mouth.

Every time William kissed me, I lost my inhibitions. This time was no exception. Immersed in his passion, I gripped the collar of his shirt and kissed him back with all I had, fully merged with the moment. Still, I couldn't stop my smile from interfering. Enjoying his mouth was one of my favourite pastimes, and it always exhilarated me. Giddy and lightheaded, I chuckled into our secret kiss and pressed myself against the length of his body while I smiled until my cheeks hurt.

Delighting me, a smile of his own soon interfered as well. When it became impossible to keep kissing each other, he pulled away to nuzzle my nose with his.

"I hate that I won't be sleeping next to you tonight," he said affectionately. I tightened my grip on his collar.

"Me too." Diving into the dreamy pool of his eyes, I found I'd be happy to drown there.

Grinning, he lowered his mouth onto mine again, and it took us mere seconds to progress into a feverish French kiss. That's when the clearing of a throat interrupted us.

"You look hungry. Good thing I brought actual food," Jason said and showed us the biscuits he'd brought from downstairs. "You trying to get caught or what?"

"Piss off, you tit. She's yours nearly every evening," William muttered and pecked my lips repeatedly.

Jason giggled. "Jealous?"

"If only you knew."

Beside us, Jason opened the packet of biscuits and tossed one in his mouth. Unashamed, he stared at us kissing while he chewed it.

Finally, William had enough. "Jason, what the fuck?"

He pointed to the staircase with his thumb. "I'm scouting the coast, man. Making sure it's all clear."

"Like you didn't just expose us a minute ago," William retorted.

The mention made me frown. "Yeah, Jason, what was that?"

Jason sighed and rubbed the back of his head. "Sorry. It was a spontaneous decision. When Dad mentioned the function, I realised some of their friends will be there as well, so I gathered they'd find out one way or another. Because of that, I thought you should probably be the ones to tell them. I'd hoped it would help you control the outcome better, but you failed – miserably."

My heart leapt to my throat. He thought we'd failed, too?

"Thanks to Cara," William said and raised a brow at me. "You should never play poker, dear."

"What?" Defensive, I sucked in a deep breath. "How is this my fault?"

With a shake of his head, Jason reminded me, "You blushed like you'd been hanging upside down since the dawn of time."

"That's because everyone was staring!"

"Or, and hear me out, it's because you're actually fucking Will and don't want to get caught."

"It doesn't matter," William said before I could try to defend myself again. "Like you said—" he looked at Jason—"they would have found out one way or another. To be fair, they would probably have been more suspicious if they'd learnt it from someone else."

"That's what I was thinking," Jason said.

Panicking, I looked between them. "So neither of you think we fooled John?"

Jason shook his head. "Nor Mum, for that matter."

Turning to William, I desperately hoped to discover some sign that he was of a different opinion, but upon the sight of his clenched jaw, I could tell it wasn't the case. "Will?"

"I'm sorry. I don't think we did, either."

That William also thought they suspected exacerbated my anxiety. "Perhaps we should call it off," I said, as if that would solve the issue at once.

William tensed immediately, eyes frosting. "Call off what, exactly?"

"Me going to the function, of course. What else?"

He relaxed. "Right."

My eyes widened as I inferred what he had feared. His instinct had been to assume that I had meant *us*, and it exposed his insecurities. I had really scarred him, hadn't I? By being so reluctant to date him in the beginning? It was obvious that he still didn't trust that I would stand by my decision, and it wounded me to know that, even though it was completely understandable. I wished I could make him see that once I made up my mind about something, I always saw it through. That meant that I intended to keep dating him even if my job was at risk, because he was worth it to me. However, to convince him of that, it was evident that the only thing I could make use of was time. Telling him clearly didn't help. He needed time to truly believe it.

Jason pursed his lips. "She had you for a second there."

William gave him a glare.

"Sorry. I should have phrased myself better." I caressed William's chest. "I obviously didn't mean us."

He shook his head. "Calling it off would only make them more suspicious at this point. Besides, the damage has already been done."

I drew in a breath while my pulse skyrocketed. Now I was really panicking. John had only just told me he'd like to offer me a training contract. Would he change his mind now? After learning about my affair with his son? "What should we do, then?"

"Should I leave you alone?" Jason asked.

William nodded before glancing at him. "Yeah."

"Cara, you'll be fine," Jason said, and I badly wanted to be as confident about it as he seemed to be. "Worst that can happen is that Will won't be qualified to be your direct superior anymore."

"That's not the worst that can happen. John could think I'm only trying to sleep my way to a job!" I argued. "This can taint his impression of me, Jase."

"Er, you clearly don't know Dad. To be honest, I'm sure he's mostly shocked that anyone would ever desire Will."

William groaned. "Jason, please. Fuck off. I'll take care of this."

"Right." Turning, Jason climbed up the stairs to join his parents.

William's eyes were tender when he brushed his thumbs across my cheeks. "Cara, calm down. Whatever the case may be, this won't jeopardise your career. I promise you."

"How can you be sure? What if he changes his mind now that he suspects? I mean, for all he knows, you might have suggested a training contract for me solely because we're dating."

He looked offended. "Cara, he's got more faith in me than *that.* Besides, you'll have to be interviewed by an objective party – Theresa, in this case – just like every other applicant. All I did was recommend you, and it really has nothing to do with my feelings for you, and everything to do with your capabilities. Fred and Violet have seen that, too, so they'll have your back where I'm disqualified from voicing my opinion."

I couldn't relax. "Do you think he's disappointed in me?"

Suddenly his eyes were alight with amusement, which bewildered me. "Absolutely not. Frankly, I'd say he looked pleased with my choice above all else. I know for a fact he's got a soft spot for you. Honestly, I wouldn't be surprised if he's secretly hoping there's something more between us."

Hearing that – and knowing that Jason wasn't too stressed about this either – reassured me somewhat. "Really?"

He nodded. "You charmed Dad to his toes the very first time you met him, Cara. He adores you – don't worry."

I huffed out a loud breath. "I really hope you're right. To get on the wrong side of John is not on my wish-list."

He chuckled. "Understandable. It shouldn't be on anyone's."

"On a scale of one to ten, how sure are you that he knows?"

"A solid eight."

"Fuck," I whimpered. "Only because I'm joining you for an event? Is that really such an odd thing to do? I mean we're friends! And colleagues. I'm your assistant. You said it was perfectly normal to bring your assistant to events like these."

He pressed his lips together. "Well, it's a combination of things. First of all, you really could have reacted less conspicuously. Dad's exceptional at reading people, and your face is an open book."

Despairing, I threw my head back. "It was the attention!"

"Second of all, had it been with Jason, Dad wouldn't have batted an eye. The problem is that this is a deviation from my normal pattern of behaviour. I've never brought a date to anything – ever. Not even female friends. So he was undoubtedly shocked to hear that I am bringing someone at all. And if there was any room for doubt after that, your reaction absolutely erased it."

My jaw dropped. "What?"

"Yeah."

"You've never brought a date to anything before?"

He grimaced. "No."

"Not even Kate?"

He shook his head. "Not to anything like this, and surely not to things where my family was concerned."

I waved my arms in the air. "And you didn't think to tell me that? I had no idea what I agreed to!"

"Hey, listen," he said softly and cupped my cheeks. "Knowing Dad, he'll call me about this later if he's got a problem with it. If he does, I am one hundred per cent sure that all he'll do is advise us to move things around at work, role-wise. If he doesn't, he'll pretend he doesn't suspect a thing, which we might as well consider as permission to continue. He'll deliberately turn a blind eye to it then, which – honestly – I think he already is."

Still alarmed, I glanced at the staircase leading to the terrace. I wished desperately that William was right and that John – if he suspected – was supportive, more so than anything else. "We should join them. They're already suspicious. We can kiss any other time."

He sighed and lowered his hands to my hips. "Never enough times, though."

Enchanted, I looked up at him with a smile. "I'd like it if you slept at mine tonight."

His eyebrows formed surprise. "Really?"

"Yeah. And, there's something else I'd like to say."

"What?"

Resting my palms on his pecs, I stretched up to steal another kiss. As I leaned away, I said, "Regardless of how this turns out, I really am so grateful you recommended me for a training contract. Honestly, I hadn't expected you to do that."

His smile was unsullied. "You genuinely deserve one, Cara."

"When did you do it?"

"Monday."

"You've kept it secret all week?" I grinned in my astonishment.

"I wanted to surprise you."

"Will, you can be impossibly sweet, do you know that?"

He smiled, eyes roaming admiringly across my face. "I'm glad you feel that way."

"I do. As thanks, I'd like to stand for all the work when we have sex later."

He chuckled. "You know I won't allow that."

"We'll see. Anyway, let's go."

He clasped my hand to stall me. "One thing."

I peered up at him. "Yes?"

"I want you to know that I would have recommended you regardless of whether you had agreed to date me or not. You've got serious potential, Cara, and I genuinely think you'll be an asset to the firm."

My eyes widened while colour increased in my cheeks. Seeing it, his lips curved into a smile.

"I guess I was wrong. *Some* praise still reaches you," he said.

I chuckled. "You're amazing, Will. Thank you for telling me."

"Thought you ought to know. Now, after you, my lady." He gestured towards the staircase.

The instant I opened the door, John turned to regard us, and in his eyes, the answer was loud and clear.

He knew.

24

IT'S NOT YOU, IT'S ME

THE FOLLOWING WEDNESDAY, I WAS LYING ON THE SOFA with Jason, watching *The Fall,* when the sound of my phone ringing in my pocket caused me to squeal. Jerking in Jason's embrace, I could feel my heart thumping in my throat. I'd been so absorbed in Spector's dark world that I hadn't realised how on edge I was.

"Christ," Jason complained and tightened his embrace of me. "You nearly gave me a heart attack."

"Sorry," I huffed out and reached into my back pocket for my phone. It was Phoebe who was calling. "Oh, it's Phoebe. I've got to take this. I've tried to reach her all week. Pause the show, would you?"

Leaning forwards, Jason grabbed the Apple TV remote to hit pause while I accepted the FaceTime call from my sister. As soon as her adorable face appeared on my screen, the anxiety

I'd experienced from watching the haunting show immediately subsided. Just like it always did, Phoebe's mere existence calmed my heart.

"Hi," I greeted with a face-splitting grin. Judging by her surroundings, she was in a hotel room.

"Hi, Sis!" she replied enthusiastically. The freckles scattered across her nose were more apparent than I recalled. She must have caught some sun lately. "I'm so sorry I've missed your calls. Bethan and I have been super busy the last few days."

"Hi, Cara!" I heard her girlfriend, Bethan, chime in the background before Phoebe turned her screen to show me her pretty, round face. Her brown eyes shined back at me, radiating warmth that I'd adored ever since I met her a year ago, when she had visited London with Phoebe to meet the family.

"Hi, Bethan. How are you?"

"I'm great, thanks, despite your sister's questionable driving skills."

I laughed. "She's used to driving on the left side, you know."

"I'm getting the hang of it!" Phoebe insisted and turned her screen to show me her face again. "She's just complaining because I took a wrong turn *once*."

"Which cost us a whole hour," Bethan added sassily.

I laughed again. "Where are you now? You're doing Route 66, right?"

"Yeah," Phoebe replied, "but we took a detour to visit Niagara Falls first."

"So you're still in New York?"

"No, we're in Columbus now, in Ohio. Left New York yesterday."

"How was Niagara Falls?"

"Absolutely stunning," Phoebe said, her neatly plucked eyebrows arching as she shook her head. "Promise me you'll go see it someday, Cara. It's right up your alley. You'd love it."

"It's a promise."

"Good. Now, how are things? How's work? It's been ages

since we last spoke."

"I know. I'm sorry. I've been very busy myself."

"Don't apologise. I'm just as shit as you are at keeping in touch." She chuckled.

"True. Anyway, work's amazing. It's a dream come true, honestly. Even despite the long hours, it's completely exhilarating. I'm definitely on the right path, Pheebs."

"Aw, I'm so happy to hear that, Cara, even if I've never doubted it for even a second. That said, I do recall you being a bit stressed about that guy who turned out to be your boss and Jason's brother…Will, was it?"

My face immediately flushed upon the mention of him. Glancing sideways, I saw Jason's lips form a crooked smile as he stared absentmindedly at the frozen picture on the television.

"Yeah, that's the name," I mumbled and gazed back at Phoebe. Her brows were knitted now.

"Why are you blushing? You're a tomato."

"Er, well…"

Jason leaned closer. "Hi, Pheebs. Long time no see. You're sorely missed over here."

Her eyes widened instantaneously, and it occurred to me upon the sight that she must have thought she'd spilled my secret. As far as she was aware, Jason still had no idea that I'd slept with his brother.

"Hi, Jason!" She sounded alarmed. "Wasn't aware you were there. How are you? I miss you, too!"

"I'm great, thanks. And William is indeed the name," Jason replied, amused.

"Jason knows," I rushed to tell her.

She released a loud groan that revealed her profound relief. "For fuck's sake, Cara. You could have warned me Jason is with you. I thought I'd just dropped the whole bomb in his face!"

"Don't worry. No harm done."

"Christ."

Bethan cackled in the background, and it was a contagious sound.

"How did you handle the news, Jase?" Phoebe asked him.

He grinned. "Bit shocked at first."

"I can imagine." She giggled. "Cara was, too, I assure you. She was all over the place last we talked about it."

"She's been all over the place for months," Jason said, still highly amused. "You've seriously missed out, Pheebs."

"Have I?"

I cleared my throat. "Yeah, listen, there's something I've been meaning to tell you. Remember when I told you about Will and I said that I'd never consider dating him?"

She was silent for several seconds, and I could tell from her wide eyes that she was struggling to believe her intuition. "Yes?"

"Right, well… I'm dating him."

"No way!"

My cheeks grew hotter. "Yeah, way."

"Are you joking?"

"No."

"You're actually dating someone?" I rarely saw Phoebe this shocked.

"Yeah."

"I can't believe this! Jason, is she lying?"

Jason guffawed beside me. "Trust me, Pheebs. I'm just as mind-blown as you are."

"This is…What? How? You were so determined to stay away from him last we spoke!"

I grimaced. "Yeah, I know. But I changed my mind. Or rather, *he* changed my mind."

"Oh my God! Have you told Mum and Dad?"

I shook my head. "No. I don't want to tell them until I'm certain it's serious – until we're official, if we ever reach that point."

"Sounds familiar," Bethan murmured beside Phoebe.

"Yeah, I get that." Phoebe nodded. "They'll be over the

moon, Cara."

"Maybe."

"Definitely."

"Hopefully."

"Are your parents aware, Jason?" Phoebe asked then.

Her question prompted me to think of John. I hadn't seen him since Sunday, but William had told me at work just today that John still hadn't expressed any concerns to him. So, if John was truly suspicious, it seemed like he was giving us the green light to continue our affair. I dearly hoped it was the case.

"I think they know, or at least suspect," Jason replied to her. "But they haven't been explicitly enlightened of it. Either way, both Mum and Dad adore Cara, so it's not going to pose a problem when they finally learn the truth."

"We don't know that yet," I argued. "Whether it will pose a problem, I mean. I'm still Will's assistant. It's possible John is still considering whether to intervene and hasn't made up his mind yet."

Jason snorted. "You'll only be shadowing Will for two more months, Cara. Dad's definitely not going to care so long as it doesn't affect your performance at work."

"Cara, stop overthinking," Phoebe said. "You always do this."

"Excuse you. Overthinking? This is a serious matter. It's unprofessional to say the least."

She rolled her eyes.

"I get you, Cara," Bethan supported me.

"You always take her side," Phoebe said to her.

"Well, that's because she's usually right."

"Or you're just looking to suck up to her."

Bethan snorted. "I don't need to suck up to Cara. She loves me already."

"I really do," I assured her, amused.

Suddenly, Phoebe frowned. "Hang on…If you're seeing Will, what does that mean for Aaron?"

My heart sank at the mention of my dear friend. "Aaron and I aren't speaking right now."

"Oh no." Phoebe's lips protruded, her features displaying her dismay. "What happened?"

"It's a long story, and it doesn't end well."

She sighed. "I think I know."

"I think we all knew," Jason murmured and entwined his fingers behind his neck to support his head. "Everyone but Cara."

"Way to rub it in," I grumbled.

"Sorry." He grimaced. "Didn't mean it like that."

"Poor Aaron," Phoebe said and glanced away. "Is he heartbroken?"

Her phrasing and reaction brought unexpected tears to my eyes. Suddenly the horrible memory of Aaron sitting on his sofa, utterly crestfallen, awakened in my mind. I could see him so clearly, his warm brown eyes pouring of despair as he stared blankly ahead of himself. Silence had drifted in the air between us as we'd both struggled to come to grips with our new reality. I'd wanted to reach out, console him, cling to him, but my nearness was no longer welcome.

I knew Phoebe had always adored Aaron, but then again, why wouldn't she? Aaron was a lovely, reliable person, and I'd lost him. The painful reminder made me close my eyes, and I squeezed them together hard, as if it would help me suppress the memory.

"Yeah," I replied, my voice trembling.

"Cara, I'm so sorry."

"I don't want to go into it. I'll cry," I warned her.

"Then we won't. Either way, I'm happy to hear about Will. I'm looking forward to meeting him."

"Yeah, he's eager to meet you, too."

"Is he?"

"Very, from my understanding."

She smirked. "That's a good sign. Means he's serious about you."

"Yeah, he's fantastic. You'll like him, I think."

"I'm sure I will. He's got to be fantastic if he's managed to charm *you*, of all people. I've often doubted whether you'd ever find someone, to be honest."

I chuckled. "Me too."

"But here he is."

"Here he is," I sighed. "His timing could have been better. He arrived a bit early."

A quick chuckle leapt out of her. "God. When are you going to realise that you can't control everything?"

"I've never thought I could. But, I did think I could control *this*."

"And how wrong you were."

"How wrong indeed."

"Can you hear Mum's 'told you so'? Because I can."

"Frequently," I chuckled.

"When are you visiting, Pheebs?" Jason asked.

"Late August is the plan."

"Nice. Will Bethan be joining you?"

"No, unfortunately. School will have started again."

"Right. She's a teacher, isn't she? Or have I got that wrong?"

"No, you're right. High School English. Good memory, Jase."

He grinned. "Thanks. Eight hours of sleep every night does that."

She laughed. "Have you read *Why We Sleep* by Matthew Walker?"

"Course."

"Course."

"Oh, I've been meaning to read that," Bethan said. "Is it any good?" she asked Jason.

"Very enlightening."

"Nice. I'll buy it tomorrow."

"You can borrow mine. I've got it on my Kindle," Phoebe said.

"Then I'll do that."

I stared at Phoebe's adorable face for a moment, and I missed her intensely then. However, it was clear as day that she was having the time of her life over in America, and that Bethan was making her the happiest she'd ever been, and that attenuated some of the pain of having her so far away. "You stay safe on the road, Pheebs, alright? I'm watching a crime show with Jason right now, and women are really not safe out there, that's for sure."

"We're being careful, Cara. Don't worry."

"Good."

"Anyway, Bethan and I are about to head out for dinner, so we'll let you get back to the show. Which is it?"

"*The Fall.*"

She shuddered. "I've seen that. Never thought Jamie Dornan could be so creepy."

"Neither did I. His acting is on point in this show."

"Really is. Anyway, speak soon, yeah?"

I raised a brow. "Soon, as in a couple of weeks?"

She smiled guiltily. "As always."

"Do check in more often, Phoebe, especially now that you're travelling. I worry."

"Promise."

"Thank you. Have you talked to Mum and Dad lately?"

"Called them just before I called you."

"Good."

"When was the last time you saw them?"

I frowned. "Got to be a few weeks ago. Haven't seen them since I started work. I've been so busy. Life's been a lot lately."

"Well, then you should visit them soon."

"I will."

"Good. Keep me posted on Will, yeah? I'm really excited about this."

"I will. Love you," I cooed.

"Love you too."

Hanging up, I put my phone on the coffee table in front of the sofa and reclined against Jason again. "Okay. Let's resume."

After grabbing the remote, he wrapped his arm around me again.

"By the way," I said before he could press play, "could you sleep in my bed tonight? There's no way I'll be able to sleep alone after this episode."

He smiled, hand rubbing my arm. "Of course."

"Thanks." I peered up at him. "You don't think Will's going to mind, do you?"

He shook his head. "No."

"Should I ask?"

He shrugged. "Well, he knows we cuddle all the time, but I suppose it can't hurt."

Reaching for my phone again, I decided to call William.

"Hi, love," he answered almost immediately, and the sound of his voice soothed my heart in a way only he could manage.

"Hi," I said, affection oozing from my tone. "Are you at home?"

"Yeah. Just walked in."

I looked at the time. "That's very late. It's nearly ten."

"Yeah," he sighed.

"You should have asked me to stay longer. I could've helped you shorten your day."

"No, you couldn't, don't worry. No offence."

I smiled. "None taken."

"Was there a reason you called?"

"Yeah. Jason and I are watching *The Fall*. Have you seen it?"

He was quiet for a few seconds. "I haven't really got time to watch TV much, Cara."

I chuckled. "Right. Anyway, it's a bit unnerving, so I was wondering if you'd be alright with it if Jason and I slept in the same bed tonight."

"Er, yeah, sure." He sounded surprised. "Thanks for asking."

"He said you wouldn't mind, but I wanted to make sure."

"I appreciate it." He hesitated. "Though, tell the naturist to wear a pair of boxers, at the very least."

Laughter surged out of me. "He hasn't dared to walk around

naked since we started seeing each other, Will."

"Good. I swear, I don't know where he got that from. Must be Granddad, on Mum's side."

"What's he saying?" Jason's eyes narrowed with suspicion.

I couldn't suppress my laughter. "He's asking where you got your naturist tendencies from."

Jason snatched my phone out of my hand to lift it to his ear. "Listen here. For the last time, the naked body is completely natural, Will. I haven't had a boner around Cara ever, apart from some mornings, but you know I can't help that, and you know that's got nothing to do with her."

I gasped at his frankness. However, Jason didn't so much as flinch when William replied, so I got the impression that the elder brother had handled the information astonishingly well.

"Yeah, don't worry. I'll wear boxers." Jason laughed. "My dick won't so much as touch her. It never has... Yeah, sleep well. Talk soon... Night." He gave my phone back to me.

"Is he still on?"

"Yeah."

I lifted my phone to my ear. "Hello?"

"He's so eccentric sometimes."

"I'm sure it's a genetic thing," I joked.

"Yeah, I love him. Anyway, just thought I'd say goodnight. I'll see you tomorrow."

I bit my lower lip as an idea occurred to me. "You know, if you want, you're welcome to come over and hold me instead? Or better yet, I could come to you?"

His hesitation made it obvious that he hadn't expected my proposal. "You know, as much as I adore you for this, I'm actually knackered. Will you be upset if I just go straight to bed?"

I was grateful to notice that the rejection didn't hurt at all. Instead, I smiled. What I took from it was that we had reached a point where we were no longer desperate for each other. Things were finally becoming more stable between us. We no longer took whatever we could get from the other, because we knew that, if we didn't grab this opportunity, another would assuredly present itself at a later time. We'd reached a new milestone, and I cherished that fact.

"No. Don't worry. Get some rest, Will."

"Thanks. It's not you, it's me."

I laughed at his joke. "Don't worry. I get it. I really do."

"I believe you. Sweet dreams, then, darling."

"You too, Will."

Hanging up, I looked at Jason with a smile that exposed how smitten I was with his brother. "Okay, now I'm ready."

"You sure? Don't want to call your parents, or your grandparents, or Father Christmas, before—"

"Start the bloody show."

He grinned.

§ § §

The next day, Olivia had wanted to tag along to help me hunt for a gown to wear for the charity ball, which was tomorrow. However, as I browsed through the options of the shop at Harrods, she was anything but helpful. With her face buried in her phone, I heard her giggle to herself while she texted nonstop, and I recognised the version of her laughter all too well. It was the lovestruck version. I'd heard it several times before, and the person that had caused it in the past was a man I absolutely detested.

Colin.

However, when I had asked who she was texting earlier, she had insisted that she was only texting her brother, Christian, so I was growing increasingly annoyed. It was blatant from the sound of her giggles that she was texting a man she wasn't related to. And Christian was hardly that funny, anyway.

"Olivia," I said and turned towards her. Even though I'd called her Olivia, she barely offered me a scrap of her attention.

Nodding, she kept her eyes glued to the screen of her phone.

My suspicion increased. While I didn't hold it against her that she had rejected Jason, I had an inkling that had rejected him because she had rekindled with Colin, despite swearing that she wouldn't.

"Are you texting Colin?" I asked bluntly and narrowed my eyes as I analysed her reaction. For a split second, her entire figure froze.

"What? No," she murmured, but didn't meet my gaze.

Her insincerity was hurtful. "Yes, you are."

"No. I'm not."

"Alright, show me, then. If you've got nothing to hide, it shouldn't be a problem."

Finally, she directed her eyes to mine. "Cara, this is a matter of principle. I haven't got anything to hide, but I'm not comfortable with you looking through my phone."

"You're lying to my face," I accused. "In case you've forgotten, you've told me your passcode, so your argument about the principle of privacy is definitely bullshit."

Her lips parted at the way I arrested her. For three seconds straight, we merely stared at each other.

"Olivia, tell me it isn't true. Please."

She swallowed, and seeing that was answer enough.

I sighed, my shoulders sinking. "I can't believe you're doing this to yourself. You're essentially asking to get your heart broken again."

She appeared to be speechless, so I continued, "You need to reconsider your targets. I get that you loved him, and probably still do, but that doesn't mean he's right for you. Sometimes – oftentimes, actually – people fall in love with the wrong person. Colin is the wrong person."

Ashamed, she glanced away. "I don't know what to say."

"So you don't deny it?"

Her pretty face contorted as she shook her head.

I grimaced. The fact that she was on the verge of reuniting with Colin made me want to grab her shoulders and shake her.

How could she do this to herself? She was such a self-destructive person sometimes, and I was desperate to save her from herself.

"Livy, I don't want to see you get hurt again. He's bad for you. You need to shut that imbecile out of your life. You know I hate telling people how to run their lives, but I feel it's my duty as your best friend to steer you away from him. He's bad news, and he's already proved that. He fucking shagged Alison on your birthday last year. What's worse, he had an affair with her for six months before *he* dumped *you* for *her*. Have you forgotten that he told you that when you confronted him about this?"

She inhaled sharply. Looking at the ceiling, she made use of gravity to make sure her sudden tears wouldn't spill down her cheeks. Seeing her like this was painful, so without a second thought, I walked towards her and brought her into my arms. "I'm sorry. I didn't mean to be so harsh, but I'm worried, Livy."

She trembled in my arms, stifling sobs. "I'm sorry."

"Don't apologise to me. I'm not the one he hurt, Livy. You should be apologising to yourself."

She pulled back to look at me. "I don't know, Cara. I don't know what I'm doing. Ever since he reached out to me, he's been begging me for a second chance, telling me he's had so many revelations since we split up, telling me he knows he made terrible mistakes and that he wants me back."

The pain in her eyes was awful to watch. I wished I could remove it, but I had no idea how to treat this. All I knew was that my gut didn't like it in the slightest. I had a terrible feeling that it wouldn't end well. He was manipulating her yet again, and I hated to see that it was working. Here she stood, entertaining not just the thought of him, but actually him, after everything he'd done to her.

What was I supposed to do? Sit idly by and watch her walk into guaranteed heartache? Then provide a shoulder for her to lean on every time she sabotaged herself, while biting back the urge to tell her "I told you so"?

"Well," I sighed, "you make your own decisions, and you know I'll always be there for you regardless of what you choose, but I've got to say, I don't like this one bit. I don't trust that he's changed, Livy. He's a manipulative bastard. Always was."

She wiped her cheeks. "I'm…I haven't made up my mind yet."

"I get it. But while you consider things, try not to think of the future you wish to have with him, but rather the past you did have. It's important you stay rational about this. Is Colin good for you? Does he exhilarate you, make you feel good more than bad? Does he uplift you or weigh you down?"

She grimaced and shook her head vehemently. "Cara, I can't have this conversation right now."

Sighing, I pulled her close to hug her tightly again. "I'm sorry you're going through this. I'll shut up."

"Thanks."

"Help me find a dress, yeah?"

"Yeah."

§ § §

I picked a maroon-coloured dress of satin. By the time we exited the building, both of us were preoccupied with our thoughts. The mood between us was dispirited, so we hadn't said much since our conversation about Colin.

I was wearing a constant frown as we stood on the pavement outside the building, waiting for the pouring rain to ease up. The scent of wet asphalt drifted in the air while the heavy traffic in the street droned in the background. I stared blankly at the road, seeing car tyres running over puddles and splashing the brown water towards us. I hadn't brought an umbrella with me, which I should have. Olivia had been wiser and was wearing a mac.

After a while, a sigh slipped out of Olivia's mouth. "You know, I know we were supposed to have dinner together, but I'm not really in the mood to hang out with anyone right now," she told me frankly. Looking over, I saw the conflict in her brown Bambi eyes, how severe her confusion was. "I think I need to be alone tonight. Clear my head, do some thinking."

I nodded. "Don't worry. I get it."

"Are you sure?"

I gave her a half-hearted smile. "Yes. Only, it's not because you're angry with me, right?"

She shook her head. "No. I know you're only trying to look after me."

"I really am. I only want what's best for you, Livy. Whatever you need, I'll give it – but not whatever you *want*," I emphasised.

Nodding, she glanced away with trouble on her brow. "You've always been my voice of reason."

"As your best friend, that's my job."

She looked back, and her plump lips tucked into a small smile. "I love you."

"I love you too, darling."

She motioned towards the street. "Would you like me to wait with you till it stops raining?"

"No, don't worry. I'll be alright."

After a nod, she stepped closer to wrap her arms around me. "Have fun tomorrow, yeah? I can't wait to hear about it. Will's going to swoon when he sees you in that dress."

Her statement made me grin. "I hope you're right."

"Oh, I'm definitely right. His jaw is going to hit the floor."

I chuckled. "Okay, don't overdo it."

"I'm really not." A grin spread across her face. "He's lucky to have you, Cara, and so am I."

"Oh my God. Stop it or you'll make me blush."

"You're already blushing."

Smiling, I rolled my eyes. "Call me if you need anything, yeah? Or if you just want to talk; air your thoughts."

Pulling away, she shrugged her shoulders. "I honestly think

I'll call Chris."

My eyebrows arched. I hadn't expected that. "Really? But Christian hates Colin."

She tilted her head with a vague smile. "That's exactly why I need to call him. Perhaps he can beat some sense into me as well."

I pursed my lips. "I sincerely hope he will."

She chuckled, albeit humourlessly. "I'll let you know."

"Do."

After another hug, she turned to head for the Tube station. I gazed after her for some time, worrying. Hopefully, Christian would provide the nail that would shut the coffin once and for all.

As I stood there, a strange urge to ring William gripped me. I wanted him to soothe me, help me think of something else. While his voice would do, what I truly yearned for was his embrace.

I took my phone out of my purse and found his number in my recent log. As I dialled it, I lifted the device to my ear and waited impatiently for him to pick up.

"To what do I owe this honour?" he answered.

"Hello."

He was quiet for a beat. "That's not the tone I like to hear. Are you alright, darling?"

"No."

Again, he paused. "What's wrong?" He sounded anxious.

I sucked in a long, deep breath. "Are you busy right now?"

"I've always got time for you."

My heart tingled. He could be unbearably sweet sometimes.

"What's the problem, Cara?"

"Livy might be getting back with Colin." I couldn't help the exasperation that seeped out of my voice.

I heard his disbelief from his brief silence. "Are you joking?"

"No."

"Didn't he cheat on her countless times?"

"He did."

"Well, then she's an idiot. Jason clearly dodged a bullet there. Christ."

"Yes. I tried telling her it's a bad idea, but I'm not sure she's going to listen. I'm worried, Will."

"Well, you did the right thing. If she's too blind to see it herself, she needs to be told. And if her best friends won't tell her, who will?"

I grimaced. The urge to smother him and nuzzle my face against his chest was extreme. Merely his mollifying scent was something I found myself missing intensely.

"Will, I know this is pathetic, but I'd really appreciate your company right now."

"Cara, that's not pathetic. You know I'll always be there for you when you need me," he said tenderly. Delicious affection coursed through my veins upon his sweet words. I was so in love with him. "I'm impressed you brought yourself to ask, though. Did you have to twist your own arm to do it?"

I couldn't help my amused smile as I rolled my eyes at him. "No. I did not."

"What progress, love. Happy to hear that. Anyway, I'll be there in an hour. I'm still at the office. Just need to finish up a few things first."

I glanced up at the dim grey sky. "Well, I'm not home yet. Just found a gown for tomorrow. Have you had dinner? If not, I can order some take-out for us on my way home."

"You'll make for the perfect partner, Cara. So efficient. But no, I haven't had dinner. Anything will do, though. You know I'm not particular."

"So, plenty of ketchup, then?" I teased.

"Ha-ha."

"I'll make sure of it."

"The only time I'd eat ketchup is if it were off your skin."

I blushed profusely upon the reminder of when he'd licked

raspberry sorbet off my body. "I'm hanging up now," I said when the memory managed to arouse me. He was so fucking exciting.

His soft laughter poured through the line. "I'll see you in a bit. Try not to think of Livy. She'll see sense – hopefully. Well, if she's got a decent brain, she will."

"Yeah," I sighed and hung up.

I'M YOUR KING

By some amusing coincidence, I ended up walking behind William as I exited the Tube station at Notting Hill Gate about an hour later. Oblivious to my presence, he stalked across the street with his brown leather bag hanging from his broad shoulder. Unsurprisingly, he was still wearing the same grey suit he'd worn to the office, but it disappointed me somewhat. I wished he'd gone home to collect a change of clothes because, if he had, it would mean he intended to spend the night. That wasn't on the agenda, but I wanted to sleep in his arms. I hadn't done it since Monday.

Nevertheless, I admired his graceful strides and ogled his proportionate anatomy the whole journey to the flat. Only after he'd pressed the doorbell outside the front door did he scout the surrounding street and notice me. When he did, his eyebrows climbed higher.

"Stalker," he accused once I'd caught up with him.

"A rubbish one. You walk so fast I was having a hard time matching your pace." I stretched up on my toes to peck his mouth.

"Long legs," he murmured against my lips and kissed me repeatedly.

"Why did you ring the doorbell? You've got keys," I asked as I pulled away.

He shrugged. "I don't like to use them unless I have to. It's not my home after all. And..." His eyes frosted for half a second. "I'm a bit traumatised, so I prefer to make sure no one's home before I go to that measure."

Before I was able to express my regret for the awful memory I had burnt into his mind, Jason's voice drifted through the speaker. "Greetings."

"Good evening, wanker," William answered, amused.

"Will? What are you doing here? Cara's not in."

"No, she's outside with me."

"Did you both forget your keys?"

"No," I said. "Just arrived."

"Oh. Well, then you may use them. William's insult has got me offended. I ain't no servant of his."

I sniggered.

"Of course you are," William insisted.

"You got that wrong. I'm your king."

"No, you're not. I'm yours. William is a king's name. Jason implies that you're the son of a Jay. Ergo, your name is pathetic and unimaginative. Open the gates, son of Jay."

"Of hell? That is where you belong. Anyway, this is *my* castle. Get your own. And just so you know, 'Jason' stems from Greek mythology, after a hero, and means 'healer'. So alright, you might have a king's name, but I'd rather have a hero's."

"William is the name of both heroes and kings, you dumb shit. Not only that, but—"

Groaning, I ignored the rest of their banter while I reached into my purse and fished for my keys. After unlocking the door, I practically had to drag William away from the intercom since he was so preoccupied with deriding his brother.

Those two were surely something else.

"You can ridicule him upstairs," I said as I tugged on William's arm.

He looked surprised at me, as if it hadn't occurred to him. *Christ*, he'd surely been caught up in the moment.

"Right."

When the door drew shut, I glanced at him over my shoulder as I climbed the stairs. "Don't tell him what I told you about Livy. I don't think he'll handle it very well."

He agreed with a nod, but I could tell from his fleeting eyes that he wasn't entirely convinced it was the sagacious course of action.

Dubious, I stopped in my tracks to face him. "What?" My head tilted.

He shrugged and turned his profile to me. "Perhaps he ought to know. It might serve as a reality-check. If she's so daft that she's willing to get back with her abusive ex, Jason might benefit from hearing it. It might even put him off the idea of her."

Uncertain, I frowned back. "It might do more harm than good, though. Is that a risk worth taking?"

"It's the truth," he argued. "And the truth hurts sometimes. But, knowing Jason, he definitely prefers it. I think he'd appreciate knowing. Sure, he'll be angry at first, but after that initial fit, he'll come to realise what a dimwit she is."

I paled at his word choice. "She's completely lost your respect, hasn't she?" I did not enjoy the idea of that. Olivia was my best friend, so if William weren't ever going to approve of her, it would certainly bother me.

Seeming to ruminate for a bit, he looked blankly to his left. "Not completely. Depends on her next move. If she does go back to him, she might've. I mean, come on. She rejects a sweet lad like Jason for a cunt like Colin? Please. She deserves what's coming for her."

I pressed my palm flat across his chest and stared deep into his eyes. "William, Livy's my best friend. She's been there for me through thick and thin for as long as I can remember. Please, don't judge her so harshly for a single mistake – one she hasn't even made yet. And, even if she does, she deserves patience. She's in love. People do stupid things when they're in love."

He steered his eyes to mine, and I saw that my words had resonated. "You're right. It's just harder to like her when it's my brother who's involved."

"I get that, but you need to bear in mind how much Livy loves Colin. It's a hard thing to fight, especially given how manipulative he is. She needs me now more than ever."

He sighed. "Aaron, Livy...Your friends shouldn't be bringing you down, Cara."

I scowled at him. "They're not. This isn't fair to them. You've no idea what you're even talking about."

He lifted his hands, yielding. "Sorry. I spoke out of turn."

I pursed my lips. "You did. I know you don't like Aaron, but if you could please be objective for a second, you should be able to tell that he was a great friend to me."

His subsequent glare was blistering. The bone of his jaw poked out below his ears as he clenched and unclenched it numerous times. Finally, he said, "I suppose that, if he hadn't shared beds with you for the past three years, I might actually have liked him. He did earn my respect when he defended you that dreadful night. I'd have done the same, had I been in his place."

Hearing that astonished me. "Wow. Can I record this?"

His eyes hooded. He was not amused. "Careful, Cara."

"Sorry, I didn't mean it like that. I'm honestly touched by your ability to look past our arrangement and judge him separately."

"Well, it doesn't really matter, does it? You still fucked regularly for the better part of three years. I'll never be able to ignore that fact. Besides, since he's out of your life, it doesn't matter what I might think of him as a person, because I won't ever have to endure his existence again."

"No, but your ability to judge him somewhat objectively does matter to me. It speaks of your character, in the sense of a bigger picture."

He rolled his eyes. I quite adored him whenever he rolled his eyes. For some odd reason, he looked rather endearing – boyish, even if I only fancied grown men. "Glad I could make you happy."

Smirking, I turned on my heel again, but I'd only managed to climb a single step by the time he grabbed my shoulder to stall me. Curious, I looked at him over my shoulder again and saw that his eyes were glued to the three things I was carrying: our dinner, my gown, and my purse.

"I'll give you a hand with that," he said and reached for all three.

After blinking twice, I tightened my grip on them. "What a gentleman. Thanks, but I'll manage."

He chuckled. "Strong and independent?"

"Mhm."

"Don't be silly."

"Fine," I sighed and handed him our dinner and my purse. My gown I kept to myself.

"That your dress?" He cocked his head towards the bag which contained it.

"Yes." I hugged it to my chest, protective. Sensing why, his lips curved into a crooked smile.

"Can't I have a look? It's not exactly a wedding dress."

An abundance of heat flooded my face. William uttering the word "wedding" forced a strange idea into my head of him as a groom. He'd look out of this world. The sheer view of him by the altar would be overwhelming. Regardless of whether or not we ended up together, he was bound to make for a striking husband to his wife, both in mind and body – and in bed.

Gosh, the wedding night of William Night.

If I weren't going to have the honour, I knew in my heart that the woman who would was going to be the most fortunate lady alive. She had better prize him for what he was, and she had better enjoy her wedding night on my behalf.

"Oh my God," I scolded myself. How rapid my thoughts were. Marriage? Please. We weren't even in a relationship.

"Oh, your God," William teased. "Let me have a look."

"No. Tomorrow," I grumbled and scurried up the remaining stairs.

"Since I essentially bought that dress, I have a right to see it," he argued after me.

I froze in front of the door before I turned towards him and took his credit card out of my back pocket. Our argument on Monday – when he had insisted on paying for my gown – had bordered on a screaming match. Just another day between William and me, I supposed. I'd barely managed to swallow my pride when he had handed me his credit card at work today.

"I wanted to buy it myself," I muttered grudgingly. "You're stepping on my dignity."

He raised a brow at me once he made it to the top of the stairs. "You're right. That was unnecessary. I know you weren't, and aren't, comfortable with it. But you've got to understand that when I essentially beg you to attend a prestigious event with me, I won't let you pay for the designer gown you'll wear to it. You're a student, Cara, for the last time. Besides…" He turned his profile to me, evidently uncomfortable. "I hate using this card, but you know full well that I can afford it."

I pursed my lips before a sigh pushed past them. "I just want to say this again, because I don't feel like I can state it a time too many. I am not sleeping with you to get a fast pass into your wallet. In fact, you may keep it to yourself for as long as we last."

Underwhelmed, he faced me again. "You don't need to tell me

that. It's obvious that you don't when you always argue with me whenever I try to pay for things."

I shrugged. "I want to earn my own fortune."

"And I both fancy and admire that about you."

I smiled and turned to head inside.

"There's my servant," Jason greeted from the sofa once we entered the living room. "Did you have a quick round outside since it took you so long?"

"Livy might be getting back with Colin," William instantly announced.

"William!" I screeched and pulled my hair. That moron!

Jason looked blankly at William. "What?"

"Yeah. Cara told me just now."

Jason shook his head, clearly unwilling to believe it. "You're not being serious."

"I am. Tell him, Cara."

"I..." I frowned, upset.

When Jason's gaze summoned mine, I saw the hope that resided in his – hope that I would reveal that this was only a bad joke. But it wasn't a bad joke, and I hated that I'd have to be the one to tell him. Watching him suffer wounded me, too. This was going to break his heart all over again.

Sympathy coloured my tone as I said, "Jason, I'm sorry. I fished it out of her when we were shopping today."

He looked rigid now. "Are you actually serious? Has she lost her goddamned mind!"

I winced.

"After everything that prick did to her, she considers taking him back!"

"She's obviously an idiot. You should be glad she's not your girlfriend," William said. "Honestly, Jason, you deserve so much better."

"William!" Jason snarled. "Not now!"

To my relief, William actually listened. Turned mute, he gazed away.

"Jason, I'm sorry. I didn't want to tell you, but Will—"

"No," he cut me off with a bark. "I'm glad you did. But that doesn't help the fact that I'm fucking fuming. What is she thinking?"

I swallowed. I'd never seen Jason this livid. It was intimidating. I hadn't thought he harboured even the potential of such ire.

Quietly, I said, "Just give her some time. Nothing's certain yet."

"She's unbelievable!" He sat up to run his hands through his hair in his evident exasperation. "I've seen her cry over that cunt so many times I've lost count, and now she might take him back?"

I sensed William hesitate beside me. "I thought you ought to know."

"I honestly can't fucking believe this." Standing, Jason charged for his bedroom.

"Jason," I called, distressed. Wanting to console him, I was about to follow him when William clasped my shoulder.

"Leave him be, Cara," he ordered gently. "He wants to be alone. Whenever he gets like this, he always wants to be alone."

Disconcerted, I looked up at William with a pout on my face. "I get that you thought he deserved to know, but there's a better way to deliver bad news, Will. Couldn't you have been gentler? This is a sensitive spot for him. He's still licking his wounds."

His Adam's apple ascended and fell with his swallow. "I – Yeah. Maybe you're right."

"You ought to apologise."

He pressed his lips together, eyes darting to Jason's shut bedroom door. "I'll do it after dinner if he still hasn't come out."

"Thank you."

Affected by Jason's morose mood, we didn't speak much until we were halfway through dinner.

"So..." William murmured and reached for his glass of

sparkling water on the table between us. "Regarding tomorrow..."

I swallowed my mouthful of the chicken stir-fry. "What about it?"

While holding my gaze, he stated, "I've booked a room for the night at the hotel it's being hosted at. I've got a feeling it'll prove useful. Knowing myself, I doubt I'll be able to resist having sex with you for an entire evening, especially when you'll be wearing a gown. I can already feel my fingers itching to peel it off, and I haven't even seen it yet."

Knowing him, I should have anticipated this. Either way, I grinned. "Is that why you wanted to see my dress earlier? Feed your fantasy?"

"Just tell me the colour."

I laughed. "No."

Disappointed, he looked back to his plate, sulking. "Regardless, I gather we can head there straight after work, have sex for a few hours, get ready together and attend downstairs, before we head back up to have some more fun."

I knitted my brows. "Is sex all you think about?"

He smirked. "Don't be silly. You know it's not – far from it. But around you, yeah, I do think about it quite frequently. You're irresistible. Can't help it."

"And yet you're not spending the night today."

Amused, he tilted his head and scoured my features. "You sound disappointed."

"I am," I admitted, but I was too bashful to look at him when I continued, "After everything with Livy, and now Jason, I'd appreciate to sleep in your arms."

"You should've said that earlier and I'd have picked up some clothes on my way here. I decided not to since I gathered your vagina will get enough of a beating tomorrow."

I groaned. "You're an idiot. I specifically said 'sleep in your arms'. There was no mention of sex."

He snorted. "That's naïve. I'd try to fuck you, and you know that."

My cheeks grew hotter. "What am I supposed to do with you?"

"Anything you want." His tone was suggestive, his smile lewd.

I nodded slowly. "Alright. I'll strap on a dildo next time. Hope you like it in the arse."

That silenced him instantaneously. When I glanced at him, he stared back at me, disturbed, till a shudder surged through him. "Dickhead," he muttered.

"That's what I'll be driving up your arse, yes."

The stony-faced look he gave me made me snigger.

"Some men like that you know. Bum-play."

He studied me incredulously. "Aaron tell you that?"

Low blow.

"No."

"Pity. If he turned out to be gay, I wouldn't mind you two being friends."

"Pity indeed. But a man doesn't have to be homosexual to enjoy it. Apparently, that's where you lot have got your G-spot. Or so I've read."

He shook his head. "So I've heard. But I am not interested in finding out."

"You sure? What if you're missing out on the most powerful orgasm of your—"

Jason opening the door interrupted my sentence. Simultaneously, William and I gazed over. Though he still looked somewhat crestfallen, he's managed to compose himself.

His eyes flickered between William and me. "Are you two seriously discussing whether to do anal sex, on *William*, over dinner in my dining room? Like that's completely normal?"

When he put it like that, the urge to laugh was vicious.

William shrugged his shoulders and replied, "Just another day between Cara and me, this. Rest assured, it's not going to happen."

Jason's lips twitched until a short laugh escaped him. "I don't think there exists a label to describe you two."

Seemingly disinterested, William veered, "Listen, about earlier, I'm sorry about—"

"Will, don't bother," Jason cut him off with a wave. "I've grown up with you. I'm aware of the defect of your social antennas. I know you meant well."

"Still, I could have been more considerate – chosen my words more carefully."

"The message would have been the same, which is all I care about."

Charmed, I looked between them. It would appear that Jason wasn't as easily fazed by William's blunt character as I had feared.

"You feeling any better?" I asked gently.

Gripping his hips, Jason sighed. "Gutted, is all. But yeah." His eyes fixed on William. "You spending the night?"

"Cara wants me to. She's upset about the Livy-situation. But I didn't bring any clothes. I could always leave earlier in the morning, though. Would you like me to stay?"

Jason chewed on his lower lip before he gave a vague nod. "Yeah, actually."

William blinked, surprised. "Then I'll stay. I'm a bit amused you both come to me seeking comfort. Do I really come across as that type of person?"

I hadn't thought of that before he said it. Indeed, it was quite amusing – ironic even. Brutal William was our safe haven.

"In your own strange way," I replied affectionately.

Jason chuckled. "Even if you are a dick most of the time, you always have our backs. Think that's why."

William reclined in his seat, seemingly pleased with himself. The smug smile on his face was priceless. "I'm a saint," he alleged jokingly.

My lips twisted with amusement as I pointed my fork at him. "You're exceptionally talented at ruining the moment with your conceited comments."

The chuckle he gave exposed how awkward he felt. "I get uncomfortable in cheesy situations. It's my way of dodging it."

"Fancy a beer, then?" Jason asked him as he headed for the kitchen.

"Sure."

After a period of silence, William started laughing to himself. Bemused, I watched him, and saw Jason mirror my reaction upon his return from the kitchen.

"What's got your laughing gear cracking open?" Jason asked.

While shaking his head to himself, William rubbed his face and continued to laugh. "This is just priceless. First, I've got to help Andy out with Chloe, then Alex with Abigail, and now you two with Livy. Am I a fucking counsellor? Why can't you all get your shit together? Honestly, I can't help but laugh."

"Oh, go do one, Will," Jason muttered. "You're going to fuck up one day, and when you do, you should be glad you'll have all of us there to support you."

"No, don't get me wrong. I don't mind. I'm honestly just amazed."

"Yes, you're quite right," I said with a nod. "You and Oprah should get together and do a talk-show."

Jason burst out laughing while William sank in his seat.

"Way to kill my joy, Cara," William muttered.

"Oh, sorry." I feigned a sympathetic frown. "Must have been painful falling from your high horse."

"It was. You'll have to kiss it better," he replied sulkily.

"I'll give you a blowjob. How's that for kissing it better?"

Slowly, his mouth took the shape of a lustful smile. "Just perfect."

"Fucking rabbits," Jason commented under his breath.

26

WHERE YOU BELONG

LONDON AND ITS VIBRANCY MIGHT AS WELL HAVE BEEN A planet away, even if we were essentially in the midst of it. Our loud panting was the only thing I heard. Sated, I turned and smiled at the stunning view. Head facing away from me, he lay on his torso, spent after our sizzling session. It had been impatient and rough, primitive even, but entirely delicious.

Sex with William was easily my favourite thing in the world. When he pushed me towards my peak, I sometimes felt capable of touching the sky. That was how high I spiritually soared.

Earlier, I'd barely had time to register my luxurious surroundings before he'd lifted me by the hips and lobbed me onto the king-sized bed of the suite. Exigent hunger had exuded from his actions when he'd swiftly lunged after me and climbed up the length of my body. All the while, his eyes had held mine captive. Only when he had hovered above me with passionate intentions in mind had I managed to swallow the drool in my mouth. He was unfairly sexy, and especially when he was impatient with having his way with me.

Reaching over, I drew invisible circles across the slabs of prominent muscle hugging the long spine of his broad back. His skin was moist beneath my touch, and it was definitely due to his savage resolve earlier.

"Mm," he hummed and tucked his hands under his head. "That feels great."

I propped myself on my elbow to rub his back. "How long have we got left till we need to get ready?"

His body sank beneath my palm with his loud sigh. "Not long enough."

I chuckled and climbed atop him to hug his frame. Burying my nose in his hair, I took his scent deep into my lungs. He smelled wonderfully masculine, but there was a hint of musk to it now. Another chuckle escaped me when I recalled that his natural odour was something I'd found myself immensely attracted to even the first time I'd caught a whiff of it. That hadn't changed.

Suddenly, he rolled onto his side, so I had to stifle my surprise and subsequent squeal. Somewhat clumsily, he rearranged our bodies so that he was sprawled on his back beside me with his arm curved around my neck to hold me close. When satisfied with our new position, he studied the ceiling and scratched his chest absentmindedly.

My eyes scanned the few hairs upon it. Some men had quite the amount of fur on their chest, but William didn't. Still, he had just enough. Playing with the strands within my line of sight, I smiled coyly to myself and dared to trail my hand lower, towards the lane of hair that climbed up from his perfect manhood. After running my palm across it, greedily, I dragged my nails up his abdomen again.

We spent a few moments basking in comfortable silence until he peered at his flaccid member. "Cara." He faced me. "Have you taken a test yet?"

"Yes. I went for a drop-in appointment when you were returning Francesca's dress to her, so a week ago. I haven't been contacted yet, but I've still got to wait another week to be sure. If the clinic hasn't contacted me by then, I'm clean."

Nodding, his attention shifted to the ceiling again. "I'm sure you are."

"I hope so."

A smile was on my face, but it faded when he suddenly turned towards me with a sober expression.

"I'm grateful to have all of you," he said, causing my heart to tingle. "I enjoy knowing what you feel like, skin to skin."

Since I hadn't anticipated such a passionate statement, I blushed profusely and hid my hot face against the side of his chest. "Same," I mumbled shyly.

"A question," he murmured as he tucked my hair behind my ear. Curious, I peeked up at him.

"Yes?"

Tenderness shimmered in the ocean of his eyes as they roamed across my face, memorising every detail. "How many dates are we at now, in your book?"

Grinning, I climbed onto him and placed my hands between my chin and his chest. It was obvious that impatience still ruled him when it came to the pace we were moving at, but, unlike previously, I found it charming now. Compared to before, I was hardly intimidated by it anymore.

Staring into the mesmerising colour of his irises, I recounted, "Well, there was the first date, and then our date last Saturday, Monday, as well as tonight, so four?"

He glanced away. "Can't yesterday count as well?" he asked with a faint pout.

I kissed his warm chest and then cuddled it with my cheek. "Five, then," I allowed.

He sighed his relief. "Only five more to go."

"What, till you get to meet my parents?"

"Yes. I'm looking forward to it."

"You're so sweet, Will. I truly fancy how dedicated you are to this – us. Many men dread meeting the parents. I'm a lucky lady," I pointed out and lifted my head to peer at him, smitten.

He grinned back and buried his hands under his head. "And I'm a lucky man, so of course I would be dedicated."

"I don't take it for granted, though."

"I'm glad you don't. Though, on a completely different note, when's your period due?"

Groaning, I covered my face with my hand. How his bluntness still managed to take me aback was honestly surprising. Would I ever grow used to it?

"I don't know," I said and dragged my hand away to look him in the eye.

"You don't know?" he queried, puzzled.

"My period is a sporadic event. Could be months, could be days, between each."

He blinked, mystified, I thought. "That can't be pleasant. What if you get it when you're not expecting it?"

I chuckled. It was endearing that he tried to sympathise with female drawbacks. "It's because my IUD contains hormones. Messes with the predictability. But it's not a problem. I never bleed heavily because of it. In fact, my period is so light that I don't even have to use tampons. I only wear pads. And I've always got an emergency kit in my purse, just in case. Why do you ask?"

He shrugged. "I was curious whether you get moody."

"Beyond that of my usual, do you mean?"

He tittered. "Since you're already sassy, I'd like to know if I should mentally prepare for dealing with the diva of the decade."

I burst out laughing. "I do get moody, but not terribly. Only impatient, really. My fuse is cut shorter. I tend to get anti-social as well."

"Well, shit. I'm fucked. I already excel at lighting your fuse."

"If you give me food, you'll be safe. Speaking of, I get the craziest cravings, and for the strangest things. Last time, it was all about biscuits."

"Biscuits?" I could see he was trying to suppress laughter.

I nodded. "Butter biscuits, to be precise."

He giggled. "Butter biscuits? I should have known. You really love your butter, don't you?"

I blinked before another laugh snuck out of me. I hadn't thought of that. "I suppose. Any shape or form. And chocolate – always chocolate. That's the only constant craving I get."

"I'll bear it in mind. Chocolates and food for Cara when she's PMS-ing. And butter." Leering, he removed one hand from beneath his head to pat my bum. "Regarding your period, though, I'd just like to say that I have no qualms about having sex while you're having it. Doesn't bother me at all."

This man. I couldn't help but laugh again. "Why am I not surprised?"

He didn't look remotely ashamed. On the contrary, he looked as though it should have been obvious. "Real warriors get blood on their swords."

"Oh my God. You did not just say that."

He guffawed as I pushed his shoulder. "I'll take you any which way I can."

"And here I thought that my period was going to be the one time when my vagina would finally catch a break."

His body continued to shake. "Sorry, not sorry."

"Have you ever had sex with a woman who was on her period before? Since you sound so sure you're comfortable with it?"

"Only Kate."

That intrigued me. "Why not the others? Violet was your bed partner for quite some time."

He scrutinised me for an extended while, and I sensed internal conflict in him. "Don't stress out, yeah?"

My mind lagged. "That's the recipe for making me stress out, William – saying that."

He rolled his eyes, but bravely continued, "I'm only comfortable doing it with girlfriends. And even if you're not my girlfriend – yet – that is my intention with you."

My pulse spiked while I stared besotted at him. I relished how clear he was about his intentions. He was quite a reliable man. There was never room for doubting where he stood, nor room for mixed signals, with him. In that, he was outstanding, and I credited it to his practice of respect. He went out of his way to avoid playing with anyone's feelings, which he had made clear not only by how he treated me, but also by how he had treated Violet and Francesca. He was constantly managing our expectations and ensuring that they were realistic. And I knew he did it mainly because he respected our feelings. He had tremendous empathy.

"Do you know what I find odd, and rather fascinating?" I asked and raised my head to draw invisible circles across his chest again.

"What?"

I had no idea where my courage stemmed from, but I wasn't about to squander it. Besides, I was confident he'd appreciate what I meant to say. "That, practically speaking, we're already in a relationship. I mean, isn't exclusivity, having feelings for each other, and adding sex to an already existing friendship kind of what defines a regular relationship? So, in practice, we're already a couple. But, in actuality, we're not, because we're still assessing our compatibility before we put an official label on it."

Seeming to ruminate over what I'd said, he looked away as a frown troubled his face. "I get what you mean," he eventually murmured and fixed his eyes on me again. "However, personally, I'm not assessing our compatibility anymore. I know what I want. I'm only waiting for you to catch up. And while I sometimes get impatient about it, I'm not really that bothered. At the end of the day, I've sort of got you how I want, which is that you reserve this body for me alone." He wrapped his arms around me to smother me against him.

I stared at him. Heat breezed my cheeks, resulting from my racing heart pumping blood to my face. A bundle of intense emotion gathered in the centre of my chest, and its effect provided the illusion that I could flutter. By now, I knew what exultation felt like, and I was experiencing it right now.

"I'll be there soon," I told him tenderly. "I promise. Just give me a little more time. I need to be absolutely sure. That's just how I work. I don't commit to things I'm not fully certain about. But I'd say I'm eighty-five per cent there. It's just that you've got a tendency to be very uncompromising, and whenever you are, I get uncertain again."

It was clear that I'd upset him. The corners of his mouth dipped down as he brooded.

Since he didn't say anything, I thought I should elaborate, "An example is when you demand that I cut ties with Aaron. I've got to admit that it makes me a bit hesitant to embark on a relationship with you. I find it controlling. That trait of yours just rubs me the wrong way because I am fiercely protective of my freedom to make my own decisions."

He glared frostily at me upon the mention of Aaron, but I refused to let it impede me from continuing.

"Listen," I said, "I know this is an irrational argument, but if you knew how I felt, you would know that I'd never do anything with him. That you don't trust me hurts, Will. My personal opinion is that, sometimes, blind faith is required in a relationship. Moreover, the fact that you're demanding I cut Aaron out could be considered emotionally abusive, you know."

He scoffed. "That's extreme. He's the only one I've got a problem with, Cara, and given your history and prior behaviour, I think most men would sympathise with my concerns. Women, too, probably."

I shook my head. "Honestly, I will never agree with you on that. I know in my heart that I'd be fully capable of being strictly friends with Aaron without doing anything remotely sexual with him. But since I'm determined to respect your feelings, I'm going to listen to you. We might not agree, but I have to choose my battles, and this is one I'm willing to forfeit for you since it obviously bothers you so much. Mum always told me that a relationship is mainly give-and-take, and now I know what she meant."

He swallowed, and I could see that he wasn't comfortable with what I'd told him. "Look, I've said before that I know I'm demanding a lot from you when it comes to him. Don't think I take it for granted. I don't. But Aaron triggers my jealousy, and that's a feeling I can't help. Perhaps, down the road, when we've been together a while, it will be easier for me to trust you. But, as it is now, I'm still haunted by your fickle behaviour in the past. I need more time, more evidence, to trust that it isn't necessarily going to repeat itself in the future." A rueful expression clouded his features.

I nodded vaguely. "And I get that. I do. I don't agree with it, but I totally see where you're coming from. I did behave poorly. But you need to understand that I only did that because I was repressing my feelings for you, Will. You're my boss. Lusting after my boss wasn't something I was comfortable with. To be honest with you, it still isn't. I'm very dedicated to my career and, at that point, I was scared that getting involved with you, sexually and romantically, would place that in jeopardy.

"You're also Jason's brother. If things end badly between us, I'm scared I'll lose him. So, of course I'd be confused about how to treat the situation. I was determined to reject the idea of you because I was scared of the potential consequences, so I acted accordingly. I maintained my relationship with Aaron because I was determined to stay away from you. So much was at stake, and it sort of still is.

"The only reason I've decided to ignore the risks is because I can't seem to kill my feelings for you. When I was trying to repress them before, I was all over the place. You've no idea of the emotional chaos I suffered. So, obviously I'd do things that were destructive. Because you're my boss and Jason's brother, I was sincerely trying to destroy the possibility of being with you.

"But you're so bloody stubborn that you just charged forward anyway. Since you refused to let go, I was forced to just accept things as they were. You clearly weren't going to give me up, so it became obvious to me that not giving you a chance would cause more damage than the alternative – which is completely counterintuitive, by the way. Simply put, I was extremely confused, Will, so it's no wonder you found my behaviour confusing as well."

"It never ceases to fascinate me how we can be so different, and yet so similar, at the same time." He sounded riveted.

"What do you mean?"

"Well, my feelings don't confuse me. They're very...clear. Simple is a better word, actually. Either I feel good about something, or I don't. If I don't, I remove myself from the source. If I do, I try to get closer to it. And you make me feel good. That's how simple it is for me. They're usually not very layered. Most often, it's either or."

I was intrigued. This didn't correlate with my impression of him at all. To me, he seemed to have enough layers to match the universe. "Do you listen chiefly to your feelings when you make decisions?" I asked, baffled.

He snorted. "Absolutely not."

What? He was so deep sometimes that I struggled to perceive him. He could claim he wasn't layered all he wanted. He was undoubtedly the most complex man I'd ever met. But I supposed that, to him, he made perfect sense.

"Then I'm confused."

He sighed. "Well, it's situational, isn't it? Depends on what we're on about. I don't normally go about feeling loads. My feelings tend to be quite placid. They're hardly even in the background. But when it comes to you, for instance, they're loud as fuck."

I chuckled. The way he phrased himself was so unique.

He resumed, "After some introspection, I've gathered that my feelings tend to be ruled by my principles, and not the other way round. I've rationally come to conclusions about what's morally right or wrong, and, depending on those conclusions, my feelings respond accordingly. Whereas for you, it sounds like your head and your heart are two separate entities. Mine work in an alliance."

Chills crawled down my spine. "How eloquent."

He smirked. "Thanks. Do you agree, though?"

I nodded. "Sounds about right."

"Good to know. Anyway, I'll bear in mind what you said. It does explain your prior behaviour, but I still need more time to trust that it's the truth."

"Don't worry. I get it. I'll be patient," I assured him. Spreading my legs, I straddled him as I leaned forward to align our mouths. With a smile on mine, I descended into a soft kiss. Burying his hand in my hair, he deepened the passionate motion of our mouths and rolled us around.

My heart thundered at the perfect synchrony of our lips. I'd kissed more than my fair share of men during my young life, probably over a hundred, but never had it felt like this – not even close. Never had another set of lips fit so perfectly on my own. Kissing him always summoned intense feelings. They had scared me before, but not anymore. Now I merely enjoyed the rapture of them. In fact, I thrived on them, and at the root of them dwelled William.

"You ready for another round?" he mumbled against my mouth.

"So ready," I replied breathlessly and ran my hands down his back. I felt his grin against my lips as he propped his weight on his arms on either side of my frame. Reaching between us, he aligned himself with my wet folds. As he slid across them, lubricating himself in my juices, he pulled away from my mouth and trapped my eyes. The crest of him pushed in, barely.

Planting his arm beside me again, he stared amorously at me. Whenever he looked at me like that, it was as though he burrowed into my spirit, demanding his place there.

"Slow this time," he purred and pushed gently into me.

God, he felt so good. Locking my limbs tightly around him, I welcomed his kiss.

"Mm," I groaned when he slowly retreated and pushed carefully into me again. I loved William's cock. He wasn't just long. The sheer girth of him was impressive in and of itself.

"May I go deeper?" he asked and pecked the corner of my mouth.

"Yes," I encouraged. Responding, he pushed all the way into me, and when it bordered on painful, a whimper of warning poured out of my mouth. He lingered there, right on the bliss-point, while kissing me fervently.

Starting a staggering rhythm, he thrust slowly, but nevertheless expertly, into me. With each shove, my breathing grew more erratic. As he continued, I closed my eyes to savour the mere feel of him.

"Cara." His voice was low and soft, the bass of it ever seductive. "Look at me."

Obeying, I opened my eyes and stared straight into his. The content of them overwhelmed me. I'd wondered before if he had fallen in love with me, and at that moment, I dared believe it. It was unmistakable. Pure vulnerability shone from their depths, but, paradoxically, it was accompanied by confidence. He was inviting me into his heart, and he was prepared to face the consequences.

The urge to kiss him was extreme.

"Will," I breathed and clasped his neck to bring his lips back to mine. Opening my mouth, my tongue danced with his while he continued to pleasure me into ecstasy. I wished we could do this forever. I wished he'd never withdraw. His affection had never been closer, never been more palpable. If only time would freeze, right in this moment. Spending eternity in it was all I wanted.

Using my legs, I pressed him tighter against me, clinging to him as I chased the affection his actions conveyed. Starving for more of it, I dragged my nails down his back, kissed him deeper than I ever had. I wanted to devour every last trace of his devotion until there was nothing left. I craved it – I craved *him*. My hands were all over him, adoring him, running through his hair and down his back again, all while I kissed him with vehement zeal. I just couldn't seem to get close enough.

Suddenly, he broke our kiss with a hiss. Pushing up onto his arms, he watched me with a sombre expression and stopped thrusting altogether. My heart missed a beat.

For a moment, we merely stared at each other. Agony spilled from his eyes, and it rendered me speechless.

"Cara, I—" He shut his eyes, jaw clenching like he was trying to break his teeth. His whole body tensed as he battled through the conflict within him. It didn't look like he was breathing anymore.

Seized by panic, my heart froze. Around it, immense emotion pained my chest, making it difficult to inhale. Was he on the cusp of confessing?

"Fuck," he cursed and faced away to glare at the wall.

Breaking out of my paralysis, I rushed up after him until my nose skimmed his cheekbone. As I cupped his jaw in my hands, it softened against my palms, but he wouldn't turn his head to look at me.

"Hey," I whispered softly and ran my lips across his cheekbone. Slowly, he dared to face me again, his agony still blazing through his eyes.

I wanted to console him, but I wasn't sure how. I wasn't ready to confess yet. Hearing him profess his love for me wouldn't frighten me in the slightest, but I feared it would hurt him not to hear it back.

Leaning closer, I nuzzled his nose with mine. Through trembling lips, I whispered, "It's okay."

"It's not," he replied, distraught, eyes closing again. "I..." He grimaced.

I pecked his lips, repeatedly, but he didn't kiss me back. He remained frozen.

When his eyes suddenly opened again, the agony was gone. He'd lost the battle, and he had acknowledged his defeat.

"I love you," he said, and from the sound, it was like the weight of a mountain was lifted off his shoulders.

But his relief was short-lived. I could feel the ensuing fear in his eyes, sense how sincerely scared he was that he'd made a grave mistake.

Unsure of how to respond, my eyes roamed across his chiselled face. This beautiful man had offered me his whole heart. He loved me back. The sheer force of my raging feelings stunned me. Everything seemed surreal.

A most uncanny feeling whispered that, at last, a vacancy within me had been filled, claimed by the sole man it had ever been reserved for. No one else would fit into the space of my heart as perfectly as he did. Unbeknownst to my mind, my heart had been searching for him all my life. Finally, it had found him, and now he was offering me his for mine.

And yet, despite that, I wasn't ready to give mine away. I knew I loved him, but I still wasn't convinced he was the one I should dedicate my future to. Things had happened so fast lately. Less than a month had gone by since I'd confronted him about his disrespectful behaviour, after I'd agreed to go on a date with him. And while he had mainly been exceptional since then, he had also demanded that I should abandon Aaron, which made me uncertain about him again. Would he turn out to be controlling about other things, too?

I needed more time. I hated that I would have to disappoint

him, but I knew I would get there soon if things continued like this. Until then, I owed it to him to be careful. Love was a grave thing to declare. Unless I truly meant it and was ready to enter a relationship with him, I shouldn't be professing it.

When I'd been silent for too long, he sighed, and it was a crestfallen sound. Resting his forehead against mine, he closed his eyes.

"Please," I said quietly, "don't be discouraged. I'll be there soon, I just...I need more time."

He didn't reply. Instead, his mouth moved to engulf mine, but the sensation was vastly different now. His kiss was vulnerable and slow, and yet his fire had never burnt hotter. In the form of his hands, it blazed across my skin, devouring every curve of my body.

Leaning in, he steered me onto the mattress again while he followed my descent. Instead of using his words, he allowed his body to speak for him. Tender in his movements, he conveyed every trace of his profound adoration while he pleasured me. The love he made to me was surreal, unbound by dimensions. It would linger in my soul, forever to remain.

As I reached the peak of my emotive orgasm, I cried his name and clung to him. His lips found mine, and his kiss was hard, like he feared I'd disappear if he ever pulled away.

When he joined me in our private paradise, he groaned against my mouth and collapsed atop me, crushing me under his weight. Tucking his forearms under my shoulders, he rolled us over so that I was resting atop him instead, all while he refused to part from my mouth. We kissed our way back to reality, and we didn't stop until several minutes had passed. I was the first to pull away, and when I did, our breathing had stabilised.

Contemplating what had just happened, I was lost for words. Had he ever told anyone he loved them before? I knew he claimed never to have loved Kate, and that knowledge increased my disbelief of the situation. Was I the first woman he had ever declared his love for? The possibility pained me. If it was true, it must have hurt him all the more not to hear it back.

I was unable to say anything. Unsure of what to do with myself, I rolled off him and onto my side, where I stared blankly across his chest.

I was shocked.

When we'd been silent for quite some, he uttered two words that broke my heart. It was a vulnerable plea.

"Don't leave."

Frowning, I glanced up at him and saw how scared he was. I snuggled closer immediately and reached for his jaw. As I brushed my fingers across it, I said firmly, "I'm not going anywhere, Will."

Since he didn't look reassured, I climbed onto him again and kissed him with all I had, anxious to dispel his fears. "I'm staying right here, with you," I vowed resolutely as I pulled away.

Swallowing, he brought his arms around me and smothered me against him. "Please do. Nothing feels better than having you in my arms, Cara."

I kissed him again. "Nothing feels better than being in your arms, Will."

He squeezed me for emphasis. "It's where you belong."

"I know."

27

I ONLY HAVE EYES FOR YOU

Running my hands down my waist, I twirled in front of the full-length mirror in the bathroom. The maroon satin gown had a naked back that ended just beneath the small of my back. Still, it clung to my curves as though it had been tailor-made for my body.

I'd always been both curvy and slender, even if my breasts were small. My bum was, without a doubt, what I was most pleased with, and I worked hard to maintain its perkiness. As of late, I'd been working harder on it than usual, and it was certainly because I knew William loved my bum. And I loved that he loved it. We had that in common. It was always nice to hear that someone else appreciated an asset of mine as much as I did – if not even more.

"Cara?" he called outside the door. "You ready soon? You've been in there for about an hour."

"It takes time to style hair, Will. Especially hair of the same length as mine."

"I wasn't complaining."

I tittered. "Sounded like it. But yes, I'm ready."

"Are you going to knock the air out of me? Should I have a seat?" he teased.

I was grateful to hear that his humour was reviving. He'd grown rather quiet after our session earlier, and while I wouldn't have reacted any differently, it had upset me. I hated to be the reason for his despondency.

"Oh, you're in for a treat," I replied confidently. I didn't think I'd ever felt quite so beautiful before. Hopefully, he'd see why.

"I'm taking a seat."

I laughed as I went for the door and opened it. Peeking through the gap, I found him sitting on the bed. For a moment, I completely forgot everything apart from him. London faded, my existence faded, until only he remained. I'd never seen him so striking before. While he always wore suits to the office, he looked divine and opulent in a black dinner suit. William wearing a bow tie was a lethal man. I'd do just about anything for him. In fact, if joining him to events like these meant I would get to see him wearing attires of the like, I would demand to join him next time.

I gawked, speechless. He looked to have walked straight out of a fashion magazine. Had he wanted, he could easily have pursued a career as a male model. Still, I respected his decision to employ his brain rather than his mouth-watering anatomy. Well, he did employ the latter, too – in bed, with me.

Really, that his body was reserved for me alone was humbling. Handsome and clever as he was, I almost felt it was unfair to other women to keep him to myself, but I absolutely would. I wouldn't share so much as one of his caresses with anyone else.

"Oh my God," I finally managed to utter. "Will, are you real?"

It was tempting to pinch myself. He was a daydream for certain. I'd never seen a man more appealing in my life. It was intimidating.

He frowned, confused. "What?"

"You look incredible."

Surprise arched his brows. "Well, thanks. But let me have a look already."

The sight of him converted my earlier confidence into nervousness. I wanted to look good on his arm, but, in all fairness, I thought I'd pale beside him. He was going to claim the spotlight whether he wanted to or not. It wasn't that I wanted all eyes to be on me, but I definitely wanted to complement him – seem suited to him. I wanted to look like I was in his league, but he was making that quest impossible.

Regardless, I dared to step out, and his subsequent reaction restored a portion of my confidence. His jaw dropped while he gaped at me, clearly affected. He'd looked similar when I had presented myself in lingerie last Saturday, but there was still something different about it this time around. After analysing him for a few seconds, I was able to distinguish the difference.

This time, he looked intimidated. I realised it when he finally closed his mouth to swallow a lump in his throat. Not only that, but his entire figure also tensed while he moved slightly away from me. At least it was mutual. He intimidated me just as I intimidated him. In that, we were perfect for each other – stupidly blind to our own appearance when we compared it to the other's.

"Cara, I..." He paused, eyes travelling across my figure for quite a long time until he shook his head to himself, as if to recompose himself. "Wow. Honestly, I'm lost for words."

"Really?"

He nodded vehemently. "You look out of this world. I'm fucking blessed. I've never doubted you're the most beautiful creature alive, but you just proved it again. You're going to put me to shame."

I frowned. "That's how I feel about you."

He looked incredulous. "Don't be ridiculous. I feel sincerely honoured to have you as my date. My ego will be repeatedly boosted as other men ogle you tonight, wild with envy. I can't wait."

I rolled my eyes. "And yet I only have eyes for you, Will."

A spark of deep affection gleamed in his eyes. "You often tell me I always know what to say. Well, darling, you just did the same."

"I'm happy to hear that. Reassuring you is important to me. But that matter aside, we should get going."

"Let's," he concurred and approached to offer me his arm. I took it with an excited grin on my face.

§ § §

Downstairs, we passed through the small security area and provided our names to the hostess, whereafter a staff-member guided us towards our designated seats. Abandoning William's arm, I walked round the table, searching for familiar names. Fortunately for us, it seemed that both Alex and Ivy, as well as Andy and Chloe, were going to be seated with us. That couldn't be a coincidence.

"If it isn't William Night," a stranger called when I'd nearly reached my lover's side again. Both of us looked over to acknowledge the male voice, but I'd never seen the owner before.

A head shorter than William – which meant he was already taller than the average person – he seemed to be around the same age as my date. Faint lines stretched across his forehead, and I noticed vague creases around his eyes, as well as the occasional grey strand interfering with his otherwise short, black beard.

Taking his symmetrical features into account, he was quite the handsome fellow. His eyes were a bit small for the square shape of his head, but his lips were rather full for belonging to a man. They looked soft. Above them, the bridge of his nose bulged out of his face, clearly masculine in its form, but it suited him. His emerald eyes were assuredly his best feature.

Despite being a head shorter than William, the man was broad. The muscles of his arms strained against his royal-blue dinner suit, leaving it obvious that he spent quite the amount of time at the gym, and perhaps on steroids. From the look of him, I dared think he was even stronger than William, but I'd never fancied men that big. It wasn't proportionate, and it didn't look natural. William's body was perfect.

William was perfect.

"Oliver," William greeted him, surprised, and hooked his arm around my waist to bring me closer to his side. I wanted to roll my eyes, but refrained. He could be so pathetic with his territorial tendencies. "Fancy seeing you here. It's been years," he continued. "How are you?"

"It has, hasn't it? I've been well. Work over at the bank has picked up pace since my recent promotion."

"Congratulations," William replied, impressed.

"Thanks. How are things on your end?" Oliver's eyes flickered in my direction before returning to Will again. Noticing it, William tightened his embrace of me.

"They're good. I'm working on a few transactions at the moment that should have a positive impact on my career. Important clients. Big brands."

"Excellent. I'm glad to hear it," Oliver replied, enthused, and nodded his head for encouragement. "Still striving for partnership?"

William chuckled. "Yes, that's still the goal."

Oliver passed him a shrewd smile. "Well, if you're anything like your father, I'd say it's only a matter of time."

"Hopefully."

"Who's this beauty, then?" Oliver queried and cocked his head towards me. Appreciative of the compliment, I gave him a smile.

"This is Cara Darby, my date," William introduced me proudly, and my heart immediately jumped to my throat. His date? We had agreed to introduce me as his assistant, not his date. What was he doing?

Gazing up at William, I realised Oliver couldn't be acquainted with John nor Daphné, nor anyone from work. Surely William would have remembered to present me as his assistant if he was.

"Well, you're a lucky man, Will."

"I'm well aware."

Oliver's eyes turned to me. "Pleasure to meet you, Ms Darby."

"Please, call me Cara."

He smiled. "Cara," he echoed, and then steered his eyes to William again. "Will you be seated by this table?"

William glanced at the table behind us before nodding. "Yes. And you?"

"No, over there," said Oliver and pointed to a table at the far end of the space.

"Well, suppose we'll see each other after dinner," William murmured as he fixed his attention on a middle-aged woman standing beside the table Oliver had pointed to. "If you'll excuse us, Oliver, there's someone I want Cara to meet."

"Of course," he replied and watched William guide me towards the woman wearing purple. Since I sensed his stare upon my back, I cast a glance at him over my shoulder. Our eyes met for only a brief moment before he averted his.

Finding his stare somewhat unnerving, I peered up at William. "Who's that?"

"Just an old acquaintance," he answered dismissively, eyes set on the woman ahead.

"A friend?"

"Not really. A friend of a friend," he elaborated, but I could hear from his tone that he wasn't interested in sharing further details.

I hadn't failed to notice that he had wrinkled his nose upon my question, so I was now under the impression he was keeping me in the dark about something.

"And which friend is that?" I probed, but, alas, I never got my answer because the woman wearing purple had noticed our approaching figures by now, and when she recognised William, she called, "William, my dear! How wonderful to see you here."

It was Alexander's mother, Anna Winton, and she turned out to be a delightful woman. However, half an hour after speaking to her, I'd been introduced to so many people that I had given up trying to remember any of them.

We were currently chatting with a middle-aged couple who were friends of John and Daphné. I was grateful William led most of the conversation because I was truly somewhat intimidated by my surroundings, even if I didn't let it show. Everything was so ostentatious, and I couldn't help but notice that most of the conversations regarded matters of prestige. "How's work?", "We travelled there and there last week", "Lovely suit. Is it Hugo Boss? Valentino?" and I disliked it. Self-importance was clearly a trend here. Narcissism at its finest. No wonder Jason had declined.

At that moment, I missed him intensely. I wondered what he was doing. He had said he was going to grab a few pints with Jon, but I suspected he'd been lying to ease my concern. Knowing him, he was probably still wallowing in his misery over Olivia, alone in our flat.

"There's Alex," William suddenly said and cocked his head towards a group of four people. I spotted Andy among them, standing next to a blonde woman whom I presumed to be Chloe since his arm was wrapped around her waist.

In front of them stood another couple. The shorter person was a girl, with brown hair like mine, though tied into a beautiful and plaited bun atop her head. Wearing a faint-pink gown reminiscent of *The Great Gatsby* era, she looked incredible.

Was that Ivy?

Steering my eyes to the man beside her, my eyebrows climbed up my forehead. He was a mountain. He towered even taller than William.

"Christ, he really is huge," I remarked.

William's groan was heartfelt. "Just barely taller than me. Always bothered me, and he likes to rub it in my face."

"You three – Andy, Alex and you – are actual mountains. What sort of mutants."

He chortled. "We've received that comment several times, actually."

"I'm not remotely surprised. Is that Ivy by his side?"

"Indeed."

"She's stunning."

He pressed me against him and lowered his mouth to my ear. "That would be you, love."

I chuckled. "Don't be silly."

"I'm not being silly, I'm being honest. Anyway, we should greet them," he said, and I could tell he wanted to kiss my cheek. Thankfully, he restrained himself. "Don't be surprised if Alex tries to pull my leg, by the way, even if he fails every time. He's not as good at comebacks as I am, but that doesn't keep him from trying. Only you can shatter my dignity in a second."

"I see it as my duty to level out your ego," I replied as I laughed.

His grin was winsome. "I'm glad I've got you to tie me to the ground, darling. You're my rock."

I sighed, besotted. "And you're mine."

As we drew nearer to them, I grew increasingly nervous. It wasn't like me to be nervous, and it had nothing to do with the fact that Alexander was a famous business mogul. His wealth didn't intimidate me, but his close friendship with William did. It was extremely important to me to attain his approval. I feared that if I didn't, it would cause friction either between him and Will, or Will and me. After everything I'd heard about the trio's friendship, it was clear that their opinions mattered tremendously to one another.

Suddenly, all eyes turned to us, and it disconcerted me. This much attention applied pressure to my conscience. Intimidated, I directed my eyes to William's profile and felt my heart calm. Merely looking at him made breathing an easier task. His presence was appeasing. Tonight, as most nights, he was my safe haven.

"Hi, Will," Andy greeted us. "Surprised you're still here. I know how much you hate these things."

"Dad bribed me to stay the whole night," my lover replied.

Amusement danced on Andy's mouth. "Is that so?"

"Yeah. Said he'd write Jason out of his will if I did."

Everyone burst out laughing, and even I struggled to contain myself.

"Naturally, I had to take that deal," William continued seriously. "Serves him right."

"Of course you had to," Andy chuckled.

"Is this Cara?" Alexander queried then.

Meeting his eyes, I saw that they were deep blue – like his mother's – but they shined of wisdom I had not expected. Frankly, their vibe made it seem as though he was years older than his actual age. Curiosity emitted from them, too.

William's mouth took a lopsided shape. "This is her," he proudly confirmed. I nearly blushed at his tone.

"Hello, Alex," I greeted and extended my hand to him. To my utter surprise, he not only took it, but also lowered his head to kiss it. What an old-fashioned gentleman.

After releasing my hand, he held my gaze as he stretched back up. "I'm delighted to finally meet you, Cara. Will's been doing my head in for the past couple of months, going on about you."

Flattered, I gave him a wry smile and then faced my date with a leer. "Months?" I echoed to him.

He rolled his eyes. "As if you didn't already know."

"Well," I cooed, "I appreciate the reminder."

"You should," said Alexander. "It's not an easy feat to catch Will's eye."

I adored that he was trying to make me feel special on William's behalf.

Before I could respond, William chimed in, "It's not an easy feat to catch Cara's either, I assure you."

"Hello, Cara," Chloe greeted me, and the sight of her warmed my heart. Finally, I could put a face to the name. She and Andy were a beautiful couple.

Blonde and pretty, she had a nose slightly too large for her face, but quite big lips made it look proportionate. Her brown eyes oozed benevolence, and I could immediately sense that she was a maternal character.

As I studied her, it was odd to think of how long she had known William for. Even stranger was it to think of how long she and Andy had been together.

"I'm so glad to finally meet you," she continued. "I've heard so much about you, both from Will and Andy."

I smirked. "Bitch behind my back, do they?"

She giggled at my joke. "Only Will," she teased back, and it was my turn to laugh.

"I'd never dare," Andy assured me.

"Only I have got the balls for that," William stated with a smirk.

While looking at him, I nudged his arm and discreetly cocked my head in Ivy's direction. I wanted to meet her, but she seemed too shy to introduce herself.

"Right," William said when he understood. "Cara, this is Ivy, Alexander's..." He hesitated to put a label on her, which amused me. He probably wanted to say something along the lines of "Alexander's soon-to-be girlfriend", but, of course, he would resist. "Date for the evening," he eventually decided.

"His new PA," Ivy specified and extended her hand to me. Oh, his PA. She was slaughtering William's insinuation. Curious. Did she not return Alexander's interest? I was intrigued.

Grabbing her hand, I shook it rather firmly. "I love your gown, Ivy. You're putting Alex to shame." Hopeful Alexander would survive my banter, I gave him a look of mischief.

He melted my heart when he said, "She surely is."

Andy changed the subject by asking William, "Where will you guys be seated?"

"With you, as it happens."

"Good."

Mindless conversation continued for the next hour before dinner, and I was grateful the men led most of it. Since I hardly knew Ivy or Chloe, I didn't want to take up too much space with my – sometimes – bold mouth. It was important to me to make a good impression. Besides, I enjoyed witnessing the banter between the three men. Truly, their friendship was honestly more similar to brotherhood in its depth.

Once dinner commenced, I settled into my seat beside William and felt him drape his arm over my shoulders, casually protective while he marked his territory. Leaning next to my ear, he placed his hand on my thigh beneath the white tablecloth and slowly trailed it upwards. To our spectators, it looked like he was only whispering, but I still feared that someone would notice the inappropriate position of his hand. I was here as his assistant, not his lover.

"After dinner," he whispered amorously, "we'll need to have sex again. I'm hardly able to control my erection when you look this appealing."

I chuckled and shoved his hand away. His touch incited lustful thoughts, and I didn't want that right now. "Maybe."

"Definitely." His lips brushed my temple, leaving me to stiffen.

"William," I whispered harshly and leaned away, towards Alex. "Compose yourself."

He merely grinned.

SEVEN BILLION PEOPLE

After dinner, I went for a quick trip to the ladies', but once I returned to the table, the whole mood had shifted from funny and pleasant to serious and quiet. Puzzled, I sat down next to William and asked, "Everything alright?"

Protective, he wrapped his arm over the back of my chair again, but his eyes remained distracted by something else.

Andy's tone was concerned when he explained, "It's Abbie."

Abbie? Alexander's ex-girlfriend?

Compelled, I scoured the crowd, but I was unsure of what to look for. However, when a drunk young lady, with long blonde hair styled to perfection, shambled around the place, I was quite certain I had located the right target. She looked to be as drunk as I had been the other weekend, when William had held my hair while I was sick in the toilet after too much tequila.

Perhaps she had seen Alexander and Ivy? Was that why she

had drunk herself senseless?

I noticed that an older man approached her, somewhat angrily, before I turned to study Alexander. Pale in his face, he watched his ex wallow in misery, and it was apparent that he wanted to end it. He was obviously a compassionate man.

"She's making a complete scandal out of herself," Chloe stated, upset, clearly sympathising with the woman in distress.

Alexander winced at Chloe's words, but just when he was about to stand up to approach Abigail, William planted his hand on his shoulder, firmly, to hold him in place.

"Alex, don't," he said tersely, and his voice was so low that my scalp prickled. I hated when he used that tone of his. He had used it against Aaron, and he had used it against me, and it exuded power that would render any person into a wimp.

"I can't just sit here and do nothing," Alexander argued, perturbed. "It's essentially my fault."

William glared back at him, and I knew at once that he wasn't going to relent. Tough love was headed Alexander's way.

"That is precisely what you'll do," William ordered. "This is nothing but a desperate cry for your attention. If you fall victim to it, she'll see that it works and will repeat it time and again. Is that what you want?"

Alexander's jaw clenched as he directed his glare to Will's. But since he said nothing, William continued to command, "You've got to think long term. Yes, if you tend to her now, it will probably appease her, but only for the moment. You can't feed her hope, which is what you'll be doing if you provide her with your attention."

"Fuck," Alexander muttered.

"Will's right, Alex," said Andy. "Just let Harold deal with her." I had no idea who Harold was, but perhaps it was the older man who had approached Abigail earlier.

"How about a dance, Ivy? I could use a distraction," Alex then pleaded.

I heard her stammer her reply, "A-Alex, as much as I'd like to help, I truly can't dance. You'll be leaving this place with ten blue nails."

"That's a price I'd be glad to pay for a dance with you."

The man was competing with William's charms, wasn't he? Well, William's easily won when it came to me, and I planned to express that to the man himself straight away.

"A dance is a wonderful idea," I said and immediately stood. "Will?"

I must have said the last thing he'd expected to hear, because he looked astonished. "You…want to dance?"

I took his hand to drag him up. "Yes. Don't let me down."

"Of course. I'd never." His grip tightened around my hand, and he held it the entire while it took us to reach the dance floor.

Once there, I turned to face him with an infatuated grin on my mouth. "Well, then. What now?"

Stepping closer, he instructed, "Put your hand on my arm, just below my shoulder, and keep your elbow raised horizontally," while he rested his free hand on the curve of my waistline. When he took another small step forward, his arm came around me. I knew he hadn't chiefly meant to intensify the intimacy of the moment, but it was the consequence either way. Blushing, I stared straight into his chest.

He asked, "I know you've said you did Contemporary Jazz for a year, but do you have any experience with partner dance?"

I cocked my head from side to side. "Sort of. Did a twelve-week course with Livy back in college, but it was Cuban Salsa – Casino, as it's called – so what I learnt isn't exactly transferable to this sort of scene."

He was thoroughly amused. "Cuban Salsa? Really?"

"Yes."

His eyes sparkled with mirth. "Suppose you wore the trousers?"

"Course. Livy was the woman. It was my present to her for her eighteenth birthday."

His lips remained stretched into a wide grin. "How sweet of you."

I shrugged. "Yeah, she's a hopeless romantic, so she was quite happy with it."

"Your friendship is extremely amusing to me."

"Why?"

"Well, because you're an obstinate realist, and she's a hopeless romantic."

A smile fought its way to my lips. "Really? And what are you, Will?"

"Me?" He pulled me closer, and his grin never left his mouth. "I'm head over heels."

That was not what I had anticipated for an answer, so I was rendered speechless. With a considerable gap between my lips, I stared besotted up at him. Meanwhile, my heart threatened to burst.

"Anyway," he tittered at my expression, "it's alright. I'm a decent lead. I won't do anything too complicated, so just follow after me."

Rebooting my brain, I swallowed my heart back down and focused. "I can manage that."

"It's a fast song," he alerted, "but we can do it at half the pace if you want."

"Half the pace is good," I agreed with a vague nod. Thankfully, there were plenty of other couples around us, so I doubted we'd stand out even if I missed a step more often than not.

Sooner rather than later, his feet started moving, and it was somewhat difficult to follow since he was holding me so intimately. We had hardly managed a few seconds by the time I stepped on his shoe.

"Sorry," I mumbled, embarrassed.

"Step on me all you like, *chérie*. I'm having a blast either way."

I tittered at his word choice. "Blast, indeed."

"You know," his eyes searched mine, "if you want, we could sign up for dance lessons together."

My smile widened. "Are you seriously proposing this?"

He chuckled. "I am. If you're going to be my girlfriend, you'll need to learn how to dance. Events like these are commonplace in my life."

"Hm. Alright." My grin stretched further. "I'll take lessons with you."

He revealed pearly-white teeth to me in the biggest smile I'd seen. It must have been the reassurance he needed. By agreeing to this, I was proving to him that I was committed to this – that I intended to stay with him.

Pulling me even closer, he lowered his head and gazed tenderly into my eyes. "You look radiant tonight, Cara."

My grin was constant at this point. "Well, Mum's always said that in a woman's features, you see her lover's character."

His lips twitched to reveal that he enjoyed the poetic take. "Hm."

"You treat me like a diamond," I said, "so I shall shine like one."

Had we not been surrounded by people, I knew he would have kissed me then. However, casting a glance at our spectators, he resisted the urge and leaned away with a groan.

We'd danced for three songs when I heard that the artist who had been hired for the evening began to sing "Hypnotized" by Purple Disco Machine and Sophie and the Giants. Recognising it, I beamed at William.

"I love this song," I said.

Grinning back, he pushed me away to spin me around. "Thanks for coming tonight, Cara," he said the instant we reunited. "You've made the whole evening more than tolerable. I'm actually having fun."

I let out a carefree laugh. "Yeah, I'm surviving surprisingly well, too. Though, I have to say, I totally get why Jason declined."

Creases formed across the bridge of his nose before he suddenly pushed me out of his embrace again, spun me round under his arm, and brought me back in. "Yeah, handling this sort of thing isn't embedded in the Night genes, I'm afraid. We're productive and even sociable when it pertains to academic matters, but we're not social climbers."

"No, you certainly are not," I agreed, amused, and peered up at him in my smitten state.

"Neither are you, though."

"No." My eyes shifted to his heart-shaped mouth where the pink colour beckoned. "Didn't you mention something about a quick round upstairs?"

A lecherous smile spread his lips. In their corners, sin lurked. "I did. Have you changed your mind?" He pulled me closer, lips drawing nearer to mine. His breath teased me, daring me to close the gap between our faces.

I swallowed. I wanted him terribly, but would our absence raise any brows? This wasn't my world, and I wasn't about to make a scandal out of myself, especially not the first time I entered it. I had no idea how much these people pried and gossiped. But, judging from the conversations I'd been privy to earlier, I suspected it was a lot. I wouldn't have been surprised if they had eyes and ears everywhere, carefully identifying leverage wherever they could.

Still, my lust for him was so extreme at that moment that my inhibitions dwindled. "What if someone notices our absence?" I asked.

"Who cares?"

"I do. Someone might start to suspect. Before we know it, word might have reached the office."

"Not if we're discreet about it."

"How can we be discreet about it, then?"

He glanced in the direction of the men's room before his eyes fixed on mine again. "How about this. I'll go to the gents'. Once I come out again, I'll head upstairs with my phone on my ear. That should make it seem like I'm tending to some sort of emergency. Some minutes later, I'll text or call you, and then you can head after me. Since you're my assistant, people will think it's work-related.

Well, even if they don't, they'll have no proof. We can claim it is."

Excited, I nodded my head. "Fine. Go," I urged and stepped away from him. There was a moment of hesitation in him after his arms lost contact with my figure. In his eyes, I heard his thoughts.

I love you.

My breath hitched upon the impact, but before I could offer so much as a caress to reassure him, he turned to approach the gents'.

Sighing, I folded my arms and observed the other couples on the dance floor. Andy and Chloe both gave me a smile as they danced past me, and, after I'd returned it, I noticed the mountain that was Alexander.

From this angle, I could only see his profile. Standing in front of Ivy, they looked about to dance together, and I pitied her. Alexander must have managed to persuade her. But, to my surprise, they hadn't moved even a step together by the time she abandoned him on the floor. From the look of her, she was disconcerted.

Had he said something?

When our gazes suddenly collided, I was certain my eyes were wide with curiosity. Even from this distance, his sigh was visible from the drop of his broad shoulders. Poor man. What had he done now?

After rubbing his neck and staring at his feet for a short breath, he approached me. "Cara," he greeted.

"If Ivy won't dance with you, I'd be happy to," I said, hoping to console him. "I might crush your toes, though."

His responding smile was sweet, but not wholehearted. Ivy must have upset him somewhat. "Crush them all for all I care."

He offered his hand, and after I took it, he wrapped his arm around my waist and pulled me closer. His scent struck me like a shock. He smelt amazing – almost as good as William. I hadn't been remotely prepared for that, and I didn't like it, either. I knew I was only human, but it still felt weird, if not even sordid, to find myself attracted to another man's scent. The reality of it caused a blush to paint my cheeks, so I was grateful for the dim illumination around us.

As soon as he began to guide me along with the music, I realised Ivy was seriously missing out. He was a wonderful dancer.

Suddenly, he stated, "You're a blusher. How charming."

Brilliant. Pointing that out, he only made it worse. "Unfortunately."

"So is Ivy. Is it annoying?"

"Quite."

He laughed. "I find it to be rather a charming quality. An honest one, too."

"Why, because we can't control it?"

"Yes. Your words may say one thing, but your bodies, thereby your blush, tells a different story."

I chuckled again. "Are you in the habit of analysing people a lot, Alex? Since you're saying this?"

"A bit," he admitted, embarrassed. "Anyway, where's Will?"

"Men's room."

"I see." His royal-blue eyes inspected me then. "You look well together, you know. You suit him."

That was a lovely thing to hear. Heartfelt. "Thanks."

"I don't know you all that well yet," he continued, "but from what I've gathered so far, he suits you, too."

"He surely does."

He seemed intrigued. "He tells me you were difficult in the beginning."

I averted my eyes, whereupon I saw Oliver head past us, journeying for the restrooms as well. Our eyes met for a second, so we gave each other a small smile of acknowledgement.

"Will is a difficult man to put up with sometimes," I replied, and steered my gaze back to Alexander's.

His dark eyebrows curved. "Tell me about it. If ever you need any advice, or just someone to complain to who will understand,

I'll give you an ear."

I grinned. I adored him already. He was obviously investing in me because he saw sincere potential for a future between Will and me. The statement between his lines was louder than his actual words.

"Thanks, Alex. I appreciate that. Fortunately, Jason's my flatmate, and he does the job rather well."

"Right. Was that why you were difficult, perhaps? And because he's your boss?"

I pursed my lips. Even if Alexander was positively charming, I wasn't comfortable being so candid with a person I hardly knew. "Among other reasons."

"Sorry. I didn't mean to pry."

"No worries."

"Truth is, I'm having a hard time pursuing the woman I'm interested in myself."

"Really? And who might this lucky lady be?"

He raised a brow. "I'm sure Will's told you. I gave him my permission."

I smiled. "You're right. He has told me."

Amusement basked in his eyes. "I'm glad to see you're loyal – protecting his potential secrets like that."

"Well, like Will, I try to respect people's privacy."

"An admirable trait."

"Thanks. Anyway, what's the trouble with Ivy?"

He sighed and glanced at the door which Ivy had escaped through earlier. "I fear she's not interested, and I don't want to harass her either, so I'm not being very clear myself. I'm trying to gauge her thoughts, but she's awfully cryptic. When I do try to be clear, she…Well, she left just now. That should say enough."

"Well, you've known her essentially all her life. Perhaps she's scared to change your dynamics in case it might turn sour? She might just feel disinclined to take the risk since it could mean losing you if things don't work out."

He frowned, and I saw him drift for miles into his mind, pondering. "What do you reckon I should do, then?" he eventually asked.

"I'm afraid I don't know. I've no idea what she's like."

Before we could analyse the issue further, Andy and Chloe arrived next to us.

"Where's Will?" Andy asked.

"Gents'," I said.

"Right."

When he started towards the corridor where William had disappeared earlier, Chloe grabbed his arm. "I'll come with you. I've got to powder my nose."

"Your nose is perfect, darling."

She rolled her eyes. "It's oily now. You dance like a madman, so my face got flushed straight away."

Smirking, he glanced at Alexander and me. "Back in a bit."

"Yes," said Alex, and behind him, I saw Ivy enter through the doors. She scoured the room, searching for a presence. It didn't take her long to locate it, towering amidst the dance floor in front of me.

Averting my eyes, I warned Alex quietly, "Ivy's back."

He stiffened. "Is she?"

"Approaching."

Was he holding his breath?

"Alex," Ivy murmured when she reached us. "I'm sorry. I panicked."

He spun to face her, eyes wide with raw hope. "No worries. I'm sorry, too. I shouldn't have pressured you to dance with me. I know how you feel about these things."

She seemed conspicuously intrigued by the floor. "I just get so embarrassed. The attention…"

"I know. As I said, I'm sorry."

She peered at me with a grateful curve of her lips. "Thanks for indulging him, Cara."

"Oh, it was actually my pleasure," I laughed. "Alex is a wonderful dancer, and I can't dance for shit either, so that says something."

The pinkness that surfaced in her cheeks was something I sympathised with. "If you'd like," she looked up at Alex again, "we could give it a try."

"Really?" Did he need me to pinch him?

She nodded. "Yes. I'll need to get better at it one way or another."

He offered his hand immediately. "I'd love to."

I noticed her hand trembled when she reached for his. Poor thing. She was evidently extremely shy.

Closing his hand around hers, Alex turned to me. "Will you be alright by yourself, love?"

I waved them away. "Absolutely. Crush his toes, Ivy. It would make me feel better about crushing Will's."

Her bashful smile transformed into a grin. "It's a promise."

I'd been standing on my own for another five minutes when I started to wonder what was taking William so long. Groaning, I looked towards the corridor leading to the restrooms. From the corner of my eye, I noticed a group of security guards sprinting towards it. What on earth?

Some trepidation entered my system while I watched them dash inside. Could an actual emergency have occurred in there? Was that why William was taking so long? Perhaps someone had had an allergic reaction to the food, or worse, perhaps someone had suffered a stroke. Rigid, I folded my arms and glanced around the room. Only a few other guests appeared to have noticed the same as me. Mirroring my reaction, they gazed around with a concerned frown before they fixed their attention on the corridor again.

I nearly jumped when a cold hand gripped my arm. Turning, I gazed into Chloe's wide brown eyes. Her face was pale. She looked as if she'd seen a ghost.

Somewhat concerned for her, I frowned. "Chloe? Are you alright?"

Her hand lowered from my arm to clench around my hand,

and it sent a shiver down my spine.

"Cara, it's important you stay calm."

"What's happened?"

Her brown eyes turned shiny and wet. "It's Will." Her voice couldn't keep a steady octave.

My heart fell completely still.

"He's been attacked in the men's room," she continued. "Andy told me to fetch you."

I twisted my hand out of hers immediately, disconnected from the present. Not a single thing made sense to me. Her words kept replaying in my head, "he's been attacked in the men's room", but I couldn't fathom them. It was as though my soul had left my body. My existence seemed bizarre even to me. All I could do was respond to impulse.

Stalking towards the men's room, I found a group of guards standing outside of it, blocking the way for anyone who wanted to enter. When I caught a look at Andy, my heart leapt to my throat. He was visibly rattled while speaking to a member of security.

The blood on his white shirt grabbed my immediate attention. Was it William's?

"Andy," I called. His gaze slid slowly towards me, and when he realised my presence, his entire face twisted.

"Cara," he sobbed, and he looked about to collapse. The sound and sight of him left my chest in splinters.

I'd never been this scared before. That a grown man like Andy was showing such obvious fear increased mine. Streaming down his cheeks were silent tears, and I could tell he struggled to hold my gaze.

"No," I breathed, aghast, and scurried over to him. "What's happened? Tell me what's happened. Where's Will?" I demanded as tears surfaced in my eyes.

I stared at the blood on him. Was it William's?

"Miss," the male security guard that had been speaking to him interposed, "we've got the situation under control. The paramedics will be here shortly."

Fearing the worst, I looked into his hard brown eyes, pleading for information. "Please, tell me what's happened. Is the blood William's? Is he alright?"

He turned to Andy. "Do you know who she is, Mr Thompson?"

Andy barely managed to look at me. "Yes, sir, it's Cara – his girlfriend," he said, and it confirmed my fears. It was William in there.

The man faced me again, but his expression was softer now. The hardness had been replaced by compassion, and I hated to see it because it meant that it was true – it was William's blood on Andy's shirt.

"Cara," he said. "May I call you that?"

"Please, tell me he's going to be alright." A snivel interfered with my plea.

"He's got a pulse, but he's unconscious. That's all I can say for now." Moving towards me, he wrapped a strong arm over my shoulders and guided my shocked figure to sit against the corridor's wall.

"Please, may I see him?" I begged.

His tone was gentle and patient, "I'm afraid I can't let you see him right now. We've got someone trained in first aid tending to him till the paramedics get here."

I thought I would faint. I could hardly keep a steady gaze on anything. The world spiralled around me while I struggled to breathe normally. The uncertainty was driving me mad. So what if he had a pulse? It might not be there in five minutes. He was unconscious!

Had his head been struck? Was that why? Then, what if his brain had been injured? What if, when he woke up, he wouldn't be the same again?

Shock gripped me. Numbness unlike any other I'd experienced spread through my system until I could only stare blankly ahead of myself, out of touch with reality.

Who would do this to him?

Only seconds seemed to elapse before the police came in, asking for a word with Andy. A moment later, a team of paramedics rushed past me and into the men's room.

Once they opened the door, I saw his legs, surrounded by lots of blood. Facing up, he lay entirely limp on the floor while they examined his injuries. The ghastly sight expelled the air from my lungs. Breathless and pale-faced, I started to tremble in my shock. That was when Andy sat down next to me and wrapped his arm over my shoulders.

"He's going to be alright, Cara," he assured me, but I could hear in his voice that he was saying it on autopilot. He wasn't sure he believed it himself.

"I don't understand," I whispered as I continued to watch the stillness of William's legs. I wished they would move. I wished he would express some sign of life, no matter how small.

"He's going to be fine," Andy repeated, and I wondered then who he was really trying to convince.

"Who did this to him?"

"I don't know. I don't know him."

"Did you see him?"

"If I saw him? I thought I would kill him." His tone was flat – empty.

"What happened?"

He gulped, gaze steering clear of mine. "I came in." He paused for a while, the sinister scene running past his eyes. "I… He was on the floor, blood streaming from his arm. The bastard was still kicking him in a furious rage, but not a sound came out of Will – he was already gone. I intervened, yelling to Chloe to fetch help." He closed his eyes, jaw flexing as he gnashed his teeth. After an unsteady breath, his face contorted while he struggled to stifle a sob. "Security brought him out the back door just before you got here."

I glanced at the door at the end of the corridor, and I imagined that the despicable creature behind this had been apprehended by the police just beyond it, about to be taken into their custody.

Looking back to the scene of the crime, I watched as two members of the paramedics lifted William onto a spinal board. I couldn't bear it. Crouching over, I squeezed my eyes shut and started to cry.

I just couldn't believe it. It was truly him. Even if I hadn't seen his face yet, I recognised that body. I would have recognised it anywhere. To me, he stood out as one in seven billion.

Because that was what he was – seven billion people on the planet, and I knew without a doubt that William had been created just for me. What I had with him couldn't be replaced. There would never be anyone else for me – not like him.

"You should ride with them," Andy told me. "Chloe and I will meet you at the hospital. Don't worry about Alex or William's family. I've got it covered. Just go with him," he urged and pushed himself up to bring me with him.

Seeing as my body wouldn't stop trembling, standing proved a trying task. Noticing, Andy wrapped his arm around my waist to support me. As I gazed up at him, I realised that I wasn't the only one requiring support. He was barely holding it together, and yet he retained the strength to look after me on William's behalf – to consider my place in all this. Sobbing, I squeezed him against me, hoping to return some of the comfort he gave. I couldn't imagine what it must have been like to come upon such a scene – his best friend – the closest he'd ever come to a brother – being beaten so viciously.

We held each other, tightly, until the paramedics finally brought William out.

I could hardly believe my eyes. Along with a head immobiliser, a cervical collar held his neck and head in place. His face – his beautiful, handsome face – was covered in bruises and spots of blood. Two inches above a wound in his left upper arm, a tourniquet was wrapped to prevent him from bleeding out.

My gaze held fast to his beaten figure. "I'm his girlfriend," I managed to say, although my voice broke. "May I please come with you to the hospital?"

"Yes," the female responded. "What's your name, Miss?"

"Cara."

"I'm Bruna," she introduced herself, but I didn't look at her. I feared that if I did, I might miss his last breath.

"He's been stabbed in his left arm," Bruna said, "which severed his cephalic vein. We've managed to get the bleeding under control, but he'll need vascular surgery the instant we arrive at St Mary's." Hearing that, tears clouded my eyes to the extent that I could barely make out William's figure. "He's got a steady pulse for now, and he's breathing fine, but he's suffered blunt trauma to the head as well, which is why he's not responding. He's unconscious, but it may only be temporary."

I barely managed to nod my head. In a trance, I followed them into the vehicle where I was told I could hold his hand as I sat beside him.

I didn't dare to squeeze it regardless of how much I wanted to. He looked so brittle where he lay, and the thought of death lurking so close made me scared of even breathing on him. So instead, I raised it to my lips and kissed it repeatedly, while I silently prayed for him to recover.

My face contorted when I thought back to only hours ago. In the bed of our hotel room, we had made love to each other again and again before getting ready for tonight, both unaware of the horror we had in wait. I saw him clear as day, smiling down at me with his hands tucked under his head. Sprawled on his bare front, skin to skin, I had admired the view of him while we basked in the comfort of our union. He was beautiful.

We were beautiful.

If I'd known then what I did now, I would have told him I loved him. I regretted it intensely. Why hadn't I told him?

"Darling, please. Wake up," I said as I kissed his limp hand. Leaning next to his ear, I whispered through my inconsolable sobs, "William, I love you."

Stay up to date on the next instalment in *The Night* series by following C.K. Bennett on Instagram (**@ck.bennett**), or checking out:

https://ckbennettauthor.com

ABOUT THE COVER

Caracolla did it again: expressed Bennett's thoughts with their beautiful art.

As mentioned before, the titles of The Night series are progressive. In this instalment, Bennett dives deeper into the characters by putting a greater emphasis on William and Cara's thoughts and feelings as they explore each other. Since Into the Night aims to go beyond William's surface (beyond his "skin"), Bennett chose to remove the handprint that is present on the cover of Skin of the Night (The Night, # 1). Cara said it best: "I was enjoying his body, but, somehow, it felt much deeper than that. It went beyond the shallow surface of the skin. I was experiencing his existence – every fragment of the stardust he was composed of, every whisper of his thoughts, and every heartbeat of his emotions. When our bodies moved as one, it was like our individual chemistry combined at a celestial level, and the result was a higher force that could never be undone."

As Cara gets to know William better, more and more of his core shines through, and what she finds there is golden, hence the gold texture of the title. Gold is, in fact, stardust, which is why Bennett thought it would be suitable to use this. And, as is true for the cover of Skin of the Night, gold is a colour frequently associated with stars, which is what one typically finds within the night. Bennett wanted to give more attention to gold and stars on this cover since Cara begins to view William as a "guiding light", arriving in her life like "the birth of a star". Additionally, Bennett wanted the text to look like it was fading a bit to hint toward how Cara is being "consumed by the night".

You might also notice the number of layers in the artwork. There are several shades of green, white, and black, blending throughout, which is supposed to allude to how layered William is.

"My heart hammered. He never ceased to astound me. There was such remarkable depth to him – so many layers that I couldn't wait to peel away. Sometimes, when his core shone through, the beauty of it blinded me."

Now, why did Bennett pick green?

The colour is frequently associated with jealousy. In William's chapters, you get a taste of how dark his jealousy is when it comes to Aaron and Cara. There might be lots of beauty (gold) to be found beneath William's surface, but there is also plenty of darkness (black), light (white), and jealousy (green).

Now, if you look at the artwork from above, you might notice the shape of a butterfly, or as Bennett likes to think of it, a moth. This instalment is all about Cara and William's explosive chemistry, their fiery personalities, their sizzling passion, like stars that never stop burning – moths drawn to each other's flames.

If you're interested in more of Caracolla's art, check out:
www.instagram.com/caracolla.art

Curious about the hardcover design? Check out
https://ckbennettauthor.com/books

Lightning Source UK Ltd.
Milton Keynes UK
UKHW010634160522
403067UK00002B/327